Tale of Two Summers

ALSO BY BRIAN SLOAN

A Really Nice Prom Mess

Tale of Two Summers

BRIAN SLOAN

Simon & Schuster Books for Young Readers

New York | London | Toronto | Sydney

SIMON & SCHUSTER BOOKS FOR YOUNG READERS
An imprint of Simon & Schuster Children's Publishing Division
1230 Avenue of the Americas, New York, New York 10020

SIMON & SCHUSTER BOOKS FOR YOUNG READERS
is a trademark of Simon & Schuster, Inc.
Book design by Michael Nagin
The text for this book is set in Times New Roman and Arial.
Manufactured in the United States of America
2 4 6 8 10 9 7 5 3 1
Library of Congress Cataloging-in-Publication Data
Sloan, Brian.
A tale of two summers / Brian Sloan.— 1st ed.
p. cm.
Summary: Even though Hal is gay and Chuck is straight, the two fifteen-year-olds are best friends and set up a blog where Hal records his budding romance with a young Frenchman and Chuck falls for a summer theater camp diva.
ISBN-13: 978-0-689-87439-0
ISBN-10: 0-689-87439-1
[1. Best friends—Fiction. 2. Friendship—Fiction. 3. Homosexuality—Fiction. 4. Theater—Fiction.] I. Title.
PZ7.S6323Tal 2006
[Fic]—dc22   2005020697

FIRST
EDITION

For Chris

Acknowledgments

In the ancient days before e-mail and blogs, people used to write letters. Shocking, I know. Well, I'm one of those people (i.e., total Virgo) who saved all of mine and a great deal of my inspiration for this book came from those prolific, profound, and sometimes even profane missives. So, thanks are due to the following correspondents of the snail-mail era: Kevin Dwyer, Laurie Montalto, Liz Lamont, Lisa Lardizabal, Ian McKinnon, John Murray, Trish Plunkett, David Roccosalva, Vanessa Spevacek, Beau Strachan, Bob Williams, and Tim Woycik. I'd also like to thank faculty advisor Andris Rutins and the amazing students at Einstein High School's Gay-Straight Alliance, who taught me a thing or two about being a teen in the new millennium versus the old one. They were not only an inspiration but also an affirmation that the future for GLBT students is only getting better. Again, major thanks go to everyone at Simon & Schuster, namely, my editor, David Gale, who is just awesome; and Alexandra Cooper, who helped make it all happen. Special thanks to my agent, Will Lippincott, as well as my friends, whose words and advice (and French lessons) shaped this book: Christopher Amann, James Hoffman, Michael Joiner, David Levinson, Mark Sam Rosenthal, Andrew Volkoff, and David Zellnik. *Zut alors*—you guys are *le mieux*!

FERRIS: If you're not over here in fifteen minutes, you can find a new best friend.

CAMERON: You've been saying that since the fifth grade.

—John Hughes,
Ferris Bueller's Day Off

Week 1

08:54 P.M.
MONDAY 07.10.06

So, right off the bat, I have to say that this whole blog thing you've set up is totally gay. Now, I know that being gay and all I really shouldn't use "gay" in such a derogatory way, but what can I say? Writing blogs is so damn GAY I can't even discuss it. But this was your idea and you're supposedly straight, which makes the whole thing somewhat disturbing, actually: that straight-old-you could come up with such a gay-old-idea for keeping in touch over the course of the summer. But I guess there's no accounting for sexuality or something.

And I know I agreed to do this when we talked and everything, but still, I just have to let you know my true thoughts on this matter before going any further with this gay exercise in futility. I just don't see why simple e-mail would not suffice. I mean, people have been using that since the beginning of time (or the beginning of the Internet—same difference) as a decent mode of effective, semi-instant communication. So I don't know why you're so set on this Xanga.com, blogosphere thing. And why, good God, did you have to go and title the thing "Tale of Two Summers"? I mean, you make it sound like some friggin' Judy Blume novel!

1

Now, I know your whole rationale for this is that e-mails are disposable and deletable and you want to have a record of our big summer apart so that when we're 30 we can look back on it and be like, man, what a couple of losers we were back in the teenage day. But believe me, I will not be longing to look back and see what a pair of idiots we were for saving an online record of our every little thought and meaningless activity, especially when, on my end at least, there is really not gonna be much to report. Except, of course, my farting. Wait a sec— I feel one coming . . . [FART]. Ah, much better.

Regardless—here is my first entry. Are you happy yet? I'm not. It's Monday night and it's been a crummy first day of you not being here in crappy old Wheaton, Maryland. If there is any place more boring on earth to spend a sweltering summer by my goddamn self, I can't think of one. And you know what? If I <u>could</u> think of a place that was more stultifying, I might even go there just for a change of scenery, because, after almost 16 years, the sheer deadliness of our little 'burb is really starting to bug me out. Then, on top of that, toss into the mix the fact that I had my first day back at good ol' Einstein H.S. for day one of "Driving Instruction and Road Safety Training" (formerly known as "Driver's Ed"; see "20th century"), and I am clearly about ready to lose it.

I said it to you yesterday in your driveway and I will say it again: You are the luckiest damn dog to go hang out at the University of Maryland for the balance of the summer and learn your craft as an actor/singer/waiter. I only wish I had some ounce of talent to join you, but, as we all know, my only talent worth mentioning (i.e., farting) is, uh, not worth mentioning. *Badump-chik!* Thank you, ladies and gentlemen. . . . I'm here all summer. That's right, <u>ALL SUMMER</u>! OK— enough bitching. I can already see you shaking your head at my misanthropic missive. Still, being stuck here all alone for the next six weeks is a major drag, especially given the fact that you're not really that far away, even, just a few miles around the old Beltway. You know, I still don't see why I can't just come visit for an afternoon or hang out with you after dinner or something. What is up with UMD's severe anti-guest policy? They act like I'm gonna contaminate the whole batch of you with my lack-of-talent and cause an uncontrollable outbreak of averageness or something. But I digress. . . .

So I guess I'll get to the business at hand, which is "keeping in touch." Christ—now I've lost my train of thought. This is why the occasional phone call would be easier!!! They must have a few pay phones there? Oh right—you said something about how I'm uncommunicative on the phone. Well, you know, this was news to me. I think I'm always pretty forthcoming and chatty on the phone, whether discussing what asshole called me a faggot in the hall that day or giving a recap of the latest heartbreak on *The O.C.* So I'm not sure what you meant by uncommunicative and—wait a second. I get it. NOW you're gonna say, "Well, why didn't you ask me when we were talking—that's being uncommunicative." So this was some sort of trap, eh? Well—all I can say is, dude, that heart-to-heart in the driveway was creeping me out. You actors are so damn emotional sometimes. What is up with that?! All right, I keep getting distracted here because it takes so much longer to write some passing thought than to just say it. And since I can't just talk to you, I'm trying to make this bloody blog work as a one-sided conversation as opposed to some old-fashioned "journal." But I will now try to be coherent and cohesive and give you a running account of [insert drum roll here] . . .

MY FIRST DAY OF SUMMER WITHOUT CHUCK

Our story begins way too bright and much too early with Valerie rousing me at 7:30 for the usual breakfast bonanza of eggs/bacon/bagels/juice/fruit cup/coffee. Fortunately, I managed to decline everything except the juice and, despite my lack of cooperation, she was kind enough to drop me at Einstein on her way to work. It was so weird to be back there in the summer . . . the place is so damn empty, walking down the halls and actually hearing the sound of your own feet and not the usual stampede of thousands. And guess what? No, no—sorry, not that either. I wasn't harassed once! The one and only plus of the day.

Our driving class was located just off the main corridor, 115-B. Where we had English last year, 'member? As for the class itself, there are about 20 people enrolled in hell with me, most of whom I don't know because they are kids from the year ahead of us (me being the sage of our class due to my August b-day) and/or they are from other county schools. One person I did know which you will find hi-lar-i-ous is Joey Kelly, from back in da day at Randolph Elementary? I hadn't seen him since graduation, but he still looked the same—that is, retarded. Just taller and bigger and, thus, more retarded. Even though he goes to Prep now, Joey is still the same old cheap-ass he was in eighth grade, evidenced by his sponging on the free county-sponsored driving class.

Anyway, Joey was wondering what you're up to, so I told him, and he made fun of the whole summer-theater-camp thing—what a shocker, right? I mean, did Joey ever have a positive reaction to anyone's good news . . . ever? Fortunately, I was able to avoid sitting next to Joey by deftly pretending I knew someone else in the class, even though I didn't know a bloody soul. Pretty good acting for an amateur. (Hey—any last-minute openings in your improv class?) So I snagged a seat in the back row next to this hot blonde chick named Brett. Have you ever heard of a girl named Brett? Neither had I, but she is definitely 100 percent girl. I know I'm not supposed to notice these things now that I'm officially a guy-lover, but DAMN—this girl has got it going on, being majorly stacked and sporting the cutest face I've ever seen. You know what? You might even like her, except for the fact that she seems like a wicked bad seed. Which, of course, is why I gravitated to her immediately (heh-heh . . .).

Our driving instructor? Uhhhh, not so cute. It's this hulking goon who also does time as an assistant coach for the football team, Mr. Tlucek. (Remember him? From your ill-fated year on JV?) OMG—this guy is such a tool! The first thing he says to us in this deeply serious "I-am-God" voice was this little gem: "Listen up, people, driving is not a right. It's a privilege." What the hell! I mean, I know it's not on the Bill of Rights or anything, but a "privilege"? I thought it was my right when I turn age 16 in, oh, 28 days, to get my driver's license and finally have the right to get the F out of Wheaton at 70 mph without looking back. But I guess I was mistook. At least according to Coach Tlucek.

Anyway, after he drops this line on us with all the seriousness of Moses on the Mount, Brett and I turn to each other, our eyes rolling way up into the backs of our heads, and start cracking up. That's when I knew we would click. She is a trip! Later, during our break, she said she couldn't give a crap whether driving is a right, a privilege, or a door prize. She's only taking the class to humor her 'rents and doesn't even want to get a license when she's done. Her attitude is like, "Why should I learn how to drive when boys are gonna take me where I want to go anyway?" I was of half a mind to be like, "hells yeah . . . me, too!" Until, that is, I realized the pool of eligible Einstein homos to shuttle me around the D.C. metro area is slightly smaller than the one Brett's working with. (Who'm I kidding—it's like nonexistent!) Actually, I even told her this line, and she busted out laughing. Check it out—she didn't seem to mind the whole gay thing at all, which was refreshing for a change, right? Go Brett! Yeaaaaa! [Insert queerleaders doing a cheer.]

So on that rare, "campy" note I will end my first entry. I hope all this useless information about my so-called life today in Wheaton (a.k.a. the Black Hole of Suburbia) has truly enlightened you and brought us closer than ever. (Yeah, right.) Thusly, I will sign off, as always, your friend, confidante, and troubled soul . . . Hal.

PS—Have you gotten laid yet at "college"?

09:05 A.M.
TUESDAY 07.11.06
Dear Whiny in Wheaton,
Well. In the one day that I have been gone from your life you have lost none of your knack for being a raving lunatic. Thank God I set this blog up so at least you'll have an outlet for your half-baked rants while I'm gone. Otherwise, you'd probably be standing outside of 7-Eleven saying these

things out loud. To people. Normal people. Which means, of course, you'd be in jail by now. And surely Wheaton would be a safer place. (ha)

I'm writing you from the fancy McKibbin Library computer center on my half hour of free time before our first workshop of the day. It's too bad we can't IM or something, but I'm assuming there are no computers in driving class, where you're currently trapped. Despite all your protests, I think you've taken to the blog pretty decently. Since we won't exactly be around to share the details of our summer adventures directly, I still wanna at least know them all indirectly. Which is why I thought the blog would be a cool way to keep in touch—longer than e-mails and, yes, something that we can look back on.

Why you may ask? Well, ignoring dark Prince Hal's typically grim predictions, I think this summer is gonna be great! For BOTH of us. You're gonna get your driver's license, which is like a passport to freedom, despite what Tlucek may say. (Voice of God—that's so true!) And I'm gonna get to live like a real bachelor and meet lots of hot chicks from all over the state who have no idea what an ass I am. Hopefully, their ignorance will get me laid. Eventually. And no, it hasn't happened yet. Yet. Implying it will. Soon. And don't roll your eyes at me like that. . . . ☺

Despite my lack of sexual action so far, there is still tons to report. So much that I don't know where to start. I've been here only two days and it feels like a month—all these new faces and places. I guess I'll start with my swinging bachelor pad. I'm on the third floor of St. Ann's Hall, an old, red-brick dorm, sharing a decent-size room with this guy from Baltimore who is also named Charles. However, unlike me, he does not go by Chuck. Not even Charlie. Get this—he demands to be known as "Chaz." I was like, whaaaaatttt?! But he was insistent about it. Said it was his stage name. Chaz. Oooo-kay.

Now, as you may have guessed from the nickname and the attitude, Chaz is a lover of men. (Gays at theater camp—shocking, right?) Not that we had a big discussion about this or anything. Nothing like your coming-out chat back in January, that's for sure. No—I found this out because in the first 10 minutes of our conversation Chaz mentioned two of his ex-boyfriends and alluded to two others. I was like, "Dude, how many exes do you have?" He said five, total, but he doesn't talk about the fifth guy, getting all dramatic about it, saying he is the "one whose name cannot be uttered." I was like, "What . . . the ex-boyfriend formerly known as Prince?"

Chaz is a serious character. Get this—last night he started getting into this whole project to "revamp" our dorm room. No joke! Chaz was flipping through an Ikea catalog till all hours and, as I type, he is sitting at a terminal next to me ordering stuff online. He said he wants to make our place feel, and I quote, "more like a cute artist's studio than a cramped dorm room." Oh yeah—we're not actors or singers. Chaz insists that we are <u>artists</u>. (?!?!) So, as you may have guessed, Chaz is slightly insane. But his madness, fortunately, is more on the positive/productive side. Unlike some people I know who will remain anonymous. ☺

Hey—you know what?! I just had a brainstorm. Maybe Chaz would be a good balance for your darker brand of insanity. You guys would be a pretty interesting couple. And I could make it happen. Hey, look at me—I'm the gay matchmaker! LOL As for me and Chaz "living together," you don't have to worry about him hitting on me or anything like that. Chaz was pretty straight about this. (ha) He said that I wasn't his type. Thanks—I guess. Not that I wanted to hit it with Chaz or anything, or even be admired by him. It's just that lately it seems like I am no one's type, gay or straight or slightly crooked or anything. Even here at UMD. Seriously.

You see, there are an outrageous number of hot SummerArts honeys who have caught my eye. So many. But so far, no one seems to be catching back, you know? I thought I'd be getting something going on instantly since a) we're all away from home and b) we're all looking for summer lovin'. But nothing.

Chaz tried to calm me down on the chick thing, saying in his deep, resonant baritone (sidebar—this guy can sing!), "we are here to learn how to be artists, not hunt down sexual game." LOL He really is serious about this "artist" thing. It's funny, because I never really thought of myself as an artist. And though The Chaz had a point, I do sorta wanna get laid too. I mean, I <u>am</u> away at college! (kinda) Even if it is only about 10 miles from Wheaton, I might as well be on another planet. I mean, dude—I have a <u>dorm</u> <u>room</u>! With no parents telling me what to do or where I'm going or when they'll be back or <u>anything</u>!!!

Well, that's not 100 percent true. There is a resident assistant, or RA, who is technically in charge. But he's a junior at UMD and very cool, saying we can do what we want as long as the lights are out and doors shut by one A.M. One A.M.?! My parents would flip . . . actually, they did, 'cause I told them when I called home last night from the pay phone at the student union. Get this—Bob and Helen were complaining that I sounded tired already because I wasn't getting enough rest. They are such worriers. Which is to say, they are such parents.

Anyway, I've gotta wrap this up as we have to get to our voice class and it's on the other side of campus. (UMD is so massive—the size of 20 Einsteins!) Later today, the faculty is gonna meet with us to talk about the show that we're gonna be putting together over the course of the next six weeks. If it's *Fiddler*, then I definitely have to play matchmaker for you and Chaz—it'll be a <u>sign</u>! LOL Seriously, though, I can't wait to find out what we're gonna be doing . . . and, of course, if I can play the lead. Yeah, I know . . . I <u>always</u> play the lead at Einstein, so you're probably wondering why I'm even questioning it. But this is the big leagues, bro. Everyone here played the leads at their own schools! So scoring a big role here would actually mean something, because everyone is so talented.

OK—I'm gonna stop being such a "drama fag" now and sign off. But one last thing. Your last entry was a little, how can I put this . . . bitter? And I know you're bummed about being left to your own devices this summer. But please do me one favor: Don't be such a dark cloud in the middle of July. You can actually be a nice guy when you're not being such a self-inflicted mope. And maybe you'll even meet some interesting guys in your class (other than that dumb-ass Joey, of course).

All right—good luck with driving, and try not to hit anything. Remember, this is real life, not "GTA: Vice City." C

01:52 P.M.
TUESDAY 07.11.06

Self-inflicted mope? Where on earth do you come up with these phrases, and what the hell do they even mean? I've heard of "self-inflicted wounds" and "moping around the house" (which, by the way, is total Bob-and-HelenSpeak—yes, you are becoming your parents, and at such an early age, too), but "self-inflicted mope"? You, my friend, give words whole new meanings. That is, ones that make utterly no sense. Thank God you are excelling in a field where all you have to do for a living is read the things that other people have written for you to say. The world will be safer this way, as will the English language.

All right—now that I'm done taking you to school on your vocabulary, there is really not a helluva lot of news to report. (A total shocker, right?) Driving class could not be deadlier. Even worse is the fact that we aren't even going to be out on the road for at least another week. This is all part of the county's new Safe-ing Lives™ curriculum, in which they basically scare the shit out of everyone for about a week before you get behind the wheel. It's in response to the record number of kids who died last year in all those drunken accidents—'member? You couldn't escape it on the news. And now I can't escape it in Driver's Ed . . . sorry, make that "Driver's Scare Tactics."

This morning, class began with a truly "tragic" movie about drunk driving, during which I was able to peg the dead kid in the opening minute (much to Brett's amusement). After I ruined the ending for her, Brett wasn't even paying attention to this trumped-up scare flick, texting through the whole thing with her friend Amanda, who is stuck in Woodbridge for the summer with her stepdad. Then, when the lights came up, Tlucek passed out a quiz on the film we had just seen. Brett was like, a test? Whaaa? I offered to let her cheat off my paper, but she didn't even bother to do that. She just started quickly circling the multiple-choice answers in a random fashion, then, when she was done, held the paper up to see if her arbitrary pattern was pleasing to the eye. Then she shrugged and fake-sighed and said in her faux-breathy way, "School is sooooo hard"—and then we both totally cracked up. She friggin' kills me!

Oh—you'll be amused by this bit. On our break, Joey was trying to pretend he was friends with me so that he could make a play for Brett. (OMG—he is so bloody <u>annoying</u>!!!) So of course I had to try to foil his efforts. Not that he really had a chance or anything, because Brett didn't seem that into talking to him at all. But still, I was able to throw off his game, as it were. And let me tell you, it was one lame game. Joey was speechifying to us about the big differences between public school and private school, which is probably not the best way to make a decent impression on Brett, who has attended public schools her entire life. (But what do I know about charm, right?) Anyway, Joey's going on and on about uniforms and cliques and all this compare/contrast bullcrap when he starts jawing about this SuperFag in our driving class, a sophomore who I vaguely remember hanging off the arm of his boyfriend *du* week last spring. So Joey is blowin' on and on about how you don't spot any fags at private schools. Smooth, right? I mean, Brett and I have our eyes poking out of the backs of our heads, they are rolling back so much. Then finally, Joey has the stupidity to ask me how many fags there are in my class at Einstein.

Brett catches her breath, her eyes going wide as she wonders how the hell I'm gonna deal with this asinine query. Needless to say, I handled it with my usual flair. I turned to Joey, smiled my biggest, dopiest smile, and said, "Gee, Joey, I don't know. Counting myself, there's probably about four." So Joey nodded like an idiot for about a minute until the actual meaning of what I'd said finally hit him. When his brain got the memo, Joey's face turned about 12 shades of red and he started clearing his throat like there was, I don't know, maybe a size-11 foot in it? Brett, not one to miss a beat in a situation like this, said all coolly and calmly, "Wow—I think there's almost double that number in my year . . . including, what did you call him—SuperFag?" Needless to say, Joey was unable to respond to Brett's question due to the presence of his other foot, which had joined the dance party in his throat, making it impossible to generate any sound other than a low, rumbling *ummmphhh.*

Hold on. Phone—

08:03 P.M.
TUESDAY 07.11.06
HEY—I'm back, what . . . six hours later? Sorry about the major blog-gus interruptus. That was Brett calling before. She asked me what I was doing and I said nothing (no, writing in the blog doesn't count as anything), so she swung by my place and we went up to Wheaton Plaza to hang out for the afternoon. And you know what? I actually had a decent time. And I met this guy, too. I don't know if he's gay, exactly, but he is damn sexy. But I digress. Here's the deal:

We wanted to check out *Spider-Man III* at the Loews but it was com-pletely sold-out, even though it was playing on something like 10 screens. So instead, we saw this flick *Harold and Kumar Discover Jack in the Box*, the sequel to that first H&K movie—as if one wasn't bad enough. I thought the whole thing sounded pretty stupid and like one big commercial for Jack in the Box, which is annoying because we don't even have them in Montgomery County. As it turned out, *HAKDJITB* was mildly amusing, and Kumar, the lead Indian guy, was pretty cute. They even showed his bare ass in the opening 10 minutes of the movie, which definitely perked me up!!! I never really thought I was into Indian guys, but maybe it's because the Indian guys at Einstein are just not movie-star cute like this guy was.

Anyway, the rest of the movie was just lots of stoner and fart jokes, which was funny at first but got tiring after an hour. I have to say, though, the most interesting part of the movie was hanging with Brett, as we both made cracks throughout the thing, much to the annoyance of a couple in front of us that was trying to use the back of the theater as their living room couch. Question: Why the hell do straight people have to be so damn flagrant about flaunting their make outs in pub-lic?! I mean, I don't care if you love the girl or simply want to get it on.

Just do it in the privacy of your own mobile home, all right? Christ—I don't want to see that shit. It grosses me out!!! Now, before you get on my case over this, I am *not* being a gay grouch or dark cloud or even sore sport about this simply because I don't have someone of my own to molest in public. In fact, Brett was with me 100 percent on the pervasiveness of PDA. Like me, she prefers to watch movies at the movies . . . or at least make fun of them.

So . . . after the movie was over, Brett and I were sitting on a bench in front of this planter outside Loews, continuing our symposium on the topic of trashy straight couples, when this guy fell into our collective laps. Literally. He came flying out of nowhere and sorta landed next to the bench we were sitting on, lost his balance, and fell backward right onto us, causing Brett to scream, the decibel level of which, in turn, caused me to fling my Diet Coke in the air.

Since this anonymous guy was now splayed across us, apologies were in order, as were introductions. Shaking his head cartoon-style, he stood up, offered his hand, and said his name was Henri, but he didn't say the *H* part because he has this funny little French accent. He went to pick up my Diet Coke, which of course was completely empty, and then offered to buy me a new one. I was like, sure, why not? But before he could head into Loews, Brett demanded to know where the hell he'd come from and how the hell he'd ended up in our laps in the first place. Henri told us he was originally from Paris, newly relocated to Wheaton as of June 1st with his mom, who works at the French consulate in D.C. However, this was not exactly the answer Brett was seeking. Henri knew this, of course, and he was clearly being a bit of a smart-ass. Then he offered a real answer to her question, which was that he ended up on top of us because he was practicing Parkour, a new sport that's sorta like urban gymnastics, or, as Henri put it most succinctly, "skateboarding without the skateboard." Henri explained that he was executing a Kong Vault over the planter we were sitting in front of and didn't spot his landing properly. Our response? Blank faces, as if he was speaking some other language and it wasn't even French.

Frankly, I didn't mind the whole Parkour incident/accident so much because Henri made up for the lack of *H* in his name with another H-word: Henri was Hot! He had this tight, athletic body and a mop of curly, sun-streaked blond hair. Brett, however, being slightly bitchy, told Henri that maybe he shouldn't practice his "sport" in front of a busy movie theater on a summer afternoon. Henri's response? He said in his cute accent, "Yes, perhaps I shouldn't," trying to be charming and European and all that, but Brett wasn't buying it at all. She's a little tough that way. So after all these quasi-pleasantries were exchanged, Henri said he had to split to go meet up with some fellow *traceurs* (that's French for "Parkour enthusiast") to do back flips off the Jersey barriers on Georgia Avenue. How insane is that?!

Once he was out of earshot, we were free to gossip about him, and Brett chimed in with this gem: "He's yours." I was like, "You are so friggin' high!" But Brett went on to explain that she was convinced Henri was a total homo. At first I accused her of saying this just because he was French and had some stylish hair going on. But she said that she had evidence that was slightly more scientific, namely, the fact that Henri did not ask for her cell number or even her e-mail address when he departed. Apparently this happens to Brett on a fairly regular and reliable basis, and lack of it indicates to her lack of interest in the opposite sex. Scientific? Yeah, I know . . . not exactly a blackboard full of equations, but arguing this point with her would be soooooo moot.

Still, I was skeptical about her homo claim, as Henri seemed incredibly sporty for a gay guy. Brett countered this by saying some of the biggest Marys she knew were on the wrestling team. Whaaaaa?!? The <u>Einstein</u> wrestling team? I think she is totally tripping on this count, but whatever . . . she definitely is a little more worldly than I, having grown up in a real city, Chicago, until the move to greater metropolitan Wheaton when she was 13. So maybe she's onto something re Henri. It would be cool if he were gay. I mean, damn—this Henri was hot. (Did I say that already?)

But, thinking about it now . . . I don't know why I'm even wasting my time writing about him. It's not like one bloody thing will come of it, because, like most of my crushes, I'm sure this one is just as equally misguided. (It certainly would be par for my tragic-romantic course.) And even though Henri said he'd see us around the mall, how likely is <u>that</u> to happen? It's not like I hang around crappy old Wheaton Plaza for kicks. Christ—I'm not 12!

Still, I guess it was cool to at least see a hot guy I was semi-attracted to and who didn't seem like an asshole. (See "Sophomore year romantic interests.") If nothing does happen, at least I've now got a nice visual that I can call up when I'm whacking off all by my lonesome for the rest of my life. I know, I know . . . waaaaaay too much information, but hey, that's why we're friends, right? Always telling each other way more than any human being needs to know. Anyway, yours in unrequited lust . . . Hal.

PS—Henri has a slammin' ass, too.
PPS—Did I mention his ass?
PPPS—Dude has some serious junk in the trunk.

09:22 A.M.
WEDNESDAY 07.12.06

So what is it with gay men and asses? Seriously. What is that about? As you know, I have pretty much come around to 100 percent acceptance of guy/guy love in the last few months. But when it comes to guy/guy lust, I have to be honest: I just don't get it.

I can sorta see the dick fascination, as dicks are fascinating. (Hey—I'm totally into mine, you know what I'm saying?) But seriously, that ass shit is just totally out there. I know—hate me or sue me or at least slander my name. But I honestly don't understand. Maybe it's because I don't get sprung for girls' asses. They're fine and all that, but I tend to fixate on other areas. Namely the frontal upper chest region—a.k.a. tits. I know I've said this before, but I will say it again: TITS ROCK! (Boy, that feels good.) I will even say it again because I know it drives you batty. Tits ro—all right all right, I won't be a total dick about it. (ha)

As to Henri and his so-called "hot ass," I don't know what to say. I mean, putting the ass aside, this guy sounds like the same old song. In fact, you referenced it yourself with your "see sophomore year" comment. Earth to Hal! Hailing Hal on all frequencies! Remember the last three crushes you had, all on similarly jocky/sporty dudes, all of whom left you crushed? ("That's why they call them crushes"—props to *Sixteen Candles*.) After all that mess, I am very familiar with your tendency to be the straightest gay guy around—that is, letting your member lead the way too often. So without saying I told you so, I will say this: Just forget hot-ass Henri and I won't have to even say you-know-what. Seriously.

I don't see why you can't just find some real gay guys who are certified homosexuals and fall head over ass for them. Case in point: What about this so-called "SuperFag" in your class? Clearly this is a guy who is at least open to digging other guys. (And I'm sure Joey is slightly exaggerating things with that nickname.) Also, need I remind you that there is still a whole world out there called Washington, D.C.? In only a month you will be mobile and can set your heat-seeking missile to some of the District's gay coordinates. Like that GLBT community center in Dupont Circle we found on Google, remember? Anyway, 'nuff said on the topic. That's my lecture for today. I will stop now because, yes, I am beginning to sound like my parents. Yikes!

Your Joey outing story was pretty hilarious, I have to admit. I definitely was LOL-ing. I'm glad you showed him up for what he is . . . a retard. But, on a semiserious note, I do worry about you outing yourself like that. I say this not because I don't think you should be open and all that. It's more that when you throw that info out to someone like Joey Kelly, he's such a moron that that's all he's gonna see you as. The reality is, you are more interesting than being "that gay guy." Shit—am I lecturing again? Not that you'll listen to me anyway . . .

All right—basically I just wanted to put the thought out there: Think before outing yourself. That's all.

[This has been a paid announcement by the committee to keep you from making a fool out of yourself in my absence.]

Yeah, I know. Completely futile to try and tell you what to do. But I'll never give up trying to save you from yourself. LOL Actually, I thought that was why we were friends? I save you from your dark moods and unrealistic expectations and you save me from being a showboating attention-whore. Though I guess I don't need your protection much these days, as I'm surrounded by like-minded musical-theater whores on all sides. (ha)

OK—gotta run to scene study. Catch you later! C

06:42 P.M.
WEDNESDAY 07.12.06
First off, on your questions regarding the male ass, all I have to say is this: What is it with straight guys and their overriding analphobia? Christ! I mentioned Henri had a nice ass like once. (All right—maybe twice.) But then I get a lecture from you about how weird I am for obsessing on the nicely proportioned form of his French derriere. Anyway, I can assure you that I am not obsessed with his ass nor do I have any sort of specific designs on it. I mean, hell—what do you think I am, some sort of ass-centric sex fiend? So what—Henri has a fine-looking caboose. That is not my main point of interest in him, or the male species in general, for that matter. But you, my friend, like all straight men, see a gay guy and are all like "Don't drop the soap, man!" Christ—that is like soooooo tired!

Believe me—you and the majority of the straight male populace do not have to worry about me humping your rear. If I liked a guy, I'd want to make out with him first and foremost. Then, if that went well, we'd certainly progress to other stuff involving my own deep fascination with the male member. But the "ass stuff," as you refer to it, is serious, and if I ever went there, it would have to be with someone I'm seriously interested in. Even then . . . I don't know. . . .

Frankly, if you have to know (and clearly you do, because you are so malinformed), I'm a little freaked by the whole concept of major man-on-man sex. It just seems, I don't know . . . sorta messy, for lack of a better word. Sure—I've heard it has its pleasures. I even downloaded some visual proof of this once, when Val stupidly left the Web-filter password under the keyboard. But still . . . when I daydream about sex, or Henri for that matter, ass-sex is not exactly the visual I'm jamming on.

You know what? I got it. I just friggin' _got it_! I think the core problem here is that straight guys equate "vagina" with "asshole" when it comes to gay guys getting it on. On the surface, sure, it's a reasonable error, as they are both orifices in roughly the same zip code. But to say they are interchangeable misses the point of being gay, if I can make such a bold proposition. (Well, Hal, I think you just did!) Though this is all still relatively new for me; at six months and counting, I think it's safe to say that I like guys as opposed to assholes. Do you get my meaning here? Now, I know you'll disagree with this statement by cleverly citing the three assholes I had crushes on last year. The point here is that I like guys 'cause they're guys. Period. If I was to subscribe to your limited ass-reasoning, that would give me the right to ask you if you like chicks simply because they have vaginas? What? You do?! Seriously?!? Well, my friend, I guess that's why guys are pigs and girls like Brett think The Gays rock. LOL

Speaking of which, Brett and I had another deadening, no-driving day in Driver's Ed. In case you're wondering, here's a quick summary of what Brett didn't learn today: that a safe driver must keep 500 feet behind a moving fire truck; that a responsible driver always looks left, then right, then left again before making a turn; and that a law-abiding driver comes to a complete stop at a STOP sign. Or as Tlucek put it, "It's not a called a slow-down-a-little sign." (OMG—stop it, Mr. T . . . you're killing me!!!) All during class today Brett amused herself by passing notes to me regarding Henri and asking me, in various and sundry ways, if I was "obsessed" (her terminology, not mine) with him. I met him once . . . how can I be obsessed? She is ridiculous.

Anyway, after we were released from Einstein at noon, Brett suggested we head up to Wheaton Plaza again to see if we could track down Henri and his gang of _traceurs_ practicing the mysterious art of

Parkour. (Cue weird Chinese gong.) Though I estimated our chances of finding him as about the same as her chances of getting a driver's license before she's 30, I agreed to this field trip as there was not much else on my busy agenda for the afternoon. So, after complaining about hanging out at the mall less than 24 hours ago, I found myself hanging out at the friggin' mall today. Can you believe it? (Don't answer that.) And you know what? The place is a disaster area . . . really. I don't mean that socially, either.

The mall is in the middle of this huge renovation to double its size, with the addition of a new Macy's and a whole new wing. Oh—and the signs announcing this transformation proudly trumpet the arrival of something called "Westfield Shopping Town." First off, what the hell is Westfield? There is no Westfield in Wheaton, last time I looked. In fact, there are no fields for anything to be west of, as farming in Wheaton ended, oh, about a hundred years ago. Second off, what the hell is "Shopping Town"? Is this a new principality coexisting in the heart of Wheaton, like some breakaway retail republic? I mean, hell, is it even going to be a <u>democracy</u>? And if so, will there be a mayor of Shopping Town? Hmmmm . . . maybe I can run. Since you've clearly found a career, I have been thinking I should get moving on that front. Lately, I've been thinking politics might be a cool gig for me. I'm certainly quite opinionated and have been a fool in public on countless occasions. Isn't that enough to qualify? Also, it would be majorly cool to have every inane thing I say printed in the Post for the world to snicker at. I can imagine the headline now: MAYOR SCHAEFFER DISPELS GAY ASS MYTHS; STRAIGHT CRITICS SKEPTICAL.

Anyway, on closer inspection of the sign, Westfield is the name of the massive corporate entity that has apparently bought Wheaton Plaza to turn it into something it is not and never will be: "a destination, an experience, a way of life." I shit you not—this is the exact propaganda listed on the sign. Wheaton Plaza, <u>a way of life</u>? I will say this once and simply: no fucking way!

As for Brett's plan of spotting Henri, exciting old Wheaton Plaza was certainly not a destination for him today. We wandered around the joint for a good two hours, hoping for him to fall out of the sky again, but, alas, it was not raining men. After our failure to locate, Brett got all consoling toward me, saying that I would see him again, that Wheaton's a small place (that's for sure!), and that he's gotta turn up eventually. She was sorta overdoing it, as I was hardly heartbroken. I mean, I wasn't even doing a so-called, self-inflicted mope. (Props to my man C!)

Still, Brett kept telling me to cheer up and all this crap. I mean, I don't know what the hell her problem was. Maybe she is actually harboring some secret crush on the frog. It sorta makes sense with all those notes in class today, even if the subject was ostensibly my interest in Henri, not hers. Despite her repeated dissing on how France sucks and how everyone there is a smoking snob, I've heard this line of reasoning before. Or seen it, actually, in those cheesy romantic comedies starring Sandra Bullock and Julia Roberts. You know, where the chicks get all like, "You are such a terrible person that I hate you more than my own mother," and then turn around 10 minutes later to be all suddenly like, "Oh crap, I'm actually in love with you!!!" Now, I know you love these movies because for some reason you think Sandra and Julia are hot (or at least their tits are), but those movies are so full of shit that they literally stink when you get a whiff of the preview.

Man—I did it again!!! I really can get off on a tangent writing in this thing. Christ—this entry is approaching term-paper length. Part of that is because I truly have nothing to do, and since you're busy as a little musical-theater bee can be, my entries are definitely gonna start dominating this blog if I don't find something to occupy my endless downtime. This whole thing will become "Tale of One Totally Friggin' Bored Lunatic." Anyway, the bottom line of all this nonsense today is that I will probably never see the freaky Frenchman again. And I really don't care. But clearly a cute girl with a guy's name does. Mark my blog. H

09:04 A.M.
THURSDAY 07.13.06

Hey—you know what? It does sound like Brett is into him, even if it is in a romantic-comedy sorta way. (ha) I'd also love to educate you on the charms of Julia's and Sandra's racks, but I have more important things to report. Namely, the announcement of the show we're going to be doing this summer. And the girl I auditioned with. OMG—the girl! The Girl!!! But first, the show . . .

The show is a Sondheim musical so everyone is totally freaking out, especially Chaz. It's a show from the early '80s called *Merrily We Roll Along*, which is about this songwriter who becomes famous, falls in and out of love twice, and basically makes a mess of his life. The twist is, the whole thing is told backward! It starts in 1980 with him as an older guy who everyone hates, then goes back in time to when he was young and full of hope/talent/dreams/etc. And the music is incredible! There are all these intense love songs and syncopated 6/8 time and complicated patter numbers. Anyway, you are probably going, "What the hell is he talking about?," so I'll stop boring you with the details. All I'll say is—dude, this show is gonna be H-O-T!

As for the girl, her name is Ghaliyah and wow, she is stunning—a dark-haired Arabian beauty with piercing olive eyes, skin the color of a mochacchino, and a rack that is just . . . perfection. How can I describe it? Hell, it's indescribable. Besides, you'd be skipping right over this part if I got into the details, so I won't even bother.

I met Ghaliyah when we got paired up for auditions and man, I was mesmerized. Hypnotized. Bewitched, bothered, and boned. LOL! And that was just from looking at her! Then, when she started singing, holy shit—her voice was unbelievable! She has this soaring soprano that is just . . . I mean, she would have blown away everyone on *American Idol*. She is that much of a superstar. Seriously. Her talent actually inspired me to rise to her level, and we both killed on the song we had to do, a ballad called "Not a Day Goes By." I think we really connected singing to each other, too! Either that or she's, like, SuperActor. One thing is clear. This Ghaliyah (oh, the sound of that name . . .) is a star of tomorrow.

After our audition, we chatted a bit in the hallway. I got her basic bio: originally from Saudi Arabia, moved to D.C. when she was eight because her parents got jobs at the World Bank, currently living in Poolesville and going into her junior year at Potomac. Now, before you give me a withering, trademarked Hal-look-of-disgust, she's not your typical stuck-up private-school chick. When I told her I went to Einstein, she was actually impressed, having heard it was an arts magnet school for the county. She even considered going there, but her folks killed the idea due to the lengthy commute.

Chatting about all this stuff and more, we truly hit it off. Seriously. I'd even go as far as saying this might be my chance to get laid. But I won't. Why? I know you'll be laughing your gay ass off about this one, but I think Ghaliyah might be a more serious thing than just getting laid. It might be the L-word, and I don't mean "lesbian." But I'm no fool . . . unlike some 15-year-olds I know who will be nameless. (Though their initials are H.S.) Which means that I'm not gonna say the actual word or write it or even think it. I don't want to jinx this.

OK—gotta book. The finer art of singing scales awaits. Yours in lust that will hopefully <u>not</u> remain unrequited, Chuck.

PS—Did I mention how hot G's rack is?
PPS—Yeah, I know, I am such a hetero perv.
PPPS—But at least I'm not ass-fixated . . . WURHD!

12:50 P.M.
THURSDAY 07.13.06
OMG—enough of the ass! Christ—you can be so bloody annoying when you latch on to one lame joke like that and run it into the ground. If the actor's problem is to repeat (as you like to say), I have to state that this is <u>not</u> your problem, Chuck . . . not at all! Which is maybe why you're so damn good as an actor. But your interpersonal skills with real people (i.e., myself) sometimes need a little fine tuning. So, I beg you, please-please-please lay off the ass riff for a while. Thank you, in advance.

Now, regarding this G-chick, she sounds pretty interesting, and you certainly sound pretty interested. That is <u>definitely</u> for sure. But as your one and only true friend in the world, I have to send up a warning flare here, and <u>not</u> just as a way of getting even for the fireworks you sent up about Henri (which, by the way, was a total waste of your precious energy since I will never see his French ass again). My warning flare for you is more based in reality: your very real propensity to fall like a tree for divas who don't give a damn about anyone but themselves. And as you were kind enough not to torture me with names from my tragic unrequited past, I will afford you the same but equal treatment and not drag your Drama Club ho's through the mud again. But you know of whom I speak, right? I don't have to spell it out other than to remind you of my least favorite four-letter word in the English language: that's right, d-i-v-a.

Now I'm sure Galyiah (sp?) is a beauty and a babe with a bust you could write home about—which, uh, is pretty much what you did in your last entry. And sure, all of that is maybe some decent "let's get laid" material. But I seem to recall a short but frightening mention of the L-word in your last entry, which has sent shudders down my spine and has in turn shaken me to the very core of my being. Thus, in my long-standing role as the voice of reason in our friendship, I have no problem spelling things out for you when it comes to the L-word. C'mon Chuck—love?! Give me a friggin' break! This girl sounds like Trouble, with a capital *T* and that rhymes with *P* and that also rhymes with *G* for Gahlyah (sp?). (Apologies to *The Music Man* and your performance as Prof. Harold Hill in last year's show.) Why, you may ask? Because she is a bloody diva! I mean, you talk about how amazing and awesome this girl was at auditions, but did she say anything about how much <u>you</u> rocked? I'm so sure that you kicked it at that audition just as much as she did, if not more. But did she compliment <u>your</u> amazing tenor? Did she have a good word on <u>your</u> impeccable pitch? Or <u>your</u> impossibly rakish and charming stage presence? Yeah—I thought not.

So here's the deal: YOU are a star of tomorrow too. I know you know this, Chuck, but you need to say it to yourself more often and not to other people like this Galeyaah (wait . . . that's not right). Hell—I will even go so far as to say you are a star of today! And now you've got this rare and unique opportunity to really strut your God-given stuff and receive the acclaim and success that you not only have earned but deserve. In a perfect world, your parents would say stuff like this to you on an endless loop, except, as we all know too well, Helen and Bob are too lame to realize your talents or, God forbid, encourage them. Thank Christ you got that scholarship for SummerArts, otherwise they'd have you locked away in some high school–level, pre-law prep course with the intent of getting a running start on what they see as your lawyerly destiny.

So it's left to me to be your promoter or publicist or something, I guess. Not that I mind the role of pumping you up, because when you become a huge star I'll at least have a job running the entourage and, thus, will finally have something to do with my life, even if it means merely riding around in the back of your stretch Humvee luring H'wood hotties with the offer of free champers. Of course, none of this will ever happen if you don't stop mooning over babes like G (I'm giving up on the spelling). So for my sake, but mainly yours, you've got to start building up your own diva factor and not worship these false goddesses, OK? Or, more basically put, you've got to nurture your ability to be a supernova in your own right. 'Nuff said . . .

As for me, I have absolutely nothing to report. That's right, nothing exciting happened in Wheaton today. (Not that that's exactly news or anything.) Right now, I'm at home post-class, which was even more boring than usual as Brett was a no-show for some inexplicable reason. (Wait—oh yeah—maybe cause she doesn't <u>want</u> to learn how to drive?) But even if she was around, I don't think we'd be doing anything of interest. It's about 100 degrees today with the "humiture," so I'm just chilling indoors watching cable and eating Doritos. Hey— maybe I'll get hooked on a soap opera again. Remember when we used to watch *All My Children*? What were we . . . like eight when you had that after-school babysitter (was it Julie or Joanna?) who was addicted to AMC and turned us into daytime junkies as well? It's probably what made me gay and you interested in drama, right?

Well, enough reminiscing about the good old times. It's mucho depressing, 'cause it only highlights the bad old times I'm having right now. To summarize: This summer eats ass.

09:02 A.M.
FRIDAY 07.14.06
Hey—I'm sorry to hear you're not having such a hot time. Well, not counting the weather that is. (ha) I know, lame joke. Sorry.

I've actually been feeling sorta bad about having abandoned you. We haven't spent a summer apart like this since the mid '90s. That's a whole other century ago! Of course, I'm having fun and all that here. But there is this sorta drag-part, too, which is that I can't share this all with you. Man, there are so many things I want to tell you—so many dumb little stories about Chaz and what an unintentionally hilarious freak he is, how Professor Eckhart, our voice teacher, wears these outfits that look like rejects from *The Golden Girls* (Dorothy's wardrobe), and finally, of course, how stunning Ghaliyah is. Oh, and that is the proper spelling, BTW.

I've met some other interesting people too in various classes and workshops. This one girl, Mary Kate, is pretty funny, namely because she refuses to be called Mary Kate. She goes by MK because she doesn't want to be associated with the Olsen twins. Isn't that crazy?! She's also kinda big for a girl, a good four inches taller than me and generally a bit larger, too. Not fat or anything. Just BIG—including her tits! But she always has something funny to say about everything. Kinda like you!

But sometimes, it almost feels like the people I meet here and the amazing things I'm doing aren't real or really happening because I can't turn to you and be like, "Dude, can you believe this shit?" I'm so used to doing everything with you and talking about it with you that it's just hard to sorta take all this in by myself. I can't start talking to myself. I mean, shit—isn't that what crazy people do? I hope I'm not losing it!

But actually, having read your last blog, I worry even more that you're losing it. Seriously. You seem pretty down, my friend. (I thought I was supposed to be the dramatic one, 'member?) Please don't get so depressed about class or summer or Henri because, separately, they are really not major problems. Really. And I don't know much about Henri, but it was what, like two days ago you met him? I bet you'll see him again. Even if you don't, there are other people in the world. A lot of them. I mean, it sounds like you and Brett have already become pretty cool pals together, and that is great. Actually, it almost makes me a little jealous. Shit, man—I thought I was your fag hag? ☺

So cheer up, Hal. Okay? Do something fun. Get out of the house, like Valerie has surely said about a hundred times already. If I know you're up to something cool, I can enjoy myself here and eventually reach that level of stardom that you have predicted for me. You and your predictions . . .

And what else—oh yeah, I will keep trying not to miss you. I know, another sappy Chuck moment. Still, it's true. Even though you won't believe this, I seriously wish you were my roommate here at UMD. Chaz is fun and entertaining and all, but sometimes I just wanna make fun of him with you, you know? ☺ C

06:32 P.M.
FRIDAY 7.14.06
Hey—on my way back over to the Tawes Center for our first big rehearsal. They don't give us much downtime here. I'm almost jealous of your dull life, as I could use a break, or at least 10 minutes to just hang out or something.

Anyway, I thought I'd stop into the library and see if you posted yet. So did you have another banner day of driving instruction filled with Tlucek's pearls o' wisdom? That guy was such a dope when he was coaching JV. Always giving us these cliché-ridden speeches about going the extra mile, being a team player, etc. Thank God I didn't make the team. I don't think I could've taken him for a whole season. I gotta run, but drop me a line or two this evening if you have time! Missin' ya—C

11:07 P.M.
FRIDAY 07.14.06

Hey—what's up, dude? No responses all day. I hope your computer isn't busted or something. Otherwise I'm gonna have to hail a cab to Wheaton and kick your ass . . . and I don't mean that in any sorta gay, sexual way either. (ha)

Right now I'm on our RA's laptop because I just had to relay the big news of the day. Get this—I bagged the lead in *Merrily*!!! And if that's not big enough news, you better sit down for this one. Oh—wait—you're already sitting. (ha) Ghaliyah is playing the female lead opposite me. Seriously! I nabbed the main role of Franklin Flippin' Shepherd and she's playing Mary, my ex–best friend who has always been secretly in love with me! Can you believe it?! Actually, you probably can't, because you have no idea who these characters are.

Seriously, though . . . take it from the expert. This is like the most challenging and tough role I've ever had! This is not some cutesy, Harold Hill, song-and-dance thing. This is major DRAMA, as well as some of the most complicated music I have ever sight-read. EVER! And the fact that I get to do this with Ghaliyah?! I've died and gone to musical-theater heaven!

We both got the news at the first rehearsal, right after I blogged you this afternoon. We had a big meeting with the director of the show, this UMD theater professor, Ryan Rodriguez. To call him a professor is a bit of a stretch because he doesn't seem that old, maybe 25 or something. In fact, he said that he doesn't want us to call him "professor," unlike the other faculty folks, and that we can call him Ryan. Anyway, he told us who was going to play which character. There are tons of great characters in the show, which is why they chose it. Oh—and get this! Chaz is playing my best friend in the show and . . . wait for it . . . his character's name is Charlie. (!!!) Chaz asked if he could change it to Chaz and Ryan said he didn't think Mr. Sondheim would appreciate Chaz's artistic license. This makes Ryan the first person to successfully say NO to Chaz since kindergarten! LOL

After that, Ryan announced me and Ghaliyah's roles and we both high-fived

each other which was awesome. My first physical contact! I know, I know—
it was only a hand-slap, more common in a football game than true romance.
But it was something. A start at least . . .

After Ryan got through the cast list, he started talking about the show itself.
He told us that he had a concept for the show but that he wasn't going to tell
it to us right off the bat. He wants us to sort of figure it out or something. I
don't know, but that seems somewhat backward to me. How am I gonna
know what he wants from me as the lead actor if he won't tell me what he
thinks the show is about? He's an odd guy, and also kinda funny looking—
fairly short, slightly rotund, and with this trendy little soul patch that looks
gross.

Even more annoying about him was this: G (as you call her) thought Ryan
was cute. I was like, whaaaaaa?, and suggested that maybe she should get her
eyes checked. I'm guessing her interest was less about his looks and more
about his role as director. She seemed in awe of how he talked to us, the way
he was using all these big master-thespian words and being Mr. Adult
Authority figure in a teen theater camp busting out with chaos. I don't know.
Who can understand what interests a girl sometimes? Like, remember how
so many girls were into Clay Aiken a couple years ago? What the hell? That
dude looked like he was about 10.

OK—I'm tired and getting a bit rambly here. I better hit the hay, but, man,
how am I gonna get to sleep tonight? The lead in a Sondheim show! Can you
friggin' believe it?! Hey . . . maybe you're actually right about my talents.
Maybe this will all add up to something, someday. I dig your image of us riding around L.A. in a tricked-out Humvee. That would be hysterical! You
crack me up sometimes with these predictions of yours. But you did predict
that I'd be Harold Hill last year. And Capt. von Trapp the year before that, so
who knows . . . maybe you're psychic! (ha)

Good night and sleep well and write me the fuck back, OK?! ☺

12:25 A.M.
SATURDAY 07.15.06

Hey—sorry about the nonresponsiveness the last couple days. I was seriously losing it by Thursday, as everything about this G.D. week was just totally dragging me into a black hole of hopelessness. Witness:

Being back at Einstein . . . sucks.

Tlucek teaching us how not to drive . . . sucky.

The sticky grip of this torpid tropical weather . . . suckiest.

I know that my gripes are small things taken separately, but as the week progressed, they seemed to multiply and pile on each other and when that happens, everything about my lame life starts to seem sorta insurmountable and overwhelming and I just kinda shut down. You've seen it before. I'm sure you'll see it again. (See "Post–New Year's.")

So I formally (if belatedly) apologize for the media blackout. It sounds like I triggered your worrywart alarm and you should not be wasting time worrying about me and my so-called life while you're charting the trajectory of your bigger-than-life life. Anyway, I can report that my mood has now stabilized, as things have gotten markedly better in a couple ways. Otherwise, you still probably would not be hearing from me. Let me backtrack a bit—

Friday started out like crap, when Tlucek sprung a pop quiz on us first thing in the A.M. It wasn't a big thing—20 questions going over the rules of the road that he's been repeating ad nauseum all week long— but any sort of test during the months of June/July/August is not only bad timing, it's just downright rude. However, the quiz went pretty well, as the class as a whole scored 90 percent or better. (BTW—Brett basically copied her answers from me.) Given the stellar results all around, Tlucek said he'd take us out on the road a day earlier than planned. That woke all of us up from our collective instructional slumber and, with a couple assistant teachers, Tlucek divided the class into small driving groups that would take to the road for the rest of the morning.

My learning carpool consisted of me and Brett (of course), this Indian kid named Rami, and yes, homophobic ol' Joey. But guess the hell what? As we're walking out to the parking lot, Joey sorta apologized to me for his supermortifying SuperFag comments earlier in the week. Still, I'm somewhat skeptical of the true nature of this turnaround, because I think the whole thing was done as a big show of tolerance solely for Brett's sake. I know you'll say I'm being typically, Hal-ically cynical in my reading here by not giving anyone (that is, Joey) a chance to redeem themselves and show their true human nature. But think about it—do you truly believe that Joey wanted to be in that car with me or with Brett? So, bottom line—his apology was really just to get on Brett's good side. Cynical? Maybe. Realistic? More like it.

As we hopped into a clunky Geo four-door sedan for our first day on the road, Joey volunteered to drive first so he could show us how cool he was. Yet, per usual, he simply made an ass of himself, driving like he was playing Xbox while Tlucek, riding shotgun, kept having to slam the safety brake to keep us all from meeting our maker on Viers Mill Road. Rami, Brett, and I sat in the backseat while Joey kept making eyes at Brett through the rearview. Ughhhh. What is his damage? Does he truly think Brett is gonna be interested in his loser self? It's like he doesn't even live in the world with the rest of us. He's in his own Joey-verse, where any babe he sets his "playa" eyes on falls for him while, at the same time, some lame, half-hearted apology is gonna turn me into his best friend. Uh, I think not.

Next, it was Rami's turn to drive, and he did decently, with some minor Tlucek interference on the braking. Then came Brett and, yeah, you guessed it, we all nearly died. As she does not pay a whit of attention in class, the girl equally does not pay attention to the road and, while driving, kept chatting with me over her shoulder. Every time she turned around to address me, the wheel sorta went with her, thus sending the entire vehicle swerving in big wavy *S*s all over Rockville Pike. Tlucek kept barking at Brett to concentrate on driving as opposed to gossiping, and finally, after his incessant badgering, she gave up on our conversation and tried to deal with the road ahead of her. But when Tlucek proposed a lane change with a reminder to check her blind spot, Brett turned to look over her left shoulder and again sorta took the whole damn wheel with her, sending the car careening into the oncoming lane of traffic.

I have to admit that, at first, this was almost exciting. Until, that is, Brett totally froze as this FedEx truck barreled directly toward us, horn wailing. Brett's response? She basically screamed, which was not exactly the defensive driving move we were all hoping for. Christ—I totally thought we were history. Finally, Tlucek had to reach over and grab the wheel himself, sending us squealing back into the correct lane of traffic and setting off a flurry of horns as people avoided our Deathcar. Then, in a straining-to-be-calm voice, Tlucek told Brett to pull over. And so, after an elapsed driving time of 3 minutes and 42 seconds, Brett's time at the wheel was thankfully cut short. Our lives, fortunately, were not.

Next up was me, and I was nervous as hell. I didn't realize driving could actually be so damn deadly until I saw that fact so vividly demonstrated by our game of FedEx chicken. None of Tlucek's gory movies or scare talk could prepare anyone for that moment when your stomach hits the floorboards and you realize the end is nigh. Who knew that death would feel like indigestion?

Anyway, I got my turn and I did pretty well, considering we were on Randolph Road at the tail end of rush hour. However, not wanting to take any chances post-Brett, Tlucek ordered me onto a maze of Rockville side streets. Even though I had no idea where I was going, driving in general was going great until I spotted someone limping along the side of the road. As we got closer, this guy turned around and, guess what—it was Henri! In a reflex reaction, I slammed on the brakes. This was not a great move, quite counter to our repetitive instruction to <u>always</u> pump the brake. Well, I pumped it, but only once, bringing the car to a screeching halt and sending Tlucek forehead-first into the dash. *Smack!*

As Brett was totally cracking up in the backseat, Tlucek started yelling at <u>me</u> for coming to an abrupt stop. As he yammered away, though, I didn't really hear him, as I was focusing on Henri, who had hobbled over to my side of the car. He said *jourbon* with a friendly grin, and I asked him why he was limping. Henri had been over at Wheaton Regional Park, practicing Parkour moves on the jungle gym, when he sprained his ankle. He blamed the injury on the cheap trainers he has, adding that he's been desperate to get a professional pair but his mom won't spring for them. So while we were chatting like this, Tlucek, highly annoyed, interrupted and said we had to get back to Einstein. I asked Henri if he needed a ride, as he seemed to be in pain, and Tlucek went ballistic, screaming about how it's against school regulations and all that jazz. Finally, I was like, "Uh, the guy can't walk!" Tlucek said there was no room for him in the back with Rami, Joey, and Brett, but I did notice an empty seatbelt in the middle of the front seat. And finally Tlucek relented.

Noticing Henri's distinct accent, Joey proceeded to ask Henri if he was from France (???), the answer to which got Joey spouting like an idiot about how he thinks France is full of cowards because they didn't want to destroy Iraq. I told Joey that just 'cause Henri's French doesn't mean he actually runs the damn country, and that pretty much ended that, thank God. Henri turned to me with a quick, relieved glance, too, which was sorta cute. After an uneventful 10-minute drive, we arrived at Henri's street. He lives over in Kensington, as it turns out, in one of those big, ancient houses in Rock Creek Hills with a serious-size yard and everything. I complimented the joint and he responded with a shy smile, saying it wasn't his. Apparently, the French government owns it and lets various people use it when they're on assignment in D.C. Still, it's a nice pad, and a lot better than any of the one-story shacks we're more familiar with in our neighborhood.

So I was pulling up his driveway to turn around when something amazing and unexpected happened. Glancing in my rearview to make sure I wasn't going to cause an accident, I noticed that Henri was looking at me in the mirror too, checking me out almost. You know that feeling I wrote about, of my stomach dropping out when Brett nearly killed us all? Well, when I saw Henri's disembodied eyes gazing at me in the mirror, I got that feeling again, but even more intense. It was like . . . whoa. Maybe Brett actually had a point—you know, about Henri being into me after all? At least that's what I was thinking until Brett chimed in with a proposition. As Henri thanked me for the ride and hopped out of the car, Brett said he should meet us up at the Wheaton Plaza for a movie sometime next week. Henri agreed to this plan almost cheerily, adding that he didn't have much else to do this summer. Then Brett tossed him a piece of paper through the back window and said for him to give a call on Monday.

At first, I was like, great—now I'm gonna be Brett and Henri's gay sidekick, sitting in the back of the Loews, munching my popcorn like a dumb-ass while they get it on to some bad teen-horror movie. But once we got back to Einstein and got rid of Tlucek, the car, and Joey (God, he is such a friggin' pest!), Brett said she had suggested the movie with Henri because she knew that I wouldn't be so bold as to make a plan myself. I was like, "Well, why the hell are you giving him your phone number, then?" And you know what she said? "Hello—I gave him _your_ phone number."

The second she said this, I got that upset-stomach feeling again, like I was gonna puke or something. Christ! I didn't ask her to do this! I don't need her to pimp me out to every hot Euro-punk in the Wheaton metropolitan area. But as I said all this, Brett just laughed and laughed, like I was making a massive joke. I SO _wasn't_!!! But she was like, "Oh Hal . . . you're so funny . . . I'll talk to you this weekend." I mean, what the hell is that?! Brett is great and everything, but suddenly she's acting like she's known me and my behavior forever? It's not like we're best friends after a week, but there she was, acting like she knows everything about me! Of course, I've known you forever and you have only an inkling of my twisted personality. So there is no way <u>she</u> is suddenly the Hal expert she thinks she is. So don't worry, bro—you're still my number-one fag hag! Brett is merely insane.

OMG—it's almost 1:30 in the morning! I can't believe I've been writing on and on like this in your stupid blog. But I guess yesterday was a pretty eventful day and I had a lot to say . . . for once. My first day driving (woo-hoo) and my first day of . . . I dunno, something resembling a cute guy in my life? Maybe? I don't know. I'm pretty damn skeptical, but who the hell knows . . . maybe there might be something to this Henri thing after all. As long as Brett doesn't tomahawk me on the whole deal. (Yikes—that would suck!) Now, I know you've stated some reservations about this Henri thing, merely because of its surface similarities to some other losers I have known in a previous life (a.k.a. sophomore year). Still, I don't know. . . . This feels different somehow, like Henri might actually dig me, which was not the case with any of the Einstein trio of tragedy.

OK—I'm gonna get to bed now for real. One last thing: Thanks for being in touch even when I wasn't. And I will try to be a better correspondent (blogospondent?) from now on. And . . . oh yeah, congratulations on your big role. I would've said this earlier and praised you sooner and all that, but it's not like it's really big news. Which is to say, uh, I'm so <u>not</u> surprised you pocketed the lead! Neither should you be. As for G, I can't really be as excited about your developing diva-worship, but whatever. Just be careful, my friend. That is all. Signing off—H

Week 2

So I leave you alone for one week and what? You've learned how to drive and are using your new skills to pick up hitchhiking frogs in R.C. Hills? I'd return to Wheaton on the next Metrobus and put a stop to all this, but unfortunately, we can't leave the drama gulag. Oh yeah—and I've got a show to do. Not to mention a couple love affairs to deal with. Both real and imaginary.

First up, the imaginary front. Since SummerArts has only given us like, oh, about four and a half weeks to get this show together, we are moving at break-neck speed. We started in on the score this weekend and my voice is hoarse from the constant singing. Dude—Sondheim can seriously wear a guy down! My favorite song right now is this ballad I get to sing at my wedding, "Not a Day Goes By." It's just a powerhouse number about how you think about the person you're in love with every day of your life. It's such an amazing song that builds and builds to a heartbreaking conclusion, because, as I'm singing it to my new wife, Ghaliyah is standing to the side of us, singing about me. How intense is that?!

As for Ghaliyah herself, we are really setting off some sparks. At least around the piano. Our fictional characters are supposed to hate each other at the

34

beginning of the show, because she's bitter and a big drunk because I never fell for her. I'm hoping that, as we start rehearsing the later stuff that shows how we became best friends, it might be better for our relationship. If there is one. Yeah—I know—I am a dope to believe there's hope. LOL . . . that's funny. Dope/hope. What the hell is that?! I'm writing Sondheim-style. I am truly mad. Or in L. Or madly in L? ☺

One thing that might complicate our storyline is Ryan, our annoying director. He still hasn't told us his mysterious concept for the show, which Ghaliyah thinks means he's a friggin' genius. I think it means the dude has his head up his ass. Seriously. He acts like he knows everything, and he's barely out of school. But I haven't said this out loud or anything. And I can hear you already: "Don't be such a wuss, Chuck. Speak up." That's easy to say, but Ryan is not just some romantic rival. He's my director and I'm his star. If we don't get along, it will be bad news for both of us.

Another song we've been working on is this insane patter number Chaz and I have called "Inside Franklin Shepard, Inc." (Franklin is me), in which Chaz's character basically rips me a new asshole for being a self-centered, egotistical bastard. Wait—don't even think it! Life does not imitate art all the time. (ha) Anyway, this particular number is really challenging for Chaz, as he has to say a billion words at a speedy pace with tempo changes every few bars. I'm starting to appreciate Chaz's talents and be less annoyed by his flamboyance.

In fact, I was thinking . . . if this Henri thing doesn't work out (correction—when this Henri thing doesn't work out), you and Chaz could make a cute couple. Seriously. He is not only wildly talented but I think a pretty decent-looking guy, too. He could be in a catalog, like J. Crew or something. He's very tall and tan and sorta preppy. Still, I'm sure he could grow into a grungier look under your fashion influence. Or lack thereof. Chaz has style, but I don't think he's uncool toward those who don't. Ooooops—was that too harsh?

Oh—before I dash off—great news! Ryan said that our performances of *Merrily* are actually gonna be open to the public next month. That means you can come check it out! Maybe it can be your first official trip as a licensed driver—it's a week after your birthday! So mark your calendar—the show is running three nights, August 17 through 19. But don't come opening night because I'll be nervous enough without my toughest critic in the house. So plan on closing night. And that would be great, 'cause there'll probably be a cast party that night, too, so you could meet Chaz. I think he's pretty hot for a dude. Seriously.

Holy shit—I can't believe I just wrote something like that! Six months ago, I would have never even <u>thought</u> something like that. Wow. But now . . . it's a whole new world, as you certainly know all too well. All right, back to reality . . . I mean, rehearsal. Later!

01:25 P.M.
MONDAY 07.17.06
OK—I have to say or write something here about your last entry. Actually, it's not just about your last entry but about something in general that's been bothering me re you. Why, I ask, do you act sometimes like me being gay is the biggest change in <u>your</u> life? Hell—I'm the one who actually is gay and has to deal with all this shit. But you act like it's rocked your world in some way that just doesn't really make sense to me.

What is so new about your world? I mean . . . you can still flirt with the same old divas that you always have and no one is going to look at you differently or scream out "Hetero!" in the halls of Einstein. And if writing that a guy is hot slightly freaks your shit, I have something else to add on this subject: Get the hell over it! How long have I had to play along with your endless drooling over cute girls? Believe me, it was pretty freaky for me to have to pretend that all those chicks we talked about pre-gay were these so-called babes. So please keep that in mind when you start to believe the grand delusion that your life is so goddamn bizzaro.

And another thing. (Yes—I am on a proverbial roll!) Please do <u>not</u> be setting me up with Chaz, either now or in the future. I am very serious on this topic. Why? OK—hmmmm, let's see. Why on earth would you think that I'd be interested in Chaz? Chaz sounds like a friggin' spaz. I hope to hell that you are not getting this arranged gay marriage going simply because Chaz shares my interest in the male species, because, if that is the sorry case, that would be beyond retarded. Now, I know you're like, "Uh, why would that be so wrong?" OK, here's the deal: You can't just set up two gay guys simply because they're gay. That'd be like me saying, "Hey, I met this random girl up at 7-Eleven yesterday who has two eyes and some tits and, OMG, you guys would be <u>PERFECT</u> together!"

Do you get my meaning here? I need a little more than gayness in a boyfriend—that's the bottom line. So, given your descriptions of Chaz to date, I honestly don't think we'd hit it off, because he pretty much sounds like someone I have very little in common with other than the gay factor. But also, I have to add here for future setup reference, I don't really dig on guys who are so über gay. Can you tell me where it is written that just because we like guys we have to act like girls? And from what you've said, Chaz sounds like a big fairy-freak. In fact, referencing back to your entry of 07.13.06 (aren't you glad you decided to do this blog thing!), I can see that you described the said Chaz, and I quote, as being "slightly insane." Now, I know I'm not the most stable dude in Wheaton, but please, Chuck . . . if you have your heart set on playing gay matchmaker, the least you can do is find me a guy who might not be such a friggin' nut case!

Sorry I'm being such a bitch about all this, but it's Monday and I think I've earned it or something. As for anything else to report, there is nothing else. We were back in the classroom this morning for driving school, which sucked big-time. And Henri hasn't called either. Shocker, right? Oh why do I even bother to get excited about some dumb random guy like this. Ugggh. It is beyond lame, wholly tragic, and in the end just a damn stupid waste of time.

01:51 P.M.
MONDAY 07.17.06

Supercalifragishitstick—you won't believe who just called! That's right, the ol' frog himself, Henri. He asked me if I wanted to go up to Wheaton Plaza tomorrow to hang. Can you friggin' believe it?! Of course, the fact he asked me if I was free was hysterical in and of itself. (Like, uh, let me check with my secretary and see if I can squeeze you into my crazy schedule.) Anyway, I told him to come by Einstein when we get out of driving tomorrow. I think I'll see if Brett can join us too, as there is no way that I'm going to spend time alone with him. At least right yet. (OMG—that would be way too datey and gay.) But isn't that <u>wild</u> that he called?

Oh—and his accent is even sexier on the phone, if you can believe it. I can't. What am I saying? I have no F-ing idea what . . . wow. I'm having a moment of incoherence. Anyway, it was just nice to hear from him and completely not what I expected, I guess. Not like it means that much really. It certainly wasn't the world's biggest or sexiest conversation or anything, but it was cool to talk to him on the phone and not feel the public scrutiny of Brett watching us, checking to see what we both might be giving away in terms of what interest we might have in each other. It sorta felt easier to talk to him on the phone, in a way, without that sorta pressure. And, well, sexier, too . . . his voice is pretty sexy. OK—I can't believe I just wrote a double sexy. That's just tacky. Undo. Undo! Why the hell is there no Ctrl-Z on this thing?!

09:42 P.M.
MONDAY 07.17.06

LOL—dude, you are killing me! One minute it's the end of the world as you know it and the next you're Gene Kelly tapping his way through a downpour. Not that you'd ever dance in public. That I know from many years spent trying to lure you out onto the parquet or the gym floor. Maybe, though, you're dancing in your mind or . . . gulp, your heart? (ha) Can't wait to hear how the big nondate goes. I want all the details. Even if it gets gross. ☺

My day here was pretty cool. We started with a movement class in the morning that was all about "claiming our personal space." I've never been Mr. Height (as you like to remind me), so it was interesting to see how I could add an inch or two by adjusting my posture, angling my head up, and imagining there's a string coming out of my head like I'm someone's puppet. I know, it sounds pretty ridiculous. But it was really great and, hey—it worked. Next time you see me, who knows, perhaps we'll see eye to eye.

Next up was our voice class, where I learned a new trick: breathing through my thighs. OK—I can see your face going slack on that one. But hold on—it's for real. Professor Eckhart was trying to get us to take deeper breaths when she said breathe through your thighs. Once everyone had stopped cracking up, we realized there was some method to her madness. It's more of a visualization thing than truly breathing through your thighs. Anyway, I noticed a huge difference in my singing after that. When I had that much air inside my lungs, projecting and sustaining my voice was much easier, and I wasn't so winded by the end of a song.

After lunch, we had our rehearsals for *Merrily* to block some of the bigger and more complicated scenes. Because of this, I didn't get in much QT with Ghaliyah. I think it's okay, though. As much as I don't agree with your opinion about her, I did get something from all your yammering about it. I thought that it might not be a bad idea to hang back a bit, you know? Not dog the poor woman. I think that's been my problem, more than what you refer to as my diva-worship. I tend to get fixated on these girls, true. But shit—isn't that sorta what love is? Getting fixated on someone? Like for the rest of your life? Just asking . . .

I think my problem is more how I tend to hang around too much and end up driving these girls crazy. But a bad crazy, not Beyonce crazy. So while we did our blocking for this big party scene, I was charming and nice to Ghaliyah but not attached to her at the hip. I even decided it might be a good idea to get to know other members of the cast too. On breaks lately, I've been hanging more with MK, who plays Beth (my first wife in the show). Despite being from Frederick ("Fred-neck," as she calls it, due to it being in the sticks), she is very, very cool and also knows tons of trivia about Broadway that puts me to shame. OH—and get this. She said she thought I was gay at first, but then, when she saw Chaz, realized I wasn't. Seriously. I suffered by comparison.

So about this Chaz setup . . . all right, it's true the guy is a bit more capital G-A-Y than you. But I was way too quick to judge him as "insane" after two days of knowing him. (And yes, I am still happy that I started this blog, even if you do throw my own words back at me.) Still, Chaz's flamboyance is his way to get attention. Being thrown into a group of 40 actors/singers/dancers who are all equally attention-junkies, Chaz went overboard the first few days to get noticed. But he's calmed down since. And even though it still creeps me out to say this, he is <u>damn</u> sexy.

Yes, that's right, Chuck used the word "sexy" to describe another dude. Ice skating in hell begins in five minutes. ☺

Yours in sexiness, C

09:18 P.M.
TUESDAY 07.18.06
Christ—I am so friggin' wired on caffeine. Two shots of espresso and a) I can't believe I never tried this before and b) I can't believe this SHIT is legal. Thus, given my state, I must present the following surgeon general's WARNING:

This entry will be slightly crazed and hyper and filled with run-on sentences because I can't stop to punctuate things in my current buzz-induced delirium because who the hell knew that the blast of a few sips of continental-style joe could set my fingers on fire like this or all of me for that matter but maybe it's not the coffee speaking but something else that one could refer to in a coffee manner as Le French Press (a.k.a. Le French Crush) which is a terrible joke but one that I found pretty damn difficult to wholly resist so sue me dammit!

Now—with that little disclaimer out of the way, I can get to the news of the day. Another morning at school, sure, blah-blah-etc., but afterward was when the real excitement began. Henri was waiting for me outside Einstein (!) wearing a pair of baggy orange shorts and a fairly form-fitting silver tee as he practiced some Parkour landings by jump-ing off the bike rack. He seemed very happy to see me, a wide grin spreading across his face in a way that struck me as highly unlikely, since Henri generally looks like a badassmuthafucka! (WURDH!)

Anyway, we were chatting amiably and somewhat aimlessly when Brett approached with Joey in tow, which was both annoying and a big relief, as I was nervous as hell talking to H for the first time after our phone call. Then we all made a plan to head up to Wheaton Plaza to check out a flick. The "we" I speak of is, you guessed it, me and Henri (that sounds like a song lyric, huh?), accompanied by Brett and Joey. See, Joey was initially not part of the plan at all and basically over-heard us talking about doing something during our break, and then tagged along in true Joey fashion, which I thought would've really pissed off Brett, but she didn't seem to mind too much. Either that or she was playing nice so that I might have a chance with Henri, which means, I guess, that maybe she wasn't into Henri after all. The mys-tery of girls . . .

Joey did make his presence at least somewhat useful once we arrived at the movie theater by talking some Goth-y college students into buy-ing tickets for us to an R-rated movie, *Afternoon of the Dead*, another sequel in that endless zombie series. We had about 20 minutes before the show, so Henri then offered everyone a toke on some weed he had scored from one of his fellow *traceurs*. Only Joey accepted the offer, trying in vain to be Mr. I'm-Cool-Too, which is, of course, utterly not the case and actually the complete opposite if you ask me. I just wanted to grab Joey by the ribbed collar of his sky-blue Izod and say, dude, didn't you watch all those lame peer-pressure antidrug infomercials they showed us in homeroom on Channel 1? Maybe Joey's head was up his ass that day—that is, he was sitting on it and thus unable to view the TV properly.

As for the movie itself, it was damn scary and completely freaking my shit out, as I kept ducking my head away from the screen and averting my eyes from the carnage. OMG—there was insanely gory stuff in it, including one of the characters getting his leg amputated with a buzz saw while he was still conscious as the blood spurted up into his face. Throughout this gorefest, I kept jumping outta my seat and clawing the armrest next to me, which happened to have Henri's arm on it. Henri didn't really appreciate <u>that</u> so much but I certainly did, because, hell, touching his bare forearm, even in a moment of horror-movie-induced panic, was pretty damn hot. Unfortunately, Henri didn't seem to share my feelings on this issue after, oh, about the fifth time I did this. In fact, he was getting fairly annoyed, which became clear after we got out of the movie and he proceeded to make fun of my panic attacks to Joey and Brett. This was incredibly, colossally, stupendously (you get where I'm going with this?) embarrassing, especially in front of Joey, who kept calling me a wussy. Even worse, though, was the fact that, as Henri kept talking about me like this, it got me blushing, which Brett was kind enough to point out to everyone, which, of course, got me blushing even more. Great. So much for playing things cool. Aaaarrrrrrghhhhhh!!!!!!!

Anyway, Brett bailed on us soon after all this public humiliation, saying she had to go to a dentist appointment, which I think was a bit of a lie as she didn't talk about this before and it actually seemed to be a fiction she made up solely for the purpose of ditching Joey. Well, that left Henri and me with Joey (crap) and the task of ditching him ourselves. Amazingly, Henri was intuitive enough to sense the necessity of The Ditch and came up with a plan that made the whole thing much more believable than if I'd attempted it myself. There is something about bold, outright lies in a suave foreign accent that works because people aren't even listening to the ridiculous things you're saying . . . they're just listening to your accent. So Henri suddenly pretended to remember that there was a Parkour meet-up at his place at 4:00 and Joey, wanting nothing to do with Parkour or *traceurs* or anything explicitly French, bid us *adieu* (though, of course, he actually said "good-bye"), and that was it; it was just me and Henri. Back to that song lyric again . . . it's pretty catchy, no?

Left to ourselves, I was like, now what? We certainly weren't going back to Henri's house for the meet-up, as that was a big lie. And there was no way I was gonna bring him back to my tragic house, having seen the style in which he'd become accustomed to living (that is, in a ginormous R.C.H. estate). But still, Henri wanted to hang out, so we boldly went where few people had gone before: On his suggestion, we headed across Viers Mill Road into the heart of downtown Wheaton. Yes, that's right—Wheaton! (Cue horror-movie music.)

I know—you probably think I have truly lost my mind at this point, but what can I say? I was just as surprised by Henri's idea of an urban trek as you probably are. Sure, downtown Bethesda's cool and Silver Spring is even manageable, with that new minimall and movie megaplex . . . but crappy ass, nowhere-central Wheaton? I think not. So, still trying to change his mind on this destination, I suggested maybe hitting the McDonald's across University Blvd. and Henri got very disgusted citing corporate globalism and American cultural impe-rialism and a few other isms I can't even recall. Next, I tried to sug-gest the new Starbucks in the north parking lot, but he cursed at that idea, too, in French, even. (FYI—*merde* means "shit" and *futré* means "fuck.") Henri kept insisting that there was plenty to do in Wheaton. So, with his eyes bearing down on me—these deep-set hazel orbs that are sooooooo sorta . . . whoa . . . I was like, uh, all right, and we crossed Viers Mill into unexplored territory.

Henri actually had a Wheaton destination in mind, a Moroccan coffee shop called Marrakesh, just off University and Georgia. The place was in one of those countless strip malls that litter the area, but once you got out of the parking lot and into the joint itself, Marrakesh was pretty cool: blood-red tapestries hanging from the ceiling and old wicker tables and chairs clustered around a few bloated velvet couches. The place almost had charm if you could truly forget you were in down-town Wheaton. When we walked in, Henri spoke French to the guy behind the counter ("*Ça va mec!*" is French for "What's up, dude?"), indicating our Frenchie is a regular and, as such, ordered up two of "the usual": double espressos and almond croissants with Nutella, this spread-on chocolate that tastes like doughnut frosting—AWESOME!

As you know, I've never really even gotten into coffee, being a strict Diet Coke purist, but I gave it a shot, mainly because Marrakesh was so full of Moroccan realness that canned soda was not on the menu. And you know what? I totally dug it! The espresso was a little bitter at first, but then Henri dumped a couple packets of sugar in mine (that was so sweet, huh?), which made it go down a bit smoother. And then, about five minutes after downing it, I experienced this incredible rush of caffeine-induced excitement that's almost hard to describe. Maybe some of it had to do with just hanging with Henri, but it was more than that. It was like the world was suddenly full of possibility. Like there were instantly a million things to do this summer and I actually wanted to do all of them and be anything I wanted to be and . . . I don't know. It's weird. I had been feeling so down since you'd headed off, and then, after those espressos, I was suddenly pretty damn happy and opti-mistic, which was nice for a change. Even if it was semi–chemically induced.

Anyway, Henri then ordered some regular café lattés and we sat there for a couple hours, sipping and talking about random stuff like school and Parkour and friends. If your ears were on fire around 5:30 today, that's because I was talking a coffee-fueled blue streak about what a friggin' star you are. Henri was very impressed by all your stage accomp-lishments, which I thought was cool, you know? He basically didn't have the usual averse reaction to musical theater . . . which maybe means I have a shot with him after all, huh? LOL

Oh, and get this—we even exchanged e-mail addresses at the end of the day! So who the hell knows, perhaps there is hope for me and my summer after all. Maybe, as you fantasized in your last entry, you will actually see me doing back flips in the middle of a hurricane à la Gene Kelly. (ROTFL—just the image of that alone makes me crack up!) I don't know. . . . I have to say that, even though Henri and I didn't make out or hold hands or anything, the whole thing felt suspiciously like a date. Crazy, huh? Yours in insanity, H

09:03 A.M.
WEDNESDAY 07.19.06

Crazy is right. Crazy like a fool. But that's okay. It's not like I've been the antifool when it comes to Ghaliyah. So maybe we can both live out our foolishness together and make each other feel less worse by acting like emotional maniacs in front of our love interests. Does that make any sense?!

Hey—that story about the movie was hysterical, and so true. Remember when we saw *Scream* at my house? You were such a baby afterward, not wanting me to leave the room even to go to the bathroom. Like I wasn't gonna come back re the rules ("I'll be right baaaaacccckk!") And then later, when the phone rang? LOL—I had to pull you off the ceiling. That was awesome!

Anyway, before I get to my latest foolishness, a little vocabulary lesson. Do I have your full and undivided attention, class? (That's my Mr. Roccosalva imitation . . . pretty good, huh?) A "date" as defined in *Webster's* is as follows: "*n.* a social or romantic engagement with a person." Note: a person. Singular. Not multiple people. (Yes, Joey does count as a person, even if he is retarded.) And though you and Henri ended up alone together at Marrakesh, that was sorta by accident, not design. There was no engagement made to be alone with this Frenchman. And sure, I guess he sorta ditched Joey, but that was pretty much the national pastime when we were growing up.

I say all this not to douse your fire but only to remind you of the realities of dating. Not that I'm an expert or anything (ha), but dude, I can read a dictionary. 'Nuff said. Wait—sorry—false alarm. I've got more on this topic. Here's the deal—I don't want to have to go through all that drama of last spring when you kept talking about going on "dates" with the likes of Todd, Bryan, and that one with the name I could never get right (Yuri? Urdi? Icky?), only to have you come bitching to me about how these guys were total dicks. And straight dicks to boot.

Now, I can sense your temperature rising, your eyes getting all bloodshot, and your ears going red in typical Hal-overheating fashion because you think I'm saying this because I don't want to listen to your gay romantic complaints. It's not that. Seriously. I just don't want to see you get all hurt again. Even worse was the way you beat yourself up over these things; it's what you do and you know it. You are the king of the self-inflicted knockout punch. So that's all on this topic. This is Dr. Phil, over and out.

As to life on Mars, things here at UMD are cool. We had a blast last night, hanging out on the big lawn in front of our dorm, singing songs and playing games until it got dark. I know, it sounds pretty childish and summer-campy, but honestly, I have never had so much fun in my life!

There was this one game that we played called Ha-Ha. It sounds so stupid when you explain it, but trust me, it was hi-lar-i-ous. Basically, it starts with one person lying down on his back, and then another person lies down perpendicular to them with the back of their head resting on the first person's stomach. Then you form a huge chain of people like this. . . . We had about 30 when we all got down on the grass. The chain we formed looked like a crazy, human crossword puzzle!

The game actually starts when the first person says "ha," then the person with their head on the first person's stomach has to say "ha-ha," and then the next person, "ha-ha-ha," and so on. But here's the trick: You have to do it without cracking up. Seriously! It sounds simple, but it was so hard, because when they "ha," it pushes their stomach up (as we've been big into speaking from the diaphragm). When you do that seven times in a row, bouncing someone's head on your belly, it's impossible not to bust out laughing.

Of course, Ghaliyah was close by during all this hilarity, my head bouncing on her stomach. (natch) I did okay the first time the chain of "ha"s got to us, but lost it the second time, which got her sorta pissed off. She said I wasn't concentrating and that, if I was a good actor, I could put the humor out of my head and just say all the "ha"s without losing it. But it was impossible to do this because it sounded so damn funny to say "ha" about 12 times.

As for Ghaliyah's theory of acting, I think she is on crack. Not closing yourself off to an experience and whatever emotions it brings up is the essence of acting. Being real and true and honest, even if it means you can't stop laughing to save your life. But me and the Ice Princess differ on this point, as she thinks acting is all about control. Sure—there is some of that, because you need to be in control of your body. (Like that whole "claiming your space" thing from the other day.) But if you're not open to the spontaneous, you're gonna look like a robot. Which she does. Sometimes. She'll let it fly when she's singing, but when it comes to our scene work, sometimes she is a little stiff.

I've noticed that Ghaliyah's kinda uptight when it comes to opening herself up. It's the toughest part of acting, to be that vulnerable. To be that open to anything. And maybe I go too far in the other direction, being a total goofball on stage. But I'd rather do that than not be alive or able to enjoy a simple game like Ha-Ha.

All right—I'm gonna be late for studio, so I'll wrap this up. One last thing: Since no matter what I say about Henri you are clearly going to be fixated on him, I thought it'd be nice to get a good visual on this character. Can you take some pix the next time you guys go on a "date" and post them here? Maybe you can show me some of his Parkour moves? Whatever you do, just don't post a shot of H toking up or we will seriously be reported to the higher hosting authorities at Xanga and our blog will get shut down.

Holy shit—I can't believe I just said that, because now you will post that exact photo and end the whole thing on purpose. Shit. Please—just post a nice, normal picture, Hal. Besides, you have to admit at this point, hasn't the blog been a lot of fun? ☺ C

08:05 P.M.
WEDNESDAY 07.19.06
You think you're so funny sometimes, don't you? Laughing at your own bloggy jokes and emoticoning your sly little winks. Well, let me be the first to tell you that sometimes you are not so amusing, especially when you are lecturing me on the meanings and/or nuances of the English language. Remember—I'm supposed to be the smart one here, so I do take some offense on being quoted *Webster's* definitions by a drama fag. Furthermore, if you will refer back to my entry regarding the usage of the word "date," I said it "felt suspiciously like a date." Which is to say, I know when a date is a date and I know that Henri

and I did not have one. All I said was that it just had that feeling, even though it wasn't officially a bona fide date. It just seemed like one and I kinda was diggin' on that feeling. That's all. Believe me, I am under no delusions about the true meaning of dating, especially after what happened with the three whose names will not be mentioned. (Didn't you get that memo? Christ!)

As for Henri and me, we are hanging out, not "dating." That's all. And I can still think he's cute and sexy and has a tight body without being in some sorta datey couple thing with him. So maybe you should save the lectures for your fellow actors . . . like G, perhaps? She might actually get something from your theory of acting. Anyway, your whole acting theorem is truly a genuine, albeit rare, case of you knowing what you are talking about. (Ha) See—I can laugh at my own lame digs as well. I could even drop in emoticons if so inspired, though don't you think they're kinda gay?

09:13 P.M.
WEDNESDAY 07.19.06
Dude. You are such a bitch sometimes, you know that? Seriously. I thought the purpose of the blog was to stay in touch. Tell each other what's going on and shit and not be a defensive ass about everything I say. All right—maybe I went a little overboard, but I guess I thought you had a sense of humor. So let's make an effort to curtail the lectures and stick to the facts. Which is to say—what is up? ☺

11:52 P.M.
WEDNESDAY 07.19.06
I love it when you get all dramatic and sassy. No wonder this MK thought you were a homo! As to what's up, frankly there wasn't much to report yesterday (thus my delayed response today), which is why I thought raking you over the coals would at least occupy some of my endless free time this summer. But then, earlier tonight, Henri called and we met up again. And no, it wasn't a date. But it was an adventure. Get this: We were up at Wheaton Plaza all night! I know, not exactly the adventure you were thinking of. But we were not just lamely

hanging around the food court or watching a dumb summer movie. Oh no . . .

At Marrakesh, we'd talked about his giving me some lessons in the fine art of skateboarding without the board. So the plan was to go to the mall after it had closed so Henri could show me some Parkour moves without being disturbed by people or security (a.k.a. "Jakes" in Parkour-ese). But when we got there, we ended up breaking into the mall's construction site—you know, where they're building the new-and-improved "Westfield Shopping Town." Now, before you flip out, as I know you will, the break-in was not my idea, it was Henri's, and it wasn't exactly a break-in. Also let me say in my defense that, even though it was sorta illegal, it's not like what we did was some reprehensible moral lapse, like stealing a car or breaking into a real person's house. It was a construction site after all. What were we gonna steal, some spare I-beams?

OH—since we've become fond of dissecting definitions lately in our discourse here, I would like to dissect the term "break-in." It is a common phrase regarding criminal activity that generally implies someone actually broke something to get into a restricted/locked space. (I didn't even have to check my Webster's for that one!) However, Henri and I didn't have to bust anything. We didn't even have to pick any locks. Basically, there is a huge fence around the new wing of the mall where they are building the Macy's (where the Giant supermarket used to be). Well, the truck gate was closed but not locked, so all we had to do was swing it open and walk right into what we thought was the first floor of the new Macy's. But get this—we were actually on the second floor, as they are excavating a whole new underground level underneath the Macy's wing, as well as underneath the entire mall itself!

We discovered this by sliding down the escalator platforms that had just been installed and finding ourselves in what we thought was the basement. But then we saw a huge entranceway that opened onto a big, cavernous area underground that was a mirror image of the mall layout above. It looked pretty wild down there, as the whole space was half finished, with wires and beams dangling and pieces of piping running everywhere. Even though they were building something new, it almost looked like the joint had exploded or been the site of some massive earthquake. It was also very, very dark. Fortunately, Henri had a laser pointer and a Mag-Lite that was sufficient to lead our way. We explored this whole new section of the mall for almost an hour—it was huge! And it's not really going to be underground, as we found that they are excavating under the north parking lot, too, so that will have two levels as well. When they're finished, it's gonna be massive!

Wandering around with our hazy Mag-Lite leading the way, I asked Henri to do some Parkour moves, but he said he didn't want to, that it might be dangerous with all the construction crap down there. I thought this was weird and told him he was being a wuss. This got Henri's ire up and he shoved me a bit, then he finally confessed that he'd gotten stoned before he got to my house, which is why he didn't want to risk any moves. It's funny, because when I first saw him tonight he seemed a little goofy, grinning like an idiot. I thought this was due to the fact that he was glad to see me or something. But no, he was just baked, though definitely in a more bemused way than he was at the movie earlier in the week.

As to your request for pics, I did get to snap a few of Henri and our descent into the belly of the mall. So check them out—I did some captions, too, for explanation and sarcastic commentary. Oh, and guess what? No. No. Wrong again. The flash on the camera got us in a bit of trouble when it caught the attention of a Jake. It was late in the game, though, just as we were about to head out of the Macy's. As the guard walked up to us, Henri started speaking nonstop French while I just shrugged and repeated a few choice phrases in what I thought was a lame French accent. (Not that the Jake was gonna know, as he himself was Indian and could barely speak English.) As Henri kept on with the rapid-fire *française*, the guard got so flustered and mystified by what we were saying (or in my case, trying to say) that he told us to leave and not to come back, locked the open gate behind us, and essentially let us go. Amazing, huh?

Once we'd walked a safe distance away from the mall, we both started busting up laughing over the whole thing. Henri couldn't stop laughing, in fact, and said he had a case of the giggles from being stoned, which was sorta funny and cute. He was—

Shit. Valerie just got home. She seems to be having some sorta active social life this summer, which is good for her, I guess. Finally back on the dating horse after dumping Big Fat Fred (thank God). I have to say, though, that all these recent outings have certainly made it easy for my escapes to the mall *sans* any explanation or justification. (BTW—*sans* is French for "without.") So she hasn't even seen or heard about—

OMG—Val just popped her head in here to say good night and she was a bit tipsy! I think she'd been smoking cigarettes again, too. (Blecch!) She said she was at Sandra's house downtown for a BBQ and took the Metro home. It's funny—she just made this huge deal about her mode of transport home solely to make the point that she wasn't DWI. Believe me, that is <u>not</u> gonna be a problem for me when I'm legal. I have enough trouble driving sober without adding a few drinks to the mix.

All right—I'd better sign off before Valerie makes a return visit to tell me to turn the computer off. Gotta say, though, it's a drag you couldn't be here for our big mall adventure tonight. It reminded me of all the semi-illegal stuff we did when we were in grade school . . . remember? Like breaking into the Metro rail yard at Glenmont when they were still building it. That was pretty cool, especially when that rent-a-cop tried to chase us through the woods and tripped over his own big feet. LOL! Thank God for clumsy adults. OK—miss you and all that crap. H

09:20 A.M.
THURSDAY 07.20.06

Wow—no one will ever accuse you of being sentimental, my friend (re miss you and all that crap). Which I guess is part of whatever charm you have, you friggin' nut.

So . . . breaking into the mall and getting away with it? You must have been seriously working the charm with that security guard, because I can't imagine your French would cut it. You got a "D" in Spanish freshman year, as I recall. And there were also your occasional tirades about foreign languages in general. Like how, as an American, there was no need for you to learn another language, as most other countries take the time to learn English. So I have to point out here that it is capital-H <u>Hilarious</u> that you are hot for someone who speaks something other than your language. (ha)

As for the Henri pics, I have to say I was a bit surprised by them. Or him. You never said anything about Henri being my evil twin. (Or me being his evil twin, depending on your perspective.) I mean, we look like we could have been separated at birth. Seriously. Not hairstyle-wise, as his blond locks are a bit more wilding than mine, but we kinda have the same square face and skin tone and even sly grin.

Now, I know you'll hate this, but I showed the pics to Chaz and he agreed that there were definitely some severe similarities. Then, he asked me a question I didn't really have an answer to: He wanted to know if you had a crush on me. Chaz said that clearly I was "your type." Then I got to thinking. . . . I know, I know. Chuck + Thinking = Danger! But seriously, I started thinking back to the whole New Year's incident and wondered if that was somehow connected to Chaz's question?

If you don't feel comfortable writing about this here, that's cool. But I <u>am</u> curious to know the real deal, as I'm truly trying to figure you out lately. It's like, the more I know about you and your sexual proclivities (OK—I learned that word from Chaz!), the more I don't know about you, if that makes any sense. You've become a bit of a mystery, Hal. It's like one door opens but leads to another and another, most of which are kinda locked. And sure, it's always been hard to get a handle on what's up with you. That's been the case since day one in first grade, when it was total chaos and you were in your own little Hal-world, calmly sitting there making volcanoes out of Play-Doh. (LOL—that image is still ingrained in my head!) I know you've never been Mr. Open with the emotional details or general info on what's spinning around in that mad brain of yours. So all I'm saying is, hey—I'd like to know more, if you want to tell me. That's it. No big deal.

As for my romantic life, my "hang back" plan with Ghaliyah is sorta working. However, there may be a bad side effect to this. It seems that the more I hang back, the more Ryan steps up. Ghaliyah has become quite enamored of him in the last few days of rehearsal and has spent the majority of her meal times with him too. Oh—and he still hasn't told us his big concept for the show. Lately, I'm thinking that he probably never will, because (*ding-ding-ding*) it doesn't <u>exist</u>! Still, Ghaliyah is just gaga about him and his big theories on acting and the stage and how he is such a master thespian at such a young age. YAWN!

The joke is, just because he has a master's degree doesn't mean he's a dramatic genius. At <u>all</u>. Every time I try to get into a discussion with him about my character, Ryan starts going on and on about all this theoretical bullcrap that has nothing to do with anything. Correction—other than inflating <u>his</u> massive ego. He'll start talking about some other production of some other play he did or some famous mentor he had at Arena Stage that no one's heard of. I mean, he'll just go on and on, trying to impress us with the fact that he's done a million shows. Of course, I don't give a shit about all his previous shows. I just want to know about <u>this</u> show. Something which he seems to have very little clue about.

Everyone else in the cast has been great, though, encouraging me and telling me I'm doing a good job even if I am getting zero direction. Still, it would be nice to have an ally in this, as opposed to an enemy, romantic and otherwise. But, as they say, "the ho must go on!" (ha) This was a stupid joke that MK and I started during lunch yesterday. It doesn't really make any sense, other than to say that we are all drama ho's or something. But who cares. The way MK says it just kills me. . . . . The ho must go on! LOL

This weekend, one bright spot is that I might get to have some quality time with Ghaliyah *sans* Ryan (to borrow some French from you). We're going on a SummerArts field trip tomorrow to the National Gallery to see some art, and then to the Folger Theatre to see *Taming of the Shrew*. I've never really seen a professional production of Shakespeare, so it should be pretty cool. And this one's gotten raves! Even better is the fact that Ryan won't be along for the ride at all. He has to stay at UMD to work with the set and costume designers, who are a bit behind getting their technical acts together.

So wish me luck on the big date. OK—OK—I also know it's not really a date, but a guy can dream, right? Hopefully, though, Ghaliyah will see I am not such a bad dude in real life. I think lately she has me confused with my character, who is a bit of a jerk to her in *Merrily*. I just hope I don't do anything foolish during the show tomorrow, like dig my nails into her arm during the scary romantic banter. ☺ C

02:10 P.M.
THURSDAY 07.20.06
OK—first off, as to your question about Henri being your doppelgänger or something, I am not even going to discuss it. Though I will provide you with the definition of "doppelgänger"—"*n*. an apparition in the form of a double of a living person." But that definition really doesn't matter one bit, because guess what? Henri does not look like you <u>at all</u>! Other than the fact that you are both pale of complexion and blond of hair, that's about as far as it goes. And as to Chaz's question about me having a crush on you, yeah—you guessed it—I'm not going to discuss that, either.

Look—Chaz is so friggin' old school, it's ridiculous. That whole gay-guy-falling-for-the-best-friend thing is so damn 20th century. I always suspected that this Chaz was older than his years, and I have to say, that sorta dumb-assed commentary proves it. Which leads me to the bottom line here: You and Henri couldn't be more different. He is a sporty French guy who smokes pot and you are a musically gifted, Broadway-bound song-and-dance man. Need I say more? I thought not.

As to New Year's, I beg of you to please-<u>please</u>-PLEASE let that day (and night) of infamy lie. Yes, it's true I did say and do some undeniably stupid things on that long, drunken eve. It's also true that the overwhelming, magical powers of champagne succeeded in beating my usually gruff personality into submission, causing me to say all sorts of sappy things that I regret. However, I don't regret the ultimate upshot of the night: me coming out and all. But getting to that revelation was a little rougher (and messier) than I'd wanted it to be.

BTW—I thought I sent out a memo about this topic being buried, no? If somehow it got lost in the voluminous interoffice mail of our friendship, I kindly ask (no, I'm gonna make that "beg") for a 10-year moratorium on any further discussion of the events of January 1. And no, don't be your usual smartass self by wondering if December 31st is fair game for discourse—it ain't. So, with that out of the way, let's talk about you, okay?

I think that's great news about Ghaliyah going for the almighty idiot whom your people call "director." They seem made for each other in a way that's pretty brilliant and alliterate, too: the diva and the dumbass. Unfortunately, I can already sense in your written tone that the spark of competition that you soooooo live for has been lit under your own unsuspecting ass. Please, Charles (can I call you Charles when addressing topics of import?) don't start gunning for G simply because someone else is making more progress with her than you are. That is the <u>worst</u> reason in the world to like someone. Yes, it's true . . . it's even worse than going for a guy simply because he has a hot ass. How? Well, you really can't do anything about the scientific and fairly magnetic attraction between a guy and some body part. However, you <u>can</u> do something about competing for the sake of competition. Save your time and energy for the show—please? If you do so, I promise that I won't have a crush on you. (kidding)

As for my own weekend plans, there is nothing big on the horizon other than . . . well, actually not a goddamn thing. Maybe Brett and I will scare up some fun by renting an unrated DVD or something—

there was a vague discussion about this on our break today. Oh—and we did get out on the road again to do some more driving today. We even went on the Beltway for the first time, which was terrifying. I told Tlucek I wasn't ready for this sorta literal acceleration in difficulty, but he was undeterred, saying that everyone had to do a spin on 495 to pass the class. Except Brett, of course, who nearly got us all killed again after only a few minutes by switching lanes in front of a semi, thus getting herself removed from the driver's seat for the day. (Not that she minded.) I am beginning to suspect she does this on purpose so that Tlucek will relieve her of driving so she can get back to what she does best: texting Amanda. God knows what they say to each other, but T-Mobile is gonna send them both personalized Christmas cards. Their parents, on the other hand, will kill them when they get those bills! ($$$)

As for my time in the driver's seat, it was insane. In. Friggin'. Sane. Trying to switch lanes on the bloody Beltway while going 60 miles an hour? And checking your blind spot at the same time? Not to mention slipping in so-called "micro glances" at your dash to check the speed limit, which no one seems to obey anyway? You know, I thought the Beltway had colossally slow traffic jams, but it was pretty free and speedy when we got on shortly after the morning rush. Anyway, I was seriously sweating out my 10 minutes of highway terror and was beyond glad to pull off at the New Hampshire Ave. exit to give Rami a turn. Which is all to say, I will never drive on the Beltway again, I will never drive on the Beltway again, I will never drive on the Beltway again. . . .

Tonight, Valerie is going to Bethesda for a dinner with some of her girl-friends from work. Again, she made a big point of saying how Marisa is going to pick her up and be the Designated Driver (caps are hers, not mine), all to impart a Valuable Lesson to me. What—as if I've never heard the term before? In scare-tactics Driver's Ed? Christ—I could spell "designated driver" backward in my sleep at this point. She needn't waste her breath, but that, of course, is the core definition of being a mom: speaking to the wind.

Maybe I'll give Henri a buzz if I'm bored later and nothing's on cable. Not for a "date" or anything but just to hang out and alleviate the boredom, which again is becoming all-consuming. When are you coming back, again? August 20-something? That long, huh? Christ.

11:08 P.M.
THURSDAY 07.20.06

Special late-night entry, courtesy of Chaz. In true spaz fashion, he got his brother to FedEx his iBook from Baltimore once he realized there was Wi-Fi in St. Ann's. So now I'm not limited to the library's net access, which is cool. The tough part will be getting on the computer, as Chaz is constantly IM-ing about 20 people at the same time. I was like, "Who the hell are all these geeks?" Then, all serious, Chaz goes, "They are my people." No shit. That's what he said. Yep—Chaz is a total character sometimes. Make that <u>ALL</u> the times.

Anyway, had to write you because I had quite the revelation in our acting workshop tonight. Our teacher there is this pint-size but bigger-than-life former Broadway actor, Mr. Allis. He's now in residence at Arena Stage downtown, coming in once a week to do these master-classy things with us at SummerArts. How it works is that a couple students are given a scene (this week's being from *A Delicate Balance* by Albee) and they have about three hours to rehearse it. Now, using the Albee show was sorta absurd, as it's about a bunch of old people losing their minds. So the two teen actors were at a huge disadvantage going in, I thought.

But after they were done with the scene and Mr. Allis started dissecting things, he said that the age of a character shouldn't matter to an actor. As a professional, he told us how he's always doing stuff that's 10, even 20 years older than he is. What matters, he said, was understanding the character, what he called their "core": what they want and need. He said most characters in a play can be boiled down to something they want or are trying to get.

Another thing he talked about a lot was how characters are not what they say but what they do. His example of this was how in *Streetcar,* Stanley is always talking down to Blanche, but his actions (grabbing her stuff, walking in when Blanche's changing, etc.) show that he's intrigued and sexually into her. That was pretty surprising, I thought. It's an interesting concept, this character stuff, don't you think?

Walking back to St. Ann's tonight, I started mulling all this over in terms of life in general and found that it applied there, too. For instance, take you. When you write all sarcastically about missing me and start complaining about "this dumb blog," I realized that these are things you are saying (or writing, in this case) but not really meaning. The reality is that you've actually been writing in the blog. A lot. More than me, even. Which means that you <u>do</u> like it and also that you <u>do</u> miss me. See—I found you out. (ha)

I know how you like to play a big, bitter game. And that's okay, since this riff of yours is usually pretty amusing. But now that my skills as an actor are being honed, you won't be able to fool me anymore. Now—don't worry about me spilling all your secrets (or not-so-secrets). They're still just as safe as they've always been. Including New Year's. And I understand totally how you don't want to get into the whole thing. So I won't harp on it in true Chuck-fashion. But Chaz wants to say a little something himself:

HI—IT'S CHAZZZZZZZ. SO WHAT'S UP WITH YOUR NEW BOYFRIEND WHO LOOKS LIKE CHUCK? HE REALLY DOES, OBJECTIVELY SPEAKING. I'M JUST AN INNOCENT BYSTANDER TOO. (WELL, MAYBE NOT SOOOO INNOCENT—LOL!!!) CHUCK SAYS YOU THINK THEIR PERSONALITIES ARE TOTALLY DIFFERENT, WHICH TOTALLY MAKES SENSE, AS HE IS TOTALLY FRENCH AND CHUCK TOTALLY ISN'T. ☺ BUT STILL—THEY ARE BOTH PRETTY SEXY. [CHUCK IS MAD I JUST WROTE THAT!] OK—THAT'S ALL I'M GONNA SAY, BECAUSE I WANT TO GET CHUCK OFF THIS THING SO I CAN FINISH SOME CHATS. HOPE TO MEET YOU SOMEDAY. CHUCK SAYS YOU'RE CUTE. SEND A PIC!

Honestly, I had nothing to do with that. That is all Chaz. All spaz, that is. (OK—now he's really mad that I just wrote that!) All right, gotta go so Mr. Social can connect with his people. Ow—he just hit me! He's pretty strong for a fag. Owwwww!!! C

08:15 A.M.
FRIDAY 07.21.06

Wait a minute—what is the deal with Chaz's special guest appearance in the blog?! I thought this was our private thing, 'member? C'mon, Chuck—what is up with that? You've really made a serious breach of your own protocol when you put this thing together in the first place. Now if Chaz is gonna be leaning over your shoulder, reading and making smart emoticon-peppered remarks while jumping into the dialogue at will and screaming at me in big, faggy caps, I don't know if I'm gonna be so into this blog anymore. Sure—what he wrote <u>was</u> semi-annoying, which is maybe partially why I'm pissed, but more disturbing was the fact that he wrote something at all. So if Chaz is so damn desperate to have a heart-to-heart with me, he can drop me an e-mail. (No IM-ing!!!) But I can't abide having him nosing in on our private stuff here. I know there is no way he's figured out the password, but please, if you're gonna use his computer, I just ask that he let you use it without his prying eyes attached. Until then, I have nothing more to say. That's not meant to be bitchy, by the way. Just clear.

11:05 P.M.
FRIDAY 07.21.06

Hey Mr. Bitch! So you know that your way with words sometimes can get a little harsh. You know that, right? Holy shit!

All right, I'm sorry about the breach of blog "protocol," as you put it so damn wordy and Hal-esque. We were just goofing off and didn't really think it was such a big deal. And if you're worried about what Chaz saw, I can assure you that he only popped in to write his stuff. Seriously. I didn't let him read any of the blog entries, yours or mine. And I definitely did not tell him the password.

I did mean it when I said this would be a private blog. I can see that Chaz's little intrusion might have given you the impression I was sharing stuff with him. But I'm not. We talk about you, sure. I mean . . . I miss you a ton and I often find myself talking about you. But I don't talk about what I write. That's between you and me, and that's it, bro. Swear to God, even if you don't believe in Him.

In L news, kinda a bummer of an evening on the Ghaliyah front. Things were very promising when I woke up this morning with the idea of a Ryan-less field trip ahead of us. Now I'm like, dude, what was I thinking. This shit is never gonna happen. Strangely, it started out great as we sat together on the bus, which was incredibly loud as everyone was belting out show tunes on our way into town. After we did some classics from *Little Shop* and *Rent*, I took center aisle with my Ethel-Merman-does-Madonna routine, which got the bus convulsing in hysterics, including Ghaliyah. I know, I know—I can see you shaking your head at my lame attempt to revive this party trick from freshman year. But the SummerArties (what we sometimes refer to ourselves as) don't know it's a lame party trick from two years ago. To them it was totally fresh! ☺

We first stopped at the National Gallery of Art to check out a big show of sculptures by Rodin, this French artist who was around back in the 1800s. Dude—his stuff is amazing! You have to check out this show. And what's really incredible is that, even though it's art in a museum, it is totally hot and sexy. Serious. Some of these sculptures of his are damn racier than anything you'll see on MTV . . . even on *Wild Boys*. The reason? Ninety percent of Rodin's sculptures are 100 percent naked, and there are some hot bods on display. Female and male. Sure, they're cast in bronze, but the detail is so realistic. And the poses he puts them in . . . wow. There was this one called *The Kiss*, and man, I have never seen a kiss like this before in a museum. Another one, *Eternal Springtime*, had these lovers in a very sexy pose, all tangled up in a way that was just like they were on the verge of truly getting it on. Man— it was hot!

So you can imagine my charge checking out this sort of stuff with Ghaliyah by my side. Seriously, dude, I was getting a stiffy! And Ghaliyah was really into Rodin too, talking about the poses and how they were classically inspired but Rodin gave them this intense sensuality that was new and almost shocking. Apparently, Potomac has an art history class, which she excelled in last semester. She was going on and on about the history of the pieces and their "contextual meanings" while I was basically getting a boner. Typical Chuck move, right? LOL

I didn't let on about my sexual state other than to say I thought some of the pieces were cool. She agreed with me but said it in a more artful way . . . like something you'd actually say. I think the word she used was "provocative." She is incredibly smart and brainy, which does remind me of you sometimes. Of course, you two couldn't look more different . . . no worries there!

So without Ryan in the picture, we were really bonding and getting along great. I was getting very psyched to move on to the next part of the field trip, the Shakespeare show. I imagined us sitting together and whispering into each other's ears about acting theories and maybe even getting some decent hand-holding in during the show. Or a little bumping of elbows on the shared armrest. Some sort of contact that would at least give me some hint of interest to hang my hat on, you know?

So we get to the Folger and are standing in the lobby when Chaz comes up and starts chatting with us. He and Ghaliyah get into this big discussion about Shakespeare that had me utterly baffled. They were talking about these theories that Will didn't write all his own plays (whaaa?) and were throwing around the names of these other ancient writers who I'd never heard of. Anyway, the upshot of this is that when the house opened and we went in, there were two rows of seats for SummerArties near the back of the theater. Chaz and Ghaliyah were so into their continuing debate that I couldn't get between them, literally. So they ended up sitting next to each other and I got stuck next to Chaz. Can you believe that shit? If I'd sat next to her, I'm sure it would have sealed the deal. Instead, she and Chaz were whispering away to each other the whole time and I was left floating in space.

The show was good, but by the end of it, I felt awful. I know I shouldn't let myself get so damn down about this. On the positive side, Ghaliyah clearly likes me when I hang with her. But, at the same time, she seems very nonexclusive. She doesn't seem to mind splitting her free time between every Tom, Dick, and Chaz in our group. So it makes me feel less special when I do hang with her, you know?

When we got back to St. Ann's, Chaz could tell I was bumming on something, so I explained the whole deal. He apologized for monopolizing

Ghaliyah's time but also said that I should have said something to him at the theater and he would've given me some room to maneuver. Of course, I'm terrible in those situations because I don't know exactly what to say without sounding like an idiot. I'm so much better with a script, as you know. When it comes to real life, I get in an awkward jam like that and kinda freeze up, which not only sucks but is also not too productive.

So Chaz was very sympathetic about the whole thing and humored my interest in Ghaliyah more than he probably should have. In fact, he even made a suggestion toward the ultimate goal of us getting it on. Chaz's idea? To throw a party in our dorm room next weekend, inviting Ghaliyah so that I can make my move in a strictly social, party environment. I think this could be a cool idea except for one minor thing: We're not supposed to have parties in our dorm rooms. But it's not like the rules have ever stopped Chaz. That's for sure. And convincing me wasn't so hard once he mentioned I'd have Ghaliyah to myself, since inviting faculty (a.k.a. Ryan) to an illegal dorm party would probably not be a good idea. (ha)

All right—Chaz is now pointing at the clock on the wall. (From across the room and not over my shoulder!) Looks like my time is up. Hope you found something fun to do this weekend. If you're superbored, you really should go check out the Rodin show. You can take the Metro down there. Miss ya . . . C

11:30 A.M.
SUNDAY 07.23.06
Thanks for respecting our privacy re the blog. I didn't mean to be come off superstrident (what you referred to as "bitchy"). Rereading it, Chaz's addition to the dialogue was actually sorta funny in it's own spazzy way. But when I first saw him in the blog, I just started getting paranoid that you were showing it to everyone in your dorm or something. I, of course, have no one to show or share this thing with at all. (It's not like I'm gonna be talking about all this gay stuff with Valerie, that's for sure.) And though I've told Brett about you, her interests lie more in guys that are tangible and present, because, well, she's just that kind of girl. So anyway, thanks for keeping this thing between us, as it should be.

That Rodin exhibit downtown does sound kinda cool, even if I'd have to wander through the governmental wasteland that is Washington to get to it. Hey—maybe I can convince Henri to take a road trip (rail trip?) on the Metro using the lure of French culture. We're actually supposed to hang this afternoon, but I think he wants to go up to Wheaton again. (ughh) But maybe later in the week we could head into D.C., if he doesn't get bored with me after today.

Hey—that idea for the party in your room sounds fun, especially if it is illegal! (Amazingly, I'm with Chaz on that count.) Maybe I could make it to UMD somehow and crash it, too. . . . That would be awesome, no? Wait—get this! Maybe Brett and I could borrow Tlucek's instructional Geo after school and pick up Henri and maybe even Joey, if he promised not to be annoying (and drove the Beltway part of the trip too!). OMG—that would be such a trip! Literally. A road trip to UMD!

Phone—BRB

It's Henri. Later!

10:11 P.M.
SUNDAY 07.23.06
Christ—what a day! Where to begin . . . well, I guess the beginning always works. Duh. If I sound a little strange, what can I say other than I'm a little strange right now. You see, when Henri came over, he had some European cigarettes with him (half tobacco/half pot) and I guess I got half stoned. I know, I know—I'm not a druggie and I don't get stoned and all that crap. But Henri assured me the weed was very light, cut with the finest Gauloise (a fancy French cigarette). But I have to say that about eight hours after the fact, I still feel about an eighth stoned. I'm kinda, well . . . spacey and racy and Macy Gray-like, you dig?

So on the Henri agenda today was another trek to downtown Wheaton, though this time we totally bypassed the mall. Henri wanted to do some shopping, which made me think we were going to the mall at first, but he said the stores in Wheaton proper were much more interesting and actually cheaper, too. Our first stop was the Salvation Army up on Viers Mill. Henri and I made a beeline for the T-shirt section and found some truly bizzaro items: a sky-blue ringer that said AMERICAN ROLLER COASTER ENTHUSIAST, a bright yellow staff shirt from the old Wheaton Triangle Bowling lanes (remember all those birthday parties we went to there?), and the pièce-tee-résistance, which was a dingy brown shirt with an iron-on that read SKI IRAQ. Henri really wanted the "Coaster" one, but I said he couldn't pull it off as he wasn't American. I really wanted "Ski Iraq" because it was so bizarre, and he said I couldn't pull it off as I didn't know how to ski. (Clearly a stoner's dialogue going on there, right?) So I got the coaster one and he took the Iraq one, and we were fighting over the bowling staff shirt when a small Mexican woman came out from behind the counter with another staff shirt, exactly like the one I was holding. She didn't say much, just handed the shirt to Henri and said, "One dollar." So we both now have the same shirt—how crazy is that?!

Sifting through some of the collared shirts, I found a bunch of old Izods. I showed them to Henri and he made a puking gesture, which made me laugh. Of course, these retro fashions are exactly the kind of things Joey loves, and I had half a mind to buy one of them for him as a joke, but they were actually eight dollars each because they're so damn trendy these days, so I passed. Henri bought some orange athletic shorts that were going at the bargain rate of two bucks. (Orange appears to be his favorite color.) I swear—you could get a whole damn wardrobe in that joint for less than 50 bucks!

Next up on the shopping agenda was Henri's favorite store, the Army/Navy Surplus, which is just around the corner from SA. Let me tell you—this was one F'd-up joint! They had the craziest shit in there you could imagine: ammunition, machetes, camouflage outfits, riot sticks, survival kits, etc. I wondered out loud to Henri if al Queda knew about this place and he smiled as I made a lame joke about how the surplus store could serve "all the modern terrorist's shopping needs—and at half the price!" Henri thought that was a riot. However, the skinhead behind the register looked pretty perturbed that I'd even mentioned al Queda and was basically giving me the evil eye the rest of the time we were in the store. What a punk!

The coolest thing Henri wanted to buy were these gas masks with instructions that were spray painted in French. Henri was like, "I really need to get this, even though it's 30 clams," and I was like, "Henri, what the hell do you need a French gas mask for?" Then I whispered that the pot was maybe making him paranoid about a terrorist attack or something, but he said he didn't want it for that, that he just thought it would look cool hanging in his bedroom. Did I mention that Henri is, how can I say, somewhat strange?

Next, we crossed the street to the back of yet another strip mall to hit this comic-book store that Henri frequents, Barbarian Comix. Henri is totally obsessed with Spider-Man and all its various incarnations. I asked if he'd seen the movies and he was totally offended, saying that no movie, especially one made by a huge American studio, could do justice to the spirit of the original Spidey. I was sorta stunned by him ragging on my man Tobey Maguire like that, so I said the movies were pretty cool, or that Tobey was at least cool. But Henri seemed quite annoyed by my comments and left me alone while he went to check out some Marvel back issues. Sometimes he gets so damn testy about something so damn stupid. Christ! It's just a movie—who the hell cares!

I was feeling a little bummed out about this dumb disagreement so I tried to occupy myself with the Buffy figurines in a back corner. But Henri got over his mood pretty quickly once he found some Spidey back issues he was looking for. After buying about 10 books, we headed out, and at this point I thought we were pretty much done with what downtown Wheaton had to offer. But as we exited the store, Henri saw something out of the corner of his eye and froze in his tracks. I was like, what is it? And he pointed to a red neon sign that said CADMUS II. I was like, so what? But then he pointed again and I read the smaller print underneath the neon: ADULT BOOK STORE. Then I froze in my tracks. I was like, dude, there is nooooooo waaaaay we are going into a porn store. But Henri was insistent.

Now, for the record, I thought this was a very bad idea and majorly illegal, too, as we were both way under 18. But Henri said it was illegal only if we bought something and, for whatever inexplicable reason, I was down with this rationale, either because a) his explanation sounded semi-reasonable or b) going into a porn store with a hot guy could be . . . enlightening? I let Henri lead the way since he looked 100 percent more confident in this mission than I did. Inside, the place was incredibly bright—I'd almost say dangerously bright, as I've never seen such explosive fluorescent lighting. It was a small store, with basically 10 racks of DVDs organized into different fetish categories, which I will not list here other than to say, some of them were truly gag-making. Hell—some even involved gags!

As we made our way down each rack, glancing at the titles (me) and ogling the hot-breasted babes featured on the covers (Henri), we eventually found ourselves in the "Bisexual" section. Henri said a few things in French that were not "oo-la-la" but seemed to be along those lines, referring to the chicks in the photos, not the dudes. But then he picked up a couple of the bi DVD cases. I pointed at the security mirror in the corner and demanded Henri put them down before we got arrested or kicked out or both. But in his dismissively calm manner, he said there was nothing illegal about getting a closer look. But what was surprising to note was that Henri seemed to be getting a closer look at the guys. Not that I'm a mind reader, but check this out—the boobs were quite obvious when looking at the DVDs from afar, but if you wanted to see more detail on what the guys had to offer, you had to get a closer, look, which meant grabbing one of the boxes for handheld inspection. Though he didn't say anything about these guys, in French or English, I could see he was checking out their packages. As was I, of course. But that goes without saying. . . .

After a few minutes of this cheap voyeurism, we silently moved on to the "Sex Toy" section, where we both started cracking up at the inflatable sex dolls with "realistic vibrating mouths." What is realistic about plastic? And—excuse me—who on earth has a vibrating mouth? As if that weren't bad enough, then Henri spotted the dildo rack and, of course, had to pick one of them up and start waving it around. I told him to put the big rubber penis down (using those exact words actually), but he wouldn't listen, and in fact started whacking me with the 12-incher. It made this ridiculous *thwack* sound on my arm, a sort of pornographic onomatopoeia. This disgusting noise, of course, drew the attention of the store manager, a severe-looking black dude who made straight for us and interrogated us about our age. Henri responded—and I quote— "Old enough to know the difference between a fake dick and a real one." The manager was not pleased at this kind of smartass response, not in the least, and proceeded to grab both of us quite brusquely by our new cheap shirts, dragging us out the door and telling us in no uncertain terms we could come back when we had money and proper IDs. That was classic, huh? This guy's problem was not that we were underage but that we were <u>poor</u> and underage. Ah—the beauty of American commerce . . .

By this point in the afternoon, we were getting quite hungry for some munchies (see "European cigarettes," ibid.). We wandered around the fast-food wasteland that is Georgia Avenue and were about to hit KFC when Henri noticed a place called Nick's Diner. It was a very old and very greasy spoon-style joint that smelled like burnt bacon and had a long counter with stools. Inside, the people working there kinda looked like burnt bacon too, semi-fried and very salty. We sat down at the counter and checked out the menu on a big board above the grill. In plastic letters, it said that Nick made "the best Ham Sandwich around," so we both went for that, and you know what? Nick was not shitting us <u>at all</u>, as it was pretty damn amazing: fried up with some American cheese and tons of butter. Though there was no bacon involved, the sandwich had a hint of that baco-taste, probably from being grilled on the same big grill that everything got cooked on.

Anyway, it was a nice snack and a nice way to end a nice day. Who am I kidding with this "nice" stuff?—we were hanging out in a <u>porn</u> store! Valerie would <u>strangulate</u> me if she knew what I'd been up to this afternoon! Would you have ever imagined such dirty wonders were to be found here in our hometown? The next thing you know, they'll be opening a gay bar in Wheaton. How friggin' freaky would <u>that</u> be, right?

Good lord—I just scrolled back and saw this entry is especially long. How the hell did that happen? Must be the lingering effect of the European . . . both the smoke and the dude. (grin) Hanging with Henri, I have to admit, is semi-intoxicating. Yeah—I know—maybe that's because I'm semi-intoxicated. But I don't know . . . there's something else at work and it's nothing like those other dopes from Einstein I was crushing on. With them it was more of a physical thing, which is not to say that Henri's not cute . . . okay, semi-hot . . . okay, damn gorgeous! LOL But what I really dig on is his craziness in getting me out of the house to do all this insane shit I would never do in a million years. All right, enough of this rambling on and on and on. I must sleep so I can wake up, alert and nonstoned for driving class in the A.M. Night-night! H

PS—Let me know the details about your party. . . .

Week 3

Crap. What a day. Sure, Mondays are supposed to be bad anyway but today it was like an all-day Crap-a-Thon. Seriously. You just won't believe the shit that went down today. And you know what got the shit storm started in the first place? It was around 9:00 this A.M., reading about you smokin' up with Henri. What the fuck, Hal?!

I was so flippin' mad that, at first, I couldn't even respond to your post other than to yell at the computer screen. C'mon, dude—what is up with you getting high the minute I leave town? Are you seriously doing this just because you don't think you're gonna hear about it from me because I'm not physically present? Have you totally forgotten what a waste-case my sister became, dropping outta NYU after failing everything except "Intro to Inhaling"? And don't even try to play it like you're not really smoking because it's some half-and-half concoction. NEWS FLASH—morons mix coke with everything from sugar to baby laxative and that doesn't exactly make it better, does it?

I gotta tell you, Hal, this Henri has really fallen in my estimation. In fact, the only thing he's got going for himself at this point is his faint resemblance to me,

69

and frankly, that's freaking me out too! If you insist on hanging with this weed-whack case, then the least you could do is not partake, all right? I don't wanna come back to Wheaton and find you off in rehab somewhere. End of story.

So yeah—THAT little bit of news really got my Monday off to a great start. Then, on our lunch break, I had a little scene with Ghaliyah in the cafeteria. Unfortunately, it was not scripted. Not by a long shot. And you know me without a script—dead in the water.

Here's the scenario: Our lunch break got moved back an hour because block-ing rehearsal ran over. Usually we have the dining area to ourselves, but there was some overlap with the Math/Science summer geeks. And yeah, I know that calling them geeks is like the pot busting on the kettle and all that shit, but seriously . . . you have to see these kids. They are G-E-E-K-S. Hard-core. We usually don't have any interaction with them because they are in differ-ent dorms and on a whole different program and schedule. Which is for the best. So I should have known to beware when geek worlds collide, as they did today.

So Ghaliyah gets in line and doesn't realize there are like five little shrimps already in line because they have their faces buried in their PSPs. So then one of them pipes up and is like, "You can't cut in line." I think the last time I heard someone say that I was in fifth grade. Seriously. So Ghaliyah turns around and apologizes, saying she didn't see them in line. Of course, they take this the wrong way. A minute later they're all coughing and saying "ter-rorist" and "al Queda" under their breath. Like this is funny?

Anyway, Ghaliyah ignores them but I can't. It's insulting! Besides, I figured that if I stood up for her in this situation it might give me some traction on the relationship front. So I turn around and ask these geeks what they are muttering, and the one in front says, "nothin'" in a little pip-squeak, prepu-berty voice. So I turn back around, and then they start up again with the ter-rorist crap. Ghaliyah just sighs heavily but I can't take it, and I turn around again and ask, in my stage voice, what the F they're saying. Ghaliyah tries to get me to calm down and leave them alone, but I am a man on a mission now. Unfortunately, I have no idea where this mission is headed.

When the lead kid denies it again, I just go ballistic and push him, saying something brilliant like, "I'll show you 'nothin'." Unfortunately, the poor kid weighs like 85 pounds or something and goes flying backward onto the floor, smacking his head on it. It was like a comic-book noise—*ccrrrrraaackkk!* One of the geek counselors picks up the kid, who is moaning and crying, and rushes him off to the clinic, even though the wimp was fine. He'd just never been in a fight before.

So you'd think after all this was done in her defense that Ghaliyah would be clinging to me, as if I was Spidey to her Mary Jane. You know, being thankful for saving her from these bigoted creeps. But get this: She turns to me and says what I did was stupid. Yeah, stupid as in not smart! Though their name-calling was retarded, she goes, "It was no reason to start a fight and hurt someone." And even though I tell her that I was just sticking up for her and her nationality, she got even angrier. Really angrier. In fact, she even tells me to go to hell! Seriously. So all those rumors that chivalry is dead—guess what? They were totally true.

Then, during rehearsal this afternoon, I twisted my ankle during this dumb dance number at the end of the act. Dancing has always been my least favorite part of shows because I can't remember all the steps. I don't know why they don't take the hint here at SummerArts and just have everyone dance around me, like they did in *Guys and Dolls* freshman year. That looked decent, right? I mean, I'm hopeless when it comes to getting these routines down and executing them in a manner that doesn't look like a handicapped person attempting to break dance.

So now I'm back in our room, ankle wrapped in Ace bandage with a cold pack (courtesy of Chaz) as I work out all my frustrations re this Supercrappy Monday in my blog to you. Man, sometimes . . . I just wish that—

Someone's at the door . . . BRB.

12:47 A.M.
TUESDAY 07.25.06

Remember how when we were kids and we'd have an awful day and our moms would say, "Don't worry, it'll get better tomorrow"? Well, technically that's exactly what just happened. Monday sucked ass, but Tuesday has gotten off to a sweet start, even though it's less than an hour old.

It was Ghaliyah at the door. Seriously. Even wilder was that she said she had to talk to me. So once Chaz made himself scarce, she blew my mind even further by telling me she wasn't just stopping by to say hi or run lines. She came by to apologize for her behavior. Can you flippin' believe it?

Here's the deal: She said the anti-Arab stuff drives her batty but she's learned to deal with it. She doesn't take it personally and tries to let it slide. (Which, of course, is impossible!) The thing that rattled her was me swooping in to save the day. She said that she can take care of herself and that she doesn't need some big, dopey guy (yeah—that'd be me) rescuing her. Then she went on, saying that that sorta attitude, that women need to be saved/protected/rescued by men, was what bothers her the most about Arab culture, where women are so dependent on men and sometimes even subservient to them. It's something she really can't stand.

So this line of talk led us into even deeper conversational territory. We got into this big chat about all kinds of family stuff. Seems her folks would like her to be a more traditional sorta girl. By this they apparently mean not so talented. Seriously! It turns out she and I are under similar pressure; her parents don't get that her interest in theater is not just college-application filler but something she wants to pursue as a career. But in her case, I gotta say, the situation is much worse.

Whereas my folks just want me to get a decent job as a lawyer, her parents are already talking about who might be a suitable husband for her back home in Riyadh. She's worried that, after high school, they'll just ship her back to Saudi Arabia and marry her off to some rich sheik and that'll be it. It'll be tough if not impossible to stay here on her own. And, as you may have guessed, there are not a ton of opportunities for musical-theater divas in the Saudi desert.

So Ghaliyah and I talked for almost an hour about families and life stuff—it was pretty intense! Our best, most real conversation yet. In the end, it turns out those stupid Mathletes have basically given me an opening. Even though there wasn't much sexual tension during our talk, there was, I dunno . . . I guess you could call it friendship traction. (ha) Now, finally, Ghaliyah doesn't see me as merely her costar but as a friend she can talk to about anything, even family stuff. And that's a pretty decent development for a Tuesday, huh?

05:05 P.M.
TUESDAY 07.25.06
Yeah—I guess that is a pretty decent development. Of course, Ghaliyah should've apologized earlier, if you ask me, but I guess it shows that she is at least one quarter human after all, even though it took her damn long enough to get in touch with her humanity. I mean, you were just trying to defend her against those ignorant Mathletes and she should've appreciated that and not gotten all annoyed by it.

Granted, your ability to escalate an innocuous argument into a full-blown fight with geek casualties even (bonus points for that!), is well-known, not to mention wholly appreciated by me. I have thoroughly enjoyed the protections you've provided me, especially in regard to the last six months of "fagging" I've suffered in the halls of dear ol' Einstein. Still, I gotta say I sorta feel for that Mathlete you sent flying yesterday. That poor kid probably has enough trouble with life as an "outed" geek—now he has to live down the fact that he got a small concussion from some drama fag. (Sorry—I couldn't resist that one!) Hopefully, though, you will rediscover your lifelong process of chan-neling your flinty temper into your acting, since, after all, it is what got you into show biz in the first place after the Ritalin proved to be a bust. Ah—the drugs of our youth . . .

Speaking of drugs (smooth transition, eh?), I have not, repeat, NOT become some sorta stoner since you deserted me here in Wheaton. Granted, I do have full reason and license to become a full-blown drug addict given the sorry state of my existence: days of instructional tedium interrupted by some mild bursts of afternoon excitability when Henri comes a-calling. If anything, I am probably addicted to Henri more than The Pot. And sure, maybe that means the rare contact high every now and again, along with the stray inhale. But give me a friggin' break, okay? Christ!

You know what? I think being addicted to Henri is much healthier for my well-being and has even focused my sexual energy in a way I've never experienced before. It's funny, because suddenly I'm not really crushing on every guy I see anymore, either . . . not that there's that many cruisable dudes in suburban Maryland. But even the guys I see on TV who used to be totally hot (i.e., Steve-O, J.T., the boys of *The OC*) are not so obsessive-making anymore. When I daydream about sex (which is often!), I tend to fixate now on an image of Henri. Hey— maybe I'm not a homosexual after all. Maybe I'm more of a Henri-sexual. That's a good one, huh? But seriously, folks, now all I need to do is figure out if Henri is a Hal-sexual. He's definitely not a homo-sexual, due to his aforementioned sportiness, Frenchness, lawless-ness, etc. But he does seem to dig on me. Or want me around a helluva lot, and isn't that the same thing?

Meanwhile, I'll get to the news of the day. When I arrived home from Einstein around 12:30 today, I saw the most remarkable thing on my computer: Henri had sent me an e-mail! That was a first. I can't tell you how seeing his name there in my inbox made my heart kinda hic-cup for a second. Then, just as I was reading it for the 10th time, he IM'd me and asked me what I was up to. The shocking answer: absolutely-fucking-nothing. Even more shocking was that I IM'd him back even though I absolutely loathe this sorta faux communication. Then, he invited me over so that he could give me my long-promised "Intro to Parkour." Though I wasn't so sure about this Parkour thing, I basically hit warp speed on my bike getting over to Rock Creek Hills, as I was somewhat excited by the prospect of hanging at his house for the first time, alone together. I mean, who the hell knew what might happen?!

Well, as you may imagine, the first thing that happened at Chez Henri was our Parkour lesson. The first move he taught me was how to land and roll. I have to say, this seemed sorta backward to me, as I thought I'd have to learn how to leap before landing, but, as Henri explained, the majority of people who get injured in Parkour do so because they have done just that: leaped before learning how to land. He said it was the equivalent of leaping before you look. By way of demonstrating, we went out to the backyard and he did a simple roll for me, which I thought looked easy because it was so damn fast and seamless. Anyway, after doing a few slo-mo rolls with Henri assisting me, I got the hang of going into the thing diagonally, which protects your spine.

Next up, we did some practice landings, jumping off the picnic table onto his patio. Once we'd spent an hour on these two building blocks of the sport, I got the chance to put them together into—drumroll, please—<u>The Land and Roll</u>. Mind you, this was not as easy as it looked when Henri did it, but he's been practicing Parkour for a good year and a half now. Like any average sport, getting stuff right is all about practice. So I practiced and crashed and burned a good many times. But Henri was patient with me and didn't treat me like a retard, totally unlike those coaches we had back at Randolph Elementary, 'member? Thinking back on my childhood athletic career, there is a true and real reason why I didn't like sports. Those coaches we had, specifically Mr. Williams in basketball, were not terribly patient with someone like myself who needed a bit of instruction and, uh, like <u>coaching</u>! (doi)

Anyway, after a couple hours getting ourselves dirty and sweaty practicing in the backyard, we then shed all our clothes and hopped into the Jacuzzi for a mad, passionate afternoon of lovemaking. (OK—not really! Just making sure you're still paying attention!) I have to say that the thought did cross my mind, as there actually <u>was</u> a Jacuzzi in the house. But instead of some hot and heavy action, we plopped ourselves in front of his computer and Henri showed me some Parkour videos he'd found online. They were amazing! One showed a British guy who looked like an actual, real-life Spider-Man, practically flying off buildings and jumping up parking ramps, but without the suit or the

webs or anything other than a sweet pair of trainers and years of training. I was totally blown away by this clip, seeing how graceful Parkour
could be . . . it was almost, dare I say, balletic?

After that, Henri toked on some pot and we just hung out in the den
while he played some French rap music for me. Even though I wasn't
stoned (FYI—he didn't even offer me any), I kept cracking up at the
CDs he was playing. Do you have any idea how ridiculous rap sounds
in French? OMG—I was dying . . . totally and literally ROTFL. OH—
later I got to meet Henri's storied mother as well. (Not sure what the
deal is with his dad . . . maybe back in Paris?) She got home from
work and, finding us in the den, pretty much kicked me out. At least
that's what it seemed like. She barely said *bonjour* to me and focused
her attention on Henri, throwing some choice French phrases in his
direction in a tone that didn't seem to be friendly. Maybe she was wise
to the weed . . . or maybe there's a ban on boys in the den due to
Henri's long history of defiling 15-year-old boys like myself. C'mon—
a guy can dream, right?

After she stormed upstairs, Henri apologized about his mom's attitude, saying that she was stressed from work. I said it was not all that
unusual on the MBS (Mom Behavioral Scale), other than the fact that
I had no idea what she had actually said. I got the gist, though, as it's
the same vibe you get from any mom who comes home from work
after a long day and is like, Christ, this place is a DUMP and you're
sitting on your G.D. ASS getting baked and listening to the most
annoying rap CD of all time while dinner's not even a twinkle in anyone's eye. You know the drill—in fact, I think we've experienced it with
Valerie on a few occasions, no?

Hey . . . before I sign off, what's the 411 with this party? Is it gonna be
on Friday still? I went to the Metro Web site and saw the green line
goes right to UMD. So with the right amount of planning and fare
cards, I think we could make it work—we being me and Henri, of
course. He's very into it. One thing I ask—just make sure Chaz has a
date other than me. Later! H

10:55 P.M.
TUESDAY 07.25.06

Bad news on the party front. Professor Eckhart overheard me and Chaz making plans during our voice workshop today. She then passed this info along to the RA, who confronted us, oh, about 10 minutes ago as we were coming back in from rehearsal. So it looks like the thing is off. Totally sucks. I was really looking forward to getting to see you and hanging out. It's been almost three weeks—can you believe it? Well, I guess we're just gonna have to wait another three. That's when the show goes up. Damn—I was really looking forward to this. Not to mention the chance to hit it with Ghaliyah. Everything was going so well. Arggghhh!

11:06 P.M.
TUESDAY 07.25.06

Hey—just tried to IM you. Where did you go? Re the party, that's a big black hole of suckdom. Henri e-mailed me earlier tonight saying that his mom had some diplomatic reception Friday so he could probably come. Apparently her issue earlier today was his cleaning his room, which Henri neglected to do. Ah well . . . I mean, even if there's no party, maybe we could still visit you and just hang out. I know it's still forbidden and all, but what are they gonna do except tell me to go back to Wheaton, right? Hey—isn't there a movie theater out there . . . maybe, if you guys could escape lockdown, we could check out a midnight flick or something? Let me know if that's a concept you'd go for because—yeah, I'll admit it—it would be cool to see you, too. It feels like three months, not weeks. *Arrggggh* right back at ya!

08:38 A.M.
WEDNESDAY 07.26.06

Guess the F what? We're going to have the party anyway! Seriously. But it's not gonna be on Friday. It's gonna be tonight. I know, last-minute notice, but I figured you could manage to clear your busy social schedule. (ha) This was all decided late last night when Chaz heard from this chorus girl, Becky, who lives in the room next to our RA, that the RA was gonna be out of the dorm tonight to see a show downtown. So Chaz suggested we take the opportunity, as we'll probably be able to get away with it!

And get this: Chaz even came up with a theme! He's calling it a Hump-Day Party. And NO, it's not what your dirty mind is thinking. This is not some dudefest-orgy, though I'm sure that concept would get your day-dreams going. It's about Wednesday being the middle day, the hump of the week. Hump-day. Sounds fun, huh? I hope Ghaliyah is into the plan . . . not sure if she'll go for being a bad girl, though. The chick can be uptight, as you know. But she does have a somewhat rebellious nature (according to her folks at least), so I'm hopeful she'll come. Chaz IM'd one of his brothers who lives in D.C., who's going to messenger some of those boxes of wine to us in a plain brown wrapper. Pretty crafty, huh? I am convinced that there is nothing Chaz cannot do.

All right—we're gonna be late for our scene study. See you tonight—9:00 P.M. St. Ann's. We're on the third floor, room 312. There'll be a pink-flamingo light in the window (another Chaz touch), so that way you can find it. Just look for a pink beacon in the night! Hope you can make it. Oh, and . . . HAPPY HUMP-DAY! ☺ Your bud, C

01:03 P.M.
WEDNESDAY 07.26.06
Hey—that sounds good. And despite your lame crack about my social schedule, I will come. I can't wait! It's gonna be a blast. As long as I don't get lost getting there. OH—I don't know if Henri can make it, as his mom will be around tonight. Either way, I will definitely be there. Valerie's going to some free concert downtown with some friends after work, which means they'll then go drinking in Georgetown after and she won't be home till God knows when. Christ—she is such the party animal these days. Go, mom!

02:11 P.M.
THURSDAY 7.27.06
Dude—I think I'm still hung over. Is that possible? I swear when I woke up this morning I was still a bit drunk. Chaz put on his *Hedwig* soundtrack at 8:00 A.M. and started bopping around the room, and (gasp) I joined him. Dancing? In the morning, even? For fun? Yeah, that would add up to me not being quite myself. But now that feeling has passed and I just have a head

that feels like a basketball that someone is playing with. Ouch-ouch-ouch. Game over . . . please?

We got an extra hour for lunch today, as Ryan's in another production meeting about our disaster of a set. (More on that later.) So I thought I'd check in with you, see how you're feeling? I hope it wasn't too long of a trip home on the Metro. Remember what Chaz said when you were heading out? "The most unfortunate thing about public transportation is the lack of complimentary lighting." Isn't he a riot?!

I was so glad you made it, Hal. And (you might wanna sit down for this) I was even glad Henri made it too. Despite your accusation about me changing the party date so that Henri wouldn't be able to come, all I can say is—dude, if I were only that crafty! But seriously, it was cool meeting Henri. It was also a bit of a relief to see that in person he doesn't really look that much like me after all. Though we are still the same general type, we are definitely very different people. Especially in the wardrobe department. What was that tracksuit thing he had on? He looked like a sorta low-rent pimp/rapper or something. OK—gotta admit, that line is cribbing from Chaz's fashion commentary.

So what did you think of The Chaz? I saw you guys talking for a little while. Were you talking about me? (ha) Or were you both complaining about me? That was probably more like it: an episode of *Queer Eyes Gang Up on the Straight Guy*. It was hard to tell from across the room. And once that place filled up . . . damn! I was like, who knew you could fit a good 30 people in our dorm room? I can't believe so many showed! I thought we'd be lucky to get 15 or so given the last-minute notice and the fact that I'd really only invited MK and Ghaliyah. But I'd forgotten to take into account the Chaz Factor and his knack for knowing just about every SummerArtie.

Ghaliyah seemed to enjoy herself despite the cramped quarters. She really liked meeting you and said that you were nothing like what she had expected. I didn't quite know what that meant. I'm guessing it has something to do with my sore lack of skills in the description department. BTW, she thought your stories about driving school last night were hilarious, and she's obsessed with Brett. You have to bring her out for the show!

As for my grand G-scheme, after you left, not much more happened on that front. In the end, getting it on with Ghaliyah was pretty much a bust, as we had no alone time. But I'm glad that you and I got some time to just hang out by ourselves up on the roof. I didn't even know you could get up there, but it certainly was quicker than waiting for the bathroom to free up. Especially once Chaz got in there with that Albert, that tiny Mathlete he picked up at the bookstore. Anyway, it was nice to just hang, though I feel like we barely got through talking about everything that's been going on lately. And what was up with that New Year's stuff? I thought you remembered everything that had happened that night. Or I'd assumed that was the case. Anyway, I hope our talk about all that didn't freak you out too much. What was freaking me out more was that we hadn't even discussed it in the last seven months. Namely the whole kiss thing.

Now, I'm not gonna deny that what went down post-midnight was a bit weird. It was. Mainly because you were so trashed on my folk's champagne that you could barely keep your eyes open. But, to be clear here, it wasn't like we "made out." You just kissed me on the cheek and the forehead and my ear, which was sorta funny and almost cute, like something our dog would do. But then, when you hit the lips, that's when I asked you what you were doing. Your answer? Well, there was none. You just passed out on the couch. And that's when I picked you up and carried you to my room and plopped you on my bed. I didn't particularly want my folks to see you sprawled out in your condition. They might think I was trying to take advantage of you or some-thing. LOL

Seriously, though—nothing happened in my bedroom at all that night and you didn't do anything embarrassing. Nothing. I slept on the floor—not because I was mad or anything but because I didn't want you to wake up and puke on me. So you really have nothing to feel bad about re that night. And I hope, now that we've cleared this up, we can continue to be the best friends we've always been. All right, not always. (I exaggerate as usual.) But c'mon, dude, it's almost 10 years, which is a long time given we're only 15. It would be stupid to lose that because of one dumb, drunky night.

The only question I have left, I guess, is something I wanted to ask you last night. Of course, I was too much of a coward to ask it live and in person. So I'm just gonna be typically, Chuck-ically blunt and throw it out there. Here goes: Were you in love me last year? Is that what led to the New Year's kiss? Is that what helped you realize you were gay? Remember—anything you write here will NOT be held against you in a court of law. (ha) I'm just curious, that's all. And trying to figure out that complicated mind of yours. A futile mission, I know. But it keeps me going, you know, dreaming the impossible dream and all that musical-theater crap.

OMG—that last sentence sounds totally like something you'd write.

Speaking of which, I thought I'd hear from you this A.M., but maybe you had trouble getting up for driving class. Did you get any action with Henri? ☺ He seemed pretty social with everyone at the party, especially MK for a bit. Did this bug the hell out of you? Why am I even asking that question—of course it did! But let me know if there are any more romantic developments. He might be a cool guy if he can get rid of that blinging tracksuit. Kidding. You know me: Life's one big one-liner. Missing you . . . again! C

04:11 P.M.
THURSDAY 07.27.06
Ugh—it has been one, long friggin' day of recovery from cardboard-encased wine. That stuff was pretty awful in retrospect . . . the kind of wine that doesn't come with a year but an expiration date. Thus, it was severely slow going this A.M., but I did barely make it to driving class and spent most of it trying to keep from falling asleep and drooling on myself. I didn't get to sleep till almost 2:00 A.M. last night! And no . . . nothing goddamn romantic happened. You think I was going to go home with Henri and lay some clumsy move on him? Wasted? I think I learned my lesson on that count on New Year's . . . that's for sure.

Speaking of which, regarding this issue of our "relationship," as you like to call it, I will give you this. To be totally honest and real here for a moment, I don't think I was in love with you last year. It's more like, I dunno . . . I sorta just wanted to be you, that's all. People always look up to you as this sort of shining exemplar of teenage perfection because of your talents and probably because you are often standing on a huge stage, which necessitates people physically craning their necks and literally, uh, looking up at you. The truth is, you are so damn self-assured and confident, which is a pretty attractive thing given how my life can be such a disaster area, especially in the last year. So it's like, who <u>wouldn't</u> want to be you? You are a total champ, whereas I am, more often than not, a total chump.

So I think that's the general idea of what was coursing through my deranged mind on New Year's when I made such a colossal fool of myself. Maybe I thought I could work some magical transference of your best qualities onto my personality if I made out with you. Yeah—I know, amazingly scientific logic, huh? On the surface it seems ridiculous, but I think there's a little something to it. You see, I thought that maybe us getting closer would cure all that ailed me, namely me. But that was sooooo the wrong approach. And I didn't want to talk about all of this shit at the time because I was still so mortified by the fact that I even thought this approach was something viable, when in fact the only viable way to like myself was to simply start liking myself . . . that is, <u>all</u> of my little gay self.

Though I'm hardly there in the self-love department, I think I've at least identified the problem at this stage and will not be prone to make the same mistake twice. With Henri, for example, I'm not interested in being him. Not at all. First off, how could I ever be a totally slamming, hot French expert on free-running. But, that technicality aside, I honestly don't want to be Henri. I just want to be with him. And I think that's a big difference, no?

Like last night, for instance, Henri and I had a pretty awesome time at the party. One thing I noticed that was different from my behavior with the Einstein Three is that I wasn't desperately clinging to Henri like he was some lifesaver carrying me downstream in the middle of a disaster. I was able to enjoy the party on my own terms and not just be Henri's appendage. When Henri wandered off to chat up MK, it honestly didn't bother me, and I didn't feel the need to be by his side—

and that was totally weird! I remember thinking, sure, him and MK are having a fun, flirty time, but in the end, Henri's going to return to me and, eventually, he's going home with me. Well, not literally, of course, but more in a general sense, as we were both returning to the Wheaton area. And that gave me this calm peace of mind, which, for me, is like beyond rare.

Of course, getting home was an epic journey that was definitely not helped by the fact that I was smashed on that boxy wine. (Christ—I am such a lightweight!) Per usual, I got very damn chatty on the ride home, which Henri didn't seem to mind too much and almost seemed amused by. Then I lost all sense of propriety and inhibition and public decency, as I started talking a blue streak to Henri about cute guys after spotting a poster for *Spider-Man III*. A discussion of Tobey led to my obsession with Ashton and even (dare I say it) the Three Losers of the Apocalypse from Einstein, who I described at length to Henri while we zoomed under the city.

OMG—I still can't believe I spilled all these beans to him. You know what? I wish I had some sort of emergency brake mechanism on me, like they do on the Metro, so that when I start getting out of control like this and spewing all sorts of intimate details about the kind of guys I dig on to (uh—hello!) a guy that I am currently digging on, someone would be able to use their common sense, break the glass, pull the red cord, and bring my conversational diarrhea to a screeching halt. (OK—I think I just mixed about five metaphors with that rant!) Anyway, Henri seemed shockingly unfazed by my lustful ramblings and basic confession that I was a huge homo. Who knows? Maybe he'd figured it out already. Still, it was the first time I'd really talked about it so brazenly.

Later, as we were walking our bikes down Georgia Ave. (too tipsy for riding), I thought that now that I had made a complete idiot of myself, perhaps Henri would be willing to share a little more about his romantic past. I knew he had one, being a suave Frenchman. (I mean, hell, isn't there a reason why it's called French kissing? They practically invented it, right?) Anyway, he told me about some girl named Natalie he was hanging out with before he left Paris and also about his best friend who he left behind, a guy named Patrice who he was in *la seconde* with, the equivalent of freshman year for them. And they were more than just friends. Check this out! Apparently, him and Patrice used to sorta fool around, too! A couple years ago, Patrice had found his dad's stash of porn DVDs, so he invited Henri over to watch them. Well, they apparently got a bit stoned and ending up jerking off to the movies. Together. That's right—<u>TOGETHER</u>!!!

Can I just say that as Henri was telling me this story, I was getting such an insane visual regarding their video wank sessions that I got totally boned! Thank God I was able to hide my unsightly bulge behind the seat of my bike as we walked, my stride a little more awkward than his. Once I regained my ability to speak, I asked Henri if he and Patrice had ever made out. He said no, a bit too dismissively, adding that it would have been "weird" because they were best friends. OK— reality check here: Jerking it with a buddy while watching your dad's porn is pretty F-ing weird if you ask me. But he wasn't asking me. He was just telling me he thought kissing his best friend was not cool. Hmmmm. Talk about conflicting signals.

Around 1:30 we got to the intersection where he turned off to head home and we said our good-byes for the evening. Oh man—that sounds so damn corny, like there was a full moon out and we both had hazy romantic lighting encircling our heads. It was nothing like that, though. We were standing under the harsh, orange glare of a standard-issue streetlamp and there was no golden moon that I saw, unless it was hiding from me on purpose. (Given my luck, it could happen.) So in the end, our good-byes were just that—both of us saying the word "good-bye." Or maybe it was "good night." Anyway, Henri did offer a quick, sporty hug, which would have been fine and innocent and all that except for the fact that I was still packing wood at the moment of friendly impact.

I think I turned about 10 shades of red, which, thank God, under the cover of the orange light was fairly unnoticeable. But he clearly must have noticed my erect member giving him a little farewell salute, no? OK—not that it's THAT huge, but still . . . it's something down there when there is not supposed to be anything down there, especially when two buds are giving each other a sporty hug. Christ! I can't believe I did that—I should have just refused the hug. But I guess that might have been even weirder and maybe sent the wrong signal, too, since I'd like to do even more than simply hugging. Though, I have to say, hugging Henri briefly like that was quite nice, even though it only lasted for about half a millisecond.

As for more happening down the road, who the hell knows? I think sometimes that maybe it's just a matter of waiting with Henri, in the way that I waited at the party and he eventually returned to me. But, on the other hand, sometimes I'll see the visual I got when I asked him about kissing Patrice and think that I am living on another planet entirely when it comes to the reality of us ever making out on this planet we know as Earth. H

09:02 A.M.
FRIDAY 07.28.06

Hey—sorry I didn't get back to you last night. Chaz was physically attached to his laptop, IM-ing Albert all night, as they are now apparently in love. If you thought Chaz was weird in normal life, Chaz in love is a whole other level of strangeness. And even though I told him I didn't want the explicit details, all Chaz could talk about this A.M. was kissing Albert.

That's what he claims they were doing in the bathroom, though I find this somewhat hard to believe. I mean they were in there for a good half hour. And knowing the sex drive of the average 15-year-old male, you put two guys together like that and I don't even wanna think about the sorta shit that went down on our toilet. Yikes. Still, Chaz insists they had the most intense make-out sesh he's ever had. Maybe—but as Shakespeare says, I think the lady doth talk about it waaaaaay too much.

Of course, this means my whole gay-matchmaker gig is up. I guess you and

Chaz were maybe just not meant to be. I know you're devastated by this development, but try not to get too suicidal. LOL Besides, it sounds like you clearly have enough to keep yourself busy with Henri. That is very interesting about your conversation with him on the way home. Surprising, almost. And if he wasn't as flipped out about all those details on your gay crushes, maybe you <u>are</u> on something of a righteous track. I say this because if I'd been there for that chat, the mention of you getting sprung thinking about two guys pulling their pud would have been tough to stomach. I know, I know— gotta get over my gay squeamishness. But still, all I can say right now is . . . blech!

As for my fine romance, things are not exactly so warm and cuddly today. I thought the party was going to be this big step for me and Ghaliyah, but it's only pushed us farther apart. The reason? Yep—you guessed it. Ryan Rodriguez. He was chatting with her in the lunch line today as everyone's yammering on about the party. Of course, he wonders what we're talking about, and Ghaliyah, puzzled, says she thought he'd been invited too and just couldn't make it due to work. I was like, whaaaaa?! Like we're gonna invite a faculty member to our illegal house party? Once Ryan was out of earshot, Ghaliyah said that he would've been "cool" about it since he's so young. Can you even <u>believe</u> this? So I said she was wrong because there are absolutely zero things "cool" about Mr. Ryan Rodriguez. Then Ghaliyah calls me out. She says I didn't invite Ryan because I'm jealous. Can you <u>believe</u> that shit? Seriously. Of course, I denied it, which Ghaliyah thought was utter bullshit. But what was I gonna do? Cop to jealously? Uh . . . nope.

Then she started going on about how throwing the party was maybe not such a great idea and showed a lack of professionalism on my part. Again with the "professional" thing. Like, she's some serious pro now? I hate to admit this but, dude, I think you were right on your diva claim. This girl is sometimes so full of herself it's enough to drive a normally talented person like myself absolutely nuts. Professional?! She is <u>unbelievable,</u> that's what she is!

Goddammit—she makes me so angry sometimes I want to choke someone. Like her. It's good I can lash out at you so that she doesn't have to see the ugly side of my nature. I couldn't talk about this with anyone here without fear of it spreading through the gossip vine, which is twisted and reaches everywhere. So thanks for hearing me out, bro. And helping me to keep my sanity barely intact. Later . . . C

11:10 A.M.
SATURDAY 07.29.06

You think you had a day. OMG—what a day I had yesterday—what an insanely bizarre and wonderfully confusing day. I'll start with the crazy shit first, though. You won't believe this, but we actually got in an accident in Driver's Ed yesterday and, no, I wasn't driving. C'mon—I know that's what you were thinking. (Thanks for the vote of confidence!) No, the maniac behind the wheel was none other than Brett, which was probably your second guess, right?

We were doing three-point turnarounds on a dead-end street a few blocks from Einstein when this all went down. My first attempt, granted, was more like a four-point turnaround, but I knocked it down to three after Tlucek gave me another chance. Then it was Brett's turn, and she had no idea what we were doing, even though we'd done it like three times already. She was too busy texting Amanda and couldn't be bothered with driving. So Tlucek explains the deal again, just for her, while Brett barely listens. Then she shifts the car into gear and hits the gas. However, the thick heels she was wearing came down hard on the accelerator, sending the car lurching straight at the opposing curb and hitting it with a dangerous-sounding *clunk* that tossed us up and over the entire curb into a formerly lovely rose garden. We finally came to a slamming stop when we collided with the metal pole of a big, ornate birdhouse, sending it falling to the ground, where it exploded into a million pieces as about 100 birds evacuated. It was hysterical! Tlucek, however, was not amused. He went crazy, yelling at Brett like he was her dad or something as the lady of the birdhouse came running out her front door in a lime-green bathrobe, screaming at the top of her lungs. The scene was utter chaos—totally like something out of a Jim Carrey movie or something. You would have loved it!

Of course, at this point, Joey and I couldn't stop laughing in the back-seat of the car, probably because we knew Brett so well and that this was all somewhat inevitable. Brett, on the other hand, actually started crying, which—and I know this means I'm going to hell—only made us laugh harder. (I know, I know . . . laughing at other's misfortunes. My weakness.) Rami, on the other hand, was seriously terrified, his body stiffened into a state of near rigor mortis.

Anyway—the upshot of all this madness was that our driving instruction for the day was seriously curtailed. Cancelled, in fact, because with a flattened tire stuck in a muddy rose bed and a metal pole encased in the grill, our car was waaaaaay out of commission. So Tlucek released us, saying he would stay with the car and wait for the insurance guy and the tow truck. So the four of us started walking the couple blocks back to Einstein to get our stuff. Brett was still pretty hysterical, even after I tried to calm her down by telling her that at least no one got killed. (Though some feathers were ruffled—LOL!) But she was still busting out in occasional sobbing episodes as we walked along Newport Mill Road, causing drivers coming in the oppo-site direction to look at her with concern. Only when Joey gave Brett a supportive hug did she start breathing like a normal person again.

Once we got our stuff from the classroom, I suggested a group trip up to Wheaton Plaza to spend the rest of the day sneaking into movies, but Brett just wanted to go home. I even asked Joey, but he declined, offering to walk Brett home. So there I was at 10:00 in the A.M. stand-ing outside Einstein with a whole Friday ahead of me and no one to play with except Rami, the mute Indian dude who still had not blinked since Brett's bird-ramming rampage. And no, I didn't ask Rami to the movies—that would've been a little too weird, as we've hardly said two words to each other since Driver's Ed started. So we cordially parted ways with a handshake and a mutual grin, an acknowledgment that we'd both survived our first car wreck with our sense of humor intact and a much deeper understanding of our mortality.

I was about to walk home when my mind drifted, as it often does these days, to thoughts of Henri. I thought to myself, he's certainly not doing anything productive today other than getting stoned. So I stopped at 7-Eleven, got a Big Gulp, and gave him a ring, having completely memorized his home number. Not that I call it that much, really . . . I just have a tendency to look at it a lot and think about calling him. Lately, I find myself often having these weird internal conversations with Henri while I'm walking to Einstein or watching TV or spacing out in driving class. I'll start to hear us having this chat in my head where I tell him how much he's changed my life this summer and he'll say that his life was equally damn boring till he stumbled upon me and that it's kinda crazy that we have become so tight in, what, less than three weeks. Of course, who am I kidding, in that we will probably never have this sorta conversation, which is why I get it out of the way in my head. But still, it's kinda weird, no?

Anyway, I gave him a buzz and he wasn't even stoned, just sitting around planning his Parkour workout for the day with some online tutorials he'd found. I told him the short version of my story and asked if he wanted to do the movie deal up at the Plaza. He said yes to the hanging out but suggested something radically different from a movie: He wanted to go on an epic bike ride to Virginia. My reaction at first was like, damn, that is a superlong way to go on a friggin' bike. And probably dangerous, too, given the way traffic is downtown. (OMG—I'm starting to sound like a parent too!) But Henri explains to me how he found this bike trail that starts in Rock Creek Park and goes all the way through Georgetown, the monuments, over Memorial Bridge, and down the west side of the Potomac River, where it makes its way to Mount Vernon. All totaled, it's something like 25 miles, and I'm like, shit, I don't know if my legs can handle that. It's not like I'm working out all the time. (You know me—sloth is my favorite sin.) But Henri tells me not to sweat it as it's all pretty much downhill, a claim I find questionable yet, when made in Henri's sexy, accented voice, one that sounds wholly and utterly believable.

So I throw on some shorts, grab my camera, hop on my bike. When I get to Henri's, he is waiting out front, his ass parked on a supersweet

Trek 4300 roadster. Even sweeter are the pair of tight Lycra biking shorts he is wearing. OMG—those legs! Sure, I'd seen them before, but never like this, wrapped so alluringly in funky stripes of black and lavender skintight fabric. As for his package, I am gonna spare you the gory details because I know it will only creep you out. But let me just say, for the record, it was equally sweet and totally distracting!

One thing that was interesting: Henri had printed out this multipage map from his computer that had the whole bike route on it. He also had a backpack filled with bottles of water and PowerBars. I thought that his being so prepared and almost responsible like that was sorta cute, you know? Not exactly what I expected from someone as laid-back as Henri. I told him all this and he replied that he and Patrice used to tool around all over Paris. He also informed me, or educated me, that the bicycle itself was a French thing, invented by a father/son team back in the 1860s. I had no idea . . . I thought bikes were invented in the U.S. by Mr. Schwinn or something. Huh . . .

So we hit the road and it was a great day for riding—not too ridiculously humid and just hot enough to make you feel the summeryness of the day. Our trip began on the bike path that goes through Rock Creek Park, which led us to the Capital Crescent trail, the one that used to be a train line. That was beautiful: tearing right through the middle of these dense woods that were so damn lush and alive and eye-poppingly green. Since it was a weekday there wasn't much bike traffic or strollers, so we really moved along at quite a clip, though I was always a few bike lengths behind Henri trying to keep up with his pace. He is a <u>mad</u> cycler!

We got to Georgetown and switched over to the C & O Canal trail, which meant slowing down some as there were a bunch of poky tourists jamming up the works. Next, we crossed Memorial Bridge and Henri suggested we go for a ride through Arlington Cemetery. I was like, why? He said it's pretty cool, which made me wonder if he had a thing for dead people. Arlington, however, was not so downhill and was in fact very uphill, so much so that I had to walk my bike a few times on some of the steeper inclines. But once we got to the top of the main hill, there was this huge house that has the most amazing view of D.C. and even Maryland (you could see the Mormon temple near Henri's house and even that one office building in downtown Wheaton!). I was thinking, this spot would be some seriously pricey real estate if there weren't thousands of corpses buried in the ground.

Apparently, this used to be Robert E. Lee's house, but when he decided to lead the enemy in the Civil War, he lost the land to the Union Army, and in a colossal act of revenge, his college buddy turned Lee's backyard into one giant graveyard. That's totally fucked up, right? That's like taking revenge to like the 1,000th degree? Hey—when we have another huge fight in the future, promise me you won't go plugging up my backyard with dead people, okay? That is just a little severe, don't ya think?

After filling up our water bottles, we hooked up with the Mount Vernon trail, which ran right alongside the Potomac. Man—it was gorgeous! Riding just a few feet from the edge of the water, with all the monuments there. Wow. Have you ever noticed how beautiful Washington can be on a perfect summer's day? And the river, too? It's just so placid and calm and actually clean-looking, which was something of a shock. Has it always been this nice? There were even some people swimming off their boats parked out in the middle of the river. Crazy, right?

We finally made it to Mount Vernon around 3:00, and we were gonna take the tour but missed the last one. So instead we just wandered around the grounds of the place ourselves. It was a little bit bigger than the Lee house and a little bit nicer, given the fact that they didn't have tons of dead people there. Except, that is, George and Martha. They were buried together in an aboveground, stone crypt. (Awww— isn't that sweet?) Apparently, crypts were common for folks who could afford it, in case you got put to rest before you were actually dead . . . something that happened a bit since they didn't really have accurate heart monitors back in the 1700s. Henri asked me if, when I died, I'd like to be buried aboveground, and I was like, "Why are you suddenly so death-obsessed?" He ignored my question and asked me again. I said I would prefer to be cremated and my ashes sent to the principal's office as a sick, postmortem prank. I started laughing my ass off at my own dumb joke, but Henri, for some reason, didn't think this was so funny. So I finally answered his question with a big NO: I would not want to be put in a stone ice house in case of my untimely death. He just nodded and, thank Christ, we moved on to other, less deadly topics. Like lunch.

After eating, we began the long trek back. Even with some post-lunch energy, I was skeptical that I was going to make it back to Wheaton, as the return was all uphill. Not majorly, but still requiring a bit more leg power than coasting. Hitting Alexandria, there was a detour in the path due to all the roadwork they're doing on a new bridge for the Beltway. Henri, of course, went the opposite direction the detour sign pointed, saying that we should check out the construction site. I was not into this at first, suggesting that we should get home before dark given the fact that Valerie would be having a parental spaz attack if I was at large after 9:00 P.M. But Henri said it would be fun, "an adventure." Always an adventure with this one, right?

The construction site was massive—they are building not one, but two brand-new, six-lane spans across the river. It was about 5:30 when we arrived, so all the workers had gone for the day, and again, someone had left one of the fences wide open. I guess all construction workers were raised in a barn (remember how Helen used to say that to us?). From the shore, we could see the huge, arching supports for the bridge way out in the middle of the river, these droopy concrete Vs that will eventually hold up the Beltway. The steel frame for the approach to the bridge was up, but not the roadway itself, so Henri, in true Henri fashion, suggested we find a way to climb onto it. And sure enough, after looking around a bit, he found a scaffolding platform that went all the way up to the deck, and he immediately started climbing like a monkey.

I told him to get down, that we were gonna get arrested, but he wouldn't listen. Then I told him he would fall and die and I'd bury him in a coffin deep in the ground and, in response, he turned around from about 20 feet up and just grinned at me. So I gave up and did what he knew I would eventually do—I started climbing up myself, though with a little more caution. When I got to the top, it was higher up than I thought, a good 40 feet off the ground. Henri, though, was unfazed by the height or the drop to the ground or anything, as he started walking out on the steel beams toward the point where they went over the bank of the river. With another wicked glance over his shoulder, he bid me to "c'mon!," and losing my mind (or perhaps leaving it at the bottom of the scaffolding), I followed, gingerly putting one foot in front of the other, trying to keep my balance like an urban trapeze artist.

When I caught up to him, we were now even higher, maybe 50 feet up, and I froze. I was not gonna go any farther. I just stood there with my camera, clicking off some more pix. (The view was pretty wild!) Henri told me not to be a wuss, but I was like, "I'm not a wuss . . . I'm just fucking scared out of my mind!" Then, walking back around and behind me for support, he said I'd be fine, that he was right behind me. I felt a tug on my pants as he hooked his fingers through the loop of my belt. Though this wasn't really safer, as it only meant that both of us would plunge to the ground together and die in tandem, I started inching forward anyway. Why, you ask? I don't know the hell why. It was stupid and dangerous and basically deadly, but it was Henri and saying no just didn't feel like an option.

As we neared the end of the beams, my pace started to slow up again as the expanse of the river came into view. Henri said that we should walk right out to the edge, and I was like, "Uh, you're on your own, buddy." So, as I turned to get out of his way, I of course lost my balance for a sec. As I tottered on the edge of eternity, Henri grabbed me around the waist to keep me from falling. My heart was in my skull by this point, beating so hard that it felt like my eardrums were going to burst. But Henri held on to me, thank God, both his hands tightly gripping my midsection, in a way that did serve to stabilize me. But you know what? It also equally served to destabilize me, if you get my meaning here. Translation for the visually impaired: The man had his hands just inches above my manhood. Sure, plunging to my death into the Potomac would not be cute, but getting a boner in broad daylight in front of Henri? Yes, there is a fate worse than death.

So, after my near brush with the great beyond, we gingerly made our way back toward the scaffolding and slowly made our descent to the ground. Oh—THE GROUND!!! The soft, muddy, shit-brown ground—have I ever been so in love with dirt?! As it was now fast approaching 7:00 P.M., I suggested we continue on our way home. And this is what we did for a few miles, until we got to National Airport, where Henri again suggested another detour. I was really getting tired by this point in the day, having been on my bike for almost eight hours. But Henri had a consolation prize: He suggested that after this final detour we could catch the Metro back to Wheaton. What could I say to this plan but a very enthusiastic "YES!"

So we turned off the bike trail into a parking lot at the edge of the main runway, where Henri said the planes took off right over your head. He wasn't kidding on that count, as they weren't that much higher off the ground than we were earlier on the span of the Wilson Bridge. We dropped our bikes and found a car that looked to have been in long-term parking for quite a long term—my guess was two months given the dirt that had accumulated on the hood and the windshield. We sat on the hood and, checking around for cops, Henri pulled out some pot and lit up. I took a little toke (only a little one!), which of course was more than enough to get me completely baked, being such a world-class lightweight. Then, as the sun set, the sky started turning these amazing shades of dusky purple as we watched plane after plane buzz over us in silence. Our silence, that is, not the planes, as they were pretty damn loud!

After sitting like this for almost, I dunno, half an hour, I noticed my watch inching toward 9:00 P.M. and suggested we hit the road before both our mothers assumed we were missing. The pot, along with the exhaustive bike ride, had made me severely sleepy, so that the minute I hit the orange plastic seat on the Metro, I lost consciousness. When I awoke with a friendly joust from Henri, I was sleeping on his shoulder, my face smushed against his shirt. This would have been cute and almost sexy, you know, cuddling up with Henri for the long train ride home, however (embarrassment alert!), my mouth had been totally open the whole time and I was drooling on his tee. Nice, huh? As I mumbled sorry, I tried desperately to wipe my pool of spit off but only succeeding in rubbing it into the fabric of his shirt. Henri laughed and said not to worry about it. He said my drooling was almost cute. Now, what the hell does that mean? OMG—he is killing me! I swear to friggin' God he better not say things like this to me unless he's figured out what he's trying to say, otherwise I will interpret it for him and come to the absolutely subjective and ridiculous conclusion that he actually likes me or something.

So when I got home, guess what? Yep—Val went completely ballistic on me about where the hell I'd been and that I didn't leave a note and all the standard mom-panic-attack stuff. But you know what? Being slightly stoned really takes the edge off these sorta dicey parental encounters. After she was done monologuing, I just calmly explained to her that I'd gone on an all-day bike ride to Mount Vernon. Man, you should have seen her face. LOL She was absolutely befuddled, and finally blurted out, "You mean you . . . exercised?" I said no, I'd gone touring, which sounded so much classier and—hey, I admit it—even a little French. She was like, "Really?" I offered to show her my digi-pix of the day, timed and dated as they were for solid evidential proof, though I would've skipped over the ones of me high-beam walking over the Potomac so as not to give her a premature heart attack. In the end, she said she believed me and that maybe she'd take a look at them later. Oh mother—

So . . . I guess that's the end of my endless Friday at the end of July. Quite the tale, no? I would have written it sooner but, after dealing with my mom, I hit the mattress and was out for a good 12 hours. I haven't slept like that since, I dunno, maybe our first day down in

Ocean City for Memorial Day weekend. Which is to say, yeah, I had that much fun. H

08:06 P.M.
SATURDAY 07.29.06

Holy shit, dude! You are in L-O-V-E. Notice how I have no hesitation spelling it. At all. Reason? That was just the wildest entry you've posted! Ever. In fact, those were some of the strangest things I've ever heard you say/write. And not just all your talk about The Man himself. It's more other things. Like your description of downtown D.C., which I recall you previously referring to as "lifeless" and "a governmental wasteland," is now suddenly beautiful and magical? You are so seeing the world through the eyes of L-O-V-E.

Now don't get too crazy though. This change in you hasn't completely changed my opinion of the frog. I'm still not so sure Henri is really the best person in the world for you to be falling for. I mean, seriously, is trouble this guy's middle name or what? But I guess it's too late for any sort of rational thought, as you have fallen. You are on the floor, dude. Struck by love. ROTFL—that's "Rolling On The Floor w/ Love"! (ha)

One thing I will say is that this does sound a bit different than those Einstein guys. That's for sure. At least Henri gives you the time of day and seems to treat you like a real human being. Bringing water and snacks on the trip was nice, like you guys were on a picnic, though saying that explicitly would have been too gay for him probably. But you get the point. He sounds like he does genuinely like you, which is a pretty good start.

All I'm saying is that you shouldn't take that fact the wrong way. Seriously. People should like you, lots more people. You are a very likable guy, really, once you get past all the cursing and superficial I-hate-everything bullshit. And Henri's clearly broken that barrier. Sounds like he may have smashed it to pieces, actually. BTW—that might not be such a bad thing. . . .

On the negative side, it still sounds like the question of his sexuality is a big one. Semi-unanswered and potentially unanswerable. Who knows? I guess the best way to figure this stuff out is to just ask him, bluntly, if he digs on guys other than his best friend. I know, I know—you've said before you can't do that, just come out and ask someone. And that <u>you</u> don't need to because you're able to figure it out through the magic of "gaydar." Listen up: calling gaydar "magic" is more like it. You thought all those Einstein guys were gay. In the end they were not even a blip on the screen. Clearly, your gaydar thing has got a few technical kinks that need to be worked out.

Hey—you know what else was really cool about your entry? I loved the way you described the whole accident with Brett. Can I print out part of that and show it to Ghaliyah? I wanted to ask you first so you don't bite my head off again. But I think she'd love it. And love your style, too. You've always been pretty funny, but lately, some of the shit you write in here is just classic. You should really start your own blog once the summer's over. It might be a more positive outlet for your inner bitch. (ha) And don't deny her—you know she's there and, despite The Henri Effect, is alive and well. She was just on vay-cay for that last light-headed entry.

Seriously, though, your writing is great. I got such a vivid picture of that whole bike trip—like losing your shit up on the bridge. I can't believe you did that?! That is like so un-you, Hal, it's mind-boggling. But then again, so is the fact that you rode your bike somewhere other than 7-Eleven. (No wonder Valerie was tripping on your excuse!) So who knows? With all of your "travel" and potential love-ing, this summer may prove to be a bigger growth spurt for you than for me.

Lately, I feel very blah. Rehearsals are really working my last nerve. Specifically, Ryan is doing that mainly. He is such a pain in my ass! <u>And</u> he keeps angling in on my territory with Ghaliyah, too. Get this—he asked her to the movies tonight over in College Park. It's our one free night to do something and now I don't have anything to do. Chaz is out with Albert, going to a lecture by the Google guys (who are UMD grads) and I'm stuck here in St. Ann's, writing to you about how lame my love life is.

You know what? Lately it just seems like <u>everyone</u> is getting some. Except me, of course. I mean, if a friggin' Mathlete can hook up with Chaz, why can't I find someone? It just seems like there's something wrong with me and

I'm never gonna find anyone. The joke is that people here think I'm taken. Like I have some princess girlfriend stashed in a castle somewhere in Wheaton. Oh yeah—like there's some sorta harem in my bedroom. Like Helen would ever allow <u>one</u> girl in my bedroom?!

I was talking with MK about this at lunch and she too assumed I had multiple ladies at home. Of course, there is not even one. And when people like MK say shit like, "I can't believe <u>you</u> don't have a girlfriend," it just makes me feel like crap. Like I have somehow screwed up my own more-than-decent odds for having one. Except I don't know what I'm doing wrong, you know? Oh yeah—maybe obsessing on a girl who's not quite interested in me. But other than that . . .

Sorry if I'm going on about this, but the topic's on my mind today. A lot. You see, yesterday Chaz asked me if I'd mind if Albert spent the night in our room. Of course, this is highly illegal and against all SummerArts regulations, like everything that interests Chaz. At first, I was pretty reluctant to agree to it, but the look on Chaz's face was just . . . so un-Chaz. It was severely sincere and almost desperate.

My bigger concern was that I didn't want to have to be in the same room with all sorts of sex going on. But Chaz said that they just wanted to be together and wouldn't be "smoking each other's bones." Holy shit! Smoking each other's <u>bones</u>?! (Have you ever heard this phrase before?) So I was skeptical, knowing Chaz is a bit of a playa. But he said that he likes Albert a lot and thinks it might be a serious deal and wouldn't want to ruin that with premature sex. Then I was like, uh, okay, who kidnapped my roommate and replaced him with this chaste imposter?

Being the ultimate softie that I am, I said yes, and little Albert spent the night. So do you think Chaz kept his word on the lovemaking? Actually, the answer is yes. They just sat around on the floor last night listening to show tunes on Chaz's iPod, cutely sharing the earphones. Then around midnight we all went to bed (not together, you friggin' perv!). I was out fast, beat from the long week. When I awoke around 8:00 this morning, I reluctantly opened my eyes expecting to see them rockin' the man-on-man action. Instead, I saw the most incredible sight. Tiny Albert was tucked up into Chaz's arms like a little baby as they both slept like, well, like babies. Albert was snoring a bit, but still, you get the picture. It was so damn cute it was heartbreaking!

Now, if you promise not to mention a word of this ever to anyone, I can tell you a shocking fact. I swear to God that I just about cried, seeing them all peaceful and content like that. Seriously. Mainly because I wished I could do the same thing with Ghaliyah . . . hold her in my bed in the morning, all curled up cute like that. Man, just thinking that thought gets me a little choked up. . . .

I know, I know—you're like, cut the waterworks, Joe Actor. Seriously, though, I am feeling a bit emotional these days. Probably because I feel like I will never find The L. And even though I'm hardly an adult, it seems like other people who are hardly adults are finding it, or at least getting it on. Everyone except me. And please, Hal, don't give me your routine about how it's impossible to feel sorry for me because I have so much going for myself because I'm so damn talented. Talent only goes so far. I want to be happy, too, you know? Happy where it counts. Like in the arms of some nice, sexy, sweet-smelling girl on a Saturday morning.

Well . . . that ain't gonna happen for me this weekend, not even on Sunday morning. That's for sure. The only thing on my hot Saturday night agenda is a trip to the ice cream parlor with MK and some of her pals around 9:00. Whoopee. Well, I better make myself presentable so more chicks can reject my handsome mug. Shit—with lines like that, I am turning into a pre-Henri Hal. HELP!!! C

Week 4

Look—I don't know what you're crying about. At least you did something this weekend other than sit around watching a *Pimp My Ride* marathon while trying to avoid your slave driver of a mother, whose only interest in me is to assist her with the laundry, fix the gutters, and mow the G.D. lawn. Sure, I know how you're totally friggin' bummed out about not being the Casanova that your handsome good looks indicate is your ultimate destiny. The problem, though, as I've said before, is wholly self-inflicted, in that there are tons of girls looking at you—believe me. The core issue here is that you just are not in the right place or mind frame to see these chicks, that's all. You are chasing a dream (a.k.a. G) and not seeing the reality, which is that life is a bowlful of ripe cherries and you should just grab some. (OMG—I don't believe I just made such a dirty het analogy!) Specifically, I speak of the oft-mentioned MK, who sounds like she could be promising because she has a hint of a sense of humor, unlike most of the girls you dig, who are so damn Serious. So come on, dude, give it to me straight—what's the scoop on ice cream night? Details, details!

07:22 P.M.
SUNDAY 07.30.06

So now you go from the longest entry in the world to the shortest? You are so unpredictable sometimes. What am I saying—ALL the times!

It's funny you asked about MK. Are you psychic? Were you getting some weird MK vibe around 12:15 in the A.M. last night? I did actually have a pretty great time at the lame old ice cream shop after all. I mean, granted, getting ice cream with a screaming gaggle of drama girls is not my idea of a smokin' Saturday night. But it was pretty fun. Mainly because I was the only guy there. Not only in our group but in the store. Seriously.

The place was jammed with hot coeds, not counting the skinny hippie dude dishing it out behind the counter. The girls were merciless to him and it was hilarious. They kept making all these ice cream innuendos about whether they wanted "hard-serve" as opposed to soft-serve LOL, and if they were interested in cherries (props to your analogy). These girls were relentless, turning that hippie's face a shade of Strawberry Cream as he surely fought to restrain the woodie in his hemp underwear. That's a good one, huh?

After getting our treats, all six of us smushed up into one booth, and it was crazy: nonstop chattering and gossiping and carrying-on, with MK as the total ringleader. She is too much. She is too-too. After ice cream, we took a long, looping walk back to St. Ann's, across the main campus. It was a beautiful night out, warm and nicely humid. You know what it reminded me of? Remember the summer before eighth grade, how we used to sneak out of the house after midnight and ride around Wheaton on our bikes till all hours? Man, that was awesome! That feeling of freedom we had, you know, that we could go anywhere and do anything we wanted. It sorta felt the same way last night, minus the bikes.

After a while, most of the girls went back to the dorm to watch SNL, leaving MK and me strolling the campus green by ourselves. So I took that moment to tell MK the story about us on our bikes, because I was having such major déjà vu. She loved hearing it too, saying it sounded like a blast. In the fall, she suggested coming down from Frederick so we could all meet up one night to do it again, going around on our bikes. I looked at her like she was crazy, telling her that you'd have your driver's license when school started up. There'd be no more need to be pedaling like that. But she said something amazing: "Just because you grow up doesn't mean you have to be a grown-up." Wow. Is she wise or did she just crib this from one of those "Chicken Soup" books? Either way, I thought it was not a bad idea. So simple but kinda true, you know?

When we got back to St. Ann's, I thanked her for inviting me along on the girls' night out. Then she goes, "Yeah, usually only the gays are allowed the privilege of our company." The privilege? Their company? Dude—this MK is so whacked sometimes! Then there was a bit of weirdness at the end when we said good night. (This is the 12:15 part.) I leaned in to give her a friendly hug and she put her hand on the back of my head, holding it and even like rubbing it a little. But basically, she was making it so that I could not pull my head away. Seriously. The girl had me in a semi-romantic headlock.

I didn't know what to do other than say, "Uh, can you let me go?" But I figured that would have been rude. So I kissed her slightly on the ear as a signal to let me go. But that signal didn't quite get through. In fact, it only made her kiss me on the cheek. Which led to me kissing her on the cheek and . . . well, yeah, we eventually sorta made out. Not major tongue-sucking action, really, but . . . all right, there was a little bit of suction. But it didn't last forever, maybe a few minutes. Five, tops.

When that weirdness was all over, I said good-bye and she goes, "Uh, you already said that." Which I had when I went to give her the hug. Of course, this left me scriptless and stupid and just stuttering like an idiot until I finally said, "Line!" which is what you yell out to the stage manager when you can't remember dialogue. And this totally cracked her up! So she goes on this riff of pretending to read to me the lines of some fake script she's making up off the top of her head (she's a bit better unscripted than I am). She's also doing it with a British accent. (?!) It was something like, "Good night, my dear friend. It was a delightful evening strolling about the grounds. I do hope we may enjoy each other's company again because, as you know, Father thinks the world of you." LOL She is so bizarre sometimes. I mean— "Father thinks the world of you"? WTF! Did I mention she is whacked?!

04:11 P.M.
MONDAY 07.31.06

Now, there's the Chuck I know and love (and I mean that in a platonic way, of course). Out on a Saturday night with a veritable harem of dirty-mouthed young ladies, tramping about the campus of UMD till all hours, and then (whoops!), accidentally making out with one of them. Props to you, bro. Kudos, even. Hell—I'd send roses if I had a dime to my name, because it's about friggin' time you got yourself a little coed action, even if it took a female wrestler to make the move, or headlock, as it were. That is too damn hysterical! I definitely remember MK and her harem at the party, clustered over in the corner by the stereo and screaming in unison every 5-10 minutes. And Henri had a lively discussion with her re music as he kept trying to force some hip-hop into the mix and she just kept hitting repeat on the *Wicked* sound-track. Typical showgirls . . .

Meanwhile, here in the real world, we started our last week of driving class today with a review of where we all stood in terms of driving hours and grades on the quizzes. It will come as no shock to you or anyone in the greater Wheaton area that Brett is pretty much failing the class. In fact, she is the only one failing the class. Tlucek tried to make this point to her, but Brett just sat there bored and basically glad that only five days were left of this torture. When Tlucek asked her, pointedly, how she was going to get to jobs in the future, she just looked at him and said, "I don't really plan on working for a living." This cracked all of us up, except for Tlucek.

He did seem genuinely concerned about her, but that's because he doesn't really know her. Brett is going to be fine and taken care of for the rest of her life because she is a babe with total friggin' attitude—apparently, guys love this. (See "Joey.") Case in point: This A.M. I noticed some anonymous hunk in a Lexus dropping her off in the Einstein driveway. When I asked her who the hell was that guy, she simply said, "Jerry," and that was that. Like, who the hell is Jerry!?

After class, I gave Henri a buzz, as we'd made a tentative plan to hang at Marrakesh. But there was no answer at his house, just the machine. I left a message and then ran into Brett out in front of school talking to someone on her cell. She looked fairly displeased when she hung up the phone and I was like, what's up? She said Jerry had a business lunch and couldn't pick her up, which made me ask how old Jerry was. I guess my tone was a bit too alarmed, because Brett just gave me her dead-level glance and said, "Older than you," and that was that. She has a way of doing this a lot, avoiding the direct question if it doesn't interest her. Conversation or engagement with Brett is on Brett's terms alone and usually that's fine, but when she's pissed off . . . watch out!

Anyway, I asked her if she wanted to go to Marrakesh and she was like, "Isn't that in Africa?" I nearly fell over laughing on that one, telling her no, it was this coffee joint in downtown Wheaton. She was incredulous. I might as well have said that Marrakesh was on Mars. I told her that it was really cool and Moroccan and funky and that they had the strongest coffee in the known universe. That seemed to be decisive and she agreed to hang.

After a couple double espressos, I was pumped and buzzing and totally inspired to gain a lot more information about Brett's mysterious life outside of driving. She was also feeling the caffeine rush and started talking a mile a minute about everything. Namely men—that is, the ones in her life. That's right, as in plural. I had always assumed Brett was sorta slutty, so this merely confirmed it. But not in the way I expected. I thought Brett was just having sex with all these random guys who dropped her off at Einstein. But the deal is that she won't have sex with just anyone, it has to be someone who might pan out into a real and truly long-term relationship. This is a strict rule for her too. She doesn't couch it in that crap of "blow jobs aren't really sex," either. As she put it in her typically Brett way, "If someone has an orgasm, then someone's had sex." I was very curious, though, how she manages to keep these multiple guys interested while toying with them at the same time—don't they get annoyed by that? "Guys like to be toyed with," she claimed, "and they especially enjoy a challenge." And she is certainly challenging.

From this discussion about her voluminous love life, we turned to my fantasy lust life, specifically, the topic of Henri. I told her what's been going on lately (the bike ride, the drooling, etc.), and she said it was all good, though the drooling did gross her out a bit. She told me that I've got Henri eating out of the palm of my hand, to which my response was: "Whhhaaaaa? Are you totally high, woman? Has Henri been slipping you some fatties on the sly?" But Brett was absolutely serious. She said I wasn't giving it up (meaning my male virginity), and that was good. Can you <u>believe</u> this? So I had to inform her that I wasn't exactly fighting Henri off, as he tried to unsnap my bra (to put it in Brett terms). But she knows he wants me and said she could see it the moment Henri and I first met that afternoon at the movie theater. Still, I was pretty skeptical about this line of hers, thinking that she was just trying to build me up (HINT: a ploy <u>you</u> might try once in a while). Then she said she could prove it . . . if, that is, I called up Henri and told him to come and meet us.

I told her that, in fact, he <u>was</u> supposed to meet us (or at least me) but had been a no-show, proof to my point that Henri's interest in me had a tendency to come and go. Brett, barely listening, tossed me her phone and told me to give him a call and demand that he come meet us, now. I told her she was tripping on too much caffeine and that there was no way that I could do that. I mean, I could call him and maybe see what he was up to, but I was not gonna be all like—"Bitch, get your ass in gear and come meet me <u>now</u>!" Brett rolled her eyes at this, and told me to stop joking around and just call him. So I did and he was at home, or at least he picked up this time. The first thing he said was this: "I've been stoned for the last 24 hours!" Not exactly the kinda hello I was hoping for, you know? Despite Brett's bitchy encouragement, I didn't demand Henri's presence at Marrakesh. I just said, "Hey, I thought we were gonna do something today," and you know what? He was totally apologetic (which I thought was sweet), and he even said he would come by and meet us at Marrakesh in half an hour or so. Wow, I thought . . . <u>that</u> was weirdly easy!

But when I hung up, Brett was displeased with my phone manner, saying I was too girly. Christ—can you believe this one? I'm too girly? Excuse me, but who's the one wearing sparkling purple lip gloss and glittering three-inch nails? What she meant was that I let him off the hook too easily at first or something. Anyway, the bummer upshot of all this is that in the end, Henri was still a total no-show. Brett said he would've stopped by if I'd demanded it. Still, I don't think that's true. Henri wouldn't have come if I phoned in a death threat to him. Reason? Henri was friggin' baked like a cake and was not going anywhere except the sofa and maybe the refrigerator. It's funny, 'cause I thought I'd made some real progress with him on our big day trip down to Mount Vernon. But I guess it was maybe only progress in my head. Which is, in fact, where this relationship seems to exist: in my head.

Brett was very sweet and encouraging as we walked home, saying that I just had to be tougher with Henri and make him want it more. Maybe . . . I don't know. I sometimes find it hard to believe he wants it at all, meaning me. I certainly want him—oh God, do I ever! (Shit—is Henri turning me onto belief in a higher power?!) Yet Brett's advice was to never let Henri see how much I want him because desperation scares off men more than anything else; she read this in *Cosmo*. But I wonder . . . do the same sorta rules apply when it's two guys? I mean, it can't be the same dynamic, right? And I know you're gonna say, "Well, one guy is always gonna be the girl in the relationship," but that is such a heterocentrist worldview I can't even discuss it. The thing about gay guys is there is no girl . . . that's why we're gay guys. I know it sounds sorta weird, but I think you get the point, right?

Even though Brett's intentions are good, I feel like I need some advice from a guy who doesn't read *Cosmo*. It is a guy I'm dealing with, after all, you know what I mean? I await your reply. . . . H

09:10 A.M.
TUESDAY 08.01.06
Sorry you had to await my reply for so long. I read your entry late last night but was so exhausted from rehearsal that I crashed. We started running the

first act all together, and it is a bear. I am onstage the whole time—not that I'm complaining. It's just I didn't realize how demanding that was gonna be. I've done leads before, but even in *Music Man* it wasn't like I was in every single scene!

So—as to the man-man question, you raise an interesting point. I guess I did think that's how gay guys got together. You know, that one was sorta more the woman and the other more the man. Like in *The Birdcage*. And lately, with all this talk about gay marriage, it seems like that was making the case even stronger. If gays want to play house, then someone has to be the husband and someone has to be the wife, right? Otherwise, isn't it like total chaos and relationship anarchy? I think about my folks, specifically, and how Helen is such a friggin' nag about cleaning around the house while Bob is always telling her to pipe down 'cause he's watching ESPN. So with two gay guys, how does that work? OH—wait a minute . . . maybe that analogy doesn't work, since no self-respecting gay man would ever watch ESPN. (ha) Unless maybe it was men's diving.

But seriously, I have to say the whole issue confuses me a bit too. So I don't know if Brett's advice to play the girl and be all distant and demanding is decent or not. Sure, maybe it works for her. But you and Brett, though you've become friends, seem like total opposites. You are definitely not wearing sparkle lipstick, at least that I'm aware of. ☺

As for Henri, my only advice at this point is something you are probably not gonna like. It is, simply, to stay away. Seriously. The more you write about him, the more this guy sounds like a total druggie. C'mon—stoned for a whole day? That may be cute in a teen movie or something, but in real life, frankly, that's just sad. And if his life is this tragic now, it's only gonna get worse. So as charming and sexy as he is, I have to put in my major reservations at this point.

And I know you're having a good time with him, which is great. However, when you're not, it sounds like you're having an awful time. Lately, your mood seems to fluctuate wildly depending on Henri's proximity to you. Case in point: The post–bike riding entry was endless and the post–dull weekend entry was only like four sentences. And yeah, I enjoyed reading the bike riding entry a ton, as you enjoyed experiencing it. But the warm, fuzzy glow of that day seemed to disappear awfully quickly, leaving you cranky and uncommunicative.

Now, I know that I'm probably guilty of the same thing in my Ghaliyah obsession. But in my defense: a) Ghaliyah is not a drug addict and b) she is not the only thing going on in my life. Oh shit—I can see you flying off the handle right now reading this. But PLEASE, Hal—don't take those things the wrong way. I don't mean it to come off as mean. I just want you to find something that interests you creatively or professionally other than guys. (And no, driving class doesn't count.) It seems you put so much stock in these guys you meet because you don't have a lot of stock in other things. Maybe if you got involved or interested in something else, it would fill your life up more, so that when things got rough in the men's department, you wouldn't go so postal. And don't deny that—because you know you do. I've been there for it!

So don't be despondent if Henri doesn't work out. Take it this way—now that Henri has gotten you out of the house a little this summer, look around. There are millions of things in the world out there that you might like. Like that Rodin sculpture show I saw downtown. You used to really like making stuff with Play-Doh—remember? I'm sure that's how old Rodin got his start. Well, unless they didn't have Play-Doh in the 1800s. (ha)

Still, you know what I'm going for here. Try stuff. New stuff. I think it would be great for you to be open to some new experiences this summer and not just planted in front of the TV feeling bummed out that some dude didn't call you back. Hey—I can even put all this advice into a short, Chuckie phrase, too: Do something, not someone. That sounds like a public service announcement, huh? All right—I'm gonna go. Take care . . . miss ya! C

09:22 P.M.
TUESDAY 08.01.06
By all rights, I should go off on you. I should really start letting you have it via an endlessly agitated and somewhat enraged stream of electronic invective. But I'm not going to do that. I'm a changed person since you left. I've realized the value of being pithy—which is to say . . . F.U., BRO!

09:25 P.M.
TUESDAY 08.01.06
And don't think you can get off dismissing Henri as a drug addict, because that is just a typical, puritanical Chuck move to demonize someone who likes to maybe have a good time every once in a while. CHRIST! The minute you see someone take a toke you're like, the devil has come to claim your goddamned soul! And I know this is all due to your wastoid sister, but still, Chuck. Give it a rest! Henri is not a drug addict because he got stoned for a day. Here's the deal: Henri likes to get stoned sometimes. Sometimes he doesn't. Sometimes it can be annoying and irresponsible and what have you, but sometimes we are all not as perfect as ideal little Chuckie, with your perfect hair and perfect face and perfect smile, voice, attendance, etc. You know how I said before I wanted to be you? Sorry, I guess I must have been high! Which is how I tend to waste all my oh-so-valuable free time these days, apparently. Spending it in a big, hazy cloud of Henri-induced wacky smoke. Ja!

11:02 P.M.
TUESDAY 08.01.06
So . . . I take it Henri didn't call you back today or something?

11:38 P.M.
TUESDAY 08.01.06
Oh—you think you're SOOOOO FUNNY sometimes, HUH? You think you're sooooooo friggin' wise? You think you know me sooooooooooooooo GODDAMN <u>WELL</u>? OK, then, here's a surprise. You know the hell what? As of today, I give up on YOU and our FRIENDSHIP and THIS FUCKING STUPIDASS BLOG. IT'S OVER!!!

11:41 P.M.
TUESDAY 08.01.06
IF THAT IS YOU CALLING ON THE PHONE, I AM NOT PICKING UP!

11:47 P.M.
TUESDAY 08.01.06
CHUCK—STOP <u>FUCKING CALLING</u>! YOU'RE GONNA WAKE UP
MY MOM!!!

02:15 A.M.
WEDNESDAY 08.02.06

Hey—still can't sleep after our talk tonight. I feel terrible. And not just for waking up Valerie and getting her involved in our fight. (FYI—I had to wake up the RA at my dorm to use his phone.) It's just . . . I, uh . . . I don't know what to say, Hal. When you started bawling on the phone like that, talking about Henri. Shit. That was killing me. It just hurt so bad to hear you hurting so bad. Even worse was not being able to do anything about it either. Except listen, I guess. And I didn't feel that was enough. Not by a long shot.

I had no idea you felt this strongly about him. Seriously. I thought it was really more like the Einstein Three, just a dumb crush, but this . . . I don't know. I've never heard you like that before, crying over someone. Hell—I don't think I've heard you cry over anything since you fell off the jungle gym in sixth grade and broke your wrist. So I guess all that crying does mean something . . . a lot of something. No matter what I may think.

Along those lines, I'm sorry I said those things about Henri being a drug addict. That wasn't fair, and you're right that I don't know him at all. A few minutes' impression at a party and a couple anecdotes is not enough to form an opinion. Especially about someone who clearly means a lot to you.

And I'm sorry about telling you what to do about it too. I gotta admit . . . I am such an ass sometimes, telling everyone what they should be doing with their lives and loves when I'm barely figuring it out myself. The loves part, mainly. But maybe I do this because it keeps me from focusing on my own problems. Or maybe I'm just an idiot. I've never been that bright, you know. You're the smart one. I'm just one big, good-looking, dumb package. (ha)

Anyway, I'm sorry about what I said, and I really do hope Henri calls you back. Seriously. I want you to be happy, and I guess it didn't sound to me like that's what was going on with your previous entries. That's why I was so critical of Henri. I thought he was on the verge of making you miserable, like the Einstein guys. But maybe, with time, the whole Henri thing can work out. I hope that's the case. Really. Because I sure don't want to have any more sobbing phone conversations at midnight like that anymore. Maybe in person that'd be okay, but on the phone? No thanks. It's just gotta be the most hopeless sound ever. Someone crying on the other end of a phone. Shit . . .

All right—I better try to sleep. I've got a long day ahead of me. Hey—and if you wanna talk tomorrow, as opposed to blog, let me know and I'll see if we can arrange a time. Miss you . . . C

05:20 P.M.
WEDNESDAY 08.02.06
Hi. So I know I was screaming and going crazy last night when I picked up the phone, but thanks for calling in the first place and being understanding eventually. And thanks for your late-night entry as well. I know what you mean about crying on the phone, that's for sure . . . it's damn depressing. Fortunately, Valerie had gone back to bed by that point in our tragic little chat, leaving her with the impression that we were just having some friendly fallout. Which I guess we _were_ having until it got into The Henri Effect, as you like to call it. I guess it's probably something more specific than an "effect" if it can make me cry like a friggin' baby. I guess I am in love with him or obsessed with him or maybe I'm just a plain old emotional basket case.

Anyway, I'm sorry I got so cunty in the blog, and even sorrier that my cuntiness is now recorded for posterity. (Is there any way to delete some of these more-than-unflattering entries?) As to the man in question, you might have already guessed that my less-than-suicidal mood combined with the simple fact that I'm actually blogging might indicate good news on the Henri front. And it does. Yeah—I did talk to and even see Henri today. He just showed up out of the blue, standing outside of Einstein as driving class let out, pretending like it was some sorta surprise that I happened to be there too. (?) Oh—and get this! The first thing he said was pretty much an apology for bailing on me at Marrakesh. He totally forgot that he'd said he was gonna come by and, when he saw Brett's number on caller I.D. later that night, he felt pretty bad about it. So to make up for it, he offered to buy me lunch up in Wheaton. How about that? So if that's not an official date, I don't know what is, right?

I thought we were gonna hit Marrakesh again and just get some hummus or some other Moroccan delicacies, but Henri had a whole different plan. We went to this Ethiopian restaurant on Fern Street that I had never even seen before called Zed. I mean, hell, I didn't even know they had food in Ethiopia . . . wasn't that a problem for a while? I even said this, which made Henri crack up and mutter something about American ignorance.

After we sat down and Henri ordered (in French so that I had no idea what we were getting), I realized something odd. There was no silverware. I pointed this out and he said that this was a traditional Ethiopian restaurant, which meant that you used your hands. At first, this was sorta grossing me out, but when the food came, I realized how it worked: Basically, you use these bready things called *ingira* to pick up your food, and when you're done, you eat your utensils. I said this to Henri, which he thought was funny too (re the utensils). So all in all it was a great lunch date, as a) the food was cool and b) Henri was laughing at about 90 percent of my lame jokes.

After lunch, we started wandering around Wheaton, but it was deadly hot out, 95 with the humiture! So Henri suggests we go swimming. I'm like, great, but Ocean City is about three hours away by car and it's still a week before I get my license. But Henri's not talking about the beach: He's referring to that swim club over on Viers Mill Road. I'm like, "Uh, you have a membership?" And he goes, with a shrug, "Who needs a membership?" Then I ask if he has a bathing suit? He says no, but he can certainly buy one for a dollar at Salvation Army. I'm skeptical about this whole plan as we head over to SA, looking for some old jams and avoiding the ones with that white netting inside, which Henri says is "deese-goose-tea-ing." (OMG—his accent kills me sometimes!)

After buying some swim trunks, we head over to Viers Mill, though it's still pretty unclear how Henri plans to get in without a membership. But he seems to have a pretty good idea. Or at least he pretends that's the case. So we walk over to the pool club and take a slow, roundabout walk through the parking lot before going to stand outside the entrance. I'm trying to figure out what's going on, but Henri says, calmly, to just wait. Every few minutes, he turns and smiles at the perky girl who is sitting at the front desk checking people in. Finally, after about 10 minutes of this waiting, I am wilting and wondering if we are ever gonna make it in, and Henri nods, giving me the signal, which is putting his finger to his lips as if to say "silence." Though I don't know exactly what this signal is about, I just follow him.

We go up to the girl and Henri starts talking in a much more heavily accented and broken English than I'm used to, telling the girl that we are foreign exchange students staying with the Paulson family for the summer and we were supposed to meet them here and blah-blah-blah. The girl instantly perks up and is like, "Oh, you're from Paris!" So Henri talks about this for a while, and then she says that the Paulsons are already inside. And Henri lights up, smiles, flirts, and basically tells the girl we are going in to meet them. So what can she do? She certainly can't do her job, which is to keep vagrants like us out of this exclusive pool club, because when Henri turns on the charm and turns up the accent, he gets whatever the hell he damn pleases!

Ducking into the men's room, I ask him who the hell the Paulsons are. Henri says he doesn't know. He just saw the name on a registration sticker on one of the cars in the parking lot. (He's too clever by half, huh?) So then Henri tosses me my new one-dollar bathing suit, a pair of green jams that are one size too large. In an awkward moment, we both turn around to face away from each other and put our suits on. (SIDEBAR: Can I say this is a bit of a technical problem with being gay—sharing intimate moments like this with the same sex. Someone needs to do something about this. . . .) Anyway, I take my shorts off and slip the jams on over my underwear. Henri, however, being French and free of any inhibitions, proceeds to whip off both his shorts and his underwear. I know this because, as I'm turning back around, I get an oh-so-tantalizing glimpse of his storied ass as it disappears into his trunks. OMG! "Just kill me now" is all I could think at the moment. That ass was dangerous enough clothed. Unclothed, it is a lethal weapon that could be employed to serious effect in the War on Terror. Though I guess, for it to work in that context, al Queda would have to be completely gay or something. . . .

Anyway, we spent the next couple hours hanging out in the pool, which was a cool, blue oasis on a dog-day afternoon. (Wow—that's not a bad sentence, huh?) However, it was also swarmed with tweens, which was somewhat annoying as they can be incredibly loud and spastic and splashy. But Henri didn't seem to mind. In fact, he almost enjoyed that sort of chaos and, well, was pretty loud/spastic/splashy himself. At irregular intervals, he would get up on the diving board and show off some of his Parkour flips and twists for the youngsters. I told him it was probably not a great idea to draw attention to ourselves given the fact that we were there illegally, but Henri was like, "What are they going to do except tell us to leave?" So I don't know how he can keep his cool in these situations, as I'm looking around the pool wondering where the hell our "host family" is and when they're gonna rat us out.

Finally, after about an hour in the drink, I convince Henri to take a break, as I'm turning a bit prunish. We wander over to a less populated area of grass and pull a couple loungers together. I wanna be in the shade while Henri wants to be in the sun, which leads to us placing the loungers so that they are facing each other. So I'm lying there peacefully when I hear a scream come from the pool. Looking up to see what the commotion is, I notice something that makes me want to scream. Henri is lying on his chaise napping, his jams baggily open on his right thigh so that I can see up his leg to where his private package is nestled. I can't believe I'm seeing this in the first place, and then, to be checking it out in such a public place, too? It almost made me wonder if Henri was intending this private show for me. Almost. Whatever his intent or lack thereof, it was sexy and disturbing and titillating all at once, so much so that I started to get a lil' stiffie myself. Fortunately, I did not go the free-ball route or I would have been kicked out of the pool, not for trespassing but for public lewdness. Still . . . the sight of him. Hell—all of him! So close, really, yet so damn far.

After a few minutes, Henri shifts in his slumber, thus closing the curtain on my private peep show. Then, when Henri finally pops out of his nap, he smiles at me from his chaise, a lengthy, odd grin. I wonder if he knows I've been checking him out? Probably. But I'm guessing Henri has no idea how much I've been checking him out. Still, he gets the basics, which, to boil it down for you, is the simple fact that I cannot tear my gaze from his fairly naked body. I'm assuming all this because once he started looking at me, I was blushing like I'd gotten an instant and impossible case of sunburn in the shade.

He asked if I wanted go back in the water and I was like, sure . . . at least the cold will put a damper on all my, er, excitement. So we spend another hour or so in the pool goofing around, and, you know, it was just the most fun I've ever had swimming. Well, all right, not counting the time that we were body surfing at O.C. last summer after that hurricane. But still, can I say it was the most fun I've had in a public pool? OK—that works and won't hurt your feelings. I know how sensitive you can be. . . .

Actually, when we were walking home, I was talking to Henri about you, and I thought it would be cool if you guys could get a chance to hang out more. Driving wraps up on Friday, so maybe after I get my license on my b-day, Henri and I can make another illegal visit to UMD, this time via car. I know it will depend on Val's permission to borrow the wheels, but I'm sure she'll go for it if I pitch the trip as some big best-friend make-up session, since she probably thinks we still hate each other from the other night. I think if you had a little more time to hang out with Henri, your opinion on him would be instantly changed. I mean, to be honest, even I thought he was a bit of a dick when I first met him. Hell—look at the first couple entries where I talk about him. I don't think I was that impressed, especially when I thought he was into Brett. So anyway, getting to hang out a little more might change your mind about him. Just an idea . . .

Also it would be great to be with you on my birthday because, after 10 years of shared b-day parties, it wouldn't really be a birthday without you there. I mean it. It would be like the cake was missing or something. So think about it and let me know. The more advance notice Val has, the more time she'll have to get over the notion of me on the Beltway. Or maybe I'll just take University Blvd., as the idea of hitting the Beltway scares me a bit too. Later! H

PS—Any more make outs with MK?

12:35 A.M.
THURSDAY 08.03.06

OK—so when did you become a psychic? When did you develop your magical, mystical third eye? How is it you know every time something is up with me and MK? I wish I had a similar minicam trained on your Henri shit. Then maybe I would have a better sense of what's going on with you two. Well, then again, maybe I'll pass on the big, hairy close-up of his pork and beans, if you know what I mean. Yikes!

As to your premonition, there was something going on with me and MK tonight. Kinda freaky but ultimately kinda cool. It happened after our first full run-through of the second act. Unfortunately, the rehearsal was terrible. The act was running ridiculously long and everyone's singing was awful, as people are still trying to figure out how most of the songs in the first act go. Sondheim's music is incredibly difficult—did I mention that before? They are not your average show tunes. And that's cool, to a point. But when you have to learn them for a show that goes up in, oh, less than two weeks? AAHAAHHHHHH! OK—now you've seen me scream like a girl. So, in terms of emotional embarrassment, I guess we're back to being equals. ☺

Anyway, the only bright point of the rehearsal was one song toward the very end of the show called "Our Time." It takes place up on a rooftop in New

York in the '50s when all the characters are really young, and Franklin (me) meets Mary (Ghaliyah) for the first time, looking for a satellite named Sputnik to cross the sky. But really, the song is not about space exploration. It's about these characters, all of them with dreams of Broadway, starting out on the journey of their lives. What's heartbreaking is that, because the show's been going backward, we know that their future leads to friendships being strained and trust being broken and relationships dying. But the younger version of these characters don't know this stuff yet: All they have is this crazy, unlimited hope for their future.

We'd gone over the song in choral rehearsals a few times, but only part by part, never all together. Until tonight. And hearing it for the first time in the rehearsal space, with everyone belting it out . . . man, this song is just amazing! The words are so inspirational and the music so soaring, but it's almost sad at the same time. It's sorta hard for me to describe it. But when we finished singing tonight, just about everyone on stage was a little moist in the eyes. Yeah—it's <u>that</u> good!

What I really love, though, is the message of the lyrics. Here's a quick sample:

> *It's our time, Breathe it in,*
> *Worlds to change and worlds to win.*
> *Our turn, coming through,*
> *Me and you, man, me and you.*

The "me and you" part is actually about me and Chaz, who's playing your part (as my best friend!). And even though Chaz isn't really my best friend, I now sorta see him as you. OH MAN—I hope that is <u>not</u> going to offend you! Let me explain before it does. It's a part of how I've learned to make our characters' friendship real onstage. I just imagine that I'm there with you singing this song about how together we're gonna change the world. And you know what . . . <u>it works</u>!

When I started singing those lines to Chaz tonight, my face sorta beaming, I swear to God he almost lost it. Yeah—I know—brag about how good you are,

Chuck. But it was pretty cool to see someone onstage get moved like that. When we get an audience in there, I swear, they are gonna be sobbing!

Also—you know how things with Ghaliyah and me have not been so great lately. We've been barely talking to each other since her interest in Ryan heated up. Well, as we were doing this scene tonight, all that seemed to go away. Toward the end of the song, the stage blocking calls for us to put our arms around each other's shoulders, and as we did so, Ghaliyah smiled at me. I mean really grinned at me, one of those goofy grins that you can't hold back or restrain or anything. The kind that takes over your whole face, making you look like a moron. Except on her, that kinda grin hardly looks stupid. It was . . . radiant.

I'd like to say that I was pulling out all the acting stops and also thinking of you when I looked at Ghaliyah to get this reaction. But, uh, that would be a big lie. When I saw her there, I saw her beauty and her talent and how she has inspired me so much this summer. It's funny . . . in my efforts to impress her, I have started to impress myself. And others, too, apparently. After the song ended, Ryan came up to me and was just unbelievably complimentary, saying how I had blown him away, not only with that last song, but with the second act in general. This was a total shock, as I thought the whole run-through had been pretty rough. But Ryan, who has a better perspective on it, seriously disagreed. Even though the blocking was sketchy and some of the songs not quite hitting on all cylinders, the emotion was there, which is what mattered. He said he actually felt me feeling the part, going through all the heartbreak and friendship drama and general shit Franklin goes through in a way that he had not seen before.

When he said this, I asked him if that was the secret. You remember . . . his big hush-hush plan about what the show was about that he wouldn't tell us? Well, you know what? Ryan smiled, because I was right. The show is about us. All of us at SummerArts! We are all aspiring to do the same stuff that the characters in this show do. Mary wants to be a writer, Beth a performer, Franklin and Charlie a pair of songwriters. They're just like us, artists (props to Chaz) just starting out on this long, uncertain journey that will take us who knows where. The show is about us. Literally. We are all putting our old lives behind us and starting these new lives as performers. And guess what—that was Ryan's secret! Can you believe it?! No wonder he didn't want to tell us, because we all would have been typically, "Yeah, right, whatever." But now, having done that song and actually understood it, too, I can see what he was getting at. So, news flash: Ryan is not a complete asshole after all. He's actually pretty smart . . . even if he is playin' my girl. (WURHD!)

After finishing the song, everyone was in such a weirdly good mood that the whole cast decided to hit the ice cream parlor. We got there just at closing time, which did not make the hippie behind the counter very happy. He was losing it trying to serve us all. Then MK realized that with this one guy working, everyone was not gonna get their just desserts. So she took action. Literally. MK and her posse jumped behind the counter, washed their hands, and started dishing out the ice cream for everyone!

At first, the ice cream dude was like, "Uh, you can't do that." But after MK pointed out that if they didn't help him out he was gonna be there all night trying to serve everyone, he agreed to the assist. So as MK's crew dished it out, the hippie took people's cash. You should have seen MK behind the counter! It was <u>hilarious</u>! Yelling at people and smarting off at them, like she was some character from *Seinfeld*. Chaz started calling her the Ice Cream Nazi, which only got her going even more. What a trip!

After leaving the hippie exhausted (but well tipped), the whole gang of us then headed back toward St. Ann's, but once we got to the main green, Chaz yelled out the magic words: "Ha-Ha!" In a second, all 30 of us were on the ground and Ha-Ha-ing like crazy. My head ended up on Chaz's stomach and MK's head was resting on my stomach, which was . . . cool. And weird. And also sorta funny to see someone I've made out with having her head way down there and, you know, not getting busy. Not that that's what I wanted. But . . . I don't know. It was just weird.

Post Ha-Ha, I was pretty exhausted and was about to go up to my room when MK suggested we head up to the roof. She was suddenly very roof-oriented after doing our second-act roof-topper, as she called it. (She is so bizarre!) So we went up to the roof and . . . oh shit. I am so embarrassed to admit this.

OK—I am only gonna write this if you promise not to make fun of me. All right—I guess if I can't trust you with this sorta information, then who can I trust? I didn't even mention this to Chaz, because I would become so instantly and publicly humiliated by breakfast tomorrow morning the way he spreads info around.

OK—so basically MK and I got up on the roof and started singing to each other. Holy shit! I feel like such an idiot for having done this. I mean, singing on stage is one thing, sure. But on the roof of some dorm at 11:30 at night! Who do I think I am, Tony from *West Side Story*?!? It started because we both were going on and on about what a cool number "Our Time" was. And then, there we were . . . two dopes full of hope (and a bit of talent) up on the roof. At first, we did it sorta jokingly, but as we got into it, it started getting even more intense than it had been onstage. When we reached the end, you can probably use your psychic powers to guess what happened. Yeah—we pretty much started making out. I still can't believe it! Not that it wasn't fun. It was, but it was also . . . I don't know. It was so Moulin Rouge—it was CRAZY!!!

I mean, even though making out was pretty cool, I guess, I'm not sure about the whole thing. MK is funny and interesting and all that, but I don't think she's exactly my type. I mean, she's bigger than me. Not in a fat way or anything, but just, you know, bigger. When she wrapped herself around me like that up on the roof, there was really no escape. Seriously. She was in charge. And it's not like I wanted to get away or anything. But still, that option would be nice to have, at least. But I was hers and she was not gonna let me go. Not that that was so terrible. . . .

Anyway, after she finally let up on me and I could breathe a little, we talked for a bit about the song . . . oh man, we couldn't stop talking about it. MK said that she wants to move to New York, just like the characters in *Merrily*. And she wants to do it right after graduation and try to be an actress/singer/dancer for real. I was like . . . New York?! I mean, that's like a real city. It's <u>huge</u>! Not to mention the biggest terrorist target in the world. But she was very blasé about that stuff, saying tons of people still moved there every day. I guess this is true . . . but New York City? That is bold.

I have to say, though, she got me thinking about it. Seriously. Maybe it's where I should be if I truly want to be a professional and eventually successful. I mean, I am not gonna be entourage-worthy hanging around Wheaton. There's nowhere for an entourage to go in Wheaton. That's for sure. And, sorry—Marrakesh is not an option, even if it is cool.

Holy shit—look at the time. I've gotta get to sleep! OH—before I forget, I think the b-day idea sounds cool. But I don't think we can have a real party-party like we did last time. That'd be too risky. Besides, it'll be a Tuesday, and I don't even think Chaz could think up a decent theme for that night. But if you guys came, I could have Ghaliyah and MK and maybe even little Albert over for a secret b-day cake get-together and some board games. Chaz, of course, has a full range of them . . . including Cranium! I know, I know—so you won't exactly be partying like a 16-year-old rock star. But you'll have plenty of time for that this coming year. I can't believe you're gonna be able to drive. That is so sweet! OK—later! C

01:40 P.M.
THURSDAY 08.03.06
New York? Now you're gonna leave me behind to go to New Fucking York?! All right, leaving me in Wheaton to go to UMD for a few weeks is one thing. But moving to another city? Somewhere like four states away? Hold on here just one damn second, OK? I mean, not to be selfish or anything, but have you even discussed this with me yet? I mean, how would you feel if I suddenly, without any warning, enrolled in an immersion French class and moved to Paris in the fall. Sounds crazy? Well, it could happen. Though actually moving to Paris would be a helluva lot easier than learning French. But still . . . that's not the point. The point is you leaving.

Now—don't get me wrong here. I think it's great about you and MK and both of you being so professionally inspired and all that crap. But there are tons of theaters and shows right here in the D.C. metro area that you two can hit before going to the Big Apple. Hell—you went downtown just a couple weeks ago to see that Shakespeare thing and that was pretty decent, right? There's also the Arena Stage and the

Kennedy Center and many other theaters that I can't name but I always see the ads for in the weekend *Post*. So this is all to say that maybe jumping on the Metroliner to NYC is a little bit like jumping the gun. Maybe you should try to get yourself going professionally here and then head up to New York in a few years . . . you know, like when you're 30.

I do think it's great you are finally getting majorly jazzed about your work and potential career. (It's about friggin' time!) I just hope that being a pro doesn't end up sending you away. Because then I'll truly be left behind and lost and without a goddamn clue re what to do with my life. Christ—I don't think I realized I even <u>had</u> a life until this year. I sooooo wish I could have such a clear and true calling as you, and frankly, sometimes I sorta hate you for it. I think that may have come out just a bit in our big fight Tuesday. Again, I'm sorry for harshing on you like that, but you have to admit, your life is sooooo much easier in that you know exactly where it's headed. Me—it's all such a bloody mystery.

All I know for sure is that there are things I don't want to be, and that's sheerly by default. For instance, I don't want to be or probably can't be an actor, because I am not nearly as big a ham as you are. What else could I do . . . rock star is probably out, given the fact that I have yet to master any musical instrument or my own voice. (Though that certainly hasn't stopped Ashlee Simpson.) And though I appreciate your effort in getting me geared toward the finer arts, I think my sculptural explorations in Play-Doh were not quite the portraits of an artist as a young kid that you've implied. So where does that leave me? Nowheres. I guess I could look to my hobbies or interests . . . hmmmm . . . what hobbies or interests? Well, Henri is my main interest these days, and who can blame me, right? (Oh wait—you can . . . sometimes.)

As to the b-day trip, I breached the subject of borrowing the car with Valerie this morning at breakfast. I even ate some of the eggs she made just to get on her good side, though I fear she saw right through this shameless ploy. I got a very skeptical look, especially when I mentioned (for the first time ever) Henri's name. I sorta lied and said that Henri was in my driving class, since I don't want her to know that I'm picking up random Parkour punks at Wheaton Plaza. That might set off a few gay alarms, you know what I mean? Oh, and I also sorta lied about it being okay for us to visit you. I mean, it's okay with you, of course, so that's not really a lie? Right? <u>Hello</u>? Anyway, the upshot of all this "sorta" lying was that Val said she would "sorta" think about it. So we shall see. . . .

Whatever happens, the countdown to my license to drive has begun. T-minus five days! And tomorrow is the last day of driving class. (!!!) That makes me majorly psyched for two reasons. One is that I can get my certificate of Driver's Education to present to the DMV and obtain my license Tuesday. Two is that from now on, I won't have class in the A.M., so my time will be freed up to do more stuff with Henri. In fact, we have planned a little celebration trip tomorrow, since class gets out early, at 11:00. Believe it or not, I'm gonna take your advice and go check out that Rodin show at the National Gallery. Not really on my own volition, though. You see, when I mentioned it to Henri on the phone last night, he nearly hit the ceiling. Rodin is apparently his favorite artist, to which I replied, "Uh . . . you have a favorite artist?" My favorite artist is Pink, but Henri said, cracking up, that she doesn't really count.

I'm also gonna see if Brett will join us on our field trip, but she seems to be hanging pretty tight with this Jerry character. He's been picking her up every day after school this week, much to Joey's chagrin. Like Joey ever really had a chance with her? He thinks he did after comforting her during the accident-inspired meltdown. But that was strictly situational. She'll never take Joey seriously until he gets a hot set of wheels and a job with some dough. But that probably wouldn't help Joey because, even if he became CEO of a Fortune 500 company, he'd still be the biggest friggin' cheapskate on the planet.

Case in point: Today in class, Tlucek was talking about what we have to do at the DMV to get our licenses. There's a computerized multiple-choice test, a vision test, a short driving test in the parking lot, and then you hand over your driving school certificate and a check for 75 bucks. So Joey starts squealing about the price—75 clams?! And then he says driver's licenses should be free! We pay taxes, he goes on, it's a government service, it should cost nothing. Tlucek very calmly says, "Joey, do you have a job?" Joey shakes his head. "Do you pay taxes?" Joey shakes his head again. "Well," he says, "even if you did, it still costs 75 bucks because . . . ?" Tlucek says this incomplete sentence hoping to get the Socratic method going . . . in a <u>driving</u> class! But you know who the hell answers? Brett pipes up and says, sounding like a contestant on *Jeopardy*, "Because driving is a privilege, not a right." LOL You could have knocked Tlucek over with a spitball, he was that stunned. Once he got over the initial shock wave of Brett's first shot at classroom participation (at the end of the course—natch), he says, in a calm, almost pleasant voice, "Thank you. Brett." And Brett, in her own special way, replies with this gem: "Anytime, Mr. T." OMG. She kills me!!!

After that exchange, we got out of the classroom and onto the road for our last trek in the Geo. I have to say that, for the first time ever, I felt like I sorta knew what I was doing behind the wheel. I almost felt, dare I say, confident as a nearly-minted driver. You may recall that, when we first started hitting the road way back in July, I was a bit terrified of commanding some big piece of machinery at speeds that could cause serious damage or death to anything unfortunate enough to be in its path. (See "Brett and la birdhouse.") But today, it was different. I finally felt like I wasn't a kid but an older, almost adult person who could safely drive a hulking automobile. It's kinda crazy to think I can do this now, because I feel like there is pretty much nothing else in my life that I <u>can</u> do. Really. There are no other skills I can point to that make me anything other than the sulky, bitter, pain-in-the-ass loser that I am. But now I have this . . . this thing. Driving. Dude—I can friggin' drive a car! Yeeeeahhhhaaaaaaaa!

Hey—maybe <u>this</u> could be my career. I could become a limo driver, or check this, maybe even a taxi driver in New York City. (Just like that game "Crazy Taxi"—remember?—that we used to play up at Galaxy Arcade in Rockville?) But driving in New York is apparently even worse than that game, more akin to something like the Beltway times 100. But there's gotta be other jobs that involve driving . . . oh, pizza delivery! (That could be sweet, and think of the free pies.) Or policeman—that would be totally boss! Driving around all day in a hot, souped-up Ford V-8 with a two-way radio and a computer on the dash. Except holding that sorta job would mean I'd not only have to obey the laws, but actually enforce them. That might not be a good fit. . . .

Man—I am <u>totally</u> rambling on today. What is wrong with me? Nothing, really. Literally. That's the problem, because I have nothin' to do. Henri had to run errands with his moms this afternoon, so I'm solo and clearly losing my mind. I mean, hell—policeman? What am I talking about!!! Anyway, I will stop wasting your time with the mad musings of a suddenly driving-obsessed maniac. BTW . . . that is great news about you and MK totally getting it on up on the roof. I hope this chick will lead to some serious H-and-H action before your time is up at UMD. But if you've already got a serious make-out going on first base, you will definitely have more than enough time over the next two weeks to round all the way to home, don't you think? You crazy stud!!! H

09:23 A.M.
FRIDAY 08.04.06
The most disturbing thing happened this morning. I had this insane sex dream about MK!

Man . . . I never even had any sex dreams about Ghaliyah. Maybe some romantic dreams that were a little sexy, but not actually sex. And some daydreams, definitely, but not full-on fantasy action. And, dude, I mean <u>full-on</u>. OK, this may be oversharing, but I gotta tell you, this was not a dry dream. Not by a long shot.

Now, as if that weren't embarrassing enough, when I got up this morning, I was sorta spacey and didn't quite realize what a mess I'd made down there. Until, that is, Chaz starts screaming like a stuck pig. I wish I were kidding, but I'm not. Holy shit—you'd think the guy would have seen a lot of sperm-splattered undies in his time, being such The Gay Playa. But Chaz lost his friggin' shit, squealing and then laughing and then falling onto the floor.

Then, to justify his laughter, he related to me this lovely tidbit: that I was apparently moaning in the middle of the night and saying things like, "yeah, baby" and "Come on, honey." As you may know, Chaz has a tendency to exaggerate, so I don't know if I totally believe that suddenly I became a porn star in my sleep. Still—I was making some sorta noise. Some kinda primal grunt—that's bad enough!

After showering and getting myself cleaned up, I thought I'd be fine. That I'd feel better and less . . . weird. Well, not exactly. I'm washing my face, brushing my teeth, getting ready for the day, when I start remembering this dream again. Shit—it was insane! It was like the person I was getting it on with was MK physically, sure, but not really her or something. It was like her big, brassy personality had been hijacked by a *Girls Gone Wild* babe.

Anyway, so I'm thinking about how totally bizarre this whole dream was when I smell something funny . . . something minty. I look in the mirror and my face is covered in toothpaste. You know what I did? Completely spacing out, I grabbed the Colgate, thinking it was the Jergens, and started moisturizing with friggin' toothpaste!

Maybe I was just tired, I thought. Or maybe it's like early-stage, adolescent Alzheimer's. Of course, it's neither. You get my drift here? I'd spell it out if I could, but it only has initials, really. M and K. What is going on? I mean she's nice and all, but not really midnight-porn-fantasy nice. Let me see if I can put this plainly. She's not the kind of girl you just want to bone, you know what I mean? She's a cool girl, definitely, and, as much as making out with her was fine (not that I had much of a choice), it's hard for me to get a great visual on us doing a whole lot more. Despite the dream. Man—that dream was bizarre. More freaky than sexy. Except that I did end up shooting a load. But still, it was a dream, right? That's all I—

Shit—I am totally late for studio.

01:40 P.M.
FRIDAY 08.04.06

Hey—sorry about the double entry. I know you're downtown at the museum today. (Congrats on finishing up driving!) But I just had to tell you about some additional drama at lunch today.

MK was with her posse over near the soda machine, so I decided not to sit with her and be the one guy breaking into the henhouse. Then I see Ghaliyah sitting by herself, going over her lines. I plant my tray next to her and we start talking, and guess the F what? She knows I made out with MK last night! Shit. I am so busted!!!

So I tell her me and MK are not really an item, desperately trying to backpedal here to save my romantic life. I tell Ghaliyah that it was just this make-out thing, you know, that we were both caught up in the moment. In fact, you know what I did? I blamed the whole thing on that song from the show and our rooftop duet. Seriously. I made Stephen Sondheim take the fall for my horny desperation! This excuse, however, was not wise, as it totally cracked Ghaliyah up. And even though she was laughing at me and not buying my excuse at all, I did like making her laugh. Always the entertainer, huh?

Still, after Ghaliyah was done being amused, I tried to be clear. I said that I didn't think I really liked MK, even though we'd made out. And to this Ghaliyah says, all thoughtful-like, "That's interesting." (?!?!) So, trying to further explain myself and/or dig my grave, I went into how I just don't see MK and myself being physical. And Ghaliyah says, like she suddenly has a degree in psychotherapy, "Well, you certainly don't have a problem making out with her, which could mean that deep down you like her but can't reconcile that with the current state of your conscious mind." So I'm like, "Uh, come again? In English?" And she goes, "Maybe you like her but just can't deal with it."

Question: Why do I get into these sorts of conversations with girls I like? Why do I continue to give them way too much information? Why can't I shut my trap sometimes before making an utter idiot of myself? Your answer to all the above is probably some smart-ass line, like, "Uh, because you're Chuck." But seriously, I'd like to know why I say this crap. Why can't I say the right shit? You know, something along the lines of, "Hey, G—you've got one slammin' body. Let's <u>do</u> this!" Instead, I get into an ultimately embarrassing discussion about my rooftop make-out with the girl I'm actually in love with. Wait a minute—I mean, discussing it with Ghaliyah. MK is not the one I'm in love with. I mean, WTF!!! Where is my script when I need one?

Hey—I just figured out the perfect job/career for you. You can be my scriptwriter for life. You'd be perfect! You can write me lines so I don't sound like an emotional retard. You can dash off witty pickups for me that will actually work. This is genius! Don't you <u>love</u> this idea? Now, I know I won't be able to pay you a lot starting out. But once I get some decent acting gigs, maybe a commercial, then you'd be set. (This chick in the chorus did a Starburst ad when she was 10 and still gets checks four times a year!) You know, we might have to invest in some Blackberrys to make this work properly. That way I could send you the 411 on the hookup and then you could text me back some sweet lines. That would be awesome!!!

This may sound like a big joke, but I'm serious. I need help! Tell me what you think when you get home. Later . . . C

11:40 P.M.
FRIDAY 08.04.06
Are you still not back? I need to talk, chat, get advice from you on something. Shit—a lot of things. I'm having a <u>major</u> emergency tonight. I'd call your house, but . . . awwww, hell.

11:49 P.M.
FRIDAY 08.04.06
So, lying like a rug to my RA, I said I had a "family emergency" so he'd let me use his phone. But no one picked up at your place. Not even your party-hardy mom. I guess you are both out having fun. But what are you doing, I wonder?

Anyway, Chaz is spending the night at the Mathlete Compound, so I'm all alone here and freaking out. You know how some days just start off on the wrong foot and don't really recover? That would be today. Friday. August 4,

2006. A day that will live in embarrassing infamy.

Have I mentioned how gossip flies here like nobody's business? Seriously. It goes at the friggin' speed of light, which is amazing considering none of us are even IM-ing or have cell phones. Thus, info has to travel the old-fashioned way, person to person. But once it gets to the right person, forget it. It's like wildfire. And today, I am the flame. Basically, everyone here now knows the details about my cumtastic wet dream. Everyone. The source of the blaze? That flamer Chaz, of course.

Apparently, he told Enrique (one of the dancers). Enrique was telling some other guy in the cast when one of MK's gal posse overheard the story. They relayed it to MK, who was apparently equally grossed-out/psyched about the whole dream-loving thing. Then Ghaliyah heard them all talking about it and was able to add the charming detail that, even though I'd made out with MK and then plowed her in my porno fantasies, that I wasn't really that into her. So . . . can you guess MK's reaction to all this? Bingo! That's right, she lost it.

MK's big breakdown happened during our last break of the evening. We were about to go into our dance rehearsal for the big end-of-act-one number, a song called "Now You Know." (How ironic, right?) As Ryan cued up the music, he looked around the stage and realized that half the girls were missing. He asked Missy what was going on, and she said that someone was crying in the bathroom and the other girls were trying to help.

Ryan told her to get the chicks outta there and back on stage. When the girls came back, it was pretty clear that MK was the one who'd been balling. Her face was all flush and her eyes red. Seeing this, I thought I was gonna have a heart attack. When you see someone like MK, who is usually Ms. Plucky, looking like Ms. Carwreck, that's serious. I mean, when you were crying, that was bad, certainly, but it almost makes some sorta sense, given your depressive nature. (Please—no offense on that one . . . I've got enough problems!) But when MK is down? Whoa—that's like, shit! It really must be serious.

So, as the girls are walking into positions, MK sorta glances over at me. Her face goes from looking sad to really angry in a second. And I'm like, hell, what did I do? I'm the one suffering from mortal embarrassment here. But she is looking at me like I killed someone, and she is not referring to the little sperms that died in my shorts this morning. (ha) I'm still a bit clueless, though, why she's suddenly angry at me. While Ryan is giving us notes, I whisper to Ghaliyah, asking her what the deal is with MK. She says that she overheard them talking about the wet dream and MK started asking her questions about our chat and she answered them. Great! I'm so friggin' pissed at Ghaliyah, betraying my confidence by saying that stuff to MK about me not really digging her. But she was like, "What confidence? All the SummerArties know about your wet dream!"

Ghaliyah says that I should probably just talk to MK after rehearsal and straighten things out. I'm like, about what? Ghaliyah gives me this withering look and says, and I quote, "If I have to explain this to you any further then you will have lost all my respect, as opposed to half of it." That was bitchy, right? I thought that maybe if me and Ghaliyah didn't make it happen, we'd at least be good friends. Some friend she has turned out to be. Shit.

So after rehearsal ends, I find MK outside the studio surrounded by her gang. The circle they have formed looks fairly impenetrable, and I'm about to give up when one of them spots me and, like magic, the circle dissipates as they all scatter off. MK looks less tragic now, postcrying and all. Which is not to say she doesn't look mad at me. If anything, she looks even madder. So before I can even say, "Hey—I'm sorry about the whole make-out-wet-dream thing," she goes off. I mean, she just explodes!

It went a little something like this: "How dare you have sex with me in a dream and then play it like it's some weird, disgusting thing that you didn't want in the first place, when all along, clearly, you've been trying to get with me and now you just act like I'm some one-night-dream-stand that you can just discard like Kleenex when you're done shooting your load!!!"

DUDE—I AM NOT <u>KIDDING</u>! She was <u>THAT RAW!!!!</u> So I was like, wait a minute, are you seriously angry that I had sex with you in my dream?! So she gets even more pissed off, saying that's not the point. Apparently, the point is that it freaked me out and that I then proceeded to tell everyone about how weird the whole thing was. OK—in my defense, I didn't tell "everyone"—everyone told everyone. But, shit, it <u>was</u> weird. And that's what I said, which only got her to start storming away from me.

Once I caught up with her (she's got a big stride), I asked her to slow down. But she wouldn't, so I kept on trying to talk to her while trying to keep up with her too. That was exhausting. And you know me: I have enough trouble putting a sentence together standing still. So, of course, as we're passing the library I totally tripped on my own two feet and came crashing down onto the pavement. At first, MK didn't even stop walking. It wasn't until she heard me say "Fuck" when I realized I'd scraped my knee that she stopped.

She opened up her purse and gave me a tissue she had, and then we sat down on the lawn and talked while not walking. Even though I still didn't get her damage, I said I was sorry. I said I wished the whole thing hadn't happened. Which got her angry again—she said, "You mean the dream?!" Oh brother. No, I said—the dream was sexy, I guess, otherwise I wouldn't have gotten so excited. But still, it was weird. And before she got angry over me saying "weird" again, I tried to explain. In fact, I explained a little more than I intended to.

I told her about Ghaliyah. You know, I thought this was only gonna make her more angry, but it actually didn't. She just listened quietly at what I had to say. I can't believe all I said, too—and without a script! Though the words were rough, I got the basic story across, which is that I like her a lot but think I might be in love with Ghaliyah. You know what she says to this? She goes, "Does Ghaliyah love you?" Well, I didn't really know for sure and said so. MK then says, to my utter astonishment, "That sucks." And I was like, "Yeah, it does suck." And saying this, I started to get a little glassy-eyed. I'm sure MK saw this, but she was cool enough not to bring any attention to it. She just said that we should probably get back to the dorm, and that was the end of our talk.

When we got back here, I said I was sorry again and, you know what? She said she was sorry too for screaming at me over a dream. Isn't that a riot? In case you're wondering, no, we didn't make out when we said our good-byes.

We just hugged. But it was a pretty long hug. (I'd say weirdly long, but whenever I say "weird" lately, people take offense.) But it was nice, too, even if a little too tight for my taste. This girl has got a grip!

So anyway, that's my emergency. (ha) I guess now that I've written all this down, it doesn't seem like such an emergency. Maybe I just needed to get all this shit out, because having it crammed in my tiny brain was killing me. That's a lot to deal with in one day. I'm so exhausted! But that could be good. Hopefully I'll be too tired to get it on with anyone in my dreams tonight.

Hope you had a fun day (and night?) downtown. Miss ya . . . C

07:53 A.M.
SATURDAY 08.05.06
Christ—I go away for one day and you have written a veritable trilogy of teen terror. Your tales of your Day of Infamy are so friggin' insane!!! I was equally laughing and recoiling, and was so entertained that I read them twice. And I'm sorry I didn't respond sooner, but when I got home last night from our field trip, I just hit the bed around 9:00 and was totally out. Which meant that, with 10 hours of sleep, I got up at 7:00 A.M. this morning . . . WTF?! But more on my amazing day later . . .

First of all, I can't belieeeeeeve Chaz saw you all spunked up like that. Hell—I've never even seen you like that (thank God). I think my reaction, however, would not have been to scream like a big drag queen but more to go mute, possibly for the rest of my life. I mean, dude . . . that is disgusting!!! Second of all, I can't belieeeeeeve that the whole damn campus found out about your adventure in self-lust. If the same scenario had befallen me, I seriously would have killed myself by now, which proves my big old point (one that I've always told you but you never believe) that you are a waaaaay stronger man than me. Third of all, I truly can't belieeeeeeve that MK got her panties in a twist over the fact that you two had fake dream-sex!!! Either this girl has serious boundary issues regarding reality vs. fantasy, or she is totally and irredeemably in love with your ass. I'm guessing it's the latter, because she doesn't seem too crazy . . . for an actor, that is.

As for me, my Friday with Henri started out squarely on the wrong foot, which didn't bode well for anything of import happening other than us checking out some art. The wrong foot in my case, however, was Henri's, not mine, in that he showed up at Einstein somewhat crispy at 11:00 in the A.M. I could tell because he was wearing his sunglasses, even though it was totally cloudy and because he laughed for about 10 minutes when I said hi. Now, I know I've hung out with him stoned before, but I guess I thought, this being before noon, that he'd be somewhat sober, but I guess I thought wrong on that count.

I didn't mention his drug-induced state at first, since Brett and Joey were there, all of us hanging outside school for a bit comparing our certificates of Driver's Education. Mine, of course, had the highest possible marks one could attain on said certificate. (Applause, applause.) Brett's, needless to say, was marked "Incomplete," as she remained a few hours shy on street driving. I asked Brett again if she wanted to come downtown with us, and she was like, and I quote, "I don't want to look at a bunch of rodents at the Smithsonian." "Rodents"—can you believe her? Henri completely lost it on hearing this and couldn't stop laughing, even when I told him it was funny, sure, but not that funny. Which really it wasn't, Brett's malapropism being more ignorant than amusing. But I wasn't half-baked before noon, so what did I know from funny . . .

As Henri and I started walking to the Metro, I called him out on being stoned and he was all like, "What's the big deal, *mon gar*?" So I told him the big deal: I thought we were going to the museum to get some culture and learn something and not just be brain-dead for the entire day. Henri tried to defend himself, saying he'd only had one hit and that it probably wouldn't last for more than an hour or two. Still, I told him that it was annoying and basically rude, because it was impossible to converse with him and/or deal with him as a real, cogent human being when he was like this. So, you know what the stoner said? "You talk too much." To which I responded—"Oh yeah, you think I talk too much? Well then, check this out . . . I have nothing more to say to you." And it was true. I was so over having any kind of conversation with him because I was so goddamn angry!

Once we got to Glenmont, we rode the Red Line in silence all the way down to D.C. Even when we got to the museum, I still wasn't ready to talk to him. I know you may find it hard to believe that I could play this silent routine for so long, but honestly, I was not playing. I was so friggin' mad at him. As we started to make our way through the exhibit, Henri started talking anyway, offering me little factoids about Rodin and his work methods and why he was so unique in the sensuality that he brought to religious iconography. Once Henri had found his way back to words like "iconography," I knew he wasn't so stoned anymore, and I started listening to him again, though not really saying too much in response. Not that I had too much to say about Rodin, really, but continuing the silent treatment like this still made it seem like I was pretty angry with him. Which I guess was a good thing, because it only got him to try and engage me more in conversation. Except how the hell was I gonna start conversing about a 19th-century Parisian sculptor? I didn't really have much to add on the topic, you know?

So we were wandering through the exhibit, slowly walking our way around each of the sculptures. I have to say that one thing about sculpture that I really like is the fact that you can walk all the way around it, that it's not like a painting where you just stand there and stare at it on the wall in one direction. Since you can change perspective and move around the sculptures, it was almost like the statues were more alive than a flat old painting, and I thought that was totally cool. And, like you mentioned before, some of these pieces were damn sexy, too. Do you remember the one called *Fugitive Love*?! OMG—that was insane! That guy splayed out on that woman's back, totally naked and ripped? Even though they were made out of metal, the people looked so realistic, with all the details of their hair and eyes and lips and muscles. That particular figure even had that amazing, sexy, arching line that guys have going from the high point of their hip diagonally down, which certainly drew my attention to the hot spot. (Henri has the same line too—as I witnessed at the pool.) Christ—my piece was going half-hard looking at this piece. I never knew art could be so damn pornographic! I hope the government doesn't try to shut this thing down or anything, because it's like 10 times racier than Janet Jackson's nipple. In fact, I wanted to get the *Fugitive* statue in the gift shop to take home with me, but they only had *The Thinker* in miniature, which was kinda boring.

Another statue that I had a more personal connection to was titled *Despairing Adolescent*. Yeah, I know—funny, right? But I really did like this one, and not just cause it was hot. The way that kid's arms were reaching up for the sky, like he was trying desperately to grab something, his whole body put into the effort but still not quite getting it. (Man, I know the feeling. In spades.) There was something so alive about the statue. You know, to call it a statue seems like a total misrepresentation, because that makes it sound like something stately and sorta dead. But man—this thing was so alive!

Of course, as I'm looking at these hot bronze guys, I'm secretly checking out Henri to see which art he was digging on more. He definitely was not ignoring the women, which is hard to do when their busts are busting out all over and their tits are pointing straight up to the sky. But there was one imposing-looking guy, a solider, I think, who was standing there with an ass that you could set dinner for two on—*The Age of Bronze*. Now, I know it actually was solid metal and all that, but you could tell that whatever French dude in the 1800s modeled for this had it going on. Henri said that when Rodin first displayed this piece, critics said it was so realistic that they accused him of making a body cast of a dead person. I can see the point though, as this thing could've started walking and you really wouldn't have been that surprised.

So, as Henri and I are checking this guy out, going around to the backside of this dude, I'm totally digging it, while Henri just sorta nods. When I come back around to the front, he stays behind the behind, continuing to take the soldier's ass in. Hmmmmmm. Interesting, huh? You could say that maybe this only shows that Henri is just a major narcissist in that he was merely admiring a butt that was not unlike his own. Or you could infer that Henri maybe enjoys the form of a male ass as much as the next guy. (The next gay guy, that is!)

After an hour of wandering through the galleries, I was starting to get a little tired. I mean, sure, the pieces were sexy, but after a while, one after another, it started getting a little repetitive. That is, until we got to *The Gates of Hell*. Man—you did not tell me about this. It was astounding! I was seriously hypnotized staring at it. It was so colossal and, according to Henri, took Rodin almost 37 years of work, and then he died, without ever seeing it cast in bronze. Thirty-seven years—that's like a whole life! But Henri said Rodin didn't even display his first sculpture till he was 36. So maybe there is hope for me doing something productive with my life! Still, 37 years . . . that's like an eternity. But I gotta say, Rodin's time was well worth it, as this is truly one of the most amazing things I've ever seen.

It almost inspired me to be a sculptor too, because making something like this would be pretty cool, even if it takes forever. I mean, there was a crowd of people five folks deep lined up at this thing, all of them with their jaws dropping as they took in the enormous, intricate majesty of it all. The detail was just unbelievable, as you could see a lot of Rodin's other statues reappearing in different forms and guises too that fit into the damnation theme of hell. Does that sound too high-falutin'? Christ—maybe I should be an art critic instead of a sculptor. However, I don't have much critical to say of Rodin other than, dude . . . you rock! (pun intended)

After Rodin, Henri suggested we head to the other side of the Washington Mall to the Hirshhorn Museum. I had no idea what he was talking about, but he said I'd probably like it if I liked sculpture. Sure enough—I did like it. (He knows me so well, right?) The museum is this big concrete doughnut on stilts that is crammed with modern art and, outside, has a sunken garden filled with all kinds of pieces, some decidedly more modern than some of Rodin's stuff. But I liked the modern stuff, too, because it almost made me think more, since I had to try to figure out what the hell the artist was trying to say when he threw a bunch of I-beams and chicken wire and concrete together on a pedestal to make something that looked like a car wreck.

It was wild, going to each, uh, thing and then playing this game with Henri where we tried to guess what the thing was all about. Henri was a lot better at this than me, as his answers were often a little more insightful than "car wreck," since he seemed to know a little bit more about some of these artists than I did. He told me that modern art began in Paris, with Picasso and all his pals, 100 years ago. Henri knows so much about things like this . . . it's almost shocking.

After all the walking and education, by 3:00 P.M. I was starving. Fortunately, the Hirshhorn had this outdoor restaurant and we snagged a table, no problem. It was about 97 degrees out, so not too many of the tourists could take the D.C. swamp feel. But me, I'm used to it, and Henri . . . he's learning. So we got a table and this slim, supermodelly waitress came to take care of us. She also happened to speak French, which ensured us the best possible service ever. Henri did all the ordering in French, which our waitress (an exchange student at G.W.) appreciated sooooooo much, grinning every time she swung by our table. I've never seen such a happy waitress in my life— maybe it was the French or maybe it was the fact that Henri was turning on his natural charms. Not that he has to do that much to make this happen. That's why they are natural, dig?

After a nice, hearty meal, Henri noticed the wine menu on the table. At first I was like, oh please . . . again with the illegality? I tried to tell him it was really not a great idea given the fact that we were not only underage but also in a very public place (i.e., an outdoor sculpture garden). But this didn't seem to phase Henri at all, just as most things of a questionable nature don't seem to phase him at all. So the next time the waitress flew by, Henri turned on the high-beam smile and started speaking French like there's no demain (that's French for "tomorrow"). Even though their whole conversation was in a foreign language, it was fascinating how much I could understand just by watching the way they talked to each other. The waitress laughed at the wine request at first, but Henri's tone was quite serious, so she reconsidered. Then she looked around and Henri got less serious, trying to play it off like ordering wine wasn't such a big deal. Then she seemed to say something about it being her job to not serve 15-year-olds wine, while, at the same time, she started fretting with her uniform. But then Henri really laid into her with the eyes and she was a goner. (I know this trick of his, that's for sure.) After a few minutes she returned with two big plastic cups . . . that just happened to be filled three-quarters of the way up with a nice '96 merlot that Henri had selected himself.

All right—I can hear you already, screaming and jumping up and down as you read about me drinking in broad daylight on a Friday afternoon. But you know what? I don't care, Chuck. Sorry. It was my last day of driving school and I was celebrating. And what's wrong with a little celebration, even if it does get you trashed before cocktail hour has even officially begun.

After we'd finished our wines (yeah, we ordered a second round—sorry!), Henri offered to pay the entire bill, which was a bit of a shock. He said it was his present to me for passing driving. He went on to say how he was so jealous of the fact that I'm gonna be able to drive because, in France, you aren't allowed to drive until you're 18. That sucks, huh? But then again, you can drink starting at like five, so that sorta makes up for it. At least that was Henri's line, which, being drunk on illegal wine, I totally had to crack up at. Sometimes Henri can be funny like that when he's not even trying.

So, slightly soused, we strolled around the Mall for a bit making our way up toward the Capitol. It's such an amazing building, even more so when you're a little inebriated. And in the middle of a summer afternoon, it is so blindingly white and stately looking. But also kinda sad these days, in that it's completely surrounded by fences and Jersey barriers and squads of police cars. I told Henri about how, when we were kids, we used to come downtown and you could pretty much go where you wanted in the Capitol. It's one of the few memories I have of my dad, going down to D.C. to do some tour of the Capitol.

Remembering that was sort of a bummer, as I then had to explain to Henri about the whole dad disaster, how he totally left us when I was six and moved to California with that woman from work. Henri sympathized with all this, which was nice, since it's not a story I really like getting into. And as it turns out, he had his own dad story. His parents are split too, his dad living in Paris, which is part of why he and his mom came here . . . to get away from *le connard*, as Henri put it (French for "bastard"). It's still a pretty raw nerve for him, as the divorce only got finalized about six months ago. I didn't get the details on why they broke up, but, whatever the reason was, it made for ugly feelings on both sides. Which partially explains his mom's deal, being so damn surly. That's for sure!

So, after having all this depressing family conversation, we got on the Metro to make the long trek home. Partially because of the wine and the down topic, I hit the seat and passed out. OK—I guess <u>mainly</u> because of the wine. When I woke up, I fortunately wasn't drooling on Henri again. In fact, this time my face was pressed up against his chest, and I could hear his heart thumping away like a big bass drum. I listened to my heart and tried to slow it down a little, to get in pace with his. But it didn't work. My heart was racing because I realized that not only was I sleeping on his chest (which was wild enough!), but he had his arm draped around my shoulder.

Whoa . . . this freaked me out so much that I immediately sprang up from the seat and was like, "Where are we?" "Silver Spring," Henri answered. "Three more stops." Then he said this, which killed me: "You wanna go back to sleep?" OMG. If he's asking me if I wanna lay my head on his hot chest and listen to his heart pound in my ear till my own heart starts flipping out like a Geiger counter in a nuclear reactor, then, uh, the answer is sure. It's beyond sure. So I did go back to sleep, but I hardly slept for the seven minutes or so it took us to get to Glenmont.

When it got to our point of departure on the walk home, it was an even stranger moment. Though we were both saying good-bye, it was clear that we both didn't want to say good-bye but, at the same time, didn't have the guts to continue the evening either. That was sorta cool and sad at the same time, you know? I mean, Henri really likes me. I saw it, literally, standing on the corner of Viers Mill Road and Wheaton Avenue as we looked at each other and, reluctantly, started walking away in opposite directions.

Hope this entry wasn't too long and boring for you. But it was really such a great day I wanted to put everything down so I didn't forget it. Hope you have a drama-free weekend! H

09:23 A.M.
SATURDAY 08.05.06
Gotta say, it was a little long, as it took me the last 20 minutes to read and now I only have five minutes to write something back. But it sounds like it was a pretty cool day. If you ignore the wine/pot aspects of it, which I will try to do. (See . . . at least I'm trying!)

I'm glad you got down to the Rodin exhibit, as I knew you'd love it. You are a sucker for the male form, that's for sure. Who knew you'd have something in common with ol' Rodin, huh? ☺ And that bit with you and Henri on the subway sounded interesting. You know what it reminded me of? That entry a few weeks ago (or was it last week?) when I was talking about Chaz and Albert in bed together, all cozied up to each other. I sorta got the same image of you and Henri like that, so I can see why you're pretty jazzed.

Now, I still have some reservations about this guy, but it seems like things are going okay, so I won't say anything more. Don't want to jinx it or anything. (Quick—knock on wood!) As for myself, I haven't seen anyone since the dramas of Friday. What a day that was! I had trouble getting to sleep last night, I was so bothered by what was going on. Mainly by the MK angle, because I'm not sure she got my meaning in our chat. I kept having these conversations in my head with her, trying to explain to her how she is very cool and sweet and all that but I'm just a very mixed-up person right now. I don't know . . . maybe I'll have a chance to tell her some more of this today. Or after rehearsal. Today is our last day in the Tawes Center before moving into our new home, the

Smith Center main stage, where we'll actually be doing the show. Load-in day is always pretty exciting!

OK—gotta run. Have a nice, sober weekend . . . if that's possible. ☺ Miss ya! C

11:42 P.M.
SATURDAY 08.05.06

OMG—I have had an astounding weekend! No, make that a stunning day! Strike that, how about a stupendous Saturday!!! As for the sober thing, OK—time for full disclosure. I am a little drunk right now, but not messy or stumbly or anything. I mean, hell, I can still write, right? ☺ I am, though, a bit New Year's Eve-y. . . . that is, kissy. You see, I just got back from a night at Chez Henri's, and (sit down for this one) we friggin' <u>made out!!!</u>

He called me earlier tonight to see what I was up to. I don't know why he even bothers to ask me "What's up" when he calls because the answer is always "Nothing." Maybe he's just being polite. Anyway, he invited me over to watch the *South Park* movie. Now, I know I've seen this about a million times, the majority of those times with you singing along to every goddamn song in the movie. But this time it was different, because we watched the movie in French! That's one of the options on the DVD, and Henri said that in French it was even better. Even though I didn't understand most of it, it was pretty damn hysterical, especially when Henri pointed out some of the translations. In that song about Cartman's mom being a big fat bitch, the French version calls her *la grande vache*, or "very large cow"! LOLOLOL Henri said there is no French word for "bitch," though I suggested one to him . . . "Uh, your mom!" To which he totally cracked up!!!

After the movie ended, Henri hit the wine cellar and got us each a bottle of merlot, and then we played some Xbox for a while. We were both sitting on the couch, jousting each other in the arm while playing Halo, trying to mess each other up, when Henri really slammed his shoulder into me. Given that I was still feeling the effects of the wine, I tipped completely sideways on the couch and started cracking up. The next thing I know, you-know-who is grabbing my controller and making me die. In the game, that is. But I'm also dying in real life, because Henri, in order to reach my controller, has to sort of crawl halfway on top of me. When I finally stop laughing, he ends up hovering over me and propped up on his arms, the ceiling light behind his head creating this crazy blond halo around his hair. I swear . . . it was like a religious vision almost, all spiritual and amazing and ethereal and shit. Until, that is, he smiled that insane Henri-smile, leaned in, and without a word, planted one right on my lips.

Yes, apparently, there is a God . . . his name begins with *H*!!!

The whole thing was pretty surprising in general, but mainly because when Henri had talked about Patrice and him fooling around, he said that they didn't make out. It was almost like it grossed him out. When I asked him about this later, he said making out with his best friend would be creepy but with me it was all right. Or more than all right, apparently. : OMG, Chuck! How the hell to describe to you what went on for the next hour. And no, you don't have to worry about this getting too gay and graphic, because we did not have full-on homosex. We just made out. But to say that we "just made out" is to almost dismiss it, which I don't mean to do . . . not at all. I mean, yeah, we were only locking lips, but Christ, they were Henri's lips, the lips of the guy I've been obsessively in L with for the entire summer! (All right—at least since you left.) BTW—I completely understand now why it's called French kissing because, hello, is there any other kind?!

Even crazier is that Henri said I was amazing . . . that is, an amazing kisser!!! I'm like, "Uh, but I'm American," which completely made him bust out. He said it didn't matter if I was Indian or German or Swahili; what matters is knowing the power of the kiss, the sensuality of it, knowing it instinctually. (This is what he is telling me!!!) And, for some insane reason, I got it down pat. So, not only do I know how to drive but I can also kiss like a motherfucker! What the hell do you think about that!?!?!?

Now, I don't know if there is a career in kissing, other than being a hooker, which is probably not gonna work for me, but I don't mind it as a hobby. Not at all. As long as Henri is the head of the Kissing Club, you can sign me up for the next two years of afterschool extracurricular excitement. I will be the president and treasurer and secretary all wrapped up into one multitasking maniac as long as *mon pede* shows up at all the meetings, get my drift? OMG. THAT was CRAZY! I am feeling so utterly insane right now!!!

On the way home tonight, I kept thinking about what happened and how great it was and how it was the last thing I ever thought would happen in my life, more or less this summer. And now . . . the totally whack thing is, I think it's going to happen again! And maybe even the full-on sex, too. I mean, it almost got to that point tonight, as both of us had raging hard-ons and were completely doing the dry hump. I think Henri wanted to go further, because he kept pawing at my zipper and belt. But, thank God, I heard Brett's sassy voice in my head telling me to make him want it. And man, did he want it!!!

But after almost an hour of this, I didn't think I was gonna be able to hold out! Fortunately for me, the whole session ended a little abruptly, as his mom came home, announced by the slamming of the front door. That was a shock at first, as we both had to grab pillows and put them over our crotches and start pretending to play a game that we both had died in. But when his mom came into the den, fortunately she didn't know what a game of Halo is supposed to look like. She just acknowledged me curtly, as she had before, and said something angrily to Henri in French, which I translated into meaning that I had to hit the road. With two bottles of wine sitting on the table there, she did not look too happy. But then again, she never looks happy.

After she left and our dicks got back to normal, Henri and I got up from the couch (oh man—that couch!) and he walked me to the front door. He said he'd call me about the b-day road trip tomorrow. I said I'd be looking forward to it. He said, "Me too." Him too!!! All I can say is, kill me now because it can't get any better than this. Can it?!?

Your lovely pal, Hal ☺

Week 5

08:15 P.M.
SUNDAY 08.06.06

Oh shit. Oh lord. Oh-my-ever-loving-God. This is serious. You are using emoti-cons. That is F-in' insane, dude! You have truly lost your mind. Or your heart. I'm guessing both given the length and feeling behind that last entry. Whoa . . .

In my entry about getting it on with MK on the roof, I was like, "Uh . . . and we made out." But you went on for two, maybe three paragraphs about the whole thing. Forget critic or sculptor or professional kisser/whore. I think you may have a future writing Harlequin romance novels. (ha)

Gotta say, though . . . I never thought it would come to this. That is, you and Henri making out. But I'm glad, because you sound like a different person almost. Or at least a happy one. Again, though, I just want to put in some friendly advice. It does seem like all your fun with Henri either comes out of or is a part of smoking pot or drinking or whatever. I know, from my sister, that that might be a bit of a problem. But I really don't know Henri enough to see if he's taking it too far or if it's just casual, stupid fun. I do know you and have not known you to be such a partier, minus New Year's, of course. ☺

Just remember: The next time H orders up a bottle of wine or grabs one out

144

of the basement, you can just say "no thanks." Don't feel like you have to do everything this guy suggests, most of which seems to be on the bad side of the law. And please—<u>don't</u> get all bent at me for saying this. I don't want to ruin your good time. Seriously. I just want to make sure it's your good time and not something he's forcing on you, you know? Maybe I'm too sensitive to all this stuff because of my sister. But it's probably better to be too sensitive than not sensitive at all, right? Especially given my choice of career. (ha)

Speaking of which, we finally got to move into the theater where we'll be putting on *Merrily*. This place is sweet! It's UMD's new Smith Center main stage, which is like a real, professional theater. Nothing like that massive "assemblytorium" we have at Einstein. It's about half the size of that monster, seating 500, with nice wood walls and hi-tech lighting and even carpet. And the seats are fancy too, red-velvety and semi-stadium style so everyone can see me onstage!

When we walked into the place this afternoon, we all stood at the center of the stage looking out on all those empty seats and you know what? That alone was a trip. It just feels like a completely real theater where real people would put down real money to see a real show! LOL Not that I'm deluded into believing we are on Broadway or anything. But even if it's gonna be our parents and best friends in the audience, at least the illusion is there that it's something semi-real. And that's pretty cool, I guess.

Backstage, there are tons of makeup rooms and dressing rooms and even showers. And there are green rooms on either side of the stage where you can wait around between scenes, watching what's going on from a TV monitor in the room so you don't miss your entrance. Not that I'll be lingering too much, given my constant stage time. But the chorus and supporting players certainly appreciated them. MK even asked if they could set up an Xbox backstage. Can you believe her? Not only does she ask the craziest questions sometimes but, dude, she's a total gamer! How 'bout that?

After all the excitement of our tour ended, we got down to work. (Yes, even on a Sunday!) Now that we're on the actual stage, the blocking has changed, so we had to run through the majority of the show again and go through all the notes on those changes. It was very, very boring and long—when we have an afternoon like this, I wonder if maybe I'm not cut out for this work after all. It was just so damn annoying, having to now readjust and relearn what we'd already done for each scene. Sometimes, it's this sorta technical stuff that I can't stand. It's such a pain in the butt, you know?

All in all, the blocking rehearsal was a huge downer after the excitement of seeing the stage for the first time. At one point, I even said to Ryan, "Why can't we just act and see where that takes us?" And Ryan, being a smart-ass, says that would be fine with him but it might take me out of my light. Which, he hastened to add, would be fine by him. So, yeah, guess what? There is still some tension between us regarding this Ghaliyah thing. Not that they seem to be some serious couple, not at all. But still, Ryan loves to publicly make an ass out of me in front of her. Unless . . . maybe I'm making an ass out of myself? It's happened before. Or maybe I'm overreacting about all this stuff. Please advise. . . .

11:52 P.M.
SUNDAY 08.06.06

Christ—of course you're overreacting. That's what you do. Acting, overreacting, etc. Besides, who gives a crap what Ryan thinks about you? And who gives two craps what you think about Ghaliyah? I thought that was over, now that MK is in the picture. Though I did take note that there was no big mention of her in the last entry. I hope you haven't gone and had more wet dreams about her and said that she sucked in the imaginary dreamland sack. Don't laugh—you know it's within your abilities to make an utter fool out of yourself. Not that I should talk. I'm doing a pretty good job of that myself these days. Or at least today.

I had a major embarrassment on the Henri front. Or *faux pas*, if I want to be French about it. Something that you will completely relate to . . . or not, if you take it too literally. But really, I'm not sure exactly how you'd categorize it, other than to say it led to a stupid fight. But I'm jumping the gun here. First, let me recap.

Since the big make-out, we've been e-mailing and even IM-ing today, but not making any major plans or anything. It was weird, or should have been weird, but it didn't freak me out too much, believe it or not. (And I know you're thinking—NOT.) Actually, it was all pretty cool, because, as Brett said, I knew that he wanted it and I was almost secure in the fact that he would eventually make a plan to get some more of it. If not all of it. Guys are like that, you know. (WURDH!)

So this afternoon I was hanging out in my room looking over my driving stuff, prepping for the big trip to the DMV tomorrow, when the doorbell rings. It's Henri, which is cool. What is not so cool is that my mom answers the door and yells that Henri's here. I nearly jumped out of my skin when I heard that, mainly because I looked like a slob and hadn't showered or shaved or anything. But also because Valerie was meeting Henri for the first time and was going to be waaaaay too curious. I would have asked Val to make Henri cool his heels while I got properly ready, but I knew she'd use those precious minutes to start grilling the Frenchman as to the five *W*'s (not to mention the *H*) of what was up with him/us/everything.

So I speed-changed into a less dirty tee and hustled to the front door before too many conversational beans were spilled. Henri was just standing there looking as casually gorgeous as ever while my mom was seriously looking at me like, "Since when do you have friends other than Chuck?" No joke—the look on her face was exactly that without saying a word. I'm becoming very good lately at reading people without them uttering a sound (or at least a sound I can understand as English). Maybe that could be a career path—professional psychic. I could be like that Jamaican woman who had that 800 number . . . Sybil or something. She was awesome and apparently made millions, which is not too bad given that she had no clue what was really going on in people's heads. Me—at least I can conjure up one or two good sentences from the form of a curious scowl on Val's face.

Anyway, once we got safely out of the house, I told Henri that he really shouldn't stop by my house unannounced like that. (Even if I was utterly psyched as hell to see him!) He didn't get the problem I had with this, saying that my mom seemed supernice. Well, shit—the Grinch would seem like a friggin' fairy queen compared to Henri's mother, who has not smiled or even shown me one pleasant glimpse of her pearly whites. Even though that wasn't the point, I was not really interested in getting into the point, which was that I'd like the opportunity to make myself a little more presentable (read: kissable) when he stops by. But I wasn't gonna say this. Christ—how would I ever say something like that. I'd sound like a total girl!

So Henri wanted to go up to Wheaton and tool around for the afternoon—you know, a little shopping, a little Marrakesh, etc. That was fine with me. As long as it all ended up back on his couch, I was cool with it all. Trying to get an idea on the odds of this actually happening, I nonchalantly asked what his mom was up to today, and he said she was having some friends over for an early dinner that afternoon, thus necessitating his exit from the house. So I guess couch lovin' was not gonna be an option, and that was a bit of a bummer, you know? I have to say that it sorta put a damper on the day knowing that all of our Wheaton wanderings were not gonna lead to anything.

We stopped in at Salvation Army to look for some old O.P. shirts, but I wasn't very talkative, or very lookative either. Henri got all excited when he found a pair of sky-blue cord shorts, but I was like, who gives a flyin' flip, and went back to half-heartedly scanning the racks while in my head fantasizing about the soft, juicy taste of Henri's lips on my mouth. You've seen his lips, in that picture I sent, right? Christ—what am I saying: It's not like you'd ever get what I dig about some guy's lips. . . .

Anyway, after spending about an hour in SA, we wandered over to the Triangle area, destination: Marrakesh. However, I saw something that caught my eye. In the strip mall near Barbarian Comix there was a new store, except it wasn't a store. It was where this tacky Mexican restaurant used to be and now it looked like a bar, since the front window had been painted over. But it was not your average bar, as a big rainbow flag was hanging on the door and a pink neon sign in the window spelled out DE LOUNGE. Henri was all like, "Is this a new French hangout?," and I was like, "Uh, dude, does that look like the tricolor to you?" Turns out he didn't know what the rainbow flag meant at all. Not that I'm an expert on it, but I tried to explain that it was a general indicator that there was something gay or lesbian or bi or even "questioning" going on inside. When he finally got the point that we'd stumbled upon the first gay bar in Wheaton, Maryland (!), he almost got a little freaked out by it. I, on the other hand, was pretty fascinated and semi-obsessed, saying we had to go inside. I mean, c'mon—a gay bar? In Wheaton? How <u>bizarre</u> is that!?

Henri protested, though, lamely claiming that we wouldn't be able to get in as we were not of legal drinking age. Uh—please—like that stopped us at the Hirshhorn?! So the role of Henri was played by me today as I strode right up to the door of De Lounge and walked in like I was entering the Safeway. Fortunately, there wasn't anyone there checking IDs or anything. In fact, there wasn't anyone in the bar, really, as it was, oh, about 4:00 in the afternoon on a Sunday. But there was some vaguely familiar music coming from a room toward the back, so, dragging Henri by the hand, I pushed aside some tacky drapes and came upon a guy who must have been 70 staring at a karaoke monitor as he belted out the lyrics to "Fame." You know that song, from the movie? OMG—it was tragic! He made William Hung sound like Elvis.

To see and hear this grandpa bellowing off-key about how he wanted to live forever and have the world remember his name was beyond scary. Which is why the room was practically empty, I guess. There were only four other guys in there, sitting at a booth diagonally across from Senior Junior, all of them downing Bloody Marys and smoking menthol cigarettes. Our entrance got all <u>those</u> creaky heads turning, that's for sure, as our mere presence brought the average age in the room down by about 30 years. One of the guys at the table, a skinny little Asian dude wearing a tank top and shorts that were waaaaay too short, came skipping over to us. Weirdly, though, he had no accent at all . . . that is, no Asian accent. But he did have a ridiculously gay accent, as he asked us, "Who let you boyz in?" (Uh, FYI, emphasis on the boyz.) I said no one, that the door was open. And then this Asian guy screamed out some name I couldn't even understand, to which the response was silence. One of the guys at the table then piped up and said that the dude with the unpronounceable name had gone to I-Hop for some food. Then the Asian guy dropped this heavy sigh and asked us how old we were. I lied and said 16, which is not such a huge lie as my b-day is tomorrow after all. (I thought 15 would definitely have meant the boot for us.) Then, smiling wryly at us, he said his name was Queng and that we could stay but could only have soda. This displeased Henri a bit, but I said sure, and we pulled up a chair for what was billed as "Slammin' Karaoke Sundays" at De Lounge.

As Henri and I sipped our Cokes, the other guys at the table introduced themselves. They were all gay too, but get this—one of them was still married. To a woman! He even had a couple kids. This intrigued Henri greatly and got him going on this big dialogue with the married guy about the fluidity of sexuality, and the Kinsey scale, and all this other stuff that was going completely over my head. As for myself, I just wanted to know what the karaoke selection was. Now that grandpa was thankfully retired from the stage, I thought I might give it a go, so Queng passed me the book. I was looking but they didn't have any of the stuff I wanted to do . . . no Smiths, no Scissor Sisters, no Dashboard Confessional. It was all poppy, crap shit, so I took a pass.

Once Henri was done with his dissertation on male sexuality, he grabbed the karaoke book and managed to find a rap song in it. It was that one from when we were kids, "Every Breath You Take," about the rapper who died. So Henri goes up and starts rapping, and you know I totally dig the guy and everything, but he is not such a performer. I mean, he wasn't worse than grandpa, but he wasn't that much better. So I'm cringing inside as Henri gets to the chorus, where the backup track sorta fortunately takes over. Henri looks over to me, seeming kind of embarrassed by his own performance and shooting me this desperate look. I'm like, whoa, that is soooooo <u>cute</u>! I smile and he smiles back, seemingly relieved that I'm with him and don't think he's awful. Of course, I <u>do</u> think he's awful, but he doesn't need to know that. And hell—doesn't that even make it cuter? You know, that I'm pretending to like him even when he's god-awfully bad because I don't want him to feel like a loser? OMG—I am becoming such a friggin' sap! Shoot me now!!!

As the afternoon wore on, De Lounge started filling up with guys that were a bit of an odd mix: some young punksters that probably went to Montgomery College, a gaggle of guys in their 20s who looked like they were trying to kill last night's hangover, and a gathering of middle-aged dudes who'd just come in from cutting the lawn. None of them were that hot or sexy, really (except maybe one of the punksters) . . . just kinda average-looking guys. And <u>all</u> of them were generally terrible at karaoke. I'd imagined going to a gay bar would be some big, racy thing, you know. Like there'd be people having sex all over the place or something. In fact, it's just like any other bar in that it's mainly a bunch of guys sitting around getting drunk with each other. The big difference, I guess, is that there are no women to tell them they've had too much to drink.

As the drunks became a little too much to bear, audibly and otherwise, I nudged Henri and said we should probably head out. I did notice, though, that there were a couple guys by the bar holding hands and I thought—<u>brainstorm</u>—maybe in lieu of Henri's couch I could make out with him here. I mean, isn't that what gay bars are <u>for</u> if you can't get smashed? So, as we were walking through the bar area, I stopped at a bulletin board and Henri stopped too. Then, as he read the community listings next to me, I looked over at him and grinned. He smiled too, sorta awkwardly, like he didn't know what I was reading or thinking or what. (Apparently, other people are not as good at this face-reading thing as I am.) So then I got embarrassed, blushing simply because he was so close to me, you know? I sorta got lost in my own plan. I mean, what was I gonna say? "Can I kiss you?" That would be so damn BOLD! But you know what the hell happened? Henri said it himself, though not as a question but sorta as a revelation: "You wanna kiss me."

I couldn't speak or say anything in response because, I swear, I thought I was gonna cry. Christ—what the hell is the matter with me? Anyway, to stave off the tears I swooped in and kissed him . . . on the lips. Whoa! I thought making out on the couch was the be-all and end-all of human existence, but hells no—making out with someone while standing up? Gripping his firm waist in my hands? Nudging my nose into his cheek as we swapped tongues? Feeling his hand against the small of my back as he starts pulling me in closer? I mean, W-H-O-A.

So we went at it like this for about 10 minutes or so, and it was sheer bliss. But what was the most incredible thing was a total surprise move. After returning each other's tongues to their rightful owners, there was this pause where we were just standing there, forehead to forehead, and I found myself kissing the side of his face, that sorta facial no-man's-land where the cheek ends and the eyes begin, and then working my way in an arc across his brow and then down to his other temple. Henri, clearly loving this and smiling broadly, says . . . "Like *maman*." And I'm like, huh? He says, "Like when your mom puts you to sleep as a kid and she kisses you good night . . . is sweet, no?"

Oh shit! Why does Henri say things like this. He is killing me!!! REALLY! Why, you ask? Because I felt the tears coming on again. So to distract my emotions or something, I went at it. Again. This time it got even more intense, as I backed up against the wall, Henri pressing into my hips so that we could both feel the unmistakable fact that we were rock-hard. And this only got Henri going more strongly, sucking my tongue like he was gonna rip it out of my mouth. So . . . in case you're thinking, uh, wait a minute, what about all this embarrassment I was talking about. Well, this is where the mortifying part comes. Literally. Yeah, that's right, as we were going to town I got a little, uh, over-whelmed by Henri's body pressing up against me like that and I just, well . . . there is no delicate way to say this. I came. Not all over the bar or anything. Just in my underwear but still . . . I totally shot it while making out with Henri, and, as Brett likes to say, if someone has an orgasm, it's sex. Except in this case, I tried to play it off like I hadn't lost my load, which I was sorta able to manage by not screaming my head off in an orgasmic yelp of pleasurable pain, which, fortunately, was a bit of an impossibility (thank God!) with our tongues intertwined.

After it was all over, Henri was standing there smiling at me, and I said I had to go, and went! I dashed into the men's room with the excuse of peeing. Again, though, I ran into that particularly gay problem of not having separate men's rooms, you know? As I was cleaning myself up in a stall, Henri comes in to take a whiz, catching me as I'm throwing out the big wad of toilet paper I used to clean up my, er, mess. I looked totally busted, and Henri was like, "Are you okay, Hal?" And what can I do? I can't lie to him about this . . . the fact that we'd just had sex. Or at least I had. So I just blurt it out—"I came." He's like, "What?" Totally confused. He was thinking I meant we <u>came</u> to De Lounge. Great—perfect timing for the language barrier to pop up. So now I'm forced to spell it out—"No, you see, I, uh, came in my pants." With a point down south, he gets it. And then he starts laughing—I mean, <u>really</u> laughing. And that's when I started crying. Really crying. That's right—my face just started leaking and I couldn't turn it off . . . didn't know where the switch was even. OMG—it was sooooooo insane!

After making a total fool of myself by first cumming and then crying about it, I brushed past Henri and practically ran out the door of De Lounge. Shit—I don't do crying, especially not in public. I was freaking out. Of course, so was Henri as he followed me, trying to play catch-up as I started running faster, telling him to leave me alone. Henri, being a much better athlete than I am, caught up to me and grabbed the back of my shirt and brought me to a halt in the middle of the parking lot. So what did I do then? I went off on him: telling him he's a terrible person for laughing at the fact that we had sex and how the whole thing was his fault anyway because he's so damn hot that I can't even control myself and blah-blah-blah . . .

I just went on and on like this, saying stuff I never thought I could say to anyone, much less someone I actually liked. Finally, Henri said he was sorry. It took a while to get to it, but he did finally say it. He kept getting distracted by the fact that I'd said he was too damn hot, which is what led to all the overexcitement in the first place. How egotistical is that? But Henri was sincerely sorry when he finally got to his apology. He even said the whole thing was bad enough without him laughing about it. And isn't that the truth! Even better than the apology, though, was this little tidbit. While walking home, he turned to me at one point and said, all serious, that he was really bummed out that he had missed it. I was like, huh? He lowered his voice and leaned into me, saying that he hoped next time, he'd get to see it. That is, me having an orgasm.

WTF—<u>next</u> time? OMG. <u>Kill. Me. Now.</u>

I was too stunned by his statement to seek details. I just nodded and smiled, and he smiled, and I don't think I have stopped smiling since.

09:12 A.M.
MONDAY 08.07.06
And the Antoinette Perry Award for Best Performance in a Publicly Embarrassing Role goes to . . . Hal Schaeffer, for his groundbreaking work in the Wheaton Triangle parking lot production of "I Came, I Went, I Lost My Shit." Sorry—I could not resist. LOL

Of course, the reason I can laugh at this and make sport of you is because we are now in the same embarrassing shoes. Both of us have now unwillingly shot up our shorts. You have to admit, Hal, it <u>is</u> hilarious. We are both so sexually starved that we are just exploding all over the place! One suggestive dream or false move and BAM! We are just spreading our love all over.

Holy shit—it's so damn pathetic, really, but I guess that's what makes it funnier, too. Seriously. If we can't laugh at our equally embarrassing situations, we are dead in the water. That's it. We might as well just give it all up, you know what I mean?

On to happier news. As the date above indicates, today's the big day. HAPPY BIRTHDAY, HAL!!! Sixteen years young and ready to get your license. I hope you can make it out here via Val's wheels tonight. It would be great to see you on the big day. Even though I am beyond jealous and green with envy. I can't believe I have to wait another agonizing seven months for mine. (Argghhhh.) What will be worse is the fact that you will surely be taunting me with your maturity from now until next March. Of course, I know the real Hal. You know . . . the guy who can't hold his sperm. And of course, you know the real Chuck, who still wets the bed. You and me will be bound to keep our summer embarrassments top secret, knowing that, if they slip back at Einstein, then we will each be socially nuked!

All right, I'm off to our special vocal rehearsal: love songs with Ghaliyah. Sigh. It doesn't get much better than that. It's certainly a helluva lot nicer than my real lack-of-love-life with the girl. Hey—good luck with everything at the DMV. Can't wait to see you and Henri later today. Oh, and break a fender! (ha)

06:52 P.M.
MONDAY 08.07.06
Hey—what's up? Where are you? Are you still coming out to visit tonight? I'm guessing that with your new freedom you're probably tooling around D.C. in Val's smokin' Taurus. (ha) And now that you figured out how to sneak into gay bars, you're surely working the downtown scene, you <u>bitch</u>! (Or *grande vache*, as Henri might say.) Just don't forget about your lame old friends in College Park. We're all waiting for you to come out for a speed round of Cranium. And MK wants to kick your ass! She is damn good. So I need some details about your itinerary. Post immediately!

07:21 P.M.
MONDAY 08.07.06
Hey—I'm in the box office here at the theater. I just talked to your mom and she said she doesn't know where you are and is worried. So I thought I'd try you again on here. And cheer you up, maybe . . . if you're even reading this. Or maybe you're too bummed out to even go online.

I'm really sorry about the driving test, Hal. That completely sucks—not passing by only one point?! That's friggin' torture. Val told me that you can take it again next month, but I'm sure that's not much consolation today. I know you must be seriously bumming right now, as it's probably put a big damper on your b-day. Look—just don't do anything stupid like get drunk/stoned/etc. with Henri. That's only gonna make you feel worse in the A.M. Believe me . . . the sight of my sister post-bender was never pretty.

I wish I knew Henri's number so I could call you and talk to you. I am almost positive that's where you're hiding out. Though I didn't tell Val, because I knew that I'd be cut off for eternity if I did. Anyway, I just wanna know that—

Shit! Stage manager's calling "places" for the second act.

PLEASE . . . don't be depressed about this, Hal. I know you were psyched about driving, but it is not the beginning or the end of the world, you know what I mean? It's just . . . driving. That's all. And you'll get your license the next time, and then I'll actually be around to celebrate the big event. We'll have a friggin' blast—I can't wait! That'll be more fun anyway, right? OK, gotta run. Miss ya . . . Chuck

12:32 A.M.
TUESDAY 08.08.06
Christ—you can be so dramatic sometimes, you know that? I mean, do you really think I'm gonna run over to Henri's after a disastrous day like today and go on some all-night drinking binge because I didn't get my stupid driver's license? Can you please maybe give me like half a credit for not being a total moron?!

I know that maybe I've not earned such credit lately, due to some of my less than legal activities, but still. You've gotta know me better than that after all this time, Chuck. It's not like I'm gonna drown my sorrows or something ridiculous like that in the face of a minor setback. In fact, I actually tried to steer clear of Henri after the DMV fiasco. Not that this was my first instinct. In fact, what I really wanted to do when I failed that goddamn stupid-ass test was run crying into his arms and have him suck the living life out of me. But, at the same time, I was so bloody mortified for having choked up on the test that I really couldn't face him. I thought that he'd think I was an idiot, which, hell, today I truly am. I mean, c'mon . . . failing a driver's test? By one point?! Someone somewhere has a wicked sense of humor when it comes to my life. I just wish that occasionally they'd let me in on the joke before it hits me like a goddamn brick.

Oh, and get this! Val tried to make me feel better on the long drive back from Gaithersburg, saying that my dad had failed his driving test something like three times before getting a license. Like <u>THIS</u> is supposed to make me feel better, comparing me to <u>THAT</u> loser and saying, well, since I'm genetically disposed to be an idiot for the rest of my life I really shouldn't feel <u>THAT</u> bad about the whole thing!!! Gee, Mom—thanks for chairing the Hal Booster Club and doing such a friggin' bang-up job!

When I got home after way too much quality time with Val, I was dying to call Henri, but then something struck me. I realized that, instead, I should probably ring the one and only person who might put this whole disaster into perspective, namely, Brett (a.k.a. The Queen of Driving Failure). Fortunately, she was home, so I biked over to her pad and hung out there for the rest of the afternoon, watching TV and listening to music and reading chick magazines. Then, around 3:00, I was like, let's call Henri and head up to Marrakesh, but Brett put the kibosh on this plan. She was like, "You are <u>way</u> too needy today and you are just gonna scare him away by clinging to him as if he's your human life preserver." OMG—she was sooooo right! That's <u>exactly</u> what I wanted to do! Brett may not be automotively skilled, but she certainly knows her way around a guy's heart.

When I checked my e-mail at her place, there were two new messages from Henri, mainly wondering what the hell was going on with the planned road trip to see you at UMD. I sent him a short e-mail back, breaking the bad news and saying that I'd call him later. But as I was writing this note to him, Brett was snooping over my shoulder and proceeded to slap her hand down onto the keyboard, stating a firm "NO." Being incredibly strident, she said that I should not tell Henri exactly when I'd call him back. She said I should be more vague and put "later" at the end of the e-mail. So, as she takes my hand, forcing me to hit the backspace key, I fix the e-mail until it's rewritten to her specs. She is unbelievable sometimes!

Later, I started getting bored and antsy and wanted to call Henri again to get my freak on, but Brett suggested we go out for the evening. She said Jerry got off work at 6:00 and could pick us up and take us wherever we wanted. My reply: "Uhmm, how 'bout Henri's couch?" Brett thought that was pretty funny but said that, no, we would find something much more productive to do with our evening other than sexing it up with Henri. I don't know what could be more productive than that, but she was clearly being the boss today, so I let her lead the way. I mean, this girl who is barely 16 has Jerry, a 20-year-old with a job and tons of cash, basically on a short leash, so who I am to question her wisdom, right?

So where did we end up, then? Why did I not get home until midnight? No. Nope. Wrong. Oh hell—you'll never guess it. We went to the Montgomery County Fair up in Gaithersburg. I shit you not. We were watching TV and Brett saw an ad for it and saw all the rides and thought that could be thoroughly distracting. I was reluctant to go anywhere near G-burg, as it would be akin to returning to the scene of my crime at the DMV earlier today. But Brett said I was being dramatic. Me—dramatic?! I told her that was your domain, but she paid me no mind and made arrangements for my second trip up-county in one day.

Around 7:00, Jerry swung by in his car, put the top down, and we sped out I-270 to the fairgrounds, and you know the F what? I had a total blast. We all did! We went on a bunch of rides and checked out all the smelly livestock and even saw a tractor pull attended by all the Barnesville hicks with their cowboy hats and Budweiser shirts. The best thing was that halfway through the night, in the middle of a spinny ride called the Mind Bender, I realized Brett's ploy had worked. I wasn't depressed at all about the driving thing. I'd almost forgotten about it, with the Mind Bender whirling us around and around and making the world all blurry. Which was exactly what I needed. It was like <u>Brett</u> had bent my mind to her own calculating purposes, which was to make me forget about being obsessed with Henri. Crazy, huh?

We stayed at the fair till closing, and then hit the highway home around midnight. I sat in the backseat, or what there was for a backseat in Jerry's sporty car, while Brett curled up next to her man in the front seat. As she nuzzled into his arm, I thought about Henri and wondered what his arm was up to. I wished I could have been nuzzling it too as I sat there alone under a pitch-black sky. But you know what? Just the thought of Henri made me feel tingly all over. I didn't even need to have him there or anything, because really, at this point, just thinking about him can make me feel . . . better. Christ—what am I saying? A little more than better. It can make me feel . . . best. Totally grammatically incorrect, I know, but emotionally, it's 100 percent correct.

HEY—just got another e-mail from Henri, which means he's online right now! Shit. I would love to IM him and say something stupid, but Brett's probably right. Clearly not being all over him today has made a curious thing happen: He now wants to be all over me. How about that?! So I'm going to show some totally uncharacteristic restraint and call him tomorrow, and maybe we'll do something then. Actually, it would be nice to get my Parkour lessons going again, now that I have more free time. And maybe we can squeeze in some make-out lessons, too. I think he's got a lot to teach me on that subject, and I am ready to learn. Remember what Mr. McKinnon always said back in third grade? How I was such a good student and always so open to learning. Well, Mr. McKinnon, you were sooooo right, it's scary. H

08:15 A.M.
TUESDAY 08.08.06
Yeah—"scary" being the key word. Henri-Henri-Henri. Is that all there is? Lately, I guess the answer is a big, fat <u>yes</u>.

You know, I gotta tell you something. I am kinda pissed off that you sent Henri an e-mail telling him about the DMV when you didn't clue me in. At all. I was sitting around at the theater all day yesterday wondering what was going on and I got nothing. Not a word. Then, later that night, I was still wondering if you were even gonna show up at St. Ann's, and still nothing. What's up with that, bro?

Despite your no-show, we did have our Cranium get-together last night anyway. Albert couldn't make it because they were having some crossword marathon at his dorm. So it was me and Chaz vs. Ghaliyah and MK. Boys against girls. Or it would have been if Chaz weren't on my team. (ha) Seriously, though, the C-Man was not very good at the game, his trivia limited to Broadway musicals and Cher's bio. So it was more like me going up against Ghaliyah and MK, who together were a dream team. They are both incredibly smart, Ghaliyah a little more book-smart, whereas MK is a little more street-smart. Needless to say, the girls creamed us. Seriously. It was no contest.

Not that Chaz minded, as he spent the whole time gossiping with MK about other cast romances. Man—there is so much loving going on here, it's wild! I was like, does anyone realize we have a full-on musical that has to be up in a week's time? Ghaliyah seconded this emotion, while MK tartly said we both needed to relax and the only reason we were stressed was because we were the leads. Basically, she was saying it was all about us. Which is really not true, because MK has a pretty decent part too in the second act. I'm definitely interested in the entire show being good, not just me. Besides, for *Merrily* to work, the whole thing has to be hitting it on all cylinders. MK wasn't really buying this argument so much, which was not so cute. I took this as a sign that she was maybe not so interested in me, which, I thought, would be just fine if she was gonna be so bitchy. But, as usual, I was wrong on this count.

After the game ended we all hung out for a while, listening to show tunes on Chaz's iBook. When it was clear around midnight that you were definitely gonna be a no-show, Ghaliyah made a motion to go, but MK, looking at me, said she was gonna hang for a little bit more. I could tell Ghaliyah got the message here, that MK and I were getting it on, which was really not the message I wanted her to get. But there wasn't too much I could do about that. MK and I hadn't fooled around in the last few days. We'd just talked a lot and hung out. All right—I guess we held hands at lunch a little and she gave me a back rub during dance rehearsal. But other than that, there was no H-and-H action. Serious. So I wasn't too happy about MK asking herself over by default when Ghaliyah left and she decided to stay. It was sorta presumptuous, you know what I mean? And then, when it was the odd three of us left, Chaz decided he'd try to go find Albert and see if he could sneak into his room. Chaz was trying to give me some space to work my mojo. But that's not what I wanted to do—at least not with MK. I really like her and all, but . . . I don't know.

Anyway, this all led to some drama, because eventually, MK asked to sleep over, and I stupidly agreed to let her. When MK got into bed, though, I just pretty much went to sleep. Or tried to. But then she kept talking, asking me what was going on. I was like, uh, I'm trying to sleep, but she kept on talking, making sleep impossible. So I was forced to address the issue again. Of her and me. She said she thought that I liked her, so why wasn't I giving her the business? I said that I liked her, too, but that I really did want to go to sleep as I was dog-tired. Of course the real reason, which she finally wormed out of me, was that I didn't want to give her the wrong idea about what was going on between us. She was like, "What wrong idea?" Holy shit—do I have to spell it out?!

So I said that I didn't want to raise her expectations too much by fooling around. Well, this got MK very angry. She shoved me and then jumped out of bed and started putting her shoes on and was like, "I'm leaving." (Scene!) I told her she didn't have to be so damn dramatic, which threw her into another round of hysteria as she went on and on about how I didn't want her to leave but I didn't want to fool around either. Oh man, she was losing it!

But what got me more annoyed was that she started drawing me into this hysterical shouting match at 1:00 A.M. about how much I did or did not like her. It got so loud at one point that the kid next door started banging on the wall, telling us to shut up! Finally, she was like, "I only want to stay if you want me to stay." And I was so friggin' angry at her at this point that I told her no, that I didn't want her to stay. Even though that wasn't exactly true. I did want her to stay. But I just wanted to go to sleep! I mean, having her there would've been nice, you know, like when Chaz slept with Albert. That would've been pretty cool. But she turned it into this <u>BIG FUCKIN' DEAL</u>!!! Talk about annoying, right? Look—just be thankful that, as a guy, you don't have to deal with this sorta chick drama. They can be so ridiculous sometimes, you know what I mean?!

Of course, after MK finally left, slamming the door and all that crap, I couldn't get to sleep. Not until about 3:00 in the morning. Reason: I was so damn mad it was driving me nuts! I was mad at MK for having such a stupid argument with me, mad at Chaz for leaving us alone to have such a stupid argument, mad at Ghaliyah for giving the whole stupid MK thing her blessing, which of course means she's totally given up on me. And finally, I was still super-mad at you for not telling me about the DMV in the first place! It made me think that maybe we're not such best friends anymore if you're telling people like Brett and Henri about this major stuff first and not me.

Anyway, I felt sorta lonely last night, like no one cared about what I felt. And I gotta admit, I'm still feeling a little like that this morning. I don't even wanna go to rehearsal because everyone has now surely heard all of the drama last night and I will be mortally embarrassed once again. All because MK wouldn't just let sleeping Chucks lie. (ha) Well, at least I can pretend to have a sense of humor about it. Even though I don't. What is MK's problem? And why is she trying to ruin my life?!

09:47 A.M.
TUESDAY 08.08.06
I have to say, that is the most pathetic story I've ever heard. A real, live girl, ready and willing and able-bodied to have sex, was in your very own bed in your very own dorm room and you didn't want to bone her? No wonder those SummerArties questioned your orientation. That is totally gay-guy behavior—or at the least, confused straight guy, which sounds like it might be a little closer to your damage in this situation. Though your confusion doesn't seem to be in regard to sexual orientation.

So—my question is, why didn't you just tell MK you wanted to sleep with her, all cute and charming like? I know you're always saying that you're not so hot without a script and all that jazz, but c'mon, telling MK that simple fact is not some Shakespearean monologue. And what are these expectations of hers that you are complaining about? MK sounds totally cool and she lives way up in Frederick County, which means that you guys are not gonna become a couple or anything post-UMD. I mean, if you want my honest opinion, I'd be more worried about having benefits with Ghaliyah, because, being such the diva, she'd probably demand you be her eternal lust slave after getting it on once. You'd probably have to sign your life over to her, inking some sorta agreement stating that you will only worship at her altar until the day you die. You'd basically become Bobby Brown to her Whitney, and that's not a pretty scenario, is it?

As to the DMV debacle, I'm sorry about not getting in touch yesterday. And no, it doesn't mean we're less friends than we used to be or anything like that. (Uh . . . jump to conclusions much?) The reason behind it has a lot to do with our friendship, but not in the way you construed it. Basically, I was so wholly embarrassed by what happened at the DMV that I didn't want to tell you for fear it would make me feel about 100 times smaller than I already felt, which by the end of the day was pretty Lilliputian. You are so good at everything you do, and the sad truth of my life is, I'm no good at anything. And no, French kissing doesn't count. So having to deal with that comparison sucks in general, and post-DMV, it was sucking even more.

This may sound bizarre, but I was looking forward to those tables being turned, if only slightly, once I had my license and you didn't. I know that may come off sounding harsh, but it's just the truth. You always have these roles and accomplishments and talents to show for your existence. And me? I don't have anything. But, if I had passed that dumb DMV test, I suddenly would have had this magic little card that said that I was a person with a skill who was also a responsible adult, or had in my possession a small laminated card that at least implied it. But the fact of the matter is, I'm still just a retarded kid who, despite being a year older, still hasn't a clue as to what his major life's purpose is and will probably remain in the dark like this for God knows how long. Hell—it took Rodin till he was 36, so, at the rate I'm going, I'll probably figure it out by 50.

Now, I know you would have been supportive and not made fun of me and all that, but just having to tell you how I'd fucked up yet another thing in my life, just like all the other things I've had to tell you I fucked up in the last 10 years (like those awful tennis team tryouts—what was I THINKING!), would have been such a bloody reminder that I am an utter failure in contrast to your utter success. And I know your life's not perfect (witness your MK issues), but on balance, your existence is a helluva lot more put together than mine. So I'm sorry for being such a loser, and that's what I was feeling yesterday.

As to all this MK drama, I know you probably don't want advice from a gay virgin like myself who can't even drive, but I do have this to offer: RELAX! Why do you have to get into such huge blowout fights with MK, anyway? You really don't need to get so invested in those sorta discussions if you don't want to. So, like, don't. But if you do get into them, realize one thing, my friend. If you're wasting that much time/energy/effort on fighting with MK, then you clearly have some interest in her. Otherwise, you wouldn't even bother. You always love a good fight, right?

The only thing holding you back with MK, I think, is some dim, dark hope that things are going to magically turn around with G in the next ten days. Now, I'm no expert on the female mind, that's for sure, but I have learned a little bit about it from my love-tutoring via Brett. And given those talks, I'd have to say, Ghaliyah is probably a lost cause. (And I don't say this to get back at you for being perfect or anything!) My intent here is to have you realize that maybe MK might not be such a bad option to consider. I mean, c'mon . . . the girl is like throwing herself on your bed! So think about that before it's too late and we both end up in some home for lonely, sex-starved lunatics that—

Oh wait—it's Henri calling. Shit. Should I answer it? Shit. I'm gonna get it. Later!

11:13 A.M.
TUESDAY 08.08.06

Hey—guess where I am? At Henri's! He's letting me use his computer, but I'm not letting him see what I'm writing. I told him our blog was For Our Eyes Only. Like that James Bond movie. James Bond was so hot. Not the new ones but the ones from waaaaay back in the '60s. Remember? I guess you wouldn't directly remember, but from cable maybe. I always thought he was cool. Connery, that is. I think I like hairy guys. Or hairy chests at least. What am I saying?!

Anyway—uh, so I'm at Henri's. Isn't that crazy! But he's not seeing what I'm writing. Did I say that already? It's a secret. Shhhhhhhh. So I had to blog you here because Henri did the sweetest thing. You know how I was so bummed about the license thing—did I tell you about that? Anyway, Henri is sooooooo sweet. You know what he did? Wait—let me ask him first. OK—no, it's not a secret. Henri called me this morning and said it was a huge drag about my license being missed by a point. One point. It makes me sooooooooo mad still. ARGHHHH!

Anyway—I'm at Henri's now. He told me to come over, that he had something for me. You know what he did? Henri baked! I mean something other than himself—HAHAHAHA. He actually baked a bunch of brownies to make me feel better. How friggin' sweet is that? You know how much I dig brownies! Isn't he the sweetest?! That was cute enough, but get this: He tells me they're <u>pot brownies</u>. You know, with pot in them. So we had a couple, and you know what? I don't feel so bad about the whole driving thing anymore. Henri says driving licenses are stupid anyway. He has a passport, and that's pretty stupid too. I mean, the picture is. He looks awful . . . like a pouty 10-year-old criminal. I just told him that. He just hit me. OWWWW!

So—I'm at Henri's now. Isn't that weird that I can write to you at Henri's, too? I didn't think I could, but I guess I can. The Internet is everywhere. It's everywhere that you want to be.™ Me? I just want to be here. At Henri's. He is so sweet, don't you think? I mean, hell . . . the guy <u>baked</u> for me? How goddamn cute is that? He's smiling at me now. Maybe he wants to make out again. LOL The couch is calling our name. More later . . . bye! ☺

06:32 P.M.
TUESDAY 08.08.06

Holy shit! I can't believe you made a stoned entry. And is it cute that Henri baked? Maybe. The guy certainly sounds like he has a lot of time on his hands. Or maybe it was from a box. (I bet it was from a box, you idiot!) Well, at least he's finally doing something productive with his summer. I guess. . . .

Oh, and is it cute he put drugs in his baked goods? Uh, not so much. C'mon, Hal—where is your brain these days?! I know you're bummed about the driving thing, but still. Don't start going toasty on me on a Tuesday morning. That is just depressing.

*** END OF PUBLIC SERVICE ANNOUNCEMENT ***

Talked to MK today. She was giving me the cold shoulder at voice class this morning, but then I grabbed her in the hallway, before going into lunch, and said what I had to say. Believe it or not, I actually listened to your online advice. (Given <u>before</u> you were wasted.) I explained to her what you said, about how I wanted her to spend the night but not get busy. Well, color me stunned, as she was much nicer about the whole thing after I told her that. Then I said I would have lunch with her if she promised no more drama. She laughed and said that might be hard . . . after all, we are in a summer drama program. (ha) So I clarified, suggesting a mutual pact that we'll both keep the drama on stage from now on.

So that was a big relief to know I won't have to worry about her anymore and I can just focus on the show. And the show definitely needs my full focus. The walk-through this afternoon was terrible. I'm still not off book for the second act, as I kept flubbing lines. How am I gonna remember all this stuff? You know what? Maybe I should work on that problem now and stop complaining about it to you. OK—later!

09:01 P.M.
TUESDAY 08.08.06

I know you're at rehearsal now, but when you get home, <u>stay home</u>. We're coming to visit! It was Henri's idea, actually, saying that best friends should be together for their birthdays. Isn't that sweet?! And no, don't worry, I'm not stoned anymore. I feel like a retard for doing a stoned entry. You set this blog up—can you please please <u>please</u> delete that entry? I will pay you cash.

OK—gotta go. Heading over to Henri's to begin our journey. OH—and we're not taking Metro! See you soon . . . H

12:14 A.M.
WEDNESDAY 08.09.06

Holy shit! You guys are so friggin' lucky! The RA came busting into the room about a minute after you and Henri headed out the window. I still can't believe you guys did that? Your landing seemed a little rough, despite the Parkour training. I just hope you're okay. And I still can't believe you drove out here! That was so insane, Hal!

That said, I have to reluctantly admit that, despite all the illegality, it was really good to see you. The last couple days have been so rough, and I was really feeling like no one gave a crap. But seeing you and seeing that we're still as good friends as ever, if not more, was cool. But I don't know . . . it was more than that too. I'm so terrible at words. It was kind of comforting. Just your presence, you know?

There was also something about you that seemed . . . different. Maybe it was the residual effects of those brownies, but you were so open for once . . . talking about your feelings and emotions and, you know, talking about Henri and how the whole thing with him has changed you. I don't think I've ever heard you talk about that stuff like that. Ever! Is that part of the effect of your being in L with Henri? Though I'm still a bit conflicted on that whole issue, seeing you two together . . . I gotta admit, you were kinda adorable. Not as a couple but more just you, staring at Henri with your silly grin and getting all goofy if Henri smiled at you. It's like, I never knew you could be so cute, Hal. Or have such a cute personality. Not that it's really ugly the rest of the time or anything. But c'mon, even you'll admit you're not the most outwardly charming person in the world.

WAIT—that sounds terrible. That's not what I mean! I like your usual bitchiness and I-hate-almost-everything attitude. This is gonna sound lame but it's always made me feel special in a way. Let me see if I can explain this. I'm a pretty likable guy. Whereas you are much more critical about what you like. So being liked by someone who hates just about everything . . . I guess that's always meant something to me. Seriously.

As for me liking Henri? I think "borrowing" his mom's car for you to drive was truly stupid. Henri knows it too. And even though he said that taking the car was part of the effort to cheer you up, it still doesn't make it not stupid. It makes it worse, really, because he's trying to justify the whole thing. But I will admit, very reluctantly, that I do like him a little bit more on the second viewing. Mainly because he seems to make you so ridiculously happy.

Anyway, I just hope you guys got home okay. Did you make out again on the couch? A simple yes or no is fine. Not so much detail this time, okay? C

08:22 A.M.
WEDNESDAY 08.09.06
OK—I'm really getting worried now. Where are you? I am on the verge of calling your house again. And you don't want me to talk to Val, do you? I might have to out you as a pot-brownie addict. So post something. Soon.

10:02 A.M.
WEDNESDAY 08.09.06
OMG! OMG! OMG! Of course I am alive and fine and all that. (You are such a drama ho!) But I'm more than fine. You won't believe what happened: Henri and I did it last night. The big S. Well, not the big S. But big enough. OMG-OMG-OMG! I am still at his house right now. He just went to 7-Eleven to get some breakfast for us. He would've cooked but there was no food here. So it's sorta breakfast in bed, which is sweet, right?

OMG!!! Can you friggin' believe it!? Well—you probably can't, because you actually don't know what the hell I'm talking about exactly. So, let me back up just a little to last night, when we made our hasty exit from your dorm room. My Parkour training did help cushion the blow of that leap, but I still got injured, cutting my palm on a broken stick. Once we got to the car, Henri took a look at it and it was a pretty bloody, though not a serious mess. He found some tissues in the glove compartment and told me to hold my hand over my head for a little while. It wasn't bleeding much by that point, just enough to make me feel like I was dying, which I kept saying over and over as we drove home.

Once we got back to Wheaton, we stopped at Henri's house to leave the car. He invited me in to fix my wound more properly so that Val would not see me making a big, bloody entrance that would raise more than a few questions, which she would not exactly want to hear the answers to. Henri did a bang-up job cleaning my wound, and then he found a bandage that was just the right size to cover it up without being hugely obvious to an outside observer. Henri's had a lot of practice dressing his own Parkour cuts and scrapes, and, thus, was a pro at it. But he was also so sweet, too, especially when I started complaining about the pain and generally being a big, skinny baby. At least, that's what he started calling me! ☺

After he was all done fixing me up, we went to sit on the couch and watch some cable. Of course, this was all a pretense for us to start making out again. Which we did for a while. But I was pretty damn tired from the impromptu road trip and the whole day in general, since being stoned can really take a lot out of you. So guess what? You may find this impossible to believe, but it is, unfortunately, true: In the middle of making out with hot Henri, I fell asleep. Can you believe it? Of all the inopportune moments to just drift off from utter exhaustion, I picked the one in which Henri is completely on top of me, his shorts tenting with a rager as he sucked on my lower lip like it was going out of style. Well, all his sexual energy combined wasn't enough to keep me conscious. I was out like a smashed lightbulb—that sudden, that severe.

The next thing I knew, I woke up in pitch blackness and was like, where the hell am I? I felt around and realized I was not on the couch at all. I was so confused and semi-freaked out because it wasn't my room at home or Henri's room either, as the walls were not covered in skate-punk posters. I could see a large window to the right, outside of which were some hazy tree shadows. Then I felt a lump stir next to me and it was Henri, lying next to me. In bed. With me! OMG!!! Henri explained that he'd carried me upstairs to the guest bedroom, taken off my shoes and shirt and shorts, and put me in bed. Sure enough, I was only wearing a pair of boxers.

I must've looked pretty startled on figuring this out, because Henri was like, "are you okay?" I was like, "Yeah, I guess." I felt so spacey and out of place and weird, waking up in the middle of the night wearing nothing but a pair of boxers. Frankly, I felt a little lost. Henri must have sensed this, because he rolled over onto his side and, staring at me, his intense hazel eyes only inches away, said, "It's okay." And I said, "Yeah," with this huge question mark at the end, and he said, "Yeah," but with a big, solid period at the end. Then he leaned in and kissed me. It was a sweet, *maman* kiss (like the one I'd given him at De Lounge), as he kissed a half circle around the top half of my face. When he was done making the face loop, he ended up kissing my eyelids, lightly, which was like . . . oh man, I can't even describe it, other than the fact that it got my whole body tingling like I was suddenly stoned all over again. When his lips finally found their way to my mouth, I was instantly sprung. I mean, it was so damn hot!

Then, as if that weren't overwhelming enough, Henri rolled right on top of me, and you know the hell what? He was not wearing any underwear at all. Nothing! I know this because I went to put my hands right on his glorious ass and that's exactly where they landed—right there on his bare ass! His real, fleshy, French ass, with no jeans or shorts or underwear to keep me away. It was all ass!!!

OMG—I can't believe I just wrote that! You're probably gagging right now with all this ass detail. Well, before you get too grossed out, let me assure you that Henri and I did <u>not</u> go that far. Not at all. But we definitely did have sex . . . both of us this time. Together. It was wild, beyond wild, spectacular! Sex with someone else is sooo much better than doing it alone. First off, it's a lot longer than jerking off and the orgasm is like a thousand times different. Holding onto another person as opposed to your own member makes a bit of difference. OMG—that's the understatement of my life!!!

In a way, the whole thing felt weirdly like a dream, waking up like that in the middle of the night, not knowing where I was, and then realizing, oh, I'm actually in bed with the world's hottest guy, who, by the way, is naked and making out with me as my hand grips his firm ass for dear life. I mean, c'mon—it doesn't get more dreamy than that, right? Literally!!! I can't believe all of this, really, thinking back on it. The whole thing just seemed surreal, the way it happened. But even more bizarre was how it made me feel . . . this wave of tingly happiness kinda washing over my entire body via the force and weight of his body. Me . . . happy? It's pretty fucking crazy, right, especially when you think back to, what, less than 24 hours ago, when I was completely losing it because I had failed the stupid DMV driving test. Today I'm like, who the hell gives a shit-and-a-half about being a licensed driver? WTF! It means absolutely nothing in the broad scope of the world or when measured up against sex with a gorgeous French guy. And I am not just saying that solely because I've realized that I can drive without a license! It's more of a general thing. I mean driving is sooooo . . . what's the big F-ing deal?!

Oh—he's back. Just heard the front door and he just yelled up to me *jourbon*. It's the backward way of saying *bonjour*, which is apparently how French guys really speak. How cute is that? I know I shouldn't be so bowled over when Henri says dumb things like "hi" in French, because, well, he's French. But I am bowled over and charmed and light-headed and, well, I think you get the point, which is that I think maybe, just maybe, I'm quite possibly head over ass in L with H. Dig? ☺

PS—Sorry I missed seeing MK last night. Now it's your turn to get some with her!

PPS—Can you believe that I'm the first one to get laid? I thought for sure it'd be you!

PPPS—Can you even <u>BELIEVE</u> this summer?!

05:50 P.M.
WEDNESDAY 08.09.06

Forget believing this summer. It's impossible to take it seriously at all for one reason alone:

I SERIOUSLY CANNOT <u>BELIEVE</u> YOU BEAT ME IN THE <u>VIRIGINITY STAKES</u>!

So does this mean I owe you a trip to Six Flags or something ridiculous like that? Remember? From that bet we made in seventh grade? Maybe it's expired by now. Or is there a statute of limitations on best-friend wagers? I hope so. Those tickets are really expensive these days!

I do have one question of a more, uh, technical nature. Not to be crude or anything, but exactly how does a gay guy lose his virginity—is that actually <u>possible</u>? Not that I'm calling your whole sex thing on a technicality. I mean, you said you didn't have any real ass-banging action, so I'm just wondering, like, what exactly goes on then.

Wait—maybe I don't wanna know exactly. (Yikes!) Or maybe I do. I don't know—I am sorta curious but also sorta scared what your answer may be. Maybe I'll leave it up to your judgment. If you think it will totally gross me out, don't tell me, and if you think it won't, then do. Does that make sense?

Gotta run—dinner. Chat you later!

07:12 P.M.
WEDNESDAY 08.09.06

"Does that make sense?" Hmmmm. Uh, well, of course not. But that's okay, Chuck, because the minute you start making sense it's a sure sign the apocalypse has begun.

As for the sex question, no, it's not that gross, I don't think. I mean, what exactly did you think we were up to? I don't imagine that it's that hard to figure out, really, but if you want me to explain it, it's no big deal. I certainly don't mind writing about my night with Henri, as, lately, it's all I've been able to think about. Basically, the whole scene involved a lot of making out all over (he made out with my nipple!) and pawing at each other and rolling around in the bed. God—when you write about it like that, in plain language, it doesn't sound that exciting, does it? But I can guarantee you, it was the most exciting thing I've ever done. E-V-E-R. I mean, Henri's body is sooooooo friggin' tight and his skin is so soft and lovely to the touch that I could just molest it for hours on end. No joke!

And yeah, if you want the down-and-dirty details, we played with each other's dicks. Okay . . . a lot! (Oh, and get this—he is uncircumcised, which was pretty unique, though he says everyone in France is like that.) But really, I have to say, my favorite part of the whole thing was after the sex and the orgasms and all the craziness was over. I was just lying on top of Henri, my head kinda tucked into the space between his shoulder and the pillow, and it was like sheer, utter bliss. Feeling his naked body under mine, feeling his hands resting on the small of my back, feeling the warm skin of his neck against my nose. That was just . . . man. I don't know. It was this sorta surprise thing that I had never even thought about when I thought about sex. And being there like that, quiet and still and resting on top of him, I felt so damn peaceful. So much so that I actually went to sleep and had just about the nicest night's rest I can remember having in a long, long time.

The only problem in all this is, now that I've had this taste of Henri, I wanna pig out, you know? I just wanna be there naked in the guest bedroom, 24-7, getting it on around the clock. Yeah—that's right— basically I want to be his love slave. OK—LOL—that sounds waaaaay too kinky! (And much too Britney!) Maybe not slave, exactly . . . how about "love consort"? That sounds so European, too, that maybe Henri would even go for it. H God—I want so desperately to head over to his house again tonight! I don't think his mom gets back from New York for another few days, so why the hell not? But Brett has advised me to lay low. Lay low? How can I lay low when, as I write, I have a surfboard in my shorts just thinking about Henri's ass? Ugggh. This is gonna be impossible!!!

Brett did say, though, that if Henri gave me a call I could consider going over, but only if I led him to believe that I was <u>not</u> going to be spending the night. Christ—she makes these things so much more complicated than I think they should be. But Brett says it's all about playing with a guy's expectations. Still, I don't know about her mind games. Hell—I like the guy! Wait. Who am I kidding—I love the guy!!! Why should I try to pretend that's not the case? Shit—did I just use the L word, fully spelled out for all to read?!

Fuck it—I'm gonna call him. Hold, please—

07:32 P.M.
WEDNESDAY 08.09.06
No answer. Where the hell is he? What else does he have to do tonight? Why didn't he—

OMG—he just IM'd me.

He's on the computer and didn't make it downstairs to the phone. He wants me to come over! Now!!! Bye!

11:35 P.M.
WEDNESDAY 08.09.06
LOL. You are killing me. You <u>are</u> his love slave. Don't even try to deny it. Besides, I don't even know what a consort is.

Well, it sounds like you're having fun. I'd almost be jealous, except for the fact that rubbing up against a naked Henri is not my idea of a good time. Which is probably fine by you. Clearly you want him all to yourself now that you are in full-on, no turning back L-O-V-E mode. That is for sure.

Anyway, thanks for your description of the sex part, too. Seriously. Because it was not what I expected. Not at all. Not to offend you or anything, but I thought you'd just be sucking each other's dicks the whole time. Though I'm assuming that was in the mix, maybe as part of the phrase "a lot"! I guess I was thinking that, if the ass wasn't in play, it was all about the BJ. My bad. But certainly your good. (ha)

Now that I'm playing sexual catch-up to you, I realized I better get to work. Otherwise you are gonna lord this virginity thing over me like a mutha. ☺ So at rehearsal tonight, I told MK about your beating me, thinking maybe it would get her interested in giving it a go again. And you know what? She was totally shocked that I'd never done it before. (Again, these false rumors about my sexual harem in Wheaton had gotten to her.) This, of course, made me feel like an ass . . . like I should have clearly had sex by now, and the fact that I hadn't meant I was deformed or something.

But she didn't make me feel too bad about it. Until it came to discussing our bed situation. Get this: She said that I had had my chance to cross the finish line Monday night. Except she used the past tense. Had. Damn—that was pretty cold, huh? But it is true, I guess. I totally had my shot with her and blew it. Man, MK really just comes out and says whatever's on her mind sometimes. No filter. At all. I told you . . . she's crazy!

After rehearsal ended, MK and I walked together back to St. Ann's, and even held hands most of the way. That was a surprise after she'd dissed me on the whole sex issue. When we got to St. Ann's, I was about to invite her back up to my room to give it a second go when she bailed. Said she was exhausted and wanted to get to bed. She was gone before I could say BOO. Hmmmm. It's weird, too, because I was thinking about what you'd written, about just being naked with Henri and how that was so cool. It got me thinking, I dunno, that that wouldn't be so bad with MK. I thought I could get into some of that action with her without dotting the big "i" (intercourse, for the heterosexually challenged). It sounds like that approach worked for you guys!

But at the same time, I'm still a bit reluctant to do even this, because I don't want to lead her on, you know? Make her think this is something more than it is (i.e., summer-camp horniness). Still, I thought that given her willingness to spend the night on Monday, she probably would be into something sexy. But in the end, I didn't even get to make the proposition, as she was down the hall before I could figure out even how to phrase it. Bummer, huh? Well, I guess I can try asking her another night. But the farther we get away from Monday, it'll just be harder. There's a window of sleepover opportunity and, if I don't use it soon, it's gonna slam shut.

I think on Friday we're having some sorta movie night, with all of us going to see a flick over at the student union. It'll be our last night free before tech weekend begins, and then a full week of dress rehearsals and the actual performances. So maybe if it's a horror movie, I can make my move. (ha) We shall see. Later . . . C

PS—Hey, you wanna invite Henri to come with you to see *Merrily* next weekend?

12:13 A.M.
THURSDAY 08.10.06
Jourbon! It's been a drama-filled night since I last blogged off. Christ—I don't know where to start. Maybe where I left off would be good, and then I'll work my way through the ups and downs of the evening.

So, just as I got off the computer and ran out of the house in response to Henri's booty call, Valerie pulls up in the driveway from work and was wondering where I'm dashing off to. I'm about to lie and say I'm going to Wheaton Plaza or to a movie or 7-Eleven when my mind just sorta goes blank. I don't have the time or energy to make up some fake story, so I just tell her I'm going to Henri's to hang. She doesn't have too much of a response to the fact that I'm heading off to Rock Creek Hills to get my freak on, which, actually, is weirdly disappointing.

(hmmmmm) Not to say that she's happy about me running off, because she isn't. However, her reason has nothing to do with Henri getting busy with her son.

Val springs on me that she wants to take me out for my birthday. I'm like, "Uh, mom, that was three days ago." To which she gets all defensive, saying that she knows when my birthday is and that she would've taken me out Monday but when she got home I was already at the county fair with Brett, and then Tuesday she had to work late, and blah, blah, blah. Meanwhile, as she is jawing on about this, my sexual clock is ticking as I'm inching my way down the driveway. But she keeps trying to stop me, saying she wants to take me to dinner tonight and even says I can bring Brett along if I want. Clearly she is not getting the point, so I say, "Mom, I've got plans with Henri," and I tell her that maybe we can do something this weekend. So, pissed that I'm ditching her, she says that I cannot spend the night at his house again and that my curfew is 11:00. Her reason is hysterical: "I don't want his mother fussing over you two nights in a row." Oh, Valerie—you know not what you say.

So after a good 15-minute delay, I get to Henri's all excited and pumped and expecting him to greet me naked *avec* hard-on at the front door. But I get there and I ring and ring and ring, but no one comes to the door, because, as it turns out, it's open. So I go in and find Henri in the den, and it's like the joint is on fire there is so much smoke. He offers me some but I decline, citing the contact high I got the second I entered the room. Henri thinks that this is hilarious and proceeds to laugh for the next, oh, 15 minutes. (Ugh) I am soooooo annoyed by him being so baked like this that I say I'm gonna hang in the backyard, and when he's done playing with his bong he can come play with me.

I thought saying something smartass and bitchy to him would make me feel better—empowered, stronger. Unfortunately, it had the opposite effect. I merely felt like a fool, because—you guessed it—Henri did not come racing to follow me outside like I'd hoped. So I'm out on the patio, inanely flipping through some copies of French *Vogue*, which was absolutely ridiculous since I can't understand a word of it. It's just pretty pictures of gorgeous women . . . not really my thing. Besides, all I can think about is Henri and how much I like him and hate him at the same time. Especially at that exact instant. I was furious . . . at least internally.

So I thought I was gonna be out there for an eternity, waiting for him till the sun dipped behind the tall oaks that shroud his backyard. But, lo and behold, he did actually show up after about half an hour. He looked sorta cowed and sullen, which was not a cute look on him. Not at all. Then I felt awful. It's not like I wanted to make him feel bad, and seeing him like this made me feel even worse. So without a word, Henri comes and sits on my lounge chair and wraps his hand around my bare calf, giving me this wan smile. He says he feels bad that I feel bad. (OMG—he is killing me!) I tell him that he smokes too much pot, and he says he knows and is sorry about it. Which wrenches an apology out of me that goes like this: "I'm sorry for being such a bitch." You know what he says in his ridiculously cute accent? "I'm sorry for being such a bong." I mean, what can you do except not laugh and fall instantly back in love with the guy, right? ☺

So the next thing he does, silently, is he starts untying my shoe and taking my sock off and pressing his thumb into the sole of my foot. OK—did you know that the foot was sexy like this? When properly manipulated? Hell—I had no friggin' idea! I mean, it seems sorta gross, because feet are not that pretty. But the way Henri was working his thumb and then massaging my whole foot with his hands—dude, I was like putty. (Correction—putty with a very stiff center!) After driving me wild with the unexpected foot action, I was certainly no longer mad at him for being such a *drogué* (that's "stoner" to you and me, kids). And he said he liked me a lot more than *le Marie-Jeanne*. Isn't that cute?

Then, taking this cue, Henri starts crawling on top of me, pulling my shirt up as he goes. At first I was like, "Ease up, bro," as we were totally outdoors. But Henri said that, with the trees, the neighbors couldn't see a thing, and you know what? Taking a quick glance around, he was right. So he takes my shirt off and then starts kissing my chest and working his way up to my mouth, and, man, I'm just at a loss to tell you what was going through my head at that point, other than one simple thought, repeated over and over as if my brain's CD was on skip: *I can't believe I'm having sex with Henri! <u>AGAIN!!!</u>*

So, as night fell across the backyard, we lost just about all of our clothes. When rolling around on the lounger started to get uncomfortable, Henri grabbed my hand and dragged me over to the lawn, where he proceeded to push me down to the ground and jump on top of me. Yep—that's right—we totally got it on using the grass as our bed. How insane is that?! Well, one thing I will say about it . . . you certainly don't have to worry about staining the sheets, as nature can pretty much take it, you know? And, man, given what we both popped off, you would have needed a whole lotta Shout to get that shit out.

But, to be semi-serious for a moment, when I came it was pretty intense. I swear, I almost started crying. No joke. This was something that was a little unexpected and a little bizarre. I mean . . . I had this orgasm that was like . . . whoa. Intense. Insane. I know this is waaaay TMI, but do you think that crying when you're having sex is a bad sign? I don't know . . . it wasn't like I felt sad, particularly, just on the verge of tears. It was . . . I don't know . . . a little strange.

After our romp and roll through the backyard, I thought the whole sex scene was over. You know that we were both spent. Back inside, Henri noticed that we were both pretty dirty, with grass and dirt stains peppering our naked bods. He said we should probably take a shower so as not to ruin any of his mom's precious furniture. So I go into the bathroom and hop in the shower, and guess the hell what? Henri jumps in too. At first I was like, "What are you doing?" I'm used to showering being, you know, a private personal event . . . like taking a dump. But Henri said he was there to help me get clean, and started scrubbing my back with soap and a washcloth. And you know what? I was hard again! As was he.

Now, I won't get too porno-movie with this scenario, as I know I'm already testing the limits of how much gay sex you can handle. But basically, yeah, we had sex . . . <u>again</u>! This time, though, when I hit the O, I was unable to stop the tears. Fortunately, with the water running all over my face, I don't know if Henri could tell I was seriously losing it, since the tears got lost in the general showery rush of things. But my breathing got pretty strange and gaspy at the same time, which Henri did notice, leading him to ask me if I was okay. I said I was just out of breath. Which was true. Out of breath because I was having a nervous breakdown post-sex. What is up with that? It's pretty freaky, right?

After I got all clean and dry, we went back to the den and hung out on the couch for a bit. I curled up next to Henri as we watched *I Love the '90s*. Every few minutes I would check the cable box for the time, because I knew this bliss had to end eventually. When it hit 11:00, I got up, and Henri was like, "Where are you going?" I had neglected to tell him about my curfew for the evening when I first got there because I didn't want to ruin the illusion that, somehow, both of us were suddenly and inexplicably living together in this great old house in Rock Creek Hills. The mention of any parents would totally blow it.

What really surprised me, though, was that he didn't want me to leave. In fact, he was almost desperate for me to stay, playfully and then not so playfully keeping me from getting up from the couch. Finally, I extricated myself around 11:30 and made my way for the door. He said that now all he had left to do was get stoned, which was some guilty trick to try and get me to stay. But I gently suggested he could just go to bed. He nodded and gave me that familiarly wan smile, and then, just as I was about to leave, he grabbed me for one last kiss, gently nibbling on my lower lip, holding it in his teeth as a final, small attempt to keep me from heading home. What a ploy, huh? I gotta say, as sweet as it was, though, it didn't work. . . .

As I was riding my bike home, taking my time as I made these weaving loops back and forth across the empty streets, it started to rain. But you know what? I didn't speed up at all. I mean, it was a true summer thunder-bumper, as my dad used to call them, the rain coming down in sheets and thunder booming just above my head, but I didn't care at all. It actually felt great getting totally soaked, and made me almost feel like I was still in the shower with Henri.

When I got home, Val yelled at me for being a big, sopping mess, saying I was gonna catch a cold. (Uh . . . in August?!) She also told me she'd made dinner reservations at some fancy French place in Bethesda for tomorrow night. French. Isn't _that_ funny? So she asks me if I want to invite anyone along for my birthday dinner and, though she doesn't mention her by name, she is clearly gunning for Brett, solely because that is the only woman in my life these days other than her. You know what, though? I told her I wanted to bring Henri. I couldn't believe I did it, but that's what came out of my mouth. Well, Val tried to play it cool, but you could tell she thought it was a little odd. So I said, "Is that okay?" And she goes, "Yeah, it's fine," flashing me one of her big, supremely nervous smiles. And so I go, "That's great because, you know, he's French so it'll be like a real treat for him." And Val looks at me again, her face going all weird, like her son has become an alien, because I sounded a little too excited about a parental dinner. So after this big pause she says, "Super!" Super! LOL Yeah, it _is_ super. Or maybe it's a superhuge mistake. We shall see. . . .

When I got up to my room, I went online and typed "crying after sex" into Google. OMG—you know what I found . . . it's a total chick phenomenon, apparently! There were three sites that had these sex advice columns with a bunch of girls asking for help with their postcoital crying. The general consensus was that sex can be a pretty intense experience (duh) that often "brings up a wide range of pretty intense emotions, one of which can be tears." One columnist said crying was fine and wonderful and an emotional release that is "something to cherish." Well, I don't know if I'll cherish a moment in which my emotions feel that totally out of control, but she's got a Ph.D. after her name, so that must mean something, right?

I did find one site that was a little more disconcerting on the topic. It

was that guy Dr. Drew (from *Lovelines*), and he said that crying indicates an incongruence in the way you feel about the relationship vs.
the intimacy you're experiencing. At first I was like, whaaaaa? But
reading on, D.D. said that people cry after sex because they maybe
expect rejection from their romantic interests and, when they experience something truly real, it sorta shows up the deficiencies in past
relationships, which make you realize that you are kinda fucked-up as
a person. (Well, he didn't exactly say "fucked-up.") Reading that, I was
like—Christ! How much more true can <u>that</u> be, because I <u>always</u>
expect things to go wrong with guys, and since they haven't with
Henri, that alone is sorta preemptively freakin' me out.

Still, reading this was kinda an eye-opener. I mean, it got me thinking about my folks, too, and how their marriage went wrong when I
was so young, and maybe that set up this sort of expectation in my
head when I was six that all relationships end in ugly, bitter, terrible
circumstances that leave everyone hating each other. And now that
I've found someone I like who likes me in a similar manner, maybe
I'm losing it because I know it will all end in shit.

Wow. This is kinda bumming me out. It makes me wanna call Henri
and ask him if he still likes me right now. I hope he's not mad that I
couldn't stay tonight. I wanted to, but it would've sent Val through the
roof. I hope he understands that he means a lot to me, even if I can't
spend every remaining night of the summer curled up next to him in
the guest bedroom. All right—I'm gonna get some sleep before I over-
obsess on this topic . . . H

08:20 A.M.
THURSDAY 08.10.06
Hey—man. Not only are you beating me in the virginity stakes, you are now
putting me to shame. I am getting creamed! (ha)

Anyway, that whole crying thing is strange but not a huge surprise. Henri has
brought you to tears before so why not again, even if it is after sex? Also, I would
like to remind you that you've never been the happiest of campers, always Mr.

Gloom-Doom. Especially when it comes to relationships. And you're probably right that you got a lot of that from seeing Val's marriage self-destruct right in front of you. I still can't imagine how that must have felt.

You know, I remember when we first met, how you were this sullen little guy, always walking around with a cloud over your head. I think that's probably what got me interested or intrigued in you, because you were so different from all the other kids. Though you were almost a year older, you seemed even older than that. Wiser. Like Yoda or something. LOL! Not physically, as you're much more handsome than some space reptile. But I think you know what I mean.

Holy shit—it's almost 8:30! It took me so long to finish reading your entry that I'm not gonna have much time to write a lot back. Besides, as for me, there's really not too much sexual action to report. My life is all about rehearsal, rehearsal, rehearsal. And then more rehearsal. Though I'm looking forward to the movie tomorrow. It's not a horror movie, though, which sucks! Was hoping MK would jump into my lap or something. (ha) We're seeing some romantic movie called *Before Sunset* . . . sounds pretty cheesy, huh?

Gotta run—have a great day with Mr. H, you big, sexy dog!

06:22 P.M.
THURSDAY 08.10.06
Hey—just checking in, post-dinner. Where R U? Damn—why am I even asking, as I know you are at Henri's, freakin' that ass. Just hold off on the crying this time, okay? (kidding!) OH—and if by chance Henri notices you losing it, just blame it all on your parents. That always works. OK . . . Blog me!

11:10 P.M.
THURSDAY 08.10.06
All right—I'm getting concerned again. I know Henri has a computer at his pad, so even if you <u>have</u> moved in, it's still no excuse to drop off the face of the planet. I know, I know—not like I'm writing much myself. But seriously, there is nothing to report! Rehearsals have become boring, repetitive, technical exercises in futility, or at least it seemed that way today.

So I wanted to live vicariously through your active sex life. I just hope things are good in the Henri department. Did he come for the b-day dinner in Bethesda? I can't even comprehend the image of him and Val at the same table. I need details. So, get to it, as your silence is worrying me. Again. Usually when you clam up it's a bad sign.

09:07 A.M.
FRIDAY 08.11.06

C'mon man, this is getting <u>ridiculous</u>! Now I'm gonna have to threaten to end this blog myself if you don't write me the F back!!! You are making me very angry, Henry Alan Schaeffer (as indicated by the use of your full Christian name). I am going to cause violence to someone. Do you want the blood of another Mathlete's nose on your hands?! (ha) Then blog me, you DICK!!!

10:24 A.M.
FRIDAY 08.11.06

Jeeeeezzzzzz—testy, testy. Give me a break and a half, okay? I've been a little busy lately, so sue me. And no, you don't have to worry yourself to death. Christ—I thought <u>I</u> was the pessimist! But I miss a couple postings and you are ready to call *America's Most Wanted* and put the county on Amber Alert. I'd tell you to get a life or something, but, of course, you already have one. I'm the one who needs a life . . . or maybe something other than Henri in it.

So—to catch you up—the majority of yesterday involved movie and a dinner. All with Henri. The movie was over at Mazza Gallerie. First, though, we took Metro over to Friendship Heights to try out some Parkour on a big parking garage behind Hecht's. I'd been out of practice, but Henri did some sweet moves, some of which I caught in mini-movie clips on my digital camera. (I'll try to post them here later.) He puts me to shame with his skills—he is a real pro! I was telling him that he could probably make a career out of it, starring in one of those hip commercials in the U.K. Or even in a movie—there's a flick called *Jump London* that I read about on the Web when I was at Henri's this A.M. Oh, yeah—we had sex again this morning . . . figured we'd get it out of the way first so we could do something productive during the day. ☺

Anyway, the Parkour was going fine and I learned a couple new moves myself; namely focusing on various vault moves to get over barriers or short walls. The coolest trick is called the Lazy Vault, which looks like break dancing if you can do it well. (ED. NOTE: I can't . . . at least not yet.) But just as I was starting to figure out the intricacies of the Monkey Vault, it started raining. Pouring. So we ran into Mazza, figuring we might as well check out a flick, and, lo and behold, the third sequel to *The Fast and the Furious* (a.k.a. *FF3*) was starting in a few minutes.

The cool thing about Mazza is they have something called Club Movies, which is basically like being in first class on an airline, because the seats are leathery and you can order fancy food and drinks that they'll bring right to you . . . even beer and wine! So yeah, big surprise here: Henri figured out a way to get us some wine. He started chatting up some older chicks sitting behind us, charming them with ye old accent and getting them to order a carafe of wine, which they passed down to us once the lights went out. I tried to protest, saying that I didn't want to meet up with my mom plastered. But Henri countered this excuse, saying that he thought my mom was a partier (which I guess she is in her own lame, middle-aged way) and that she probably wouldn't even notice. I know, I know—very questionable reasoning. But when Henri says these things, it's hard not to believe them. So we had some wine and watched the movie, which, like the previous two, also sucked. But the wine was pretty tasty!

After, it had stopped raining, so we hopped on the Metro to downtown Bethesda and met my mom at La Miche, this fancy new Franco joint on Norfolk Ave. When we got there, Henri started cracking up at the sign. He said La Miche translated into "The Round Loaf." Granted we were both a little tipsy, but you have to admit, it's pretty damn hysterical to name a swanky restaurant the round loaf (as in dropping a loaf!). It's disgusting . . . or *degout*, as Henri kept saying. LOL

Anyway, Val wasn't there yet, so we found a nice table outside where things were somewhat less fancy. When she finally showed up, Val wanted us to move indoors, saying it was too hot to eat outside and that she had just done her hair, which would get ruined . . . you know, all the usual Val neuroses. I would have bowed to her request except that I didn't want to look like a child in front of Henri. So I just said, surprising myself, that we were eating out here because it's my birthday and that was that. Then, get this!!! She tried to pull my line on me, reminding me that my birthday was on Monday, not today. But I wasn't having it. Fortunately, Henri piped up and started complimenting Val's hair, and that distracted her enough to get her to sit down and focus on the nice young Frenchman at our table. Henri's charms are absolutely magical, no? If you could bottle them and sell them at Hecht's or something, you would be a billionaire!

So the waiter comes up and Henri starts chattering away with him in his mile-a-minute French. When he talks like this, it's hard to even believe he's speaking another language. To me, other people's languages are great and cool and I love the sound of them . . . it's almost like music, really. But I don't even get that they're communicating, somehow . . . I mean, people in other languages speak so goddamn fast, it's like there's not even a break in the words, just a constant streaming of sounds. But somehow the waiter not only understood everything he said, but was chuckling with him about some extra comment he'd made about the décor (probably that it looked very faux French!).

When we finally got around to ordering, Henri totally grossed me out by getting the calves liver with onions. BLECH! He said it was a traditional favorite of his, his *grand mère* used to make it for him all the time when he was growing up. Val, feeling all French and fancy, ordered a roasted duck breast and *haricots verts*. I was like, what the hell is that? You'll never guess—it's green beans. (?!?!) So I'm like, why do they have to go and screw up a perfectly simple name for something like green beans . . . *haricots verts* makes it sound like a friggin' disease! As for my order, I kept it basic . . . *le steak frites*. Simple, easy to pronounce, very clear.

Just at the waiter was about to leave, Henri very slyly threw out some

French that caused him to produce a wine list. At first, Val demurred. But then Henri turned the accent up to 11 and said it was a celebration and that we should be festive and have some vino. The waiter wondered about the celebration and Henri mentioned my birthday to him. With a wink, the waiter told Val that he could serve us some wine too, since we were with her. And that was Henri's plan all along, apparently, as indicated by his grabbing my knee under the table and smiling like a Cheshire cat.

The food and wine was great and Val was pretty well behaved. Until, that is, my big lie about Henri being in my driving class popped up, courtesy of Val. Henri seemed surprised by this too, and unable to cover as he usually can when anything less than the truth comes into play. Finally, I told Val she had it wrong, saying that I'd met Henri after driving class up at the mall. (I hoped that all the partying she's been up to this summer would lead her to believe she'd somehow gotten her facts crooked.) I wasn't even gonna get into the whole Parkour thing, because I'm sure she'd have a friggin' heart attack if she knew I was trying to learn a sport. Of course, this didn't stop Henri from making it topic number one. Thanks, buddy!

But you know what? Val was truly stunned that a) I had taken an interest in a sport and b) that I'd taken an interest in anything other than cable television. Thus began a discourse on the finer points of freerunning, led by the honorable master *traceur* himself, Mssr. Henri Broussard. In the midst of chatting on and on about this with Val, though, Henri kept shooting me these killer looks . . . quick micro glances (if I can borrow some Driver's Ed terminology) that got me totally boned, even though we'd already had our sex for the day. I kept getting nervous that Val was maybe picking up on them, but frankly, I think Val thought Henri was pretty cute herself. Which was cool, because maybe when she finally does the math and figures out I'm a homo, at least she'll be happy to see that I share her good taste in men. ☺

Walking to the car after all this talk of Parkour, Val demanded some demonstration, so Henri did a few of his tricks, namely the Kong Vault, a few Tic Tacs, and one stunning Rail Precision jump that made Val squeal with delight in a way I haven't heard her squeal in . . . well, forever. Moms aren't supposed to squeal, right? When we got back to Henri's house, I decided to exploit all this good will toward men (ha) and asked Val if I could hang out at H's for a while, and you know what? She was so damn charmed by our night with Henri that she gave me a big fat yes (though she did say I had to get home by midnight).

So the minute we got in the door at Chez Henri, we started making out. Amazing! We ended up back in the guest bedroom, where we went at it for, oh, a couple hours, I guess. When I realized it was approaching the witching hour, I said I'd better get some clothes on and head home. But then Henri picked up the phone and called Val directly, turning the accent up. He told her that I was so tired from the wine and good food that I had fallen asleep on the sofa. Then he hung up. Can you believe him? So I was like, what did she say? Grinning, Henri said that she told him it was fine . . . that she'd leave the back door unlocked for me if I got home after she left for work in the morning. Unbelievable, huh? I mean, I've really gotta keep Henri around if he is gonna make Val this damn agreeable.

After securing me for the night, I thought we'd hit the sack, but Henri said he wasn't sleepy and fired up *un petit pétard* ("a little joint," that is). I tried not to get bitchy about this, but it was hard to hold my tongue. I mean, it sorta bummed me out. I'm like, here I am, this naked guy in bed with him, and he's more interested in some smelly weeds rolled up in paper? That's really not making me feel so special, you know? Not a great boost for the old self-esteem. Eventually, I did lure him back to bed after a few tokes, and we started making out again. At first, though, the taste of the pot in his mouth was a little too much to take. But after a while I forgot about it, because kissing Henri is a generally overpowering experience in which one tends to forget everything.

After a few minutes of tongue action, it was clear we were both exhausted, so Henri says to me, "Let's hit it in the morning." I'm like, sure, and I'm holding his head in my hands and staring at his face, and I feel like I'm gonna start crying again. Henri looks at me like, "What"? And I just say, outta nowhere, "You are . . . beautiful." Henri's response? He gives me this embarrassed grin, looking away and reaching for the lamp, and I'm like—"Don't turn it off," 'cause I wanna see how beautiful he looks for just a little bit longer. Henri tells me I'm being silly. So getting one last look at his mug, I say it again, adding his name this time because I love saying his name: "Henri, you are truly beautiful." His reply—he turns out the light. Not what I was going for exactly but, well, I think he was tired too.

Anyway, I'm still here at Henri's as I write this. I got up a little while ago, but he's still in the guest bed, asleep. I don't know if I should try to wake him up or just head home. I mean, he did say we were gonna hit it in the A.M. . . . but he is completely sound asleep. I know his mom is coming back from New York this afternoon, so maybe I'll try to clean things up a bit. This place looks like a couple of teenagers are living here. Later!

08:34 A.M.
SATURDAY 08.12.06

Hey—sorry I didn't get back to you yesterday. I felt it was my turn to pull a Hal, as it were. And I guess I forgive you for not being such a great correspondent, because, when you do actually put fingers to keyboard, you have quite a few tales to tell. Not to mention a few choice phrases in which to tell them.

That bit about Val and you and Henri at dinner together had me ROTFL! That was a riot. (*Haricots verts?!* You are such a nut case.) And I can't believe Val was totally clueless about the situation. Henri sitting right across from her, charming her son's pants off. And that you both think Henri is hot?! LOL Well, dude, I gotta tell you: It's going to be the shock of her life when she realizes you are getting lucky with the Frenchman! I just hope, when that bomb drops, I am in another county. Or another state.

So, as I write to you, guess who's sleeping in my bed? It's not me, obviously. (I may talk in my sleep, but writing would be tough.) And it certainly isn't Chaz, though I love the guy like a big gay brother. Give up? Who am I kidding—I'm sure you figured it out with that first sentence. You're bright that way. ☺ Yes, MK is curled up in my tiny single bed. However, unlike you crazy gay guys, she is fully clothed and remains unviolated. Sorta . . .

So how did this come about? I guess I'll back up a little to the night before, when we all went to the movies at the student union. I wish *FF3* was here—I thought the other two were pretty cool! The movie we saw was a sequel too, but a pretty weird one. It was called *Before Sunset*, and was the follow-up to *Before Sunrise*, a movie from 10 years ago about a guy, played by Ethan Hawke, and a girl who spend a day together hanging out in Vienna, falling in love, and then leaving without even exchanging phone numbers.

Unlike the first one, the sequel didn't even take place in one day—it took place in one hour and 20 minutes. Real time. It was about the same characters meeting again, this time in Paris, 10 years later. They haven't seen each other since Vienna, though they were supposed to meet there, I guess, but the girl blew him off (typical) because her grandma died . . . which we're supposed to believe! Anyway, the whole movie is just them walking around Paris and talking about life and love and their no-starter of a relationship.

I gotta say, though, it was kinda dull at first, because there was just so much damn talking. (And I thought I had a lot of dialogue to remember!) But the more Ethan and the French girl hung out, the more they talked about how their lives had become so unhappy since they first met. Their day in Vienna was like their youthful innocence, and now they were both old and bitter, with kids and jobs. At one point, I leaned over to MK and said, "Damn, this shit is depressing." You know what she did? She elbowed me in the ribs!

After an hour it started getting slightly more interesting. The French girl said something that really hit me. She said that when you're young and you meet someone you can connect and relate to, you think you're gonna have all sorts of those connections in your life. But the fact is, you don't. You only get one or two, and if you blow them (like she did), that's it. You are totally fucked!

And I guess that was sort of a wake-up call for me. Maybe I'm blowing some big chance with MK, who is truly someone I get along with and am attracted to (at least in my dreams). This is sorta what the French girl realizes. You can see it in her eyes, 'cause she doesn't really say it. But when she invites Ethan up for tea, they're going up this big, curvy staircase and they're both checking each other out, and suddenly you know it's gonna happen. They are gonna get together and get it on after 10 long years!

So I was waiting for the big, full-on sex scene, but it never came. I thought at least I would get to see some sex in a movie, since there is none in my actual life. But the movie ended abruptly, with the chick putting on a weird song and dancing around as Ethan smiles at her. Really smiles at her. (Reminded me of one of your goofy Henri grins!) Then she goes, "Uh, I think you're gonna miss your plane." And then the screen goes black. Weird, huh?

Afterward, everyone except me thought it was brilliant. Not that I didn't like it. I just wanted to see some sex, that's all. The thing was rated R after all. When I said this to MK, she elbowed me again! We all then hung out in the student union coffee shop having this big discussion. Going to see the movie was Ryan's idea, as he thought it related to the show. So all the girls were wildly talking nonstop about how intense it was and meaningful, and the guys were kinda quiet. Ryan noticed this and, of course, called on me to give the male perspective. (He is still picking on me!) I said I liked it but didn't understand why Ethan Hawke even gave the French girl the time of day when she blew him off at that first meeting. All the girls screamed at me— "BECAUSE HER GRANDMOTHER DIED!!!" I was like, "You really believe that?" They all groaned and said I was being cynical. And you know what I thought: *Maybe I'm turning into Hal!* AHHHHHH!

Once the commotion over this died down, we did end up having a good discussion. The reason Ryan wanted us to see *Sunset* was because it deals with two characters in love at two different moments of their lives, when they meet and when they come back together years later. Which is sorta similar to *Merrily* in that both characters had regrets over the way they'd behaved. They'd both made mistakes 10 years ago and could see them more clearly with age. Ryan said it's often hard to see anything you do in your youth as a mistake, because you always think you're right. But this movie proves that, not only can you make mistakes, but you can be completely blind to them at the time. I thought that was pretty deep for a movie, you know? I guess that's why it was an indie film. That and the fact that Paris didn't get blown up or anything.

After our chat, it was almost 11:00, and we all headed back to St. Ann's. MK was with her posse, but when she saw me walking alone, she got the message and ditched them. We had a nice walk back, talking about the movie some more. Or debating it. MK kept going on and on about how amazing it was, the naturalism of the dialogue, the realism of the time frame, the sex boiling underneath the whole thing. I was not too crazy about it, probably 'cause it bugged me. Relating it to my life, the movie basically said that my obsession with Ghaliyah probably meant nothing, while this MK thing might be the thing I'm totally ruining.

So finally, I had to tell this to MK, because she was driving me nuts with all her praise of the film. And when I did, she just stopped in her tracks. Seriously. She kinda froze. I was like, "What's wrong?" And she said nothing was wrong. I said, "That's cool." But she kept staring at me, and it was getting ridiculous. Fortunately, I remembered your entry about you and Henri at the gay bar, when you were just staring at him and he knew what was up. I think that's what was going down here, that MK suddenly wanted me to kiss her. But for some reason she wasn't attacking me like she'd done before. So, being suave for once in my life, I didn't even ask her if she wanted a kiss, I just leaned in and planted one right on her lips. And then she attacked me!

Dude, we made out for about half an hour sitting on the lawn in front of the student union! People were walking by and laughing at us, we were making such a spectacle of ourselves. LOL I wanted to stop but was also enjoying being a big PDA spectacle, so, uh, I didn't. Once I was able to catch my breath, I asked MK if she wanted to come back to my room, as Chaz was surely ensconced in Albert's lair, and she said sure. No problem. I was like, man, that was easy!

But once we got into the room and on the bed, she started talking again. About the movie! (Oh brother!) She wanted me to sing her a song, like the girl did for Ethan Hawke, and I was like, "Uh, can't we just have sex?" And I got elbowed . . . AGAIN! Of course I was serious about this sex request, even though I said I was kidding. MK then got serious about the sex issue and said she'd rather not hit all the bases in one night. That was cool, I guess, because a couple bases was fine by me.

So we made out for a little while longer and fell asleep in bed pretty much fully clothed. It was like your first night at Henri's . . . we were so beat we just passed out! Unfortunately, neither of us had enough energy to strip the other one naked. Otherwise, like you, we might have had more success sexually. But really, it was fine. Even though I am jealous of your success. Then again, you've been working Henri for a full five weeks now. And sure, I've known MK just as long, but I didn't even think of her as anything other than a brilliant performer until, oh, about 10 hours ago. So give me a flippin' break!

All right—time to wake the girl up. I set the alarm for 8:00, but she didn't even hear it. She was so beat from rehearsals that I figured I'd let her get an extra hour before we headed down for breakfast. She really needs it, as it's gonna be a long, rehearsal-filled weekend. Tomorrow is the big, dreaded tech-in, a.k.a. BLACK SUNDAY. But I'm excited, too. And not just about the show anymore. ☺

Week 6

12:33 P.M.
SUNDAY 08.13.06

I am hungover and depressed. That is a deadly combo if there ever was one, because being hungover is already like being depressed, so you really don't need a whole other level of true psychological/romantic depression layered on top of it. It's enough to make me sick. Which it did, oh, around 9:30 this A.M. I thought that'd make me feel better, you know, clearing out the system and all. But it didn't. I realized the only thing that would make me feel better is if last night had not happened at all.

So in case you're wondering—this all has to do with Henri . . . shocking, right? Since his mom got back on Friday, I hadn't seen him, but we'd been chatting on the computer a lot. His mom was pretty mad at the condition of the household and, since her return, had been keeping Henri busy with all sorts of cleaning. He was not happy. I wanted to go up to Wheaton with him yesterday, but he couldn't get a work release from Madame Broussard, so I went solo, shopping at SA and sipping some espresso on my own at Marrakesh.

On my way home, I was walking by De Lounge and saw Queng hang-

194

ing out in front, dealing with a beer delivery. He was instantly all friendly again, wondering where I had been and saying that I should come by more often, blah, blah, blah. Then he said this, which killed me: "Where is that cute boyfriend of yours?" My boyfriend? OMG—that was a trip, hearing it from a complete stranger who actually didn't even know that Henri and I had truly been getting it on. Anyway, Queng said we should stop by the club that evening for an all-ages dance party, and that he would put us on the list (meaning FREE). I was a little skeptical about the whole thing, though, because dancing at a gay bar on a Saturday night sounded a little, I don't know, stereo-typical or something. Not that I was gonna say this to Queng, but I just didn't know if Henri'd go for something that out-and-out gay, that's all. In retrospect, I sooooo wish he hadn't, because it ended up being a disaster.

When I got home, I pitched the idea to Henri via e-mail. He shot me back a quick response, totally excited to do it, adding that his mom would even let him out of the house, since he'd done a bang-up job cleaning house. Then Brett called and wanted to know what I was doing. I told her about De Lounge and she said maybe Jerry could drive us and we could all go. *C'est chouette!* (What Henri says when something is great or awesome!) So Brett and the Jerry-mobile came by my place around 9:00, and I told Val we were going to the movies. She, of course, was going down to Georgetown with her girlfriends and said she might stay at one of their places in Rosslyn if it got too late. So this got me thinking—hey—maybe Henri and I could come back and hit it at the homestead later on. Having Henri in my own bed? Wow—the idea of that alone got me all tingly and excited for what was gonna be a banner Saturday night. If only . . .

Arriving at Henri's, he came strutting down the driveway, looking absolutely amazing. He'd actually washed his mop of hair, which was shinier, even blonder that usual, and his face was slightly tan, his cheeks a little rosy and flush. OH—and get this! He was wearing the Wheaton Triangle Lanes staff shirt that we'd bought up at SA. This was wild, because guess the hell what? I was wearing my shirt too.

Brett saw this and said it was sooooo cute that we were wearing the same shirt. However, Henri seemed sorta annoyed by it. He said I should have told him that I was gonna wear the shirt, and I said I wanted to surprise him, as the shirt hadn't been seen in a couple weeks. Then, getting a little annoyed with him, I said maybe he should've told me he was gonna wear his. He smiled that smile of his (his teeth are so perfect!) and, reluctantly, admitted that he wanted to surprise me, too. We both laughed a little at this, and I thought things were fine.

Arriving at De Lounge, Henri wanted to fire up a little *petard* action before hitting the club. This also annoyed me, and I said he was on his own. Unfortunately, Jerry said he would join in the endeavor, which sucked, because I wanted Henri to feel like the lone stoner out. Anyway, once we got inside De Lounge, the place was much more crowded than it had been on Karaoke Sunday. It was downright happening, jammed with an assortment of kids that were generally under 21 and dancing like maniacs to some slammin' house beats. I asked Henri if he wanted to dance and he looked at me, looked at our matching shirts, and then whipped his off, revealing his bare chest to the whole crowd, thus causing a ripple effect of swoonage shock waves that fanned out across the bar and onto the dance floor. I swear to G-O-D my heart just about stopped. He really needs to give me a warning or something before doing this shit, especially in public! Seeing his naked chest, I really had to restrain myself from leaning in and just making out with his right nipple (like I had the day before!). I grinned uneasily at him and he grinned quite easily at me as he turned the shirt inside out, put it back on, and headed toward the dance floor.

Usher was playing so we got busy groovin'. Even Brett and Jerry joined us, though Jerry seemed a little freaked by the freaks of De Lounge. It was pretty gay-all-the-way, and Jerry, wearing one of those tacky Big Striped Shirts that seem to be way too popular with the 20-somethings, stuck out a bit. Henri, though, tried to make Jerry fit in a little by unbuttoning the top three buttons of the shirt while we were dancing. Jerry was a little taken aback by this, and frankly, I was a little jealous of Henri stripping some other dude, until I saw Brett cracking up and realized, oh yeah, Jerry is straight. I mean, I can't believe I got like that, but when I saw Henri revealing someone else's chest, it just made me crazy! This, as it turns out, was a harbinger of bad things to come. . . .

After dancing for a while, we headed to the bar, where Queng was holding court with the quartet of smokers from karaoke night. When he saw Henri and me, Queng got all excited and welcoming and hugged us both. Then Queng started talking to Henri about Paris and how long he'd been in Wheaton and generally chatty stuff, which was fine and, I could sense, almost boring to Henri. Until, that is, Queng got to the question that hit the fan: "So how long have you and Hal been together?" Henri looked at Queng quizzically, then at me, as if I had asked Queng to ask this. And then came the real bombshell . . . Henri's answer. Brace yourself for this one: "We're not boyfriends."

So suddenly it was like a five-alarm fire going off in my heart. OMG— the flames were basically shooting out of my chest, licking the tip of my chin, and singeing my eyebrows. My eyes even began to water a little until I realized that a few lame tears were not gonna be enough to stop this sorta emotional inferno, so I willfully jammed up the water-works. (Thank God.) Then Brett came up behind me and asked me if I wanted Jerry's drink, as he was feeling a little too baked. I had no plans to drink at all until my heart caught fire, and then—I mean, hell, what could I do? I figured a Long Island Iced Tea would be cool and refreshing enough to douse the flames, but you know what? Alcohol is totally flammable, of course. (I knew I should have paid attention in chem lab!) So that drink, and the many that followed, only served to make things worse.

Once I'd downed my Iced Tea like it was actually iced tea, I pulled Henri aside for a tongue lashing. (No, not the make-out kind.) I asked him about the not-boyfriends line, and you know what he did? Henri simply rolled his eyes at me and told me to stop being so dramatic. Me? Dramatic?! He's the one setting off relationship bombs in the middle of a packed nightclub. So I say this to him, and you know what? He says that making dumb analogies like the one I'd just made was even more dramatic! UGH! So, trying to calm my literary reflex to apparently make an analogy out of a molehill, I spoke in simple English and said to him that I thought we were boyfriends. Period. Henri sighed and said that he liked me a lot and that I was really sweet and all, but he wasn't looking for a boyfriend. Well, I said, I wasn't looking either until he literally fell into my lap last month. He thought this was amusing, shooting me that killer half smile of his, and said I was funny. My response? "I don't wanna be funny, I want to be your boyfriend." And again he gave me that goddamn half smile, though this time it was not so cute. Not at all.

So we got into this huge discussion about how Henri was not "into" relationships. Nice conversation for a Saturday night out, huh? He went on and on re this topic, saying that hell is other people (which is apparently something famous some French philosopher said) and that he gets sick of new people after like 10 minutes, and all this the-world-sucks-ass crap. The bizarre thing is that he pretty much sounds like me, right? I mean, he was totally quoting from the Hal Playbook, right? I mean, I don't like other people either. (Except him, that is.) But Henri kept saying that's not the point and, as the effects of my Iced Tea took hold, I was getting incredibly confused and wondering exactly what the goddamn point was, then.

Henri then tells me that I'm getting dramatic again, and yeah, I AM getting dramatic, because even though I hate the world and most of its people, I seem to love him, and it's beyond annoying to be suddenly lumped in with the rest of the humanity that bores him after 10 minutes. I mean, not only is it not fair, it's simply not true, and I try to explain this to him. I say how we have not only spent days together but whole nights, too . . . hours and hours sleeping beside each other in the same bed, not to mention dicking around with each other too. In summary, our summer has been like 10 minutes times 100! But Henri keeps shaking his head, telling me that I don't understand, I don't understand. But you know what? I do friggin' understand, because we feel the same way about everyone on this stupid planet except each other. (OK—except you . . . and maybe Brett.) But Henri doesn't want to hear this sort of truthful statement and claims that I'm yelling and, hell, maybe I was, but I had to, because he wasn't listening to what I was saying. Not at all!!! But you know what? The reason Henri couldn't understand me was because he was friggin' high as a kite, which tends to make comprehending a rational argument fairly impossible. Which is exactly what I told him at full volume. And that's when he left. No good-bye. No nothing. He just turned around and headed out the door.

Two seconds later, Brett comes over and asks me what's up with Henri's hasty exit. I tell her that I think I just blew the whole friggin' thing, and Brett says that sucks. Sucks? That is hardly the right word, not nearly severe enough. But I just nodded and said, "Yeah, it sucks all right." Jerry comes back from the bar and, on hearing this news, offers me his drink as consolation, which I guzzle in a second because, by this point, my fire has turned into an raging inferno. And then Brett tries to get my mind off Henri by bringing me out to the dance floor. I'm kinda feeling wasted now and start dancing like there's no tomorrow . . . which basically there isn't, as there seems to be no more Henri in my life, so what's the point of another day.

Then, during that Killers song, I notice this husky blond dude dancing next to us who is kinda checking me out and, since he kinda generically looks like Henri, I decide to flirt with him. I do, and we start dancing and then chatting afterward. He's 22 and just graduated from Montgomery College and is nice and cute and boring and sorta keeping my mind occupied for the time being, especially since he keeps letting me have sips of his drink (gin and tonic?). And this is where things start getting a little sketchy. There was more dancing. Some making out. Dancing again, with Queng joining us. Brett telling me to stop being such a slut. Making out while dancing—yikes. A couple cigarettes, even. Then the MoCo grad (oh shit—I can't even remember his name—Tyler? Trevor?) has me near the bulletin board where Henri unwittingly defiled me the first time and I try to repeat history with this guy . . . can I call him Tyvor? And this is actually starting to work, as he presses me against the wall—he is a seriously beefy dude! But in the midst of this "passion," Brett comes storming over and literally shoves this guy off of me, ruining the not-so-romantic moment. Tyvor was sorta stunned and I was sorta pissed, telling Brett to leave me alone and that she had no right to tell me who I could or could not make out with. Then I feel this hand on my wrist and I turn around to see Jerry, who starts walking me out, saying the party's over. And he's right, but it actually ended when Henri said that we were not a couple.

All the way in the car home, I was fighting with Brett about how she had ruined my night with Tyvor. She said that when I woke up today I would thank her, and you know what? I wish she had knocked me to the ground and dragged me out of that joint unconscious the minute Henri left. I was a total wreck and dealt with it in the worst way (i.e., getting plastered and making out with a stranger). Why am I such a moron? I didn't want Tyvor at all . . . I was just trying to occupy my mind so that it wouldn't race itself to death, thinking about Henri and whether or not this thing is over just when it was starting. Of course, Henri is back on my mind full force today, and, in fact, thinking about it all now is even worse, because this sorta emotional turmoil is not something you want to think about when you're already recovering from a night of drinking other people's cocktails.

I don't know what was up with Henri last night. Maybe it's that his mom is back in town and he suddenly feels like he has to be more careful and discreet. However, Brett's theory on all this strangeness was a little more grim: She claims I blew it by letting Henri have what he wanted. But I don't agree with her reasoning and actually find it highly flawed, namely due to the fact that Henri liked what we did and logic would dictate that he'd want some more where that came from, no? Still, Brett countered that sure, guys always want more pieces of ass, but that doesn't mean it necessarily has to come from the same person. She says that "repeat ass" (her term, not mine) freaks guys out because they don't want to be dependent on just one person, especially a girl. But I think it's different in my gay situation dealing with a guy, *non*? She said no and, according to Dr. Brett, men are men when it comes to sex, meaning that they want it where they can get it as long as they don't have to pay the price, which is commitment. I don't know . . . maybe. Who cares though, really? I don't want to learn these sorts of harsh life lessons. I just want Henri, over and over and over. I won't get bored of his repeat ass at all. I promise!

Oh Christ—what am I gonna do?! Brett says under no circumstances should I call him. None. But that is ALL I want to do this morning! It's all I wanted to do last night after he left De Lounge. All those drinks and dancing and dicking around with Tyvor were merely activities to keep my hands occupied so that I didn't pick up the pay phone and start drunk dialing. Today, though, I've got nothing to occupy myself with except cable, and nothing is on at all. Blogging has kept me busy for a bit, but once I log off I know I'm gonna reach for the phone and dial. Arrggghhhh!!!! Maybe I'll jerk off for a little bit. That'll take, what, a good five minutes. Shit—then what? I am such a goddamned mess of nerves and anxiety and ennui!!! I am not gonna make it, Chuck. I swear to you, I'm really not. . . .

11:23 P.M.
SUNDAY 08.13.06
Holy shit—you are in the zone, man! I wish I had known earlier. I could have called to keep you occupied, but I was away from 9:00 A.M. until now, over at the Smith Center for tech-in (a.k.a. Black Sunday). Though it definitely sounds like it was a pretty bleak Sunday in your neck of the woods too, eh? (ha) But kidding aside, I hope you found something better to do than call that dick. Brett is right. You cannot do that! Seriously. He will not respect you at all, not that he seems to respect you very much now. Or maybe ever . . .

Also, I think that was so cold of him to say that shit to Queng. I mean, you guys <u>are</u> boyfriends. What planet is he living on? Planet Henri, sounds like, where he is the king, queen, and country all rolled into one mean package. And don't worry, because I'm not gonna even say I told you so, because even though I had my reservations, I didn't really tell you so. Actually, I thought that Henri had proven himself slightly more worthy, if only due to the fact that he made you slightly more happy. But I guess I was wrong on that count. My bad. But your worse . . . literally and figuratively. Shit—maybe I shoulda been more forceful about my thoughts on Henri. But I guess you probably wouldn't have listened anyway. Though you do seem to listen to Brett—does she have more influence than me now when it comes to keeping you from doing stupid things?

Well, if it's any consolation, my life has not been a bed of roses today either. Though more in a professional way than a personal way, with our 16-hour tech marathon. We slogged through all the light cues and music cues and scene changes in the whole show, trying to make sure everything was working and people were standing in the right places. The reason they call it Black Sunday is that you are basically stuck in a dark theater all day. Also, after the 10-hour mark, everyone's mood was verging on the homicidal, making for a grim experience all around.

The thing that took the longest was setting the lighting cues, as you gotta stand on your spot forever while they focus the instruments and fix the gels. Missy (who did the commercial) said that on TV sets, they have people to do the standing around for you, called stand-ins. That way you get to sit in your trailer and eat M&Ms while someone else who is your same height and coloring stands on your mark, boring themselves to death. Hmmmmmm—maybe I'd be better off in that world. But Missy says you have to move to L.A. New York is far, but L.A. . . . that's like another country almost!

The only excitement today was that, for the first time, we had our full pit band in place. We've just been rehearsing with a pianist all this time, so to hear the orchestrations for the first time—it was awesome! The band's much bigger than anything they ever had for us at Einstein. And the musicians are a lot better, too, with very few wrong notes and tempos like a metronome's. They're all semi-pros like ourselves, from the SummerArts music division.

As for MK, I won't bore you with the good news on that front. I'm sure it's the last thing you want to hear today, given the current state of your affair. (ha) Sorry—I've gotta stop joking like that. It's a bad, entertainer reflex reaction I have. Sorry. Anyway, it was cool having MK around, because it did make

Black Sunday slightly more bearable. Her part actually doesn't come into the show until the end of the first act, so when we got to it around 5:00, I was downright loopy. It was sort of a relief to see her, as she kept cracking me up.

When MK and I were stuck in our lighting spots, she'd start making these faces at me that were hysterical, since the scene we were teching was all about our characters getting a divorce. In the second act, Ghaliyah shares a few scenes with MK, as they are both in love with me. (Not too shabby, eh?) And MK was having a good time with this, being playfully bitchy toward Ghaliyah while we said our lines over and over again for light and sound cues. She even started calling Ghaliyah "G" (like you do!), which Ghaliyah did not like at all. Not one bit. MK didn't get what the big-ass deal was, because she's been going by her initials since the sixth grade. But The Almighty Diva was not diggin' it at all and said as much, saying that calling her "G" made her sound like some rapper's ho. Can you believe she said this? And she was not joking! Seriously!!!

I swear, that woman has no sense of humor lately. Ghaliyah was constantly getting annoyed by our antics and said that both of us were highly unprofessional. Sound familiar? Meanwhile, MK could give a damn and was only interested in trying to lighten the mood and make our Black Sunday a Gray Sunday at least. (OK—I cannot take credit for that joke, as it was totally MK's!) She really is pretty funny, huh?

SHIT—I almost forgot the big drama of the day. And maybe this will make you feel less alone in your romantic troubles. Chaz and Albert had a huge falling-out during tech. Albert was sitting in the audience for a while, patiently providing moral support for Chaz. I thought this was above and beyond any relationship call to duty, as I would not wish something like that on my worst enemy, much less someone I had feelings for. But since the Mathletes have Sundays free, Albert agreed to do it when Chaz asked him. Then, during Chaz's big patter number in the first act, I saw that Albert had fallen asleep. At first, Chaz didn't notice this, as he was wrapped up in his big song and dance. But then Albert started snoring, and guess the hell what? Chaz did not think it was so cute. In fact, Chaz was furious at him! Then Albert got mad at Chaz, saying that Chaz was full of himself, and then he just up and left.

The Mathlete stormed out on the star! I never would have imagined <u>that</u> scene could happen.

So maybe it's something in the August air. Relationships are all upside down lately, it seems. Look at the evidence: I'm diggin' MK and Albert is hating Chaz and Henri is avoiding you because he has his head up his French ass. But don't worry your big, overanalyzing head about all this. I think it'll all pass. But it does seem like there is something wrong with the universe these days, since I have zero interest in Ghaliyah. Weird, huh? Shit, there I go using that word again. MK is gonna kill me! (ha)

HEY—if you're still feeling low, let me know if you wanna talk in real time, 'kay? Miss ya . . . you big romantic dope! C

07:08 A.M.
MONDAY 08.14.06
You know what? It's really not cute to call me a romantic dope during the biggest emotional panic of my whole entire life! Christ! Like, do I even have to <u>tell</u> you this? I am in a full-blown crisis mode here and you're making light of it?!?! That's sooooo not cool, Chuck. Not at all.

BTW—that joking reflex really has got to go! Though I may lean to the dramatic sometimes, you, my friend, lean to the anti-dramatic, avoiding any sort of uncomfortable conflict as much as possible because the real drama of life freaks your shit out! In fact, now that I think about it, maybe this is why you like being in plays and all. You dig all this stage stuff because it's drama that's all neat and tied up in a nice pretty package with good lighting and nice sound and, in the end, a totally predictable outcome. Well, wake up, Chuckles, because life is not like some stupid musical, okay?! Though I know you're always trying to find parallels between the stage world and the real world, they don't exist. Not at all! Those shows you do are like totally made up and completely fake and anyone seeking or trying to discern meaning in them might as well look for it in *FF3*!

Oh yeah—so did I mention I'm in a bad mood this morning? I mean, hell, it's barely past 7:00 A.M. and I'm actually awake, which should tell you something right there, as I never see this side of noon when I don't have to get my butt out of bed for schooling. Suffice it to say, I did not get much sleep last night. Probably a couple hours drifting off, if I was lucky. I had half an urge to break into that box of wine that's been sitting on top of the fridge since Val brought it home from her office party, but I thankfully recalled my De Lounge devolution and thought I'd probably be better off awake and sober. Also, by remaining alert and keenly aware of my ability to do senseless things, I'd be much less likely to start buzzin' or e-mailin' or IM-in' Henri like a madman. Which didn't happen, thank God. Somehow I've managed to keep my insanity to myself today and, as Martha might say, "That's a good thing."

So what is the secret to my self-centered self today? I've been occupying most of my time with the Weather Channel, completely wrapped up in their coverage of Hurricane David. Did you hear about this? It's been pounding the shoreline down in the Carolinas and now they're expecting it might come ashore near Virginia Beach tonight and head up the Chesapeake toward D.C. (It's a Category 4, which is just one step shy of a catastrophic killer!) They had some insane footage showing the hurricane tearing the roofs off peoples' beach houses and floating folks' SUVs into the drink. Now, I know this is gonna sound terrible and make me the worst person ever, but watching all this natural calamity has made me feel slightly . . . better. At least I've come to realize that my life is not being destroyed by an uncontrollable force of nature. I mean, I still have a house (even if it is in Wheaton) and Val has not been swept away by a storm surge (even if she can be bloody annoying when she wants me to spend my Sunday vacuuming the entire house). ARRGGHHHG!

Anyway, on balance my life may be a pain in the ass right now because of this Henri blackout, but at least it's not a real blackout, you know what I mean? Christ—enough with the weather-related analogies, as I—

Uh-oh. Henri just e-mailed me. Shit—what is he doing up so early?

Oh man . . . it says he wants to talk. Jesus Christ!!! I can't take this. Talks are never good things. Why do people even say this— "Can we talk?" It's really the most asinine construct in the English language. First off, "Can we talk?" is a moot question, since, of course, we all <u>can</u> talk. Yet even more annoying is that it's so vague while at the same time being underhandedly specific, too, by its inferred meaning. Frankly, I just wish that people would come out and say it, you know? What they really want to talk about, which, generally, is breaking up? Why don't they just say, "Oh yeah, hi, I just wanted to tell you what a loser you are and how this is never gonna work out and thanks for playing Fall-in-Love-with-an-Asshole"—*click!* But I guess if people actually said that shit, then the person wanting to "talk" would never in a million years get the other person to come over and listen to them. No friggin' way!

You know what? Fuck it. If Henri wants to "talk" to me, he's gotta get his French ass over <u>here</u>. Period. OMG—Brett would be so proud of me. I'd say you would too, but you hate Henri and are probably glee-ful I'm getting a "talking" to. That's okay, though. I forgive you for hating the one person in my life I've ever loved. Really . . . it's okay, Chuck. Don't stress about it. Seriously, though, I guess it's only fair as I certainly didn't care much for good ol' G, that hip-hop ho(!). Fortunately, you've been lucky enough to have MK take up some of your emotional slack, but with me, there is no slack-taker. Just Henri. So sue me for being a "romantic dope," but at least today I'm gonna be a hard-assed romantic dope. (WURDH!)

OK—just e-mailed him back. Waiting . . . waiting . . . waiting. You know what? The instantaneousness of the Internet can be incredibly annoying at times like this, because when you e-mail someone and know they can respond to you in milliseconds, a minute's wait for a goddamn return e-mail can seem like a friggin' eternity and—

Wow—guess the hell what? He's coming over. Huh . . . I told him to wait till after 9:00, when Val leaves for work. Shit—I've gotta wash my hair. And shave. I look awful!

01:10 P.M.
MONDAY 08.14.06

So yeah—we just had sex in my bed. A lot. So I guess this means we still like each other. A lot. Either that or we are both sex-crazed maniacs who are basically using one another to get our respective freaks on. OMG—it was crazy, this sex: fast and furious when it came on but then long and slow as it went on. And on. And on . . .

Rewinding here—Henri was supposed to come over for a talk. The Talk. And we did start off talking for a little bit. The first thing he told me, though, was that he'd talked to Brett yesterday, which was news to me. Get this—Brett told him I'd hooked up with some college guy at De Lounge and so Henri was wondering if she was just making that up because he found it somewhat hard to believe. Well, Christ, I wish she <u>had</u> made it up, because I not only found it hard to believe but embarrassing as hell! In fact, I got completely flustered when the subject was raised, turning stop-sign red, as it was just about the last thing I expected Henri to say. As for his face, it just went sorta slack, as he could tell by my reaction that Brett's tale wasn't made up.

I started trying to explain the whole thing and that I didn't have sex or anything with the De Lounge dude, but Henri said he didn't want to hear any more about it. I told him it happened because I was mad when he left and he said he was mad at me because I was being a pain over Queng's stupid "boyfriend" comment, which is why he had to leave. And then we were both silent for an eternity. Finally, I asked Henri what was up, and he didn't say anything. He just walked over to where I was sitting in the kitchen and started making out with me, and that was it. No more talking—just kissing and groping and undressing, and I was like, shit, who the fuck wants to talk anyway!

Henri's in the shower right now so maybe we'll have more of a chat when he gets out. At this point, I don't know if there's too much to talk about. Besides I feel all warm and sexy right now and actually I don't hate him at all. Well, there is that whole boyfriend issue but I—

OMG—what am I gonna do about these <u>sheets</u>?!

09:22 P.M.
MONDAY 08.14.06

I'm guessing you're in dress rehearsal hell, as it's only three days before opening night. But don't worry, I won't hold your blog absence against you because I'm not that kind of guy. (Uh, unlike you!) You've got a busy, glamorous life and I don't. Thus I will proceed to bore you with the details of our talk, which was The Talk after all. Let's see if I can make sense of this. . . .

Once Henri got out of the shower, I had to get this talking thing going myself by asking him what was going on. At first he was like, "I feel great after having taken a shower and maybe we should go get some lunch in Wheaton." So I had to clarify. "No—what is goin' on . . . with <u>us</u>?" He said nothing was going on and that got me very angry. Though he didn't mean it that way at all but it set me off. And so I talked—man . . . did I talk.

I wish I'd had a tape recorder, because if you had a chance to hear it, you would never again say I'm too reticent about my feelings and emotions. I basically told Henri that he means a lot to me—well, the world to me—and that this whole summer would have been shit if I hadn't met him, a statement that is completely true. I mean, hell, without Henri my blog entries would have been one or two sentences about the entropy of my existence surrounded by endless chapters about your adventures at UMD. Christ—you would have had to rename the whole thing "Tale of One Summer"!

Anyway, he listened to all this and seemed kinda surprised by what I was saying about how I'd never really felt like this before . . . ever. When it was Henri's turn to talk, he surprisingly played the old role of me and didn't have nearly as much to say. What he did say was not half bad . . . but it wasn't civil union bells ringing, either. He likes me . . . a lot. He said I am his *petit chou*, which translated means "little cabbage." I was like, wait a minute—I'm a round green thing made of wrinkley leaves, whaaaa? At first, I was sorta insulted, until he explained that, in France, it's a big term of endearment. Still, I'd much rather be his big sausage or something, which I told him and he laughed, saying my sausage was more than sufficient. (!!!!)

Anyway, regarding the Saturday night De Lounge debacle, he said that even though I am his favorite small vegetable, he still is not interested in having a boyfriend. (FYI—this is the half-bad part.) To which I countered, "What the hell are we if not boyfriends?" He said we were friends, maybe even best friends, but boyfriends sounded too serious and committed for him. He said he's never really been into having boyfriends or girlfriends or any friends for that matter. (Hmmmm— sound familiar?) Then he went off on his whole I-hate-people riff from the club, which on second hearing is such bullshit, if you ask me. He actually does like people, as he is Joe Social (like the day he landed in our laps). Still, I just listened and tried not to call him on this because I don't want us to be broken up, even if we were never quite together. Oh shit—does that make sense?

What am I going to do? I want Henri so badly and he doesn't want to be my boyfriend but wants me in some fashion (see "Multiple morning sex acts"). Shit—what does that mean? None of this adds up. I feel like I'm missing something, like this is an algebra equation that I keep doing and I'm sure it's positively right but the number at the end keeps coming out wrong. Well, after going in circles around and around this topic for a good hour and a half, Henri said he was tired of talking and wanted to go to Wheaton and get some food. I was like, "Do you want me to come too?" He said, "Sure, if you want." Which is better than "No" but still not as good as "Hells yeah!," which is what I was secretly hoping for.

So I went along with him anyway, and you know what? Even though I was somewhat bummed by our chat, a field trip to Nick's Diner and a round of the best ham sandwiches in the world took my mind off it. Maybe I think about all this stuff too much. Do you think this is the case? Henri sorta hinted at it toward the end of our chat when he was getting worn down by all my talking. He was like, "Why can't things just be what they are?" What the hell is that supposed to mean? That he's some New Age French philosopher or something? Why can't things just be what they are?! Hmm—I dunno . . . maybe because I want a boyfriend and it seems I have a new best friend, according to Henri. Of course, as you know very well, that position is sorta taken. So I don't see what the point is of having two best friends . . . it would just be a helluva lotta work, you know? All right—you know what? Henri's right. I am talking/thinking/writing too much about all this. Ugh. Am I crazy? Or just crazy for Henri? Please advise.

Your one and only best friend, H

PS—Can you reserve two tix for Henri and me for Saturday's show?

09:02 A.M.
TUESDAY 08.15.06
OK—let's make a deal. I'll make the tix reservation if Henri gets with the program and realizes he is your boyfriend. Otherwise, forget it.

All right—I'm sorta joking. But also sorta serious. That's really so not cool of him, you know? To get a gayer perspective on this, I talked a little bit with Chaz (don't get mad!) to see what he thought. He said Henri's side of the conversation sounds like double-talk for someone who has problems getting close to other people. Intimacy issues, he called it. So maybe that's what's up. I mean, it's very very obvious to me (and Chaz) that he likes you. The guy got instantly jealous when he found out you'd made out with that MoCo dude. Chaz said that, if he was you, he would've worked _that_ for all it's worth!

You know, there was one thing I was thinking about that might be helpful with all this. It was that thing I told you earlier in the summer, from our drama teacher. Remember—"Characters are what they do and not what they say." If you apply that to Henri, the situation looks a little better, because you guys are certainly doing it. And then some. On top of that, Henri still wants to hang out with you in general, even when you're not having sex. So Henri's talk doesn't really jibe with his actions and is maybe just some lame defense, a last line of resistance against your charms. (ha)

So, considering all that, maybe you should just relax, you know? Try to keep your cool about this Henri stuff. I know that might be hard for you today, but it might be for the best. Just try to remain calm, make no sudden movements, and see how things play out. Maybe Henri's a big thing. Maybe he's a summer thing. Who knows? Who can tell after a few weeks?

If I've learned anything recently it's that you just have to see what happens in the real world and not live in some romantic fantasy world in your head. That was my mistake with the whole Ghaliyah thing, you know? It was like I'd imagined this play in my mind where we were both in love with each other and we started having this amazing love affair. Of course, none of this ever happened, and now it looks like just the opposite has occurred: I'm into someone else entirely.

So try not to make any grand statements about your whole romantical situation and just take things for what they are. I mean, it sorta sounds to me like you're having a lot of fun lately—going to clubs, seeing dumb movies, and, oh yeah, having a ridiculous amount of sex. And sure, there's been some drama, too. But nothing tragic so far. Right? Hello? Are you there? Are you listening to the voice of reason? I hope so, because you have got a sweet life right now. No responsibilities, no school, no musical in which you are the lead. So please—ENJOY IT!

WEATHER BULLETIN—Chaz just told me that hurricane you mentioned is apparently heading our way. It's supposed to hit the D.C. area late Tuesday night and maybe last through Thursday. In fact, they might have to postpone some of the show dates, which would totally suck. I'll let you know for sure, but hopefully it'll all blow over before the weekend. See you soon!

08:42 P.M.
TUESDAY 08.15.06

So, after a nice night's sleep (finally!), I woke up this morning and made an interesting decision: I took a Henri-hiatus today. Believe me, it was not easy. I figured it might be a good idea after all the talking and sexing of yesterday. (Hell—the last seven days.) Now, don't get too crazy and think I actually took your counsel either. It just felt like it's been nonstop Henri since we drove out to visit you last Tuesday. OMG—I can't believe that was only a week ago—it feels like it's been a month!

To help manage my withdrawal symptoms, I called up Brett, and she was more than game for some Wheaton action, as long as we stayed within the safe confines of the mall. Not that she hasn't warmed up somewhat to Marrakesh and downtown W-town in general, but she wanted to do some shopping and it wasn't for comix or porn. So Brett and I met up at the food court around noon and had some sandwiches at Arby's while she filled me in a bit more on her heart-to-heart with Henri Sunday afternoon. Apparently, he'd left his weed in Jerry's car and was calling her to see about getting it back. Initially, Brett said she was pretty cool to him on the phone, as he wasn't saying a word about me, almost acting like nothing unusual had happened. (Can you believe it?!) Then Henri asked her if we had all had a decent time after he left De Lounge, to which Brett offered up the statement that I certainly did. This piqued the Frenchman's curiosity, and so she told him about Tyvor, leaving out the messier and less attractive details (i.e., her shoving him off me!). So she basically made Henri jealous of a situation that didn't even warrant it! I told Brett she should be a writer or maybe a diplomat, with her deft conversational skills, and Brett just laughed and said she'd rather just be a professional gossip columnist. OMG—I could totally see her doing that!

Anyway, hearing the story behind this story made me feel that maybe Henri's sexual interest in me on Monday was only due to the fact that he thought someone else was into me. Brett said that was good news, but I don't know . . . I have to say it sorta bummed me out. I don't want to have his interest in me be based on half-truths and semi-invented gossip. I want him to like <u>me</u>. Period. But Brett says this is just part of "the game," and that is how romance works in the real world. You've gotta play "the game." Ugh. Whether she's right or wrong (and I'm suspecting it's a little of both, actually), it depressed me nonetheless. It just seems like this whole Henri thing is becoming a bit of a mess now . . . one that I have no idea how to get myself out of.

After lunch, Brett and I took a walk around Wheaton Plaza. They have really made huge progress . . . it looks totally different, which made me sorta miss the crappy old Wheaton Plaza. Half the fun of hanging out there was complaining about what a dump the place was. But now it's all sleek and almost fancy. (They've even shut down the Dollar Store!) Our first stop was Target, and Brett bought a baby-doll tee that read BUY ME THINGS! Then we headed over to Hecht's (jewelry) and Aldo (shoes). I wondered how the hell was she able to afford all this stuff? Jerry had given her his credit card (!?), so I asked her how she managed that? "Playing the game." God—I thought that was sorta depressing. Maybe she was sorta kidding about this, but I doubt it.

Around 4:00, we swung by the Loews to see if there were any good bargain matinees playing, but there wasn't anything of interest, really. Then I noticed the place where we had first met Henri and my heart sorta sank on seeing this. You'd think it'd be the opposite, really. But I was already kinda bummed from seeing how much the mall was changing, as well as Brett's game-based shopping, that this sorta capped my depression. It was weird to see this totally innocuous looking bench in front of a big, anonymous planter and realize that this was the exact spot where my life had changed. Hell—this is where my life was going along fine and then took this huge, screeching right turn. Seeing that spot again, it just seemed so sorta plain and undramatic. Hey—maybe I should petition the new owners of Westfield Shopping Town to affix a plaque saying something to the effect that, "On July 7 in the year of our Lord 2006, this is the place where Hal Schaeffer was sitting on his bored summer ass when he collided with Parkourist Henri Broussard, thus causing his life to take a turn for the worst." Or was it "the best"? Or will it <u>be</u> best? I don't know . . . today it's kinda hard to say, and I guess that's what was making me feel so damn low.

When I got home, I was drained from the day with Brett. Val was home for once, actually, and making a real dinner. She asked me what was going on and I told her about my day at the mall, but Val was looking for a deeper answer. She said I seemed kinda down. I said I was just hungry and left it at that. When we sat down to eat, she said Henri had called a couple times that afternoon, and this would have gotten me incredibly excited and spastic and racing to the phone to return the call immediately. But I was like, oh great, and said I'd call him later. Which I still haven't done . . .

You know, I thought my Henri-free day would make me happier. However, I think it had the opposite effect and made me more depressed. (Ugh, like that was even possible!) Val said that, with the hurricane approaching, the air pressure was really high, which can cause fatigue. And, you know what, it did feel strangely heavy out today. But it's more than the weather. It's Henri and the fact that I want to call him but, at the same time, don't want to call him if it's gonna make me all happy until I hang up, which will then send me into a screaming, roller-coaster-size drop of feelings that will make me even more depressed in the end.

I think I'll just go to bed early and deal with him in the A.M. It's not like he's going anywhere, that's for sure. Signing off—Hal

08:52 A.M.
WEDNESDAY 08.16.06

Man, you sound awful. And not your usual fake-yet-excitable awful where you just complain about everyone and everything till you're blue in the face and I'm sick of hearing about it all. No, this sounds like a genuine sort of awful. The kind I don't think I've seen since, well, since the day before you met Henri.

But you know what, maybe it is the weather. Everyone here is cranky and irritable and full of piss and vinegar, as my granddad used to say. And to top it off, it just started pouring here, which I guess means the hurricane's arrived a little earlier than expected. Not that it should matter to us, as we'll be indoors most of today, doing not one but two full-dress run-throughs of the show. Opening night is tomorrow and—surprise, surprise—no one is ready.

In other bad news, you might want to forget about that advice Chaz offered. It looks like Casanova broke up with lil' Albert late last night. It was another high drama incident too. They were hanging and sharing the iPod again when suddenly Chaz started flipping out. Apparently, Albert had a few Eminem songs in the mix and Chaz was beyond offended. Albert didn't get what the big deal was, but Chaz said Eminem was a homophobe and a fag basher. Albert was like, "uh, he's a musician and a songwriter," but Chaz was not hearing this. He just got enraged in a way I'd never seen him get before and basically threw Albert out of our room. All because of some songs on his iPod?!

I thought Chaz was overreacting at first. But once Albert was gone, Chaz went on and on about how Eminen uses "incendiary language" (i.e., "faggot") to put down gays. And I remember hearing something about this on MTV, but I didn't really think it was a big deal, more like a made-for-MTV controversy. Of course, that made Chaz even angrier, saying, "Of course YOU didn't think it was a big deal, because no one yelled those words at YOU while running for your life down North Charles Street." Apparently, some guys in downtown Baltimore tried to jump Chaz last fall but he got away from them. And this is why he got so angry at Albert over Eminem, because the topic of fag bashing hit close to home. Holy shit—pun totally NOT intended. Seriously!

Anyway, after Chaz had calmed down a bit, I told him that maybe he should've clued Albert in on what happened instead of ripping him a new one. But Chaz was having none of this and just kept going off on Albert and people in general, saying stuff like, "You think you know someone and then they pull something like THAT." But how well can you really get to know someone in six weeks. (Or four, in the case of him and Albert.) After all, consider you and me. I mean, we've known each other almost a decade, and I am still constantly surprised by the things I find out about you. You know . . . your ever-growing freakiness. And I'm not even talking about the gay thing. (ha)

You know what? It's amazing that we haven't stopped being friends at all given our huge differences of opinion, demeanor, outlook, etc. I think part of that is because we listen to each other as opposed to throwing each other out of the room when something goes wrong. But, I guess it's also the tolerance we have for our differences and the way we're equally amused by them that has probably kept our friendship tight all this time. And that's pretty cool, huh? ☺

As for me and my romance, MK is good. Haven't had any sleepovers recently, as we're all just exhausted by the final days before the show. But we do hang out a lot at rehearsal. Oh—one cool thing lately is that MK gives the most amazing back rubs. In fact, her whole posse is like back-rub central. Whenever we have a break, they've taken to servicing all the sore backs in the show (even some of the musicians). Last night, during intermission, they formed this circle of back rubbing in the lobby that MK started calling a "borgy," because of all the moans of pleasure emanating from it. LOL!

OK—off to b-fast. And to buy an umbrella. Later!

11:30 A.M.
WEDNESDAY 08.16.06
Bummer about Chaz and Albert. But then again, who were they kidding, right? Let's face it—summer romance never lasts. Just look at *Grease*. Though I guess things got a little better for Olivia Newton-John after she whored herself up. Christ—that movie has a terrible moral, now that I think about it. So, you want the one you want? Then you better tart your shit up, yo, and then and only then will that man WANT you! How depressing. Why did we watch that movie over and over when we were nine? Oh—I remember—John Travolta was H-O-T! And you couldn't get enough of those goddamn show tunes. What a pair we were . . .

As for Henri and me, what can I say. It's friggin' crazy! The minute I stopped caring about the whole thing is when he suddenly started acting like I'd died or something and he was calling/e-mailing/IM-ing me like no tomorrow. Can you believe it? Brett said it was totally predictable, but I think she just says stuff like that when it fits her skewed worldview. Just this morning, he's e-mailed me a couple times and called me once (which I let the machine get). It's not that I don't want to talk to him. Hell—I <u>do</u> want to talk to him, but you know what? I actually think I got something out of Chaz's warped advice: I've decided I'm gonna make him sweat it a little.

OK—I'm gonna give him a call now. It's almost noon. Man, it is pouring!

09:38 P.M.
WEDNESDAY 08.16.06
Hi. Actually, more like, "High." We've been having some of Henri's sweet sweets. Yeah, I know, you don't even have to tell me: bad, bad, bad. I probably need to be spanked. But H stopped by this afternoon and brought some of his brownies to celebrate the hurricane, and he was so excited to see me and give me some that to say no would have been worse than bad. Isn't that worst? Who the hell knows. I am still a bit spacey.

Henri is soooo sweet, though. Especially when he makes me brownies. He made them himself, and no mix either. Should I believe him? Should I believe anything he says? Should I stop having sex with him? Should I stop asking myself rhetorical questions on a computer that can't speak?

Where are you today? Oh—your show. I hope it is getting all showy and ready to, you know, show. Is that why they call it a show? Hmmmm. Val's not home because it's too dangerous to drive and she's staying at her friends' in Rosslyn till the worst part of the hurricane passes over. They're having a hurricane party, so she's having fun anyway. Drink, mom, drink!!! So she'll be back tomorrow, then Henri will have to—hold on . . .

Jourbon, c'est Henri. Je suis complètement blasté en ce moment, mais Hal m'a indiqué pour t'écrire quelque chose que tu ne pourrais pas comprendre. Il croit que ce sera drôle. Je crois que ce sera stupide de chez stupide. Mais il dit que c'est la revanche pour l'écriture de Chaz ici le mois dernier. Je n'ai aucune idée ce qu'il me voudrait faire. Qu'est-ce que c'est un Chaz? Je te verrai ce week-end au théâtre. Baisers, Henri.

Wait a minute—I may not speak French, but did he just sign this "Love, Henri"? Or "Kisses"?

OK—so now Henri says he loves a lot of people. That's news! I thought he was loveless. Heartless, maybe. Or at least friendless. I'm trying to remind him of this, but he seems to have forgotten all of The Talk from . . . when was that? Monday? That seems like a whole year ago! But maybe that's the pot talking or typing. LOL The pot typing. I just had this image of a *pétard* dancing around on my keyboard, plucking out a little love letter to someone. Maybe to Henri. I can't write love letters. That would be waaaaaaay too embarrassing.

So we ate Henri's brownies today. We had a bunch and then ran outside while it was hurricane-ing and windy, and I actually got knocked over by a big gust. I got totally muddy, but Henri cleaned me off. (You can use your imagination on that one!) I saw on the news tonight that they think we might get tornadoes in the area. Like in *The Wizard of Oz*. Henri says there's some CD you can watch . . . I mean play . . . that follows the movie, and it's like the soundtrack or something. An old band from the '70s, Pink someone . . . but not <u>my</u> Pink. Have you ever heard of this?

Now the news says there is a tornado warning in effect. I told Henri he is staying here, but his mom wants him to come home. There's no place like home. LOL! But it's too dangerous out. Besides, I'm not done having sex with him. Is he done with me? We'll find out shortly. Oh yeah—and one last thing. Hurricanes are much more fun when spent with a hot French dude. Bye-bye!

02:17 A.M.
THURSDAY 08.17.06

That entry is totally freaking me out. I would be pretty angry with you for fucking around with Henri (again), for getting high (AGAIN!), for running around
in a killer hurricane (WHAT?!), and so on, but I can't right now. Why? Well,
I've had the most scary/extraordinary day. And that alone is freaking my shit
out enough. So much so that I cannot sleep tonight. At all. I'm sorry that I can't
even deal with all your madness right now. I mean, I can't even understand half
of it—in French? Give me a break, dude!

So about those tornado warnings. Well, they were not just warnings over here.
There were real, bona fide tornadoes! Seriously. Two of them, actually: one that
touched down on campus near Byrd Stadium and a second one that hit just on
the other side of the Beltway. We were on our intermission break during our
final dress when the first one hit around 7:30. I was hanging out in the lobby
with MK and her gang when everything got really dark, which was weird, as it
was still about an hour before sunset. Then we heard this huge noise, like a
freight train, and could see this dark funnel just start dipping down toward the
parking lot behind Byrd. It was totally surreal!

You could see stuff like benches and trashcans flying straight up into the air.
Meanwhile, we were watching all this through the big wraparound window in
the lobby. I was thinking it might not be such a great place to stand during a
big, windy tornado, and so I suggested that everyone head back into the theater. And just as we started filing back into the auditorium, something went flying into the glass and the whole center panel shattered. Instantly, all the girls
started screaming and all kinds of trash started blowing into the lobby and the
noise level about tripled.

Once everyone hustled back into the theater, the house lights went out and all
the girls screamed again. Girls screaming in a crisis is the most useless thing
in the world. All it does is freak everyone out and doesn't do a thing to help the
situation! Anyway, after what seemed like forever but was really only a few
minutes, the wind and the roaring died down and it was all over. Fortunately,
no one was hurt and the building really wasn't seriously damaged, other than
the smashed lobby window. Over by Byrd, though, the twister had picked up a

few cars and relocated them to the woods behind the athletic center. Thankfully, no one was injured, as there weren't too many people around UMD on a Wednesday afternoon in August. But still, it was quite a scare.

The girls, especially MK, were pretty shaken up. MK could not stop shaking after it was all over, so I kept holding her tight and telling her it was okay and eventually she calmed down. Since we didn't have any power and/or lights, Ryan told us that we'd have to finish the dress rehearsal Thursday afternoon, right before we open. Not the ideal way to run a show, but when nature intervenes, what can you do. . . .

So, after all this excitement ended, they called a shuttle bus for us (because it was still pretty stormy out) and drove us back to St. Ann's. On the short drive over, MK started panicking again thinking there was gonna be another twister, and I had to hold her all the way back. At first it was annoying, but when I saw she was truly losing it, I sorta felt good that I was maybe helping her keep it together.

Back in the dorm, the power was still out, so the RA gave us all candles. MK said she was too scared to go to her room and asked if she could hang in ours. I said it was no problem, so we headed up with Chaz and played a candlelit game of Cranium to try and take our minds off the weather. Midway through the game, little Albert showed up, and when he saw Chaz, the kid started bawling, because he'd heard a rumor that the tornado had made a direct hit on the theater. So guess what? Yeah, Albert and Chaz pretty much made up, which was cute and I guess sorta inevitable. That fight was so retarded anyway.

Around 11:00, we all decided to hit the hay: Albert and Chaz and MK and me. Quite the freaky foursome, huh? And no—it was not an orgy! In fact, Albert and Chaz went right to sleep, as indicated by Albert's now infamous snore. MK was not as tired and still pretty freaked by the storm. Every time some rain hit the window or a gust of wind howled, she'd be freaking again thinking another twister was on the way. So I just started holding her tighter and then decided that maybe if we made out it would distract her. ☺ So we went at it for a while, getting our shirts off too, and then, you won't believe this, but she grabbed my dick! Seriously. It was certainly making its presence known, but she pulled it right onto center stage. (ha) And joking, like I do, I said maybe if we had sex she would <u>completely</u> forget about the storm. And she goes, not joking, "Maybe you're right."

So I thought I'd totally scored! However, I only partially scored. I mean, someone had an orgasm, so I guess we had sex by good old Brett's definition. But we didn't really have all-the-way sex. Basically, MK jerked me off. Not that she really had to work that hard at it. Damn—it was so much easier having another person do it than me doing it myself. But what was much better than going solo is that, as it was going on, we were kissing and I was grabbing her tits, and when all that is going on at the same time . . . wow! The whole thing was overwhelming, you know? What am I saying . . . of course you do. You are such the sex-pert lately!

Now, I know I made fun of you and your "accident" with Henri at the bar, but I can't blame you. Because when it all feels that good, it's pretty hard to restrain yourself, you know what I'm saying? And I couldn't, so now I've got that same issue with the sheets too. Whoops. All right—well, I don't know what else to say about all this other than I'm pretty psyched about the sex. Almost too psyched. It's nearly 3:00 A.M. and I still don't feel tired and I've got a show to put on. I mean, if dealing with <u>that</u> weren't overwhelming enough . . . now adding sex to the mix is like, shit! I feel like my brain has overloaded and will not be able to process all this good stuff happening at once. But I really do need to sleep, otherwise my body won't be able to process anything, sexually or musically.

I'll try to drop you a line tomorrow, after opening night. As long as we have power. They had already started cleaning up the glass in the lobby when we were heading back to the dorm earlier tonight. The show must go on, as they say. ☺ (Who are the "they" in "they say" anyway?) So give me the old break-a-leg vibe tomorrow around 7:30 P.M. C

PS—Despite my better judgment, I have two tix for you and that French dude for Saturday.

10:06 A.M.
THURSDAY 08.17.06

Wow—so you finally did the deed. I gotta tell you, I was starting to think it wasn't gonna happen. I thought theater chicks were maybe just not so easy to get with. But I guess you proved that theory wrong, along with a little help from Mother Nature.

I read in the paper this morning about those tornadoes. Man, that must have been severely intense! They said the one that hit UMD was an F2 and the one that hit Beltsville was much stronger, an F3, with winds approaching 150 mph. It even tore the roof off the Home Depot on Route 1! So you guys were very lucky you got the weaker one. But still, I can't imagine how bizarre that must have been, to see a real, live twister. You know how I was saying before that your life is like a big play? Well, yesterday sounds like it was a big disaster movie/porno flick all wrapped up into one! A scary/sexy double feature! To which I can only say—that sounds <u>awesome</u>!!!

As for my night in the storm, Henri ended up sleeping over, but it was not as much fun as I thought it was gonna be. He was a bit cranky as the day turned into night and the effects of the brownies wore off. Once we got into bed, he was also not so cuddly, either, which was odd. He kept telling me I was smothering him and that there was a whole other section of the bed that I could use, even though there wasn't. I mean, it's a single bed and a little bit small, but still, we could both fit on it if we were sleeping somewhat together. Unfortunately, Henri seemed to want to sleep apart for some reason. I don't know why. I've given up trying to figure out his mood swings. On Monday he couldn't keep his hands out of my pants and then on Wednesday he was getting all freaked out if I even touched him. I think you and Chaz have a point on that intimacy thing. It's almost like the sex part is fine by him, but the more mundane stuff, like sleeping in the same bed together, can be a pain. Unless, that is, we're both baked or have passed out or something.

But it gets even more confusing. After all that debate and drama about sleeping together, we're in the bathroom this morning and Henri kept trying to pull my underwear down, which was damn annoying. I hadn't slept too well and was grumpy, and you'd think Henri going for my business would make me less grumpy, but it was just goddamn maddening, you know? He can't stand having my hand draped on his shoulder while we sleep but he will suck my dick at the drop of a hat? I don't know what to make of this. Again, mathematically, I'm having trouble adding this up. . . .

Henri left here about an hour ago, and even though I miss him already, I also really don't want to hang out with him any more today. (Maybe tonight . . . we'll see.) Henri wants to hang out today, actually. Even though it's still pouring out, he wants to take the Metro down to the airport and see what the river looks like. I said I'd call him later about this, but right now, I'd really rather just sit at home and watch TV and try to forget about him for a little while. Have a Henri-free afternoon. Maybe I'll see if Brett wants to see a movie. . . .

Hey—I'm sorry about that stoned entry from yesterday. God—when I'm stoned I sound like a friggin' moron! Please—when you get back next week, remind me as much as possible how stupid I am when I'm baked on brownies. I really don't want to do that anymore. The only reason I partook is because Henri was so damn forceful about it, and I knew that, if we got stoned, it would lead to some sort of sex. (Which it did: post-running-around-in-the-hurricane.) But I don't want "some sort of sex" anymore. I want real sex, you know . . . like you had with MK. That really sounded hot! Getting it on where both parties are clear-headed and can look each other in the eye and have intense feelings that they aren't scared of.

I mean, sex with Henri has certainly been fun, that's for sure. All right, and perhaps semi-mind-blowing a few times! But I've realized what that post-coital crying thing is about. (Which still happens every time, BTW . . .) I think Dr. Drew was right about the incongruity factor. With Henri, I'm feeling that I really love him and suspect that maybe he doesn't really care about me all that much. He likes me, sure, but maybe that's about it. And even though the sex is great and hot and mechanically happenin', in the end it leaves me feeling kinda sad, because to him we're just friends with benefits, as opposed to something more serious.

Now, I know you and Brett and Chaz are all like, he <u>does</u> like you. Yeah—I guess he does in his own fucked-up way. But I think I want someone who likes me in a less fucked-up way, you know? Hey—does MK have a big, gay brother with a hot ass? OMG—that would be perfect! You know, Queng was saying there's some big gay bar up in Frederick with a huge dance floor where guys go two-stepping. That would be a riot! Maybe we can make Frederick our first road trip when I get my license (hopefully) next month. Only if MK has cute gay siblings . . . or knows a few at her school who would go dancing with me.

Christ—I can't believe it's still friggin' raining! It's been like almost two days now! When is all this hurricane-ing gonna stop?! I just checked weather.com and they said it should be over this afternoon, but frankly, I don't believe them. Anyway, I hope your show doesn't get affected— not that I'm too concerned about it. I know you'll be brilliant anyway. As for Saturday, thanks for the tickets, though I could have done without the judgment call. (Not that that's news to you.) Anyway, can't wait to see the show. Oh yeah—and you. Later!

04:47 P.M.
THURSDAY 08.17.06
So guess who keeps calling me on my Henri-free afternoon? (Well, it ain't the pope, that's for sure!) Yes, it's true. The French One keeps pestering me about going down to the river to see it flooding or something. I don't get what the big deal is, but Henri insists we'll see all sorts of freaky things floating downstream, like people's houses and cars and mobile homes. But I don't know how he thinks he's getting down there, as Channel 9 said that Metro has stopped service on the Blue Line to the airport due to some track flooding. When I informed Henri of this fact, he told me we could ride our bikes down. So, yeah—he must be totally high again, because that would be physically impossible as it is

still raining buckets! I mean, really . . . biking in the middle of a hurricane?! I don't know what he is thinking because, of course, he's not thinking. He's just friggin' toasted again. Henri doesn't know this, but I can soooooo tell when he's stoned, because his voice gets higher and sounds almost girlish, sped up even, in the way he talks and—

Someone's at the door. Shit—it's probably Henri.

05:11 P.M.
THURSDAY 08.17.06

OMG—you are not gonna believe this! Or maybe you will, given Henri's disposition toward danger. So it was Henri at the door—with his mom's Audi! Yeah, that's right. Henri, who is not only without a license but also without any instruction in the finer art of driver's education, drove his mom's car over here in a hurricane with the intent of having me join in unlicensed driving from here all the way down to Virginia. Now, I know that I already did this to come visit you last week, but a) I was maybe a little more in love with Henri at that time and susceptible to collusion and b) going 10 miles out University Boulevard is a little different from driving through downtown Washington and over to Virginia! If I got caught driving without a license in Virginia I'd probably be executed because they don't fool around with criminals.

Well, I did not take Henri up on his offer. Not only was it incredibly dangerous and stupid, but there was also the severely annoying fact that he thought he could use his sexual charms to convince me to actually do something that dumb. I mean, he basically took for granted the fact that he could get me to do this insane thing, and that was pretty damn insulting, don't you think? I mean, come on! I'm not that spineless, really—I know I may seem that way sometimes, but really, I'm not. And especially when it comes to something as dumbassed as this idea. I mean, there is a full-blown hurricane going on! One that is spawning tornadoes!!! What is his brain damage?

Finally, I told him he should just turn around, drive back home, and call Domino's to deal with his munchies. I just hope he took my advice. I think my rejection really bummed him out. He was almost mopey, with an expression not unlike one of my own on a bad day (i.e., every day lately). But I'm sure he'll probably forget how mad he is at me in a few hours, like he always does. The question is, will I forget how mad I am at him? I don't know. . . .

06:42 P.M.
THURSDAY 08.17.06
I just called Henri's house to see if he was home and his mom answered and started yelling at me about her missing Audi. I just hung up as quick as I could. Goddammit—he didn't go home! What a total DICKHEAD!!!

09:11 P.M.
THURSDAY 08.17.06
Are you back from your show yet? Can you call me at home ASAP when you get this? I'm sorta losing it right now, because the police just left. They came over here with Mrs. Broussard, who was hysterical, claiming I had taken her car because she knew I could drive. When I told the police what had really happened, how Henri
wanted to go to Virginia and all, his mother got even more hysterical, but in French. OMG—I should have gone with him, even though it was illegal. Or I should have at least driven him back home. Or taken the keys. I hope he's okay. I mean I was mad at him but I didn't want anything to happen to him. This is bad, could be bad, even awful . . .

10:52 P.M.
THURSDAY 08.17.06
Jesus Christ—how long is your show? Call me! They still haven't found him. . . .

08:23 A.M.
FRIDAY 08.18.06
Hey—thought I'd check in again and see if there's any news yet. And see if you're feeling better this A.M. Didn't I tell you that I couldn't do any more of these sobbing phone conversations? Seriously, though, I know you were upset

last night, but I'm sure Henri's fine and is probably just hanging out at some coffee shop downtown making everyone panic because he can. He certainly does like to be the center of attention, you know?

Bottom line—no matter what happens, you can't feel guilty about it. Not at all. You are not Henri's parent or guardian or bodyguard. Even if you were his actual boyfriend, you're still not responsible for his not having common sense. Henri is old enough to know better, and you should be old enough to know that some people will never know better. And there's not too much you can do about idiots like that. I don't mean to be harsh on him, but even you have to admit that what he did was beyond stupid.

Anyway, I've gotta get to our postmortem. We have a lot to go over, since opening night was, well, a little rough to say the least. But we made it through and had the house about three-quarters filled, despite our broken lobby window. Get this: Someone who hadn't heard the news actually thought the shattered glass was some sorta modern art piece. Isn't that a riot? OK—if that doesn't make you laugh, then you're a goner.

Miss ya . . . Love, C

12:37 P.M.
FRIDAY 08.18.06
Well, at last there has been news of Henri. Not all of it great, but news nonetheless.

When I got up at 7:00 this morning, after another night of not sleeping, I gave the police a call to see what was happening, and they hadn't found anything. I suggested they check out the Wilson Bridge construction site, and, sure enough, a couple hours later they discovered a very wet and muddy Henri sleeping soundly on the scaffolding abutting the bridge deck. After he left my house, he drove all the way to Virginia, headed to the construction site, and parked the car by the river. After getting stoned, he then climbed up to the road deck, and sat there in the middle of the storm, tripping as he watched the raging waters of the Potomac rise up and over the bank. Unfortunately, he

didn't notice that the water had crept up to where he'd parked the Audi, and poor Mrs. Broussard's car was swept downstream. Stranded, with the Potomac River raging on all sides, he climbed down to a part of the bridge that was less exposed and took a nice, long nap, which ended abruptly when the state police woke him up around 9:00 A.M.

Though he'd broken countless laws, Henri was covered under diplomatic immunity and didn't get charged with anything. (I guess this partially explains why he was so bold about his pot smoking here, there, and just about everywhere.) There is the cost of replacing the car, but, like their house in Rock Creek, it was the property of the French government, and I guess they can afford a new Audi. Still, despite the material and criminal infractions, it's not like Henri's getting off scot-free. Knowing his oh-so-disagreeable mother, I'm sure he's in some serious shit with her and will probably not be let out of the house till he's 18. Still, I don't really know what's up, as I haven't heard from or seen Henri since they found him this morning. I heard they took him into the police station for a while but he was released to his mom around 11:00, so I'm assuming he's at home. But I'm not racing to the phone to call him.

Frankly, I am so friggin' mad at Henri right now and, I have to say, even madder at myself. I know it's not my fault that he lost his mom's car and slept on an unfinished bridge in the middle of a hurricane. But it is my fault that I know him and that he's become this huge part of my life in the last two months. I mean, Christ—what the hell was I thinking? Why didn't I just stop the whole train wreck before it left the station? I guess I just wanted to see what was going to happen. I mean, meeting a guy who was so bloody hot who (gasp) actually liked me?! Nothing like that had ever happened to me before, and, given that there was not too much else on the schedule this summer, it seemed like something to do. But the problem I guess, was that I totally fell in love with him. And in the end, I don't think he fell in love with anything other than himself and his weed. I don't know, maybe that's a bit harsh. But it's certainly how I feel today. . . .

Well, thanks again for listening to me lose my shit over the phone last night. Again. God—who knew I'd end up being such a crybaby, huh? You know what? Maybe I _am_ just as emotional as you are after all, but have merely done a much more thorough job of hiding it all these years. It certainly seems like it lately, as the floodgates have opened. I don't know, this whole Henri thing . . . it's all a little overwhelming to me. I'm just glad that I have someone I can talk to in these mortifying moments who is not gonna hold it against me. Or at least hold it against me in public. I'm sure I'll never hear the end of it privately, but that's okay. Hell—you'll never hear the end of what a fool you were for Ghaliyah. What is up with her these days, anyway? She seems to have dropped off the face of Planet College Park.

So, with Henri under house arrest, it looks like Val will be my date for the show tomorrow. She's excited about the whole thing, of course, as she's probably a bigger fan of yours than I am, if that's possible. Oh—FYI—I still haven't given her the whole score on Henri, so please don't get too chatty with her on the subject. She just thinks he's a friend . . . albeit a pretty stupid one at this point. But, like me, she was pretty charmed by him at first. How can you not be? That's one of the most depressing things about the whole Henri thing: He is such a charming guy, but he uses those powers for evil, not for good, you know? Well, maybe this whole incident will wake him up or something and make him switch sides. Who knows . . .

11:22 P.M.
FRIDAY 08.18.06
Well, I'm glad to hear that all's well that ends semi-well, as the old Bard said and I just mangled. I know you didn't believe me, but I was sure all along this wasn't gonna be some tragedy. Henri is a smart guy, despite himself. And he could be a decent guy, you know, if he got his act together. After all, someone who sorta looks like me can't be half bad, right? ☺

It's funny you mentioned Ghaliyah, because I have some weird news on that front. At the top of the show, while Ghaliyah and I were waiting in the wings for our entrance, we were listening to the overture and getting totally psyched

for what was going to be our first real show (as Thursday's felt more like a preview). I was feeling my typically goofy self, so I took Ghaliyah's hand and we started couples-dancing to the overture. It was pretty silly stuff, doing dance moves that were more Carol-and-Bob than Janet-and-Justin. Anyway, MK was hanging out on the other side of the stage and saw this and totally got the wrong idea. She thought Ghaliyah and I were suddenly getting flirtatious. Of course, the truth is, we were actually getting along as friends for the first time this summer, which is pretty ironic, given what happened later.

So the first act went great (finally), giving me a total performance high! Then, during intermission, MK came up and totally popped my bubble, telling me what a terrible person I was to be two-timing her. Fortunately, Ghaliyah heard this in the women's dressing room (as MK was being so loud!) and came out to intervene on my behalf. Ghaliyah laughed when MK asked if there was anything between us. That sorta stung, even though any other response would've sent MK through the fly space. But I guess my fantasies of Ghaliyah and me were still there somewhat, until that moment pretty much blew them away. Talk about good news/bad news!

Needless to say, the second act was not so hot, because of all this unnecessary drama. And not just on my count. There were some seriously missed cues, dropped lines, and misplaced scenery, as everyone was weirdly off their game. Well, just before the final scene, when we go up to the roof for that big song I told you about before, Ghaliyah has to enter through this trapdoor in the stage floor that makes it look like she's coming up to the roof. Well, she completely tripped on her way up the steps to the trapdoor and smashed her knee on the stage. Somehow she was able to ignore the pain and do the whole number, but when we got backstage afterward she basically collapsed as she couldn't put any more weight on it. She couldn't even come out for the curtain call! You know it's serious when a diva passes up that opportunity, right?

After the show, Ryan went with her over to the campus infirmary, and we haven't heard anything since. I'm sure with some ice and Ace bandages it'll be fine. At least I hope so. Anyway, I can't wait for you to come see the show tomorrow . . . and see her, too. Even though it didn't quite pan out with me and G, I still think she is a super talent. And MK's not too bad herself,

either! ☺ Holy shit—DO NOT tell her I said that or I'm DEAD MEAT! SERIOUSLY!!!

See you and Val tomorrow . . . can't wait! C

03:20 P.M.
SATURDAY 08.19.06

Hey—so I finally talked to Henri this afternoon. He gave me a ring about an hour ago when his mom left the house to pick up the new car at the consulate. It was a pretty depressing phone call, I have to say, on a number of fronts. Man, where to start. Well, first things first: Henri is going away. When he confessed to being stoned during his hurricane adventures (not to mention a good portion of the summer), his mother did more than simply ground him. She is sending him back to Paris to stay with his dad and get enrolled in a drug rehab program that a doctor friend of theirs runs. Madame Broussard has come to the conclusion that Henri is addicted to pot and, believe it or not, Henri kinda agrees.

I mean, I knew he got stoned a lot, but I didn't think it was anything superexcessive. But as we were talking about this, Henri told me that he was stoned more than I knew about. A lot more. In fact, all those times I thought he was out doing Parkour with his friends, he was actually just doing indoor smoking sports. Can you believe it? What am I saying . . . of course, you can believe it. You've been pretty much hinting at it all summer long. Please, just don't give me the ol' I-told-you-so. Things are hard enough without that sorta snarky comment.

So anyway, now Henri's leaving Wheaton to clean up his act, which also means that I won't see him for quite some time. I know that yesterday I was mad at him and could have given a shit, but today . . . I don't know. Two months is a long time! And I won't even get to see him before he goes, as his mom thinks that I'm sorta part of the whole problem, even though Henri has been trying to stand up for me. Apparently she thinks I'm his dealer or something. Isn't that an unintentional riot!?

I think the thing that really sucks about this whole Henri disaster is a more general thing about my life. Remember how at the beginning of July when you left I was so bummed out about everything because I didn't know how I was gonna deal with you being gone? Well, it feels like the minute I got over that with the help of Henri's entrance into my life, then Henri goes and gets taken away from me too. WTF—it's like I can't catch a break, you know?! Now—this is <u>not</u> to say that I'm not looking forward to you being back in town. In fact, I can't friggin' wait till Sunday and things start getting back to normal around here. It has been one insane summer, that's for sure, and though it was fun, insanity is fairly draining as well. So your presence here will be more than a relief. But at the same time, Henri's departure will be tough. I mean—what about the sex?! OMG . . . sex was sooooooo awesome, and now I've got to go back to wet dreams and self-inflicted hand jobs. It's like, how can you start eating fast food again once you've gotten a taste of four-star dining?

I really know how to pick 'em, huh? First I go for you, a totally straight dude. Then, the trio of flirtatious/jocky losers who are all equally unavailable. And then finally, I hit the jackpot with the hot French foreign exchange student (like in a teen movie!) who happens to be a massive pot addict. I'd be LOL-ing if it all wasn't so SOS. I just feel like I'm going down today, you know, sinking into a deep, dark funk. It would be scary if it weren't so familiar in a way. It's what I like to call the Funk of the Year, as I've retreated into its icky, warm embrace at least three or four times already. So it's more like back to the familiar . . .

All right—I'm not gonna wail on and on about this any more than I have to. I just hope your show has some uplifting moments in it that can help pull me outta this hole. It is called *Merrily*, right? Oh—wait a minute. I think you said the thing was pretty dramatic and depressing? Maybe I shouldn't come after all. I'll just be a big black hole in the audience, sucking the energy out of the room. Besides, going out with Val is not exactly my idea of a hot Saturday night. Would you mind too much if I didn't make it? Don't they usually tape these shows anyway, on someone's DV-CAM? Maybe it might be more fun to watch it together when you get back Sunday night. How 'bout that?

I'm gonna go take a nap. I need to lie down for a bit and not think about any of this for a while. I don't feel too great. If I don't make it to the show, don't take it personally, okay? I'm just really depressed . . . about everything. H

05:10 P.M.
SATURDAY 08.19.06
OK—so I know you're a bit down because of Henri's sudden departure. Granted, it sucks. And I certainly know your tendency to crawl into your own little black cocoon the minute something goes wrong. Granted, that sucks . . . majorly. But if you think that's a real excuse not to come see the show I've been working my ass off on all summer long, then you have not only lost your boyfriend but maybe your best friend too. Seriously.

Here's why: I have known you for 10 times 10 times 100 times the amount of time you have known Henri for. So if you can't get your shit together to come see your oldest friend for something that means the world to him, then we really might as well just call this whole friendship off. I'm not kidding, Hal.

I just hope you're still online and reading this and getting your head on straight. S-E-R-I-O-U-S-L-Y. And just to be clear, notice how I am not joking or making light of this at all. For real. C

05:22 P.M.
SATURDAY 08.19.06
Christ—you actors are so friggin' emotional! Well, excuse me for having feelings too. Just because I'm not on stage showing them off to the entire world doesn't mean they don't exist somewhere deep inside my shrinking heart. They do, and today they're just a little too overwhelming—a fact that I'd hoped you, of all people, might understand, given that emotion is your trade. But I guess that, even with you, I can't catch a break today.

So if it's that big of a deal, yeah, I'll come to your goddamned show because basically I really can't afford to lose every single person in the world who means anything to me in less than 24 hours. But don't mistake my presence for anything other than that because, trust me, I'm not gonna be happy about being there. Even if it's amazing.

05:38 P.M.
SATURDAY 08.19.06

Don't do me any favors, Hal. Just forget it. You're impossible when you're like this. Absofuckinglutely impossible! I don't know what I was thinking. I mean, trying to get you out of a self-inflicted funk is futile.

I just thought you might show me and our 10-year-plus relationship some respect, that our friendship still counted for something. But, I don't know . . . maybe after Henri, a boring old best friend just doesn't mean that much to you. I guess that's understandable, since we're not fucking around like gay bunnies. But, at the same time, it kinda sucks too.

I really hate to end our whole blog on a bad note, but what can I say? Not coming to my show was your idea. So this rough end will all be your doing. And, now that I think about it, it's always what you do: take something nice and then ruin it with your uncontrollable depressive streak.

05:40 P.M.
SATURDAY 08.19.06

OMG, Chuck! Don't go all "me" on me! That is totally NOT FAIR!!! I'm coming, okay? You win. Christ!

05:56 P.M.
SATURDAY 08.19.06

Did you get that last post? I know you don't have to be at the theater till 7:00. Where did you go? I'm really coming, okay? Look—just call me if you took back the tickets or something retarded like that. Val can buy them herself anyway. But we <u>are</u> coming. So don't have a flippin' panic attack!

11:49 P.M.
SUNDAY 08.19.06

So my iTunes is on right now, downloading a couple songs from *Merrily*. My first show tunes—can you believe it? I can't. But I had to have them, because I basically can't stop thinking about the show. I feel so ridiculous now for even having threatened not to come, because if I'd done something that stupid I would have missed out on THE highlight of my summer. All right, well, maybe it's a close tie with the first time I spent the night at Henri's. (At least I'm honest, okay?) But it was still just as extraordinary and emotional and amazing and . . . unforgettable? Is it too damn corny to say that about a stupid musical?

I thought this was gonna be something silly and standard like *Music Man*. I mean, the title sorta indicates that it's not that deep—*Merrily We Roll Along*. And even though you'd mentioned a couple times before how it was really different from your other shows, I didn't know that it would be THAT different. I mean, the story was so damn depressing— I LOVED IT! OMG—it made me feel so much better about my life, which is not nearly as screwed up as Mary and Frank and Beth and Gussie and all of them. What a tangled web they friggin' wove, huh? And some of the characters were so mean and bitter, especially in that opening scene when you guys were all old and shallow and full of problems. Ghaliyah was hysterical as Mary in that scene, being such a drunken mess and causing all sorts of trouble and then throwing that vial of iodine in the young starlet's eyes! That was vicious and awesome at the same time!!! I didn't know musicals were allowed to be that severe.

You know what I got into even more (which I can't believe at all) was the music itself. Granted, a couple of the songs were a little too cutesy, but I really liked most of the lyrics and what they were saying. Especially that song that you and Ghaliyah and MK and Chaz all did together, "Old Friends." That was really cool! I thought it captured the way that friends can be bitchy toward each other and still be friends (uh, sorta like us earlier today, huh?). And it was great the way you guys slowly kinda turned it into this big dance number without getting ridiculously over-the-top Broadway about it. Though, when he has to, Chaz can really do those high kicks like a goddamn Rockette!

Now I know we talked a lot about your performance after the show and all, but I gotta say it again, Chuck: you were just . . . WOW! I mean it was incredible, because you really were onstage every second of the show except for when the scenery was moving around, and you handled it like it was no big deal. Of course, I know it is a huge deal to be singing and dancing and acting and trying to remember everything, but you made it seem like it was just another day at the office. I mean, did you even break a sweat under all those lights? But even more interesting was that, in the beginning, when you were supposed to be older, you really <u>seemed</u> older . . . a lot older, and not only because of the makeup, but more in the way you moved and even looked at people (especially Gussie, that old cow!). Because of that, it was really cool to watch the show move backward and see how you got younger and more youthful as it went along.

Also, as you predicted, that scene at the end really got me. I mean <u>really</u>. I was losing it sitting there in my seat, totally bawling toward the end of that song, when you and Chaz and Ghaliyah were up on the rooftop. I'm playing the song again right now, actually, and getting a little emotional just hearing it . . . man, what a beautiful tune! I think that scene was so moving because you get to see how all the characters didn't start out being so mean and horrible to each other but it happened over time. In fact, way back then, they were all in love with each other, and because of a series of misunderstandings and mistakes and missteps, things slowly began to fall apart. So when you get to the end, which is actually the beginning of their lives, and you see how all their friendships began with that one moment up on the roof, it was just kinda beautiful and heartbreaking at the same time. Which is, I guess, why I started crying. I know . . . I'm the new Mr. Softie, what can I say?

Hey—I just hope that we don't ever start hating each other the way these people eventually did. I know you went nuclear on me this afternoon about my mood and near-miss no-show. But PLEASE, Chuck—whenever I'm being insanely stupid and an asshole to you, just tell me off like you did today, and I'll try to not be such a dick. I know I'm not easy when I get depressed like this, but I don't want it to end up ruining our friendship. I don't want to lose our friendship like the people in the play did because of stupid petty things that just sorta piled up over time. I want us to keep being friends even as we grow older and more cynical about love and life and everything. Or maybe you won't get that way. You are pretty damn optimistic, but then again, so was Frank. So, beware—it could happen to you, too!

Thanks also for inviting me and Val to the cast party. That was really nice, especially for Val. I think she had more fun than I did, chatting with all the cute chorus boys. I didn't have the heart to tell her that most of them were homos. LOL! Maybe she knew this already? It was sorta obvious to me, that's for sure. Especially when you see Chaz in the center of the flock. He was a riot in the show, by the way. I have to give him props for playing a pretty good best friend. And a straight one, too! That was going above and beyond, you know, and he turned in a staggeringly believable performance to boot. Val was totally convinced!!!

It was great hanging out with MK again, and even, dare I say, Miss G. Believe it or not, when you and MK went off to get some snacks, G had some pretty remarkable things to say about you. She said that she thought you were hugely talented and definitely the best male voice in the cast of that show, or any show, actually, that she'd ever been involved in. That's pretty high praise from the diva herself! Of course, it would have been nicer if she'd said this stuff to you directly, but she probably didn't want to fully compromise her divaness. But anyway, thought you'd like to know that, even if she isn't in love with you, she certainly is in love with your talents! That's not a bad consolation prize, huh?

I better get to bed, as I'm really beat. But I can't imagine how exhausted you must be from the last six weeks, not to mention the run of the show.

Hell—just seeing it once was draining enough for me! OH—one last thing. When we were driving home from College Park, Val and I had a pretty interesting chat. (And no, I didn't come out to her!) During that rooftop number in the show, Val said she noticed that I was crying and was wondering why. So I tried to tell her some of the stuff I just wrote above, how it was this beautiful and heartbreaking moment, and she agreed. And then, after I was done talking, she looked over at me and said the craziest thing; totally unprompted, she goes, "You really miss Chuck, don't you?" And before I could even say yes, I started getting teary again. OMG—suddenly I'm Mr. Emotional, even around Val. What is <u>wrong</u> with me?

I expected Val to get all goopy about this, but she was actually nice, saying it was okay for me to miss you. So this is all to say that I really did miss you this summer, so much that I can't even write about it or I'll start getting all soggy again. And even though Henri has meant a lot to me, don't worry, because basically he can never displace you. A best friend like you is not really a replaceable item, I fear. Which is probably another reason I was crying. Seeing you up on that stage, your talent outshining everything, I just know that you are gonna be gone for more than six weeks in our future. Damn, Chuck—you have such a big life ahead of you! As for me, who knows—maybe it's too early to tell (remember our late bloomer, Rodin). But you are <u>definitely</u> going places, and I probably won't be trailing along . . . unless, of course, you hire me to manage your entourage.

So I guess what I'm trying to get at here is that I don't know how to deal with this impending, irreplaceable loss. In some ways, I think that maybe I fell for Henri so fully and got so damn obsessed with him because I thought it might fill the hole of your absence this summer. But it didn't. That's what I realized seeing your show: Friendship matters the most over time, even more, maybe, than hot and heavy love. Definitely more than sex . . . that's for damn sure! (Sex lasts for a few minutes . . . all right, 20 if Henri's in charge.) But it doesn't go on and on for 10 whole years, right? And that was my revelation on seeing your show. I mean, who knew I could actually get something out of a Broadway musical?!

OK—I'm gonna hit the sack. What time do you get back tomorrow? What do you want to do when you get home? Maybe we can go up to the mall and I can give you a tour of the new and not-so-improved Shopping Town. Or maybe I could show you Marrakesh, which will probably never get a makeover as no one cares what strip malls look like. One thing's for sure, though: We are not going to De Lounge for Karaoke Sunday. Those queens would go insane with you turning out the show tunes, and we would never get outta there!

See you soon! Love, H

03:12 P.M.
SUNDAY 08.20.06

Wait a minute . . . did you just sign you last blog with L? To me?! Dude, I thought you said you <u>didn't</u> have a thing for me? (ha) All right, just kidding. One lame Chuck-joke to end this whole thing.

Holy shit—I can't believe it's time to pack up. Wow. I swear it seems like a week ago that I got here and met Chaz and thought he was a freak. Remember that? Now I know the truth . . . that he <u>is</u> a freak but a great friend, too. He's over at Albert's right now, as they are saying their good-byes.

Oh man—it's been a rough day here all around with all the good-byes. You think you were losing it last night during the show? Today everyone is just falling apart here. Seriously. It's like, going from the highs of last night's final kick-ass performance to the lows of everyone getting into their parents' cars today. I can't take it! None of us can, and the tears have been flowing freely.

As for MK, she didn't spend the night here unfortunately. But it was not due to a fight or anything. Totally a mutual decision. In a way, we thought if we did that it would be too painful to say good-bye in the morning, being all curled up and cozy in bed together. As it was, saying adios without any sex or making out was bad enough.

Her parents came down from Frederick early this morning, around 11:00. I helped her with her stuff, getting it into the car and all. I even got to meet the folks, who were very nice and generic and parenty. Then, when it came time for the big good-bye, we hugged each other, and MK would not let go. (Remember this from before?) Then she got the crying going and I followed suit, because I didn't have much choice, clutched to her chest and trapped in her trademark love-induced headlock. The whole time, her parents looked on with this weird bemusement. I don't know why they thought it was funny. Man, it was the exact opposite of funny! Sometimes I don't think adults have hearts, you know? Seriously.

MK and I did exchange e-mails and snail mails and cells and land lines and everything except our social security numbers. So it looks like we'll be staying in touch, which is cool. And I'd love to do that road trip up there once you get your license. Chaz put MK's address into GoogleMaps and it said that, door-to-door, it's only 42 minutes driving which isn't too bad . . . pretty much a straight shot out I-270. Also, MK's older sister is starting at Georgetown in the fall, so maybe she'll be down to visit on some long weekends, too. So it looks like there is hope for us despite the distances involved. That should make me feel better, but right now, I'm just feeling down about it anyway. I mean, I've been hanging with her 24-7, it seems like, for the last three weeks. I'm gonna have some serious MK-withdrawal symptoms, and I don't think a shopping trip to Wheaton Plaza is gonna distract me from my pain.

OH—speaking of pains, Ghaliyah stopped by here about an hour ago to say her good-byes. (ha) That's really surprising, those things she said to you. I never would have guessed she felt I was that great. She's incredibly critical of herself, so I just thought she was equally critical about me, some of which I heard in rehearsals if I made a mistake. Even though my fantasy about her never played out, I'm really glad I met Ghaliyah and that we are gonna be friends. That's what really matters in the end. And I gotta say, I was impressed by her professionalism and maybe even inspired by it too. She talked about it so damn much, how could it not rub off on me. Especially amazing was the way that she made it through that last show with her leg injured like that. That is truly a pro. I'm sure she'll be on Broadway before any of us get out of high school, replacing the Wicked Witch in *Wicked*. Holy shit—she'd be so perfect for it! ☺

Well, it's almost 4:00, which is when Bob and Carol are due here at ol' St.

Ann's. I'm still not done getting my clothes together. (BTW—I threw the sex sheets out and am hoping the folks won't notice!) I'll give you a call when I get home and we can make a plan for something later tonight. I'm sure my parents want to have some big welcome-home dinner, and maybe you could come over for that. I'll check the menu first, because if it's Carol's cooking vs. Bob's bbq-ing, I know you'll want to opt out.

You know what would be fun tonight? Why don't we just get on our bikes and ride around W-town? I've been thinking about that ever since MK made such a big deal about it that night we were up on the roof. Wouldn't that be a blast from the past? We could go to 7-Eleven, get some Slurpees and Suzy Q's, and then just do a loop around the Wheaton/Kensington Metroplex. We could even stop into that Marrakesh joint too, as I'm curious to see what all the hubbub was all about. But get this straight: We are <u>NOT</u> going to the porno store!!!

OK—guess that's it. My last entry in the blog. I gotta say, as much as I missed having you around, I think I'm gonna miss having this blog around, too. It's been pretty cool to write all this shit down. I think that, 5 or 10 years from now, we are gonna get some good laughs looking at this thing again. And maybe even more than that, depending on how everything turns out in the romance department with MK and Henri. Who knows . . . this summer could be the start of something big, as they say. I know you're pessimistic about things right now, but maybe Henri will get his act together and prove to be a stand-up guy in the end. I mean, my sister did pretty well once she realized she had a problem. Getting her into treatment was the hard part. After that it was sorta all downhill. So don't sweat it . . . this all might be for the best (says the crazy optimist!).

Bob just honked the horn. Gotta hit it, but I'll see you soon . . . you big nut! Signing off, your bestest friend . . . C

8/24/06

Dear Diary . . . or journal . . . or whatever the hell this is. Dear
computer? I just had to write all this down immediately, as I'm so
blown away by what just happened and, since Chuck's not home
yet, I couldn't wait to tell somebody. Or some-thing. Anyway, Henri
just stopped by on his way to the airport! When I got to the door, I
was floored. Totally. Not just by his being there but his appearance, too. Henri looked oddly adorable, all dressed up and presentable in real pants and an actual button-down shirt . . . it was a
trip! He even had a whole new, responsible haircut too. I have to
say, I sorta missed his rough and tumble style but cleaned up, he
was very preppy-hot, which is not too bad either (if not exactly my
type).

I was soooo stunned that he was there that I didn't know what to
say at first. So I just made jokes about his makeover and he told
me that it was, of course, Madame B's idea. As was the fact that he
was on my doorstep in the first place. Apparently, she wanted him to
apologize for all the worry he caused by his disappearance. And even
though it was her idea, he said he wanted to apologize too. I told him
that he didn't have to, but he said that, yeah, he did, and that what
he'd done was not very "nice." Nice? Well, I think his English was
off on this statement, as I told him that "stupid" was perhaps a
more appropriate word choice. I was half joking about this, but
Henri got all solemn and actually nodded his head in agreement.
Henri—agreeing with me? Maybe rehab had already begun?

As we chatted, Henri said some surprisingly nice things to me in
our five-minute conversation. The most shocking was that he really
liked how I said what was on my mind, unlike most Americans he
knew or had met. I thought this was pretty
hilarious, because if I'd said half of what was on my mind I would
have been arrested for lewd and public indecency the day I met him!
But Henri was serious, saying he admired this quality I had. He went
so far as to say he even admired my fearlessness, and I was like—

WOW—I've never thought of myself as fearless, especially when I'm the one who has to literally be pushed out on the edge of a girder over the Potomac River. But I guess he didn't mean it so literally. He meant more that I was fearless in my thoughts and ideas and that he wished he could be articulate about these things in a similar manner. So I said to him (feeling like I couldn't resist this one), "Maybe without the weed you'll suddenly become a fount of knowledge!" He laughed, saying he doubted that would happen.

When Mrs. Broussard started honking the horn, I wished him well with his trip and dealing with his dad and the rehab and all that supportive sorta crap. He said thanks and flashed me that killer grin. Damn. Of course, what I really wanted to do was make out with him while his mom waited in the car, but that wasn't gonna happen. (That would've totally freaked her shit out!!!) But I could tell in that silent Ethan-Hawke-movie sorta way that Henri probably wanted to make out too. He might have even done it if not for his mom's presence. Hmmmm, maybe . . .

Anyway, just before he left he gave me a brief hug, and I thought that was gonna be that. But then Henri leaned back in for a surprise attack: a kiss on both cheeks, international style. I got all tingly from this and suddenly had the urge to come up with a scheme to rescue him from his mother's evil clutches. But, uh, I didn't—so much for being fearless. Before I let him get away, though, I said he should send me an e-mail when he's settled so we can keep in touch. Henri smiled at the thought and got this funny look on his face. And then he blew me away: He suggested we could start up a blog, like the one I had with Chuck. Can you believe it?!

I mean, that's pretty crazy, huh? Henri starting up a blog!? Even crazier was me agreeing to this idea. I know, I know—after all my complaining about Chuck's blog? But, in
retrospect, that blog was a great way for us to keep in touch, so hopefully it'll do the trick with Henri half a world away. In fact, I feel

like Chuck and I have actually gotten closer being away from each other for a while. It sorta defies the laws of physics or something, but it's true. After all those TALE entries, I certainly know more freaky stuff about Chuck (see "Wet dreams") and he knows tons more insane stuff about me (see "Broussard, Henri") than we would have ever told each other in the real world.

You know, sometimes it's almost easier to write down these super-embarrassing things. And a relief, too. It just gets them off your mind or something. Also, I know that when I tell Chuck about Henri's surprise visit and the blog proposition he's not gonna be too thrilled about it. But what the hell—
I AM! So at least I can be thrilled for a moment writing about it here before reality brings me down. Though, I gotta say, it's good to have at least some voice of reason (i.e. Chuck) in your life when your heart is certainly not gonna give it to you straight. So to speak.

Shit—Chuck's here. All right, more later. Lots more . . .